FROM AN ANTIQUE LAND

First published in 2021
by Black Spring Press
Grantully, Maida Vale,
London w9, England, UK
United Kingdom

Cover design and typeset by Edwin Smet
Author photograph Jennifer Johnson
Printed in England by TJ Books Ltd, Padstow, Cornwall
Edited by M. Pinchbeck
Proofread by I. Lewis-Dodson and T. Swift

ISBN 978-1-913606-46-6

This book is a work of fiction. The characters, incidents, and dialogue
are drawn from the author's imagination and are not to be construed
as real. Any resemblance to actual events or persons, living or dead,
is entirely coincidental.

BLACKSPRINGPRESSGROUP.COM

FROM AN ANTIQUE LAND

A NOVEL BY

STANLEY JOHNSON

THE **BLACK SPRING**
PRESS GROUP

ALSO BY STANLEY JOHNSON

FICTION

Gold Drain

Panther Jones for President

The Urbane Guerrilla

The Marburg Virus (republished as The Virus)

Tunnel

The Commissioner

The Doomsday Deposit

Dragon River

Icecap (republished as The Warming)

Kompromat

NON-FICTION

Life Without Birth: A Journey Through the Third World
in Search of the Population Explosion

The Green Revolution

The Population Problem

The Politics of the Environment

Pollution Control Policy of the EEC

Antarctica: The Last Great Wilderness

World Population and the United Nations

The Earth Summit:the United Nations Conference on
Environment and Development (UNCED)

World Population: Turning The Tide

The Environmental Policy of the European Communities

The Politics of Population

Survival: Saving Endangered Migratory Species (co-author Robert Vagg)

Where the Wild Things Were

UNEP: The First 40 Years

MEMOIR

Stanley I Presume

Stanley I Resume

PRELUDE

The new Millennium has begun. George W. Bush is President and Hillary Clinton, former First Lady and now Senator for New York, already has her eye on higher things.

Life in Washington DC, the nation's capital, is getting back to normal after the trauma of September 11, 2001 (9/11).

One morning Su Soeung, who first came to the US as a child refugee from Cambodia and the horrors of Pol Pot, receives a letter with an interesting job offer: would she like to work at a senior level for SAVE, a Washington-based international charity specializing in relief work in Cambodia?

Su's return to Cambodia, on assignment for SAVE, sees the beginning of an extraordinary trail of events. Her efforts to discover the fate of her father seem to be inextricably intertwined with politics at the highest level.

CHAPTER 1

The three-storey brownstone was at the junction of P and 14th, not far from Logan Circle. Less than a decade previously, Logan had been a no-go area, a crack-dealers' haven. The storefronts were chained day and night and if for one reason or another you found yourself driving through the district, you made sure your car's doors and windows were locked and you kept your foot on the gas. But during President Clinton's second term, things had begun to change. The economic boom had gone on and on and the wave of prosperity had spread east, flooding previously run-down neighbourhoods with a new respectability. Even though the economy had wobbled following the terrorist attacks on the World Trade Center and the Pentagon on September 11, 2001, the Logan Circle area kept coming up in the world. It wasn't Georgetown or Kalorama but if you were a young and aspiring middle class professional, and you didn't want to spend a million dollars or more on your first home, you could do far worse.

That at least is what Su Soeung told herself when she first put down the deposit on the apartment. And on the whole in the two years she had been there, she had had little reason to regret her decision. On one occasion her bicycle had been stolen, but that was because she had locked it to the railings in front of the house instead of carrying it inside. Apart from that, she had no complaints. No-one had mugged her or even accosted her in an unfriendly manner. The fact that she was Cambodian probably helped. This part of Washington still had a substantial ethnic population, and she supposed she blended in fairly well.

She unlocked the front door and paused in the hall to collect her mail. Sometimes the postman came before she left for work in the morning. Most often, one of the other occupants of the building would pick up the letters and papers from the mat and stack them on the table at the foot of the stairs.

One of the features of her apartment which Su most enjoyed was the balcony with its view over the towering plane trees of Logan Circle and the distant glint of the great dome of the Capitol building. She made herself a cup of tea and took her letters outside. November was often a magical month in Washington. The trees had turned but not yet lost their leaves. The sun often shone from dawn to dusk but the heat and humidity of the summer months had gone for good. As she sat there, a sense of wellbeing came over her. So many others, she thought, had not been half as lucky as she had been. She had been seven years old when she first came to the United States, escaping with her mother from the cataclysm which Pol Pot had launched upon Cambodia. Twenty-five years later, like so many immigrants before her, she felt at home in America. This surely was where she belonged. She had never been back to her native land. She wondered now if she ever would return.

As always, much of the day's mail was routine – the new Sears catalogue, the fall programme of lectures at the Smithsonian, a credit card statement. But one envelope in particular caught her eye. It was an expensive oblong cream-coloured missive bearing her name in heavy black type. On the reverse of the envelope the word SAVE with a Massachusetts Avenue address had been embossed in capital letters.

'Dear Ms Soeung,' Su read as she opened the letter. 'As you may know, SAVE is an international charity specialising in relief work in Cambodia, notably the rehabilitation of victims of landmines. We currently have an opening for a person of your experience and qualifications to join our staff at a senior level and would welcome the chance to discuss with you the possibility of you accepting an assignment with this organisation.' The letter gave a contact telephone number and was signed, 'Andrew Mossman, Chief Executive Officer.'

Su Soeung read the letter twice, then she put it back in the envelope, gathered up her papers and went inside. She already knew a bit about SAVE. In recent years the charity had made quite a name for itself with some high-profile fundraising and publicity events in Washington. And anyone who read the Style section of the *Washington Post*, for example, had to be aware that Andrew Mossman and Caroline, his attractive, high-powered lawyer wife, were well on the way to becoming a celebrity couple on Washington's social circuit.

Su switched on her computer and quickly logged on to SAVE's website. Ten minutes in front of the screen told her all she needed to know – at least for the moment.

★★★

'Mossman? Andrew Mossman? SAVE's CEO?' Prescott Glover was intrigued. 'We were at Princeton together. He came to Washington just about the time I went off to New York for my first job with *The Times*. I've seen him once or twice in the last few months at various do's. He and his wife are a bit glitzy for my taste. But SAVE's doing a good job. Or seems to be. I'll give you that.'

Su Soeung felt strangely defensive. It wasn't that she had said yes to Mossman. She hadn't talked to the man yet. She didn't even know what the job was or whether she would wish to do it. But she detected a snide tone in Prescott's remarks.

'You think Caroline Mossman's just a bag-carrier for Hillary Clinton, don't you?' she challenged him.

'Whatever Caroline Mossman is, she's not a bag-carrier. But yes,' Prescott replied, 'Caroline seems to be a leading light in Hillary Rodham Clinton's so far undeclared campaign to be the next or at least a future President of the United States and I'm not sure that's good for SAVE. When charities become politicised, they lose credibility pretty fast.'

Su still felt defensive. 'Andrew Mossman runs SAVE, not Caroline.'

'Are you sure?' Prescott Glover smiled. 'Women seem to run most things nowadays.'

He poured them both some more wine and raised his glass. 'I think you should go for it anyway whatever it is. You're thirty-three. You need a career change.'

'You think ten years in academia is enough?'

'Two years would be enough for me!'

It was their regular Tuesday-night dinner in a French restaurant in Georgetown. Su Soeung had been 'going steady' with Prescott Glover for over two years, having met him first at a State Department reception. Su was an associate professor in Georgetown University's Asian Studies programme. Prescott, before *The New York Times* sent him to Washington to join its bureau there, had served two years in Beijing with a further spell in Hong Kong covering Britain's handover of the colony to China. He discovered he had much in common with Su Soeung besides their interest in the Far East.

As a matter of convenience, even though they 'lived together,' they maintained their separate apartments in Washington. Sometimes Prescott spent the night at Su's place; sometimes she went to his place. They were both professional people. This was the modern way. It was also, paradoxically, the old-fashioned way. Both of them knew, without explicitly saying so, that if one of them ever moved in with the other on a permanent basis, it would be when they were married.

Prescott leaned across the table and placed his hand on hers. How lovely she was, he thought. Like so many Khmer women, Su had a wide-eyed beauty about her. Her dark hair, thick and glossy, fell almost to shoulder length, contrasting subtly with her pale olive complexion.

'Did you like the piece in *The Washingtonian?*' Prescott asked. 'I thought it came out quite nicely.'

Prescott was referring to a recent magazine article about the careers of Cambodian refugees in the nation's capital. The article had followed a number of refugees in different fields – music, the arts, journalism, film and so forth. Su Soeung had been picked as the representative of Cambodians in the academic world.

'I'm glad they printed the photo of you with your father and mother. That was very moving. Has your mother seen the article? She should be proud of what you've achieved.'

'I mailed it to her. She should have received it by now, but I can't be sure. Deliveries in the Seattle area seem pretty haphazard nowadays. The mail really hasn't recovered from all the disruption caused by the anthrax scare.'

'You ought to get out to the Coast and see her soon. Your mother's a lovely lady. Life dealt her a crummy hand, but she came through. You both did.'

As they left the restaurant, Prescott helped Su on with her coat.

'I can manage,' she protested.

'Not with me around, you can't. Remember I'm an old-fashioned kinda guy!'

Prescott ducked his head as they walked out onto the street. He was not only two or three years older than Su; he was six inches taller. His sandy-coloured hair had begun to recede from his forehead, and he had acquired a pair of gold-rimmed reading glasses which gave him a faintly professorial air.

'You're not old-fashioned,' Su laughed. 'You're just well-mannered. For some of us that still counts.'

They went back to her place after dinner. Listened to music. Watched television. Were ready for bed by midnight.

The light switch was on Prescott's side. As he went to turn it off, his eye fell on the empty photo frame on the table by the wall.

'Didn't *The Washingtonian* send you the picture of you and your dad back?' he asked. 'I'll give them hell if they've lost it.'

'No, they sent it back all right. I've got it in my purse. I just haven't put it back in the frame yet.'

Prescott turned out the light, leaned over and kissed her in the dark – companionably.

'I've got an early start tomorrow,' he said. 'The Democratic National Committee is putting out a statement on the subject of campaign finance.'

'So soon,' she murmured, already half asleep. 'Seems to me we've only just had an election. Why are they worrying about the next one now?'

★★★

SAVE's international headquarters occupied two floors of a modern office building on M Street, between 20th and 21st streets. Su Soeung arrived at five minutes to three in the afternoon for a three o'clock appointment.

The receptionist smiled at her. 'Mr Mossman's expecting you.'

Su followed the young woman down a carpeted corridor to a corner office. Her limp was barely noticeable. Whoever had fitted the artificial limb had done a good job.

'Are you Cambodian?' Su asked her.

The woman half-turned her head as she nodded. 'I was one of the lucky ones. I only lost one leg.'

As Su entered his office, Andrew Mossman bounded out from behind his desk. 'I'm so glad you could come.' He shook her hand warmly and guided her to a white leather sofa, while he pulled up a chair. He looked bronzed and fit, full of energy. Behind the desk, Su noted the glory-wall. Two photographs had pride of place. One showed Mossman and a good-looking blonde woman Su recognised as Caroline Mossman with Bill and Hillary Clinton; the other showed SAVE's CEO and Princess Diana, kitted out in protective gear visiting what Su took to be a minefield somewhere in Asia. In the photograph, the Princess was being helped on with her helmet and visor by an attentive Mossman.

Andrew Mossman caught the direction of her glance. 'Princess Diana was amazing,' he said. 'Quite amazing. We wouldn't be where we are without her. It's as simple as that.

13

The reason one hundred and twenty-three countries signed the Ottawa Convention on Landmines in December 1997 was because Diana put the issue on the map. They tried to stop her, of course. Lots of people tried to stop her, our own government included. There are a lot of vested interests out there. A lot of people are still making money out of weaponry, including landmines. But Diana got the press and the media behind her. She created a storm of interest and it worked.'

Mossman surprised her. Su had imagined that she was being interviewed for a job, but it didn't come over that way. Instead of asking her questions and checking her answers, Mossman leaned forward in his chair. 'How much do you know about landmines?' he asked.

'Not enough.'

'Do you mind if I take you through it for a moment? You have to understand the background.'

Su wasn't sure she knew where Mossman was headed but she nodded anyway, 'Go ahead.'

'Landmines have been around for years,' Mossman began. 'They've been used on a large scale since World War I. They kill or maim whatever triggers them: soldiers, civilians, animals. They are a weapon of war, but civilians pay the price in peacetime.

'It's common to associate the damage created by landmines only with the horrific injuries resulting from a mine blast, but that's just the tip of the iceberg. If the victim is the breadwinner, the family's income is wiped out and the immediate family has to cope psychologically and financially. If the victims are children, their whole future – whether they can go to school, marry, find work – hangs in the balance.

'For countries like Cambodia, the financial burden, particularly the strain on the health system, can be crushing. Cambodia probably has the highest incidence of mine amputees per capita in the world. One amputee per 236 to 425 inhabitants. Estimates of the total number of amputees vary from 18,000 to 40,000. That means hundreds of new patients a year and literally thousands of prostheses and crutches.'

'Can't they get rid of the mines?' asked Su.

'You're talking about the Labours of Hercules here. Do you know how many mines have been laid in Cambodia over the last few decades, beginning with the sixties and the seventies when Cambodia was drawn into the Vietnam War and continuing right up almost to the present?'

When Su Soeung shook her head, Mossman continued. 'If you take the fields and the forests and the rice paddies of Cambodia together, we're talking about one of the most heavily mined countries in the world. There are an estimated six to ten million landmines compared to a population of eight or nine million inhabitants.'

Mossman rose from his chair and walked over to a map of Cambodia which was hanging on the wall. Pointing at the map, he continued: 'Almost every province has minefields, but the main mined areas are to be found in the heavily populated and productive crescent around the northern tip of the Tonle Sap Lake.'

With a sweep of his arm, he showed Su what he meant. 'Look, the worst minefields stretch from Pursat in the southwest through Battambang, Banteay Meanchey and Siem Reap to Preah Vihear in the Northeast. These fertile lowlands, plus those along the Mekong River, represent only thirty percent of the land area, yet support ninety percent of the population and practically all of Cambodia's economic activity.'

'Why are you telling me all this?' Su Soeung asked quietly.

Andrew Mossman resumed his seat. 'I'll tell you why. SAVE is planning to appoint a Congressional liaison officer – a Cambodian, of course, but one who holds an American passport and green card. That person is going to have to have a deep understanding of the problem. That means going to Cambodia, getting a feel for the situation on the ground, seeing what SAVE is doing there. But it also means working closely with SAVE headquarters here in Washington. We need to take the message from Phnom Penh, from Siem Reap or wherever and sell it on Capitol Hill and to the media.'

'Why me?'

Andrew Mossman gave her a frank, appraising look. 'We've known about you for a long time, Su. May I call you "Su?"' When she nodded, he continued: 'As you can imagine, SAVE takes a close interest in the Cambodian community in Washington. We didn't need *The Washingtonian* article to tell us that you have emerged in recent years as one of the leaders of that community. We think you have the stature and abilities we are looking for. What do you say?'

Su Soeung took her time in replying. She couldn't say she was surprised by Mossman's offer. The letter she had received two days earlier made it clear that some kind of proposal could be in the wind. But now that Mossman had spelled out in detail what SAVE wanted from her, she felt both elated and alarmed. Elated, because she realised she would now have a chance to revisit the land of her birth, the country where her father and so many of her relatives had died. Alarmed, because she wondered – frankly – whether she was up to the job.

'I was a child when I left Cambodia,' she told him. 'I've never been back. There wasn't a chance to do so till now. Don't you have local people, Cambodians, you can use out there?'

'Of course, we have local people,' Mossman said. 'We have people all over the country. But for this particular job we need someone who can straddle both worlds, if you see what I mean. As I've explained, you have to visit Cambodia. Indeed, we expect that you will spend a good deal of time there. But, as a Cambodian with twenty-five years' experience of America, you will be able to bring the message back over here and you'll be able to work with that message in a way that a local Cambodian coming here for the first time would find quite impossible.'

'I've never worked in the voluntary sector before. Isn't it rather special?'

Mossman brushed her objection aside. 'My contacts in George Washington University tell me you're a fine administrator as well as a good scholar. And you know how to work with people. That's what counts.'

Sitting there, listening to him talk, Su could understand why Andrew Mossman had got where he was. He was tremendously charming and persuasive. And you felt he believed, passionately, in what SAVE was doing.

'You won't have to do any fundraising,' he smiled. 'We'll take care of that.'

Su smiled back. 'That's a relief! The university is always trying to push me into fundraising but so far I've fought them off.'

They talked for a long time that afternoon. Mossman put all his calls on hold except for one.

'I'll have to take this one,' he apologised. 'It's my wife.'

Su listened with half an ear as Mossman spoke into the telephone. At one point she heard Mossman say: 'So the Senator's coming tonight, is she? I'm delighted. I'll tell the people at the Smithsonian straightaway, so they'll know to look out for her when she arrives.'

Resuming his seat, Mossman told her. 'We've got a major do at the Smithsonian this evening for SAVE's tenth anniversary. Hillary Clinton's office has just confirmed that the Senator will be attending which is great news for us.'

Su remembered what Prescott Glover had told her about Caroline Mossman's links with Mrs Clinton. She was beginning to appreciate the way things worked.

'Having a high-profile Senator as one of your patrons must do wonders for an organisation like SAVE.'

'If you join us, you'll be meeting the Senator, that's for sure,' Mossman said. A thought struck him, 'I know we haven't dotted all the i's and crossed all the t's yet, but do you think you would be able to come along this evening? Bring your partner too.' It was clear that Glover had read *The Washingtonian* article from beginning to end. He knew about Su's longstanding relationship with Prescott. 'As a matter of fact, I'm rather a fan of Mr Glover's writing. Fine journalist, if I may say so.'

When she left the SAVE headquarters a few minutes later with two engraved invitations to that evening's charity dinner in her hand, Su Soeung felt more than a little overwhelmed. So much had happened so quickly. Her life, her horizons seemed suddenly to have expanded in all directions. Had she actually said 'yes' to Mossman, she wondered?

She hailed a cab. As she sat down, she pulled out her mobile phone to call Prescott at his office. She knew Prescott on the whole hated black-tie dinners, but she felt confident that on this occasion at least he would be more than intrigued.

★★★

It was striking how much power and confidence radiated from Mrs Hillary Rodham Clinton, Su Soeung thought. She was only the Junior Senator from New York, less than half-way through her first term of office but when she entered the room, all eyes turned towards her. Of course, she was wearing a pants-suit – by now it had almost become a personal trade-mark. This evening's version was lime-green, a colour which Su readily conceded suited Mrs Clinton well.

The SAVE anniversary party was being held in the Smithso-nian's Dinosaur-Fossil Hall.

Andrew and Caroline Mossman stood beneath the tower-ing skeleton of Tyrannosaurus rex, talking animatedly to the Senator while other guests hovered nearby hoping to have a word.

Mossman went out of his way to make sure that Su met Hillary. Seeing her standing by herself a few yards away (Pres-cott with his long experience of such events having gone in search of a quick refill), he beckoned her over.

'Come and meet the Senator, Su,' he called. He explained to Senator Clinton: 'We hope Su Soeung is soon going to ac-cept our offer to become SAVE's Capitol Hill liaison officer. She was born in Cambodia. Her father died there under Pol Pot.'

'I'm so sorry.' There was genuine concern in Mrs Clinton's voice, as she shook Su's hand. 'We mustn't ever forget about

Cambodia. We bear a great responsibility.' She turned to a staffer, a striking dark young woman who had come with her to the reception. 'This is Jessie Low, my foreign affairs assistant. You two should keep in touch.'

Just at that moment Hillary Clinton saw Prescott Glover re-emerge at Su's side. 'Oh, hello, Prescott,' she said rather flatly.

Prescott Glover gave no sign of noticing the lack of enthusiasm in the Senator's greeting.

'Good evening, Senator. I'm so glad...'

Before Prescott could continue, Andrew Mossman had shepherded Mrs Clinton away.

'Not one of my favourite personalities,' Prescott murmured in Su's ear.

'What did you do to upset her?' Su asked.

'I wrote a piece in *The Times* soon after she was elected to the Senate suggesting that even though she was a former President's wife, she would still have to earn her spurs.' Prescott laughed. 'Apparently she didn't like it.'

Later that evening, when they were ready to leave, Andrew Mossman once again buttonholed Su. 'Before you go, I'd like you to meet the Chinese Ambassador, Ting Wei-Ju. Excellency, this is Miss Soeung and Mr Glover.'

Ting Wei-Ju was a suave, well-spoken diplomat, over seventy years old but still looking tanned and fit. He wore an impeccably tailored suit and a Polka-dot silk tie.

When he learned from Mossman that Su was about to join SAVE in a senior role, Ting Wei-Ju said: 'Most important work. Very many congratulations. As you know, China has already ratified Ottawa Treaty. We believe all countries should ratify. China is ready to help in any way. Good luck in your assignment.'

The Ambassador shook hands warmly all round before moving on. Mossman lingered a moment with his guests. He looked around the now fast-emptying room. 'I think it went very well, don't you? Hope my speech wasn't too long.'

'Just the right length,' Prescott said diplomatically, thinking that actually – Mossman had pitched his appeal perfectly.

'Tell you what,' Mossman continued. 'If you two have a moment later on, why don't you stop by for a drink? Caroline's longing to meet Su. 3239 O street. Just off Wisconsin. Would nine p.m. suit you?'

Su glanced quickly at Prescott. 'Nine p.m. would suit us fine.'

★★★

'How much do you remember of the Pol Pot days?' Caroline Mossman asked her. The two men – Prescott Glover and Andrew Mossman – had gone off into Mossman's den to watch the last few minutes of a major league play-off. Caroline Mossman had stayed behind with Su and was now submitting her guest to a gentle but well-directed interrogation. As they sat side by side on the richly brocaded settee which seemed to occupy the whole of one wall in the elegant, Georgetown sitting room, the two women provided a marked contrast. Caroline Mossman – tall, blonde, expensively-tailored – looked every inch the Washington "power" woman. Su Soeung was shorter, darker, black hair cropped to the collar with high Khmer cheekbones lending a touch of the exotic.

'I remember enough,' Su replied quietly. 'I remember how the Khmer Rouge came to our house the very first day they arrived in Phnom Penh. April 17, 1975. My mother and I never forgot that date. They came on trucks and tractors waving flags. At first the people cheered. But by afternoon, the nightmare had begun.'

'What happened? Are you sure you don't mind talking about it?'

'No, I don't mind. Actually, it helps. Sometimes I'm afraid that I'll forget just how terrible it was. I don't want to forget. My father deserved better than that.'

'Did they take him straightaway?'

Su lowered her eyes. 'They were looking for him. The leader of the gang had a list in his hand and my father's name was on it. They beat him about the head with their rifles and shouted, "American spy," at him. I remember clinging to his legs and begging him to stay with us, but they kicked me away. Then they bound his hands and threw him into a truck. We never saw him again.'

'Did you ever find out what happened to him?'

'No, never. He vanished without trace. Just like so many others.'

'What was your father's name?'

'Hong. Hong Soeung. Of course, I called him "father."'

In spite of herself, Su was overcome with emotion. Caroline proffered a handkerchief which Su gratefully accepted.

'I'm so sorry,' she said. 'Sometimes I think how wonderful it would be to see him again though I know that's impossible.'

'You should take some time out while you're there to find out more about your family. Do some research. Ask some questions.'

Su looked at her with some surprise. 'That's exactly what I have been thinking myself.'

Caroline Mossman's face broke into a broad smile. 'So, you're going to take the job? That's wonderful!' She rose to her feet, walked to the door of the den and called to her husband.

'Andrew, did you hear the news? Su's going to join SAVE.'

Moments later, Andrew Mossman came back into the room with Prescott in tow. He threw an arm around Su's shoulder. 'Marvellous. Absolutely marvellous. Don't you think so, Prescott?'

'I do indeed. I'd been hoping Su would say yes.' Prescott looked at Su fondly. 'There comes a time when the ghosts of the past have to be laid – that is, if you want to move on in life.'

'I think this calls for champagne,' Mossman said. As he opened the bottle, the doorbell rang.

'I'll get it, if you like. You're busy.' Prescott went to the door and returned a minute later with the young woman who had been at the Smithsonian reception earlier that evening.

'Look what I found on the doorstep,' he said.

'Come in, Jessie,' Caroline Mossman called. 'Your timing is perfect. Shall we tell you the good news? Su Soeung is going to quit GW to join SAVE. She'll be on her way to Cambodia within the next few days.'

Jessie Low accepted a glass of champagne and looked at Su with transparent curiosity. 'This could be really important. For all of us. The Senator's really interested. I had a word with her after the reception. She wants me to keep in touch. In fact, she insists on it. We must have that lunch soon. Very soon. Certainly, before you leave. Do you promise?'

As far as Su Soeung was concerned, it had been one amazing day. Suddenly she seemed to be the most popular girl in the class. Was it nerves, was it the champagne or was it the faint sense of unreality which she was experiencing? Any or all of those, perhaps. She found herself almost giggling as she replied: 'Of course, some time soon. Lunch. Yes, definitely.'

Later, as they drove back to Su's apartment on Logan Circle, Prescott said: 'That was quite an evening, wasn't it? They come on a bit strong, don't they?'

'Who?'

'The Mossmans. Andrew and Caroline. And how come Jessie Low showed up like that? It all seemed pre-planned somehow.'

Su Soeung, still on a high, shrugged. 'I don't know what you mean. They probably asked Jessie like they asked us. On the spur of the moment. Are you saying I shouldn't have accepted the job?' She was beginning to sound miffed.

CHAPTER 2

Jessica Low called Su Soeung three days after their first meeting. She sounded harassed. There appeared to be some kind of shouting-match going on in the background.

'Su, this is Jessie Low. Good to talk to you. Lunch is going to be difficult. We're under a lot of pressure here at the moment. Could you get over here to the Senator's office? I'd like you to meet Jack Rosen before you go. Jack is the Senator's Communications director. How about tomorrow? Say, three p.m. in the Dirksen building.'

Su didn't care about missing out on lunch. She was pleased anyway that the Senator's people wanted to talk to her before she left for Cambodia though. She was also a bit surprised. Of course, she had met Senator Clinton's staffer at the Smithsonian reception, but she hadn't really expected the follow-up.

★★★

'The Senator's going to be in the Chamber most of the afternoon. We can use her office,' Jessica Low said, ushering Su into an airy room filled with the memorabilia of Hillary Clinton's years in the White House. A richly tasselled US flag stood in one corner of the room. The deep, leather chairs reeked of power.

Jack Rosen, in his shirtsleeves, came to join them. He was

a compact, bustling man, around forty, with dark, wiry hair beginning to go grey at the temples.

'I wanted you to meet Jack,' Jessica said, 'because in addition to being communications director, he's the Senator's senior policy adviser. I'm her legislative assistant. That means I look after the Committee work, particularly the Health, Education Labor and Pensions Committee. Mrs Clinton is on the Health as well as the Budget Committee. Jack keeps an eye on all her other interests, including foreign affairs.'

'Particularly Foreign Affairs,' Jack Rosen interrupted. He leaned forward in his chair. 'Let me spell it out. Jessie has just explained that the Senator is on the Health and Budgets Committee and as you know she's taking her work there very seriously. She has hit the ground running. But she doesn't want to stop there. People expect her to be interested in health particularly. Christ, it's what she did when she was in the White House. I won't say she's tired of it, but she wants and needs to expand her interests in the non-domestic area. Of course, the Senator's not a member of the Foreign Relations Committee – they're not going to hand out that kind of plum to a new girl even if she was once First Lady. So, we've been thinking about how to build up her foreign policy profile in other ways.'

'Is she going to run for the Presidency?' Su asked. It was the question everyone else in Washington was asking, so she didn't see why she shouldn't.

Rosen shrugged. 'Who knows? These are still early days. The Clinton name isn't always an asset! But whenever she runs, be it 2004 or 2008 or whenever, she has to have a track record in foreign affairs. One of the ideas we've come up with is Cambodia. We think Cambodia could be important. Of course, the focus is still on Afghanistan at the moment but I believe Cambodia's going to move rapidly up the foreign affairs agenda. With the Khmer Rouge trials finally about to start, we think things are about to liven up in a big way.'

'Of course, the Senator has to have a plausible reason for visiting Cambodia at this time.'

Rosen continued, 'That's why this whole landmine rehabilitation business is so important. It gives her a reason for getting out there if she has to. Christ, getting your legs blown off has to be a health issue. In the meantime, we could use some advance information, someone with their eyes and ears open. Cambodian eyes and ears. Nothing formal. We can't pay you. We'd just like you to help.'

'What kind of information?' Su was interested but she wasn't sure what Rosen was getting at.

'Apart from the health aspects, landmines and so forth, the Senator's particularly interested in the foreign policy and human rights issues. Those Khmer Rouge trials are going to stir up a lot of mud. Why do you think it's taken over twenty years to set up the tribunal, line up the defendants, few as they are, set up the terms of reference...? Let's just say the Senator wants to know what's going on, the inside dope if you find any. We think you could be ideally placed. What do you think? Will you do it?'

He'd pitched it exactly right. Su felt flattered. 'You may be over-estimating my abilities.'

'I think not,' Rosen smiled. 'The Senator's a pretty good judge of character. She knew about you before she met you and, when she met you, she liked what she saw.'

After Rosen had left, Su spent some more time with Jessie

Low, talking over the details of how and when to communicate, 'email's probably the best,' Jessie said. 'If you need to encrypt, we have a pretty good system here – or we think we do. Nobody seems to be reading our email at the moment. None of our enemies anyway. We'll set you up.'

Su wondered momentarily whether she wasn't getting in over her head. Was it too late to pull back? Any doubts she might have had on that score were overcome when, a few minutes later, the Senator returned from the Chamber.

Hillary Clinton remembered her immediately, 'Su... Su Soeung, isn't it? How good of you to stop by. Did you meet Jack? I'm so glad. He keeps on telling me that Cambodia has to be top of the list of my foreign affairs priorities. Let's have a proper talk when you come back?'

'Maybe you'll get out to Cambodia?' Su suggested.

'I believe Jack and Jessie are working on it,' the Senator laughed.

As the Senator turned to discuss business matters with her legislative assistant, Su said goodbye and made her way out into the anteroom. She walked out of the Dirksen building and around to the front of the Capitol. This was where, she reflected, the Presidential inauguration was held every four years. Most recently, a son had succeeded his father in the nation's highest office. Would a wife succeed her husband?

She picked up a cab on Pennsylvania Avenue. It was time to get back to George Washington University to clear her desk.

★★★

Three days later she was on a plane to Seattle. Her mother had wanted to come to the airport to meet her but Su had refused. Speaking Khmer to her over the telephone, as she always did, Su had said: 'I'll take a taxi. Let's have a proper Cambodian dinner together when I arrive. I haven't had one in ages.'

Sita Soeung, in her mid-seventies but well-preserved, lived in an apartment block on the edge of Chinatown. Though they were relatively new arrivals, the Cambodian refugees who had made their way to the United States in the late seventies and early eighties had found a hospitable welcome in Seattle. It was one of the few places on the West Coast where a large and varied Asian community – Chinese, Japanese, Filipinos, Cambodians – managed to live together in reasonable harmony. Outbreaks of racial or ethnic rivalry or violence were rare.

'It's the gentle climate, Su,' Sita would say. 'It doesn't often freeze in winter and it doesn't get too hot in summer. As for the rain, well, it rains in Cambodia too. I like the rain.'

As far as Su was concerned, it wasn't just the climate which made her love Seattle. It was the sheer beauty of the place. Sometimes she would walk down to the waterfront and stand there looking out at the range of snow-clad mountains across the bay, and marvel at her good fortune. So many of her countrymen and women had never had a chance to build their lives again.

It had been an emotional reunion. Su's plane had landed early and Su had reached Sita's apartment sooner than expected. Her mother was still preparing an intricate dish involving steamed fish and a variety of specialist ingredients which she had purchased that morning in one of the Chinatown street markets. Without removing her apron Sita Soeung had rushed to the door to embrace her daughter.

'Su! It has been so long!'

'Too long, mother.'

Su helped her mother with the meal. As the two women sat there at the kitchen table, peeling and chopping and shredding the vegetables and preparing the fish, Su explained the changes in her life to Sita.

'Of course, it's sudden, I know that,' she said. 'When SAVE made me the offer, it just seemed to be such a golden opportunity. America is my country, of course it is. Life here has been good to me. But Cambodia is my country too. I feel that now more than ever. I need to find out more.'

Sita shuddered. 'I will never go back. I could never live through that time again.'

Later, as they ate their meal together, Su said, 'When I am there, I am going to try to find out more about father. Why he died. How he died. I feel I owe him that.'

Sita Soeung spat out a piece of fish with a sudden vehemence. 'Be careful, Su. You may learn more than you wish to know. Isn't it better to leave things in peace? Put the past behind you.'

Su took her mother's hand for a moment. It was a gesture full of love. 'You have your ways of doing things, mother. I have mine.'

'So, you are using this organisation – what is it called, SAVE? – for your own purposes?'

Su nodded. 'Up to a point, that's true. But I have a job to do it and I'll do it to the best of my ability.' Then she added, thinking about her recent meeting with the Clinton staffers on Capitol Hill, 'Others may be using *me*.'

When she explained to her mother the nature of her unofficial assignment as "eyes and ears" for Senator Hillary Clinton in Cambodia, her mother was all the more sceptical. 'That woman! She is thinking of her own future and nothing else. You shouldn't meddle in politics. Certainly not in Cambodian politics.'

They talked late into the evening. Sita wanted Su to go through *The Washingtonian* article. 'I wish they'd written the piece in Khmer!'

Su laughed. 'Nobody reads Khmer in Washington.'

Su began by translating the text of the report on a paragraph-by-paragraph basis.

Sita Soeung was clearly delighted by the piece. 'You have done so well, darling. I am so proud of you. I meet people in the street nowadays and they say 'Oh, you must be Su Soeung's mother!'

Su smiled, 'I tell people I am Sita Soeung's daughter.'

'And Hong Soeung's too, never forget that.'

'How could I?'

For a moment the two of them sat there, with the magazine open on the table in front of them.

'I'm glad they used the photograph. Did the paper give it back to you when they had finished with it?'

'Funny, Prescott asked that same question.' Su rummaged in her bag and fished out the photo. 'I thought I'd take it to Cambodia with me. Somebody might recognise father even now and remember what happened.'

Sita Soeung held up to the original photograph to the light. It was creased and faded but the image, as the magazine editors had found, was still sharp.

'I had that photograph all the time we were on the move,'

Sita was deeply touched. 'First when we marched to Kompong and then when they drove us on to Battambang. It was the only picture I had of your father, of the family. I just grabbed it from the frame when the Khmer Rouge forced us to leave our house in Phnom Penh. I used to hide it wherever I could, in my clothes before they turned to rags, or under the floorboards when we stopped in a hut. The Khmer Rouge would have killed us if they had found it. But I ran the risk. It was the only picture I had of him, of us.'

'Who took the photograph, mother?' Su asked. 'It's more than a snapshot. It's a high-quality picture.'

The older woman frowned in concentration as she tried to remember. 'Gaetana. I'm sure it was Gaetana Enders. I used to help her with the welfare centre for widows which she ran. I invited her to the house one day and she brought a camera with her. Later, she sent me the photo. Gaetana was Italian, but her husband was American. Tom Enders.'

'I remember Gaetana. She had such a lovely smell. Expensive perfume, I suppose. But what did Tom Enders look like? Did I ever meet him?'

'He was a giant of a man. Six foot eight tall. Imagine that in Cambodia! You may have met him. I'm pretty sure you did. Do you remember a man as tall as that?'

As her mother spoke, Su Soeung had experienced an uncanny sensation of flying backwards through time, as though someone had pressed the fast rewind button on her life and the tape was whistling back to her early childhood.

'Sometimes, on a Sunday morning, father would take me to the golf club. Once or twice, I remember him playing with a very tall American. I would walk along behind them, carrying a bag of golf balls. I don't think I had ever seen such a tall man. Could that have been Tom Enders?'

'That would have been Tom all right,' Sita said. 'I believe he died some years ago but Gaetana is still alive. Sometimes I think I should try to make contact with her. Some group she was involved with helped to sponsor us when we left the refugee camp in Thailand and came to the States. But then I ask myself what the point would be. I try to forget. That's the best way.'

'The best way for you maybe,' Su reproved her mother gently.

Su helped her mother with the washing-up.

'Are you and Prescott still together, Su?' Sita Soeung asked. 'I hope you don't mind my asking. I like Prescott. He's a good man. You two should get married. I don't understand how it is with you young people.'

Su smiled at her mother. 'I know how you feel.'

'In Cambodia, the families would insist.' Sita was too delicate to spell out what she meant but Su took the point anyway.

'I think we will soon get married,' she said.

Sita Soeung gave her daughter a great hug. 'You'll get married in the Cambodian style, right here in Seattle.'

'If I'm going to be married Cambodian style, I'd prefer to be married in Cambodia,' Su said quietly. 'You'd have to go back to Cambodia for that.'

Sita grimaced. 'That's the only thing that would get me back there, I promise you.'

'I won't let you forget you said that,' Su laughed.

Before she went to bed, Su called Prescott in Washington. He sounded grumpy. 'Do you know what time it is here?'

'It's important,' Su apologised. When Prescott was fully awake, she asked him: 'Does the name Tom Enders mean anything to you? Apparently, he was in the US mission in Phnom Penh in 1974.'

'It certainly does mean something to me. For those who followed developments in Indo-China, Enders was a bit of a legend. He was the American deputy chief of mission in Phnom Penh. He virtually ran the show out there for a time.'

'His wife, Gaetana, tried to look after the widows and orphans the US bombing created. My mother used to help her.'

'Well, that was just one of life's little ironies, wasn't it? Gaetana was – still is – a lovely lady. She'd try to pick up the pieces wherever she was. She's a widow herself now, of course. Tom died a few years back.'

'Mother told me that. Why did he die?'

'I think disappointment may have had something to do with it. Truth to tell, his career was stalled after Cambodia. Too many people in this town were out to get him. As I suspect you may discover, Cambodia is a hot potato, politically speaking. Why do you want to know about Enders anyway?'

Su was non-committal. 'I'm trying to work things out in my mind.'

Next morning at breakfast, before she left for Seatac airport, she asked her mother, 'Why did daddy know Tom Enders?'

Sita was surprised at the question. 'Your father was one of the top officials in the Cambodian Ministry of Culture under Lon Nol. He knew many people at the US Embassy, and he worked closely with Enders. They were friends as well as colleagues. That's how I got to know Gaetana.'

Su took a sip of her tea and sighed. 'No wonder they came looking for him. Poor father.'

'We were lucky they didn't take us too,' Sita said.

'Why didn't they?'

'I guess our names weren't on the list.'

Two hours later, after promising her mother that she would stay in close touch, Su Soeung left Seattle on the next leg of her journey.

★★★

Tired after the long flight across the Pacific, Su spent the night at the Regal Hotel in Hong Kong's new international airport. Early next morning, she flew on to Phnom Penh. It was a short hop, less than two hours. Around ten a.m. the plane came into land and Su had her first view of the Mekong River and the green expanses of the paddy fields below. She felt a lump in her throat.

Amid the jostling crowd of Khmers at Pochentong airport, she caught a glimpse of a fair-haired man with a moustache who carried a board with her name on it.

'Hello. I'm Jules Barron,' the man shook her hand, before helping her with her case. 'Welcome to Cambodia. I'm in charge of SAVE's office here.'

'I know that at least!' Su smiled.

The SAVE car was at the curb outside, a white four-wheel drive Nissan jeep. Jules told the driver to go straight to the Cambodiana Hotel. When the driver looked hesitant, Jules grew emphatic. 'Try it anyway!' he instructed.

Turning round to talk to her, Jules explained. 'We're in the middle of the three-day Water Festival. They call it Bon Om Tuk. The Cambodiana's located right in the thick of things at the junction of the Mekong and the Tonle Sap. Most of the streets are closed to traffic. There will be thousands of pedestrians milling around. We'll just have to see how we get on.'

As they bumped along the potholed road which led into town, Su asked, 'How long have you been here?'

'Three years,' Barron replied. 'Before that I worked with *Médecins sans Frontières* in Vietnam.'

'You're French, aren't you?'

'Can't you tell?' Jules smiled. 'The French used to run this country. Not anymore. We used to call it French Indochina. Indo-Chine. Vietnam, Laos, Cambodia – you could get croissants anywhere! Damn good croissants too, better than in Montmartre! When we pulled out of Indochina, the Americans thought they could take over. They learned their lesson, didn't they?'

'I suppose they did.' As the driver swerved to avoid people and livestock cluttering up the highway, Su concentrated on the road. She could catch up on the politics later.

'We'll probably be able to drive along Monivong Boulevard till we reach Preah Sihanouk,' Jules said. 'After that we shall have to see. We may have to walk the last bit.'

As they neared the river, the numbers of people hurrying on foot to the site of the Water Festival increased dramatically. At the first roadblock, Jules passed out a handful of notes to the policeman on duty and they were waved through. Two hundred yards later, the same thing happened again.

'The closer you try to get to the heart of the action, the more it costs,' Jules explained. 'It helps having a white car with a blue logo. They think we're United Nations. The UN still carries a lot of clout round here and some of it rubs off on organisations like SAVE.'

'I just want to get to the hotel,' Su said.

'You picked the wrong day!'

Half-an-hour later, still in their vehicle, they had managed finally to force a way through the crowds to the hotel. Two bellboys rushed out to help Su with her luggage.

'You'll probably want to rest.' Jules said. 'Why don't we meet in the lobby later, say at six p.m.? We can go and watch the fun and have some dinner.'

'That sounds great.' Suddenly Su felt overwhelmed. It wasn't just the noise, the crowds of people garlanded with festive flowers, the hooting of mopeds and motor-rickshaws – all the sights and sounds and smells of Asia. It was the fact that at last she had made it back to the land of her birth. To the land where her father was buried.

Ten minutes later, when the bellboy had left with a fat tip in his hand and she was alone in her hotel room looking out at the great river where the pirogues were already lining up to practise for the evening races, she felt a tear trickling down her cheek.

★★★

Su Soeung was fast asleep when the telephone rang. It was Jules Barron from the lobby.

'Take your time, we can wait,' Barron said.

'I'll be right down.'

When, feeling much refreshed, Su emerged from the elevator into the lobby of the Cambodiana Hotel, she saw Barron sitting by the door talking to a pretty Cambodian woman dressed in jeans and a white long-sleeved blouse. Su guessed she was about her own age.

'I've brought Lina along,' Jules rose to greet her. 'Lina Chan. Lina is my partner.'

The two women shook hands. 'I think we will be friends,' Lina smiled.

'I'm sure we will,' Su replied politely.

'We'll have dinner later. There will be plenty of time for you two to get to know each other then,' said Jules. 'We had better go now, otherwise we'll miss the action.'

If anything, the crowds were even denser than they had been earlier. They pushed their way along Sisowath Quay dodging the motor-scooters and bicycle-rickshaws, the vendors of fruit and flowers, the pulsating masses of people.

'Stick close to me,' Jules called, forging ahead. 'We don't want to get split up now.'

The Tonle Sap River lay to their right. Through occasional gaps in the crush, Su could see the huge colourful pirogues, each manned by around sixty oarsmen, thrashing up and down.

'What are they doing?' she asked.

'These are the heats,' Lina explained, keeping close to Su in the throng. 'Later on, we will have the finals.'

'Do they do this every year?'

'The Water Festival was banned for a long time but now it's permitted again. We celebrate the change in the direction of the river. During the rainy season, the pressure of the water coming down the Mekong causes the Sap River to change direction and flow upstream. Then, when the rains are over, the Tonle Sap flows back towards the sea.'

'Sounds like a miracle. Maybe this is a land of miracles. I hope so.'

'Why do you say that?' Lina asked.

'I'm not sure. I just have a feeling.' She did have a feeling, too. Su Soeung glanced at her companion. How many miracles had Lina seen in her life, she wondered? How much sadness had that young woman witnessed? Leaving one's country was painful enough, but for those who stayed so many things must have been unendurable.

They passed the Silver Pagoda and the Royal Palace on their left and a few hundred yards further on caught up with Jules outside the Foreign Correspondents Club of Cambodia.

'We'll have a grand-stand view from here,' Jules said.

They followed him up two flights of stairs into a large open room decorated with faded photographs and press-cuttings. There was a much-frequented bar in the middle of the room, as well as tables and chairs for those who were tired of standing. A long balcony looked out over the river.

'We're lucky!' Jules said. 'It looks as though they've kept a table for us. Pays to be a regular customer.'

The barman waved them over to a table at one end of the balcony. Jules waited till Su and Lina had taken their seats, then headed for the bar.

As they waited for Jules to return with their drinks, Su took in the scene. 'Who are all these people?' she asked Lina. She spoke in Khmer. Somehow it seemed more natural when it was just the two of them.

'Quite a few journalists, of course,' Lina replied, also in

Khmer. 'This was a famous meeting place for the press corps once. Sydney Schanberg, Jon Swain, Dith Pran – they all came here in the old days and now the place is picking up again. Most days you'll see someone from Reuters or the BBC or Agence France Presse. You'll see embassy types too. They pick up news and gossip here. Even some businessmen. The Chinese and the Koreans are trying to expand their activities. It's hard work though. The country is so poor. There is such a long way to go. That's why you'll see plenty of UN types in the club too. There must be twenty different UN aid programmes in Cambodia, quite apart from the work that non-governmental organisations like SAVE are doing. And of course, the UN is supervising the tribunal.'

'You mean the trial of the Pol Pot people?'

'Exactly,' Lina replied. 'You came at a good time. The sparks are about to fly.'

'You mean the shit is about to hit the fan.' Still speaking Khmer, Su was delighted she remembered how to express the phrase in colloquial Cambodian.

Lina laughed, 'All those years you've lived in America and still you speak Khmer so well.'

'I'm rusty. I may be able to speak Khmer, but I don't read it very well.'

'I'm sure you'll get plenty of practice while you're here.'

As Lina spoke, they heard a roar from the crowd outside.

'Looks like the races have begun,' Jules said, re-joining them. 'Here have an Angkor beer.'

With glasses of cold beer in their hands, they stood up to get a better view of the regatta.

Su found the spectacle entirely engrossing. Boats and

crews seemed to have been entered from all over the country, each one being decked out in a distinctive livery. Since this was the third and last day of the Water Festival, only a select few had made it through to the final rounds. The skill the oarsmen displayed was extraordinary. Sometimes, they would remain seated, rowing together in perfect timing. But sometimes, when they needed to put on a spurt, sixty lithe, brown bodies would rise as one and they would paddle furiously, using the extra leverage of their standing position to increase both the rate and thrust of the strike.

As it grew late, the floodlights came on and the final heats were completed in near darkness.

'The revelry will go on all night,' Jules explained. 'King Sihanouk himself may even appear. Sometimes he comes out of the Palace to address the crowd and hand out the prizes. There'll be dancing in the streets. Do you have a room facing the river? You do? That's all right then. You shouldn't be disturbed too much.'

Later, they had dinner together on the upstairs terrace. It was only her first day in Cambodia but Su felt she had so much to learn, she hated to waste time.

'How old is King Sihanouk?' she asked.

Jules looked at Lina. 'King Norodom Sihanouk? How old would you say he is, Lina?'

'I know my Cambodian history,' Lina smiled. 'I was a teacher once. Sihanouk was crowned king in 1941. He was eighteen at the time. So he was born around 1923. That means he's over eighty now.'

'Good heavens!' Su exclaimed. 'Has he been king all that time?'

'Yes and no. Once he abdicated in favour of his father. And during the Lon Nol years, he was exiled in China. He came back when Pol Pot took over.'

'Was Sihanouk a supporter of Pol Pot?' Su persisted.

Jules gave a wry smile. 'Cambodian politics is pretty complicated. Sihanouk has been at the heart of it for over sixty years. One of the enduring enigmas has been his relationship with Pol Pot. When he was in exile in China, he was the titular head of the Khmer Rouge. Pol Pot brought him back to Phnom Penh after they took over in 1975. But they kept him under virtual house arrest; they murdered members of his family. So, was he a supporter or not of Pol Pot? That's a hard one to answer. Even now, I doubt if we know the whole story.'

At that moment, Jules spotted a tall, sun-tanned figure wearing a bush hat come up the stairs onto the terrace. Obviously happy to be able to change the subject, he waved energetically. 'Hello, Geoff, come and join us.'

'That's very kind of you.'

Jules introduced the new arrival. 'This is Geoff Jackson. Geoff is an Australian who has been appointed by the UN Secretary-General as his special representative to oversee the upcoming trial of the Pol Pot veterans.'

A broad smile came over the Australian's craggy face. '"Oversee" isn't quite the word we favour. This is a Cambodian show, you know. They're in charge. There will be some foreign jurists on the panel, but the UN's role is purely that of an observer, to see fair play.'

'Fair play for Duch and Ta Mok, two of the worst murderers in human history?' Jules exploded.

He turned to Su, 'In case you didn't know, Duch was the

principal interrogator at the notorious Tuol Sleng torture centre. Ta Mok was one of Pol Pot's warlords. A one-legged walking terror known as the Butcher.'

'Hey, I haven't even had a beer yet.' There was a hint of steel in Jackson's mild tones. 'Even these two gentlemen are innocent until proven guilty.'

Geoff Jackson stayed with them, knocking back the beers, for well over an hour. 'By profession, I'm an academic,' he explained. 'A human rights lawyer from Melbourne University. I was Australia's representative to the UN Human Rights Commission and I guess that's where Kofi Annan spotted me. In real life, of course, I'm just a hard-drinking Aussie!'

Though reluctant, as he had already indicated, to be drawn on the detail of the proceedings or to speculate on the final outcome of the trial, Jackson was happy enough to throw out a few titbits of information.

'As far as I'm concerned, Duch – real name Kang Kek Ieu – is the fascinating one. Did you know he's "got religion?" When they arrested him, he told them he was a born again Christian!'

'And do you think he really is one?' Su asked. Her first day back in Cambodia was turning out to be far more fascinating than she could ever have imagined.

'Who knows?' Jackson shrugged. 'I haven't asked. Whenever I see Duch, he's surrounded by vast piles of paperwork. He's got a team of lawyers and they're sifting through the evidence.'

'What kind of evidence?' Su persisted.

'He seems to be going through the old Tuol Sleng records, the so-called "confessions" trying to show that he was never implicated, that he even wasn't there.'

'Like Macavity the mystery cat?' suggested Jules.

'Just so,' Geoff Jackson laughed, picked up his bush hat from the table and rose to his feet.

'I've got to be getting back,' he said. 'We've got a long day ahead of us tomorrow. The panel is hearing the prosecution's opening deposition. Could take days. Could take months. Be seeing you.'

As Jackson strode off into the night, Jules said, 'Geoff is a terrific fellow. Straight as an arrow. They couldn't have picked a better man.'

Lina Chan, who had remained quite quiet while Geoff Jackson was with them, nodded enthusiastically. 'I so agree. So much of what happens here is going to depend on the documentation. What the tribunal allows in evidence. Jackson's role in steering the tribunal could be vital. If the case against Ta Mok and Duch is going to be made, it's not going to be done through witnesses. There aren't any witnesses. Or very few. What matters is the record, the documents, the Tuol Sleng files, the photographs. Do they stand up or don't they?'

'Well, you ought to know about that, Lina,' Jules said quietly.

Su caught the glance that passed between them.

'Lina works for DC-Cam,' Jules explained.

'What's DC-Cam?'

'The Documentation Centre of Cambodia,' Lina told her. 'It has hundreds of thousands of pages of documents on the Khmer Rouge. Some of the Tuol Sleng "confessions" are even on microfiche.'

'You gave up being a teacher to work at DC-Cam?' Su asked.

'Exactly. I felt I didn't have a choice. This was something I had to do.'

'You have photos too? Photos of the victims?'

'We have images of more than five thousand victims,' Lina told her.

'Oh, my God!' Su held her hand over her mouth. She felt suddenly sick. She got up from the table and went to the balcony, allowing the night air to waft over her.

When she returned to her seat, Jules Barron and Lina Chan were looking at her worriedly.

'Are you all right?' Lina asked.

'Yes, take it easy,' Jules said. 'You've had a long day. We had better get you back.'

'I'm alright,' Su said. 'It has been rather an emotional experience, coming back.'

Lina looked at her sympathetically. 'My family would have left too if they had a chance. But we were in the wrong part of the country. We were never able to make it to the Thai border and the refugee camps. Maybe that makes it easier for us now. We've been able to get used to the horror. After all, we have had to live with it for so long now.'

While Lina spoke, an idea was taking shape in Su's mind. It was a long shot. It would be incredible if it worked. But she had to try.

'Can I come and visit DC-Cam one day?' She asked. 'Is that allowed?'

Lina took her hand briefly across the table. 'Of course, it's allowed. It's encouraged. We're here to help. One of our tasks is to make sure people never forget.'

'I shall never forget, never,' Su said quietly. As she spoke, she had the clearest mental image of her father standing on the veranda of their old house just off Norodom Boulevard, with his pipe in his mouth watching the stars.

Before they left the club that night, they were treated to a spectacular display of fireworks. When it was over, a hush fell on the crowd.

'It looks as though King Sihanouk is going to speak,' Lina explained.

In the distance they saw the gates of the Royal Palace open to allow a convoy of cars to emerge. A burnished throne had been constructed by the waterfront to which the royal party now repaired. Soon the night was filled with the broadcast sounds of Sihanouk's address.

Though they were too far away to hear what the King was saying, there was no mistaking the effect his words had on the throng. They were listened to with rapt, almost reverential, attention.

Old habits died hard.

CHAPTER 3

Su was up early the next morning. She spent a magical half-hour in the hotel pool as the sun came up over the Mekong. As she towelled herself dry, she looked at the turbulent front of water where the now seaward-flowing Tonle Sap joined the larger river. There was not much sign of the previous night's festivities, apart from some debris floating in the quieter eddies near the shore. In the middle distance, where the low hummocks of the Chruoy Chang peninsula held the eye, she could see that half a dozen local fishermen had spread their nets.

'G'day, lovely morning! You're out and about early!'

Su turned to see Geoff Jackson standing behind her. The tall Australian was dressed in crisp, white, short-sleeved shirt and neatly pressed slacks.

'Wish I could join you for breakfast,' he said. 'Unfortunately, I've got a business meeting. Damn defence lawyers! I've told them that if our Khmer Rouge friends plead guilty, we can be out of here by Christmas. But they won't go for it. Mind you, I'm impartial, of course. Wholly impartial!'

Su found herself warming to the man. Her experience to date of UN bureaucrats had led her to believe that they were a bunch of stuffed shirts. Geoff Jackson seemed to be a refreshing exception.

'Good luck,' she said. She noticed two middle-aged Cambodians, both carrying briefcases, come out onto the terrace above the pool where tables were set for breakfast.

Jackson noticed them too and excused himself. 'I see my guests have arrived. I had better get going.'

An hour later, the driver came to pick her up for her first appointment of the day.

Back in Washington, Andrew Mossman had briefed her on the extent of the landmine problem in Cambodia. He had given her the statistics. So many million mines laid: so many thousands of amputees. But nothing had prepared her for the shock of walking into SAVE's Phnom Penh clinic on a normal working day.

There must have been forty people in the waiting-room, ranging from children as young as six to old men who must have been well into their sixties.

Jules Barron, who had arrived ahead of her at the clinic, explained the set-up. 'We've more or less divided the country into half. This clinic services the southern and eastern provinces, particularly Kompong Thom, Kompong Speu and Kampot. We use our Siem Reap clinic for the northern and western provinces. We run mobile clinics from both locations as well, since a lot of the injured are quite simply unable to travel long journeys.'

As they stood there in the waiting room, a young man in a white coat came to join them.

'This is Dr Borei Pen,' Jules said, as he introduced Su. 'Borei is the director of the Phnom Penh clinic. He supervises a team of doctors and therapists here. The clinic is open five days a week, from eight in the morning to five in the evening. And I can tell you the activity never stops. That's right, Borei?'

The young Cambodian doctor nodded. 'We have as much

work as we can possibly handle. If we had the funds, we could double the size of the clinic and still we would only scratch the surface.'

'That goes for Siem Reap, too,' Jules added before going on to explain: 'Su Soeung is SAVE's new Congressional liaison officer. Her job is to make sure the US Congress understands how important your work is here.'

'Will she find us more money too?'

'I shall certainly do my best,' Su said.

Su spent the next two hours witnessing at first hand SAVE's noble work of replacing shattered limbs. Since the Phnom Penh clinic doubled as SAVE's administrative headquarters, Jules was able to retire to his office while Dr Pen showed Su around. He took her through the waiting-room first.

'It's the children who are the most at risk,' Dr Pen explained in Khmer. 'Of course, they are warned about the mines, but they forget. They're playing in the road, they chase a ball or each other into a field, and suddenly – bam! – they've lost a leg. Maybe both legs. Look around. You'll see leg injuries are by far the most common, particularly among the young.'

With his arm he gestured to a group of children waiting patiently to be examined. Some of the lucky ones – those who still had one serviceable leg and at least one arm as well – had managed to install themselves on the wooden chairs which lined the walls of the waiting room, using a variety of crude, homemade crutches to propel themselves or else relying on the assistance of friends or relatives. Others, worse off in so far as their injuries had deprived them of the use of both their lower limbs, had been allocated space on the floor. When it was their turn to be examined, they would be lifted bodily and carried into the surgery.

Having always had (thank God!) the use of all four limbs, Su found it hard to imagine what it must be like to live like this. Of course, she had watched the Paralympics on television where muscular men and women overcame horrendous handicaps to perform spectacular feats of athleticism. She had no wish to detract from those achievements. But what must it be like to live on a pavement day after day with both legs amputated above the knee?

Dr Pen seemed to understand what she was thinking. 'We offer them hope,' he said. 'The prostheses we provide are necessarily complicated items. Some of them we even manufacture locally, using local workmen and local materials. But these pieces of equipment – an artificial hand, an artificial leg – can work a miracle in these people's lives. It's not overnight. They have to learn how to live with the prosthesis, how to use it to the best advantage. Sometimes they have to come back to the clinic to have the fittings adjusted, though we try to discourage return visits if we can – there are simply too many people to see. If we started seeing everybody twice, we would be even more behind than we are.

'As I said, what SAVE has given these people is hope,' he continued. 'I see it in their eyes. Sometimes I meet in the street people I have helped professionally. Their gratitude is touching, overwhelming. We have in a very real sense been able to transform their lives. Of course, we are fighting an endless battle. Every time we fit one artificial limb, there are five more victims queuing up behind, waiting to be treated.'

'What happened to the de-mining programme?' Su asked. 'That was meant to make a difference.'

'It goes on; it's important. But it's too slow. At the current rate of progress, Cambodia will not be free of mines till the end of the twenty-first century. That's why organisations like SAVE are so vital. They offer immediate help for immediate needs.'

Later, Dr Pen took her into the treatment room itself. She sat on a chair, unobtrusively. The doctor said: 'Stay as long as you like, you won't disturb me. Feel free to ask questions. It's a bit like a conveyor belt when we get going, but that's the way it has to be. We don't have time for the niceties.'

For the next two hours, Su watched as the clinic progressed. Where patients had already had the benefit of a preliminary examination, new prostheses were fitted. Where a full examination had yet to be conducted, Dr Pen's technique seemed designed to combine speed with accuracy. Su's occasional questions failed to disturb his concentration. He answered without pausing or looking up from his task.

Once, when she asked him what degree of mobility a young man who had lost his leg from mid-thigh might expect to have, he replied: 'We are working on a new knee joint, which gives seventy or eighty per cent flexibility. Even a footballer doesn't need much more than that!'

'That's marvellous,' Su murmured from behind her curtain. She meant it. She found herself, quite literally, marvelling.

As the day wore on, she began to see her job with a totally new perspective. It was one thing to understand, theoretically, what SAVE was all about. It was quite another thing to experience it at first hand. How right Andrew Mossman had been to insist that she should see for herself at first-hand what the organisation was doing – on the ground, in the field – before trying to "sell" it to Congress.

Towards the end of the day, Jules Barron put his head round the door.

'You should get back to the hotel, Su. You're going to need a break before your next assignment.'

'What's that?' Su whispered.

'Lina just called. There's someone rather special we wanted you to meet. It turns out he's free for dinner tonight. We hope you'll join us.'

'Delighted,' Su said. Her time in Phnom Penh seemed to be crammed with activity.

A few minutes later, she proffered her warm thanks to the doctor and staff of the clinic, found her driver waiting for her and headed back through the busy afternoon traffic to the hotel.

★★★

'May I introduce Narong Sum,' Lina said. 'We are very privileged to have Narong with us this evening. His paintings have become famous in Cambodia. And now we have been discussing with him whether we may display them on the website which the Documentation Centre of Cambodia-DC-Cam has developed.'

A thin, white-haired gentleman who was, Su supposed, in his late sixties or early seventies rose to his feet to greet her.

'I'm very pleased to meet you,' Narong Sum said, 'I know about the work which your organisation is doing. When we destroy, we must rebuild. But of course, we must never forget.'

Jules Barron arrived with a tray of drinks on the veranda of the simple, suburban house which he and Lina shared.

'Soft drinks, beer, whiskey? Take your pick.'

Both Su and Lina, as well as Narong, chose a soft drink. 'I gave up alcohol many years ago,' Narong explained. 'I am still trying to paint things as I see them. I find alcohol distorts the vision.'

'Luckily, I'm not so talented.' Jules poured himself a whiskey. 'You must see Sarong's paintings before you leave Cambodia. At least the Tuol Sleng series.'

Over dinner, Narong seemed quite ready to talk about his experiences.

'I was in the first batch of prisoners brought into Tuol Sleng. Duch made us all write out our biographies. That was part of his technique. I wrote that I had been a painter and I think that intrigued him. Soon the torture stopped. He told me I had to paint a historical record of the prison and that is what I did.'

'Narong's paintings are still on display there in the prison,' Lina said. 'DC-Cam had them examined not long ago. They may need some restoration here and there, but on the whole the paintings are in good shape.'

'I painted what I saw,' Narong said. 'When Duch told me to paint the tortures, that is what I painted. Only seven men escaped alive from Tuol Sleng. I was one of them. If Duch hadn't wanted the paintings to be completed, he would never have let me live.'

Narong Sum spoke so matter of factly that Su found it hard to imagine how he could have endured years of unimaginable hardships in Pol Pot's most notorious gaol and still have lived to tell the tale.

'The other survivors, are they still alive?' she asked.

Narong looked at Lina. 'DC-Cam may know the answer,' he said.

Lina explained: 'DC-Cam tries to keep track of the Tuol Sleng survivors. We believe all other six besides Narong are still alive. Or at least they were until a couple of years back.'

'So, you know all their names?' Su asked.

'Oh, yes, we know all their names' Lina said. 'One thing the Pol Pot regime was good at was documentation. Tuol Sleng is probably the best documented torture centre in the history of mankind.'

Over dinner, Narong Sum seemed to slip into a kind of reverie. For a moment Su thought he had dozed off. She would not have blamed him if he had.

Then suddenly the old man opened his eyes and said, harking back without apology to the previous conversation: 'I sometimes wonder whether there weren't some other survivors after all. Seven, just seven! That seems such a small number. Think of how many prisoners came to Tuol Sleng and were either tortured to death there or sent on to execution at the Choeung Ek killing fields. What are the figures, Lina? I know you have the figures.'

'At least thirteen thousand,' Lina replied. 'We have firm documentation for that number.'

'Exactly!' Narong Sum exclaimed, quite awake by now. 'Why should not there have been some other survivors? It seems extraordinary that there would not have been. Maybe Duch knew there had been escapes but said nothing.'

Lina shook her head. 'I don't think so, Narong. The record keeping was too precise. We know all the details. There was no room for error.'

The old man stuck stubbornly to his point. 'At least in the first year. There was much disorder then. I know, I was there. Sometimes you saw a prisoner and then he was gone. Had he died under torture? Had he been sent to Choeung Ek? Or had he escaped? Did the records always show the truth, or were they possibly falsified?'

Lina thought about that for a while. 'Possible, not likely,' she said finally.

Narong Sum burst out laughing, 'You concede my point.'

'I concede the possibility,' Lina corrected him.

Jules decided that the conversation was taking a rather macabre turn. In Cambodia, where so many families had been touched by decades of war, to say nothing of Pol Pot's genocidal activities, it was difficult – even at mealtimes – to avoid mentioning the unmentionable. But Su had already had a long and intense day. He felt she deserved a break.

'I'm sure you both have a point,' he said amicably.

Jules' diplomatic efforts were rewarded when Narong's face broke into a broad smile. 'Let us indeed hope so.'

Soon after, Narong took his leave. Jules retired to his study. Su and Lina were left alone at the table.

'In this country, we all have different ways of dealing with the past,' Lina said. 'Take Narong Sum. The paintings he made in Tuol Sleng are in a sense the high point of his career as an artist, macabre though this sounds. And do you know what excites Narong most at the moment? It's the fact that a whole cache of his sketches has turned up in Tuol Sleng, work he's forgotten he'd even done. He's busy sorting and cataloguing them at home at the moment. When he's finished, we'll probably put on a special exhibition for him.'

Even though she had only known her for a couple of days, Su felt very close to the other woman.

'Thank you for inviting me tonight. Meeting Narong was a rare privilege. I know I can see the paintings in Tuol Sleng, and I'll do that. But do you think he would let me see his sketches too?'

Lina laughed, 'I think you made quite an impression on the old man. I'm sure he'd be happy to show you his work.'

The two women sat together in companionable silence. Su found it hard to believe that it was less than forty-eight hours since she had left the shores of the United States. Though she couldn't quite say why, she felt that extraordinary things were happening to her and that when she returned to America after this visit to Asia, she would be a much-changed person.

'I wonder if you and I could conceivably have ever met before,' Su broke the silence at last. 'Could you have been on the road with all the other people who were driven from Phnom Penh in April 1975? Even though I was only seven at the time, I can still remember it. The fear, the hunger, the lack of medicine. I think we were lucky. They took my father away before we left, dragged him off from the steps of our house. But somehow my mother and I managed to stay together. I had a brother too, an elder brother, two years older than me, but he got dysentery and his stomach swelled up and there was no medicine – it was a crime even to ask the guards for medicine, they could beat you to death for that – and soon he died. That was terrible, of course, but judging by some of the other stories I've heard, I don't think we had the worst of it. We escaped to Thailand quite soon. I remember being hidden under some sacks on a truck with my mother warning me that "they" would kill us if I made a noise. I didn't know who "they" were, but I was as quiet as a mouse anyway.'

'There are so many different stories of that terrible time,' Lina said. 'With the work I do, I hear these stories every day, I read the documents, we try to keep the records. Each person has his or her own memories. Each one is valid, authentic. These things happened. In 1975 and 1976, 1977 and 1978, these things happened. I never cease to be amazed.'

'What about your own story?' Su persisted.

'My family came from Battambang, not Phnom Penh. My father was a high school teacher, my mother was a tailor. They only had one child – me. The Khmer Rouge drove everybody out of the town, just as they did in Phnom Penh. They told the people that the Americans would drop bombs on the city, so everyone had to leave. We were sent to a forced labour camp near Siem Reap. They shot my father two months later. He was only a junior teacher, but they accused him of being an intellectual. They made him sign a confession and then they killed him. My mother died a few months later. I think the shock killed her.'

'I'm so sorry,' Su felt that anything she said would be inadequate.

'Don't be sorry. I lived to tell the tale. So many others didn't.'

Su felt she needed some air, some movement. She walked to the edge of the veranda and looked out at the lake. She could make out the dim shapes of a couple of fishing boats not far from shore. How peaceful, how serene it was, away from the hustle of the city. But that only made it all the more difficult to envisage the tornado of violence which had engulfed this gentle land.

'How did you escape?' Su asked, returning to her seat with her emotions once more under control.

'I didn't escape.'

'What do you mean?'

'There was nowhere else for me to go. Nothing else for me to do. I became one of the young guards. They gave me a uniform of sorts. Sandals made out of old car tyres, a red kerchief, a wooden rifle to carry. Half of it was psychological. In their attempt to rebuild society, they wanted to destroy the family unit, turn the children against the parents.'

'Did they force you to beat people? Did you have to kill them?' Su didn't really want to ask those questions, but she felt an irresistible desire to know the worst.

Lina smiled a tired, wan smile. 'You mean did I as a seven-year-old, eight-year-old child help commit murders? The answer is no. Even for those monsters, I was too young for that kind of work. I knew others who did. I don't blame them, truly I don't blame them. In the children's guard unit, the brainwashing was intense. Killing was a duty. Something you did for the greater glory of Angka or the party. Don't forget the Khmer Rouge was a communist movement from the start. Pol Pot or Saloth Sar, to give him his real name, used to boast he was leading the most successful communist revolution the world had ever seen.'

'What happened to you after you joined the youth brigade?' Su asked.

'After a while, I was brought back to the city with about fifty other children. We were housed in one of the old convent schools the French nuns used to run. We even received a rudimentary education. Then in 1979, when the Vietnamese invaded and drove the Khmer Rouge back into the jungle, my life was suddenly transformed. There was if you like a return to normalcy. The schools, the university reopened. I grew up, got a degree, got a job. End of story.'

'And the children who were in the brigade with you? Do you ever see them?'

'Sometimes. Once or twice a year I bump into people I recognise but we don't talk.'

Su didn't want to outstay her welcome. As she stood up to go, she said: 'Last night, at the Club, you said I could visit your centre. Did you mean it? It would mean such a lot to me.'

'It would mean a lot to me too,' Lina replied. 'Come tomorrow if you can.'

'I'm going to visit the clinic again in the morning, but I could come in the afternoon.'

Lina, impulsively, kissed her on the cheek. 'Marvellous, I'll wait for you.'

Just at the moment, Jules came out. 'Mosquitoes driving you away?' he joked.

'No mosquitoes,' Su said. 'Just time for bed.'

'So glad you two had a chance to talk.'

'So am I,' Su said. 'You can't imagine how glad I am.'

As she was driven back to the Cambodiana, she couldn't help reflecting that but for the throw of the dice, she might now be in Lina Chan's shoes, and Lina in hers.

How strangely things had turned out.

Back in her room at the hotel, she debated whether to call Prescott. Should she tell him she planned to visit DC-Cam? In the end she decided against it. Prescott might try to talk her out of it. But this was her life, her story. She was going to follow the thread wherever it led and just for the moment she preferred to do it without outside comment or interference, however well-meaning that might be.

She slept well that night. The crowds from the Water Festival had long since departed. An occasional firework exploded but the noise failed to disturb her.

CHAPTER 4

Next morning, Su's driver arrived at the hotel before eight.

'We beat the rush,' he said smiling.

Starting early helped. So did the fact that they were headed for the suburbs where DC-Cam had recently relocated and most of the traffic was coming in the opposite direction. What chaos it would be, Su thought, when all the bicycles were replaced by motorbikes and the motorbikes were in turn replaced by cars. The fabric of the city, already stretched to bursting, simply would not be able to cope.

Fifteen minutes later they arrived at DC-Cam, a newly constructed, two-storey, brick building. The foyer was spick and span. The telephone in reception worked and within seconds Lina had appeared to greet her first visitor of the day.

'We only moved in a few weeks ago,' Lina explained as she beckoned Su to follow her to her ground floor office a few yards from the door. 'It's pretty smart, isn't it? Some of our international donors were quite generous. This is a great improvement on the old premises.'

Lina picked up a pile of papers from a chair so that Su could take a seat.

'Let me explain what we do here,' she began. 'DC-Cam has been in business since 1995. We were first created as a field office for Yale University's Cambodia Genocide Program, but we became an autonomous Cambodian institute in 1997. For the last five years, we've been acquiring new and previously unknown primary documents relating to the Khmer Rouge regime, many of them from within the top-secret Khmer Rouge security services, known as the Santebel. We've been cataloguing and classifying these documents which now run to hundreds of thousands of pages.

As part of a parallel process, any individuals mentioned in the documents are also coded for entry into a second computer system, the Cambodian Genocide Biographical Database. This now comprises records of more than eight thousand individual Khmer Rouge Political cadre and military personnel, as well as many victims of the Khmer Rouge.'

'What about photographs?' Su asked.

'I'm coming to that. In addition to the bibliographic and biographic databases, DC-Cam has also constructed a photographic database. This contains images of more than five thousand victims of the Khmer Rouge, tortured and executed at the "S21" security centre, known today as the "Tuol Sleng" prison. For the vast majority of these photographs, the identity of the victim is unknown.

'Finally, we have a geographic database. Prisons, execution centres and mass graves from the Khmer Rouge era are being systematically surveyed and entered into a digital mapping database. With their continuing deterioration over time, the physical genocide sites are gradually disappearing. At Choeung Ek, for example, the heavy rains have brought a lot of flood damage. The mapping project preserves the factual details of every single genocide site investigated. It serves as a crucial source for both historical research and legal enquiry.'

Su listened fascinated as Lina continued.

'One of the most unique services provided by the DC-Cam is its Family Tracing File System. Virtually every single family in Cambodia had loved ones disappear during the course of the Khmer Rouge revolution, never to be seen or heard from again. Some of these victims of the Cambodian genocide no doubt died anonymous deaths, unrecorded and unremembered by anyone. But many of them, on the other hand, were formally processed through the Khmer Rouge internal security system, which kept records in sometimes astonishing detail.'

'What kinds of records?'

Lina paused. 'Many of them consist of the so-called "confessions" of the Tuol Sleng prisoners. The first thing Duch, the head of the Tuol Sleng regime, insisted upon was that each new arrival in the prison wrote out his or her own biographical history, a life story, which would then form the basis for the subsequent interrogation. And then we have the interrogation records themselves. Some of these documents have already been scanned into the system and are now part of our database. But this is a slow process and there is still a long way to go. The bulk of the records in Tuol Sleng are piled up just as they were when the Vietnamese kicked the Khmer Rouge out in 1979 and decided to turn the place into a Genocide Memorial Centre. In some ways, it's a race against time. We need to get the records onto microfilm before they decay.'

Lina turned to a computer and monitor set up on a side-table in her office. 'All four databases are fully computerised and online.'

'You mean I could sit at my desk in Washington and access your records?'

'In Washington or anywhere else in the world. Of course, the computer records only provide a pathway. Unless a particular document has already been scanned into the system, you will only find a summary reference to it. Date – if known, number of pages, that kind of thing. If you want to read a document which is not already in the system, you'll have to go the Archives in Tuol Sleng. You can't do that sitting at your desk in Washington.'

'What about the photographs?' Su persisted. 'Are they all available online as well?'

'Many of them are,' Lina replied. 'I mentioned that we had images of more than five thousand victims. That includes the mugshots of the prisoners taken in Tuol Sleng. It also includes in many instances what we call the "death confirmation pictures" where a prisoner died following torture or was executed.'

'Can you look up Soeung?' Su asked quietly. 'Soeung as family name. First name: Hong.'

Lina looked at her. 'Are you sure you want to do this, Su?'

'Quite sure.'

'Very well, then, I'll try all three databases – the bibliographic and biographic as well as the Tuol Sleng photographic database.' Lina tapped in the words *Hong Soeung*. Seconds later the computer screen flashed up the information. *No records found matching your enquiry.*

'I'll just try "Soeung,"' Lina said. 'Ah, now we're getting somewhere. Here's a Chor Soeung. Record B 10448; Gender – Male; Organisational Unit 1975-1979 – K.B.546; Prison History – S-21, Phnom Penh, 18.6.77; Sources – Tuol Sleng Catalogue of Confessions (Cornell University), doc.no. C 458.'

'I don't know why my father would have been known as Chor Soeung rather than as "Hong Soeung,"' Su said. 'Do you have a photo for Chor Soeung?'

'I think we do.' Lina brought the image to the screen and Su studied it carefully.

'That's not my father' she said. 'I'm sure of it.'

Dextrously working the keyboard, Lina pulled up records for three more Soeungs: Hun Soeung, Nguyen Soeung Vi, and Mil Soeung. In all three cases there was a photograph of the subject. In the first case, the photo showed an ID number but no name. In the other two cases, the photo showed both name and number.

Lina went out into the lobby, filled two paper cups with water from a water-cooler and came back into the room.

'I've got an idea,' she said. 'We can do this another way. Do you have a photograph of your father? If you do, we can scan it in. We have a programme which allows us to check for basic, physical resemblances between the scanned-in image and images on the photographic database.'

'I've got the photograph which they used in a magazine article in the States a few weeks back,' Lina replied. She found the photo in her bag and handed it over. 'Can you use it?'

'I don't see why not.'

Lina placed the photo on the scanner, then cropped it so that it became effectively a mugshot of Su's father. She saved the image.

'You may wonder why we don't try to search manually one-by-one through all the images on the database. The answer is: we can do that if we have to. Before we had the system up and running, families would go to Tuol Sleng and spend hours or even days staring at the photos on the walls of the prison hoping to identify a loved one. It is a tremendously harrowing ordeal, even if you do it just from the database without visiting the prison.

'Having your own image to scan in makes the search that much easier. The programme will throw up the five closest matches. Then you look at those and decide.'

'I understand.' Su could barely bear to watch as Lina tapped the keys.

This time the search took a little longer. Ten... fifteen... twenty seconds elapsed while the computer clunked and whirled. The photographs emerged jerkily.

'The nearest match will be top left,' Lina said. 'That's the way we've set it up.'

Finally, all five pictures were on the screen. Su stared at the images trying not to imagine the circumstances under which the photos had been taken. The top-left photo showed a name and a number beneath the face. Su looked at the picture.

'That's someone else. It says so. There's the name and number. And anyway, I'm sure that's not my father. Look!' She picked up her own treasured photograph and held it next to the screen. 'Nothing like him. I don't know why that was the first choice.'

Lina tapped the screen. 'What about this one? No name. Just an ID number. Could that be your father?'

Su gazed long and hard at the screen. 'Maybe, yes I think it could be. It's been so long since we saw him. We have nothing but memories. The image is not good. Could we look at the original? Would we find the original in Tuol Sleng?'

'Of course, we can do that, if that's what you want to do.'

'Oh, I do!' Su exclaimed. 'I very much do want to do that.'

Lina searched the database once more. 'The photos are displayed in many of the rooms at Tuol Sleng. I need to know where this one is.'

A few seconds later, she had the information she needed. 'Block C, ground floor, room three, north wall, top row, eighteen from the right. That should do it.'

Lina was about to close her computer down when another thought occurred to her. 'I'm just going to search the bibliographic database again.'

'Why?'

'We have an ID number now – 01746. That's clearly visible in the photo,' Lina said. 'If this man is your father, then that number is your father's ID number. There are thousands of documents in Tuol Sleng, many of which have never been read and certainly not microfilmed. But we have been trying to make sure that where there are ID numbers on the documents, that information is catalogued and entered into the system. That way, if a relative comes looking for a loved one, trying to find out as you are what happened to him or to her, we may be able to help them not only identify a photograph but even find the relevant document or documents.'

'What do you mean precisely?' Su asked.

'It's hard to take, I know,' Lina reached out to take Su's hand briefly. 'I'm talking about confessions, about interrogator's notes, reports to Duch, that kind of thing.'

'Oh my God!' Su exclaimed. 'I'm not sure I'm ready for that!'

As she was speaking, the reply to the query came up on the screen.

'We're in luck if you can call it that,' Lina said. 'There's a file out there with a number which corresponds to the D number 01746. According to the record, it's not a file which anyone has had a look at yet. It hasn't been read or evaluated, let alone microfilmed. It may have decayed or rotted, or the writing may be illegible or the mice may have eaten it. But in theory at least it's still there in the Tuol Sleng archives. Or at least it was there when this catalogue entry was made about five years ago.'

'How soon can I go?' Su asked. 'Is Tuol Sleng open every day for visitors? Could you come with me when I go there?'

Lina glanced at her watch. 'Tuol Sleng is open every weekday and on Saturdays till two p.m. Or should be. And of course, I can come with you. That's part of my job. If we can't help people like you, what is DC-Cam here for? What's your schedule like? I'd be free tomorrow.'

'Tomorrow would be fine. In the afternoon. I think we're seeing the Minister of the Interior in the morning.'

'I remember, Jules told me,' Lina said. 'Why don't I pick you up at the hotel around two o'clock'.

'I'm so glad,' Su said. 'I'm not sure I could do this by myself.'

Lina put her arm round the other woman and steered her to the door. 'Sometimes it's best to know the worst, Su. Then you can get on with your life.'

In the lobby of the DC-Cam building, they encountered a middle-aged Cambodian who looked as though he was just returning to his office after an outside meeting.

'Ah, Professor Hak!' Lina exclaimed. 'I'm so glad you have returned. I'd like you to meet Su Soeung.'

After they had shaken hands, Lina explained to Su that Professor Hak was the director of DC-Cam. She added that Su was working for SAVE and that she was visiting DC-Cam out of personal as well as professional interest.

Dr Hak adjusted his glasses and listened intently. Lina was a senior member of his staff and he clearly valued her.

'Most interesting,' he commented when Lina had finished. 'A word of warning, though. Be prepared for disappointment. Or for surprises. I have seen it so often. People think we will have all the answers. But we don't have all the answers. Or, if we do, sometimes they are the answers which people do not wish to hear.'

Gravely courteous, he bowed his head to them briefly and went on in.

★★★

Su spent the rest of the day in the hotel, writing up her notes and trying to get her email to work by plugging her laptop into a telephone socket in her room. After several frustrated attempts, she went down to the hotel's business centre where she had better luck.

Among her messages, she found one from Prescott. 'Why so silent?' Prescott wrote. 'Call or write soon.'

Feeling guilty, Su sent Prescott a long email covering the events of the last few days. She sat at one of the guest-terminals with a pot of green tea beside her to keep her going.

> 'One of the reasons I haven't been a better correspondent,' she wrote 'is that I've been completely thrown by my visit. It's not just the work itself though, given the nature of the injuries most of these landmine victims have, that is traumatic enough. It's more that I feel I'm skating on the surface of a deep dark pond and I don 't know what lies beneath.

Tomorrow we meet the Minister of Home Affairs, Khin Lay. He's in charge of the security forces but he also has overall responsibility for the de-mining programme. We're trying to encourage the government to speed up the programme otherwise we'll be faced with a never ending task. Khin Lay is a FUNCINPEC minister, that is to say he occupies one of the cabinet seats allocated to FUNCINPEC under the current arrangements.

FUNCINPEC is Prince Norodom Ranariddh's party and is in an apparently uneasy coalition with the Cambodian People's Party led by Hun Sen. As you know, Hun Sen used to be a Khmer Rouge working for Pol Pot, but in 1977 he fled to Vietnam and then led the Vietnamese forces which threw out Pol Pot in 1979. Ever since then he has been trying to secure his position as the strongman of Cambodia.'

Su took a sip of tea. She also wanted to tell Prescott about the forthcoming visit to Tuol Sleng, but she didn't want to betray the excitement, the sense of anticipation that she felt. So she chose her words carefully.

'It's a very long shot indeed,' she wrote. 'First, the identification may be wrong. I couldn't rely on my own memory of what father looked like. It's far too long ago. So we've relied on a machine to come up with a match taking the photo they used in The Washingtonian article as a basis. The hope is that we'll find some documents. Can I handle it? The answer to that is: I'm not sure. But I'll never know unless I try.'

She signed off, 'All my love, I miss you,' and pressed the SEND button.

One of the things about email, she reflected, is that once you pressed the button, there was no bringing the message back. Your out-tray was – instantaneously – someone else's in-tray.

Su stayed another half-hour in the centre, surfing the net. She wasn't in a hurry. What a shame it was, she thought, that her mother didn't have a personal computer connected to the internet. If she had, Su realised she could have downloaded the mugshot of Prisoner No 01746 and sent it over to Seattle as an attachment. Her mother would have known for sure whether or not it was her father.

As she sat there, an idea occurred to her. She clicked onto the DC-Cam website, then tapped in the ID reference – 01746 – and pulled up the image of the Tuol Sleng prisoner which both she and Lina Chan had studied so carefully that morning. She then downloaded the image and sent it as an attachment to Prescott in Washington with the following message: '*Please try to find a way of getting the attached to my mother in Seattle. Does she think it could be a picture of my father? Much love, Su.*'

Once again, she pressed the SEND button, before packing up her papers and heading for the pool.

CHAPTER 5

Jules Barron picked her up in the hotel lobby around nine a.m. the next morning. During the short ride to the Ministry of the Interior on Norodom Boulevard, he briefed her more fully about the Minister, Khin Lay.

'He's a busy man. The Ministry covers an enormous range of matters. Customs, the de-mining programme, museums, antiquities, prisons, police, drugs and internal security – you name it, the Interior Minister is likely to be in charge.'

When they reached their destination, they had to wait for twenty minutes in an anteroom before the minister was ready to receive them. Khin Lay was a strikingly handsome man in his late sixties. As Jules and Su entered his large, sumptuously furnished office, he stepped out from behind the desk to greet them.

'Mr Barron, so good to see you again. We appreciate so much the work your organisation is doing.'

When Jules introduced Su, explaining that Su was a Cambodian who had been living in the United States and who had recently joined SAVE as Congressional liaison officer, Khin looked at her appraisingly.

'You still have family here, Ms Soeung? Parents, relations?'

'Not as far as I know. But I'm still looking.'

Khin hesitated as though he wanted to say something but then thought better of it. 'Please let me know if I can help in any way,' he said. He sounded perfectly sincere.

For the next few minutes, the minister briefed them on the progress of de-mining operations throughout the country. He clearly had the facts at his fingertips. Pointing to a large map on the wall of his office, he said: 'We have made a little progress in the east and south of the country, in Kampong Thom, Kampong Cham and Kampot, for example. Our real problems are in Battambang, Banteay Meanchey and Siem Reap provinces. If we are to get on top of things, we need to have a massive expansion in the de-mining programme, though heaven knows how that is to be achieved given the shortage of resources.

'In the meantime, we have to do our best to alleviate the sufferings of our people with programmes such as those provided by your agency.'

The Minister turned to address Su directly. 'I understand that your work, Miss Soeung, is specially with the United States Congress? I am sure you will do your best to make them understand how vital our needs for assistance are. My colleague, the minister for health, told me only the other day of the number of artificial limbs which would need to be fitted each year just to keep pace with demand. And then there is the repair and renewal problem, is that not correct, Mr Barron?'

'Indeed, it is,' Barron replied. 'Happily, thanks to your personal intervention we are now able to ship repairable prostheses directly across the border to Thailand. That is particularly the case for damaged prostheses coming out of the northern provinces. Sometimes we can fix them in our Bangkok workshop, sometimes they have to be sent back to the United States. Either way, minister, we much appreciate the help you have been able to give SAVE in dealing with customs formalities.'

Khin Lay laughed in a modest, self-deprecating way. 'There are some advantages in having a varied portfolio.'

They knew it was time to leave. The appointment in any case had never been intended as more than a courtesy visit and, in the circumstances, the minister had already given them a lot of his time.

'Please give my best regards to Mr Mossman and his charming wife,' Khin said, as he said goodbye. 'Will they be visiting us again soon?'

'I don't know that they have any immediate plans,' Su answered.

★★★

After they left the Ministry of the Interior, Jules suggested an early lunch at the Foreign Correspondents Club of Cambodia.

'I know you and Lina are going to Tuol Sleng this afternoon,' he said.

A few minutes later, when they reached the Club, they found CNN's Bangkok correspondent, Mark Kelly, already seated at the bar. Mark was an Englishman, around thirty, with reddish hair and a moustache.

Jules introduced Su and the three of them took their drinks over to a table.

'We're having lunch. Please join us,' Jules said.

'Delighted,' Kelly replied.

Over lunch, Mark Kelly explained that one of the reasons he was visiting Phnom Penh was that CNN was making a half-hour documentary about the destruction of Cambodia's famous temples.

'We're at a crisis point,' he said. 'It's not decades of war which has destroyed Cambodia's cultural heritage, it's the bloody international art market. Goes all the way back to An-dré Malraux in 1924 when, with his wife, he pillaged Banteay Srei of some of its finest pieces and tried to sell them on the market. Hasn't stopped since. In Bangkok, where I spend much of my time, there's an antiquities hypermarket, with most of the pieces coming from Cambodia. It's called River City, on the Chao Praya River, just a couple of yards from the big hotels, the embassies and China-Town. You can pick up a catalogue and more or less order the piece you want. You want a statue of Laksmi or Vishnu, a linga or a carved bas-relief, they'll find it for you.'

Su was shocked. 'Surely the export of antiquities from Cambodia is banned? How is the stuff reaching Bangkok?'

Kelly laughed. 'Over the border. A hundred different routes and pretexts. Some of the temple complexes are only twenty miles from the frontier. If you're a refugee in a camp on the Thai side and you know you can make thousands of dollars by slipping across into Cambodia and robbing a temple, why wouldn't you? But it's not just the refugees. The military is implicated in a big way. The other day the Cambodian bor-der police intercepted a military truck loaded with ten tons of sculpture taken from Koh Ker temple, that's about sixty miles north-east of Angkor. Mind you, that was probably a mistake. More often, you'll find the military and the police working hand in hand! If you can't stop the pieces leaving the country, you've had it. Thailand couldn't care less. They never ratified the UNESCO convention about stopping the import of stolen works of art and they don't intend to.

'The real culprits, of course,' Kelly continued, 'are the unscrupulous buyers in the United States, in Europe, in Japan. That's where the demand is. Some of our most famous museums have bought pieces whose provenance is dubious to say the least. How many of those pieces have been hacked with chain-saws or chisels off the temples or filched from the depository at Angkor? My advice to you would be, go and visit the temples before it's too late. Are you planning a trip up-country to Siem Reap?'

Su looked at Jules. 'I'd like to do that. I could visit SAVE's clinic in Siem Reap.'

Jules nodded, 'We're working on that now.'

Twenty minutes later, Kelly looked at his watch. 'I've got to run. We're filming in the Ministry of the Interior. We want to get Minister Khin Lay on camera telling the world that protecting the Angkor temples from further despoliation is his number one priority! Whether we believe him or not is a different story.'

Leaving a handful of large denomination riel notes on the table as his share of the lunch, Kelly hurried off.

'These television journalists are the real stars nowadays, aren't they?' Jules reflected. 'The Minister won't keep him waiting.'

***

Jules took the car to go back to his office, leaving Su in the lobby of the Cambodiana to wait for Lina Chan.

Lina, who had her own vehicle and driver, arrived punctually at two p.m. They headed south on Monivong Boulevard before turning west on Street 320. A few blocks later they drew up in front of the prison.

The two women got out of the car. A large sign outside the complex said, in Khmer and in English, INTRODUCTION TO THE MUSEUM OF CRIME. The guard at the entrance waved them in. 'They know me well here,' Lina said. 'If it wasn't for the support DC-Cam gives it, the museum would be in a bad way.'

Away from the traffic of the street, Su found the silence sinister. There was an eerie emptiness about the place. Apart from a couple of mynah birds hopping along the abandoned, grassed over paths there seemed to be no other signs of life.

'Must be a quiet day,' Lina said. 'Usually, we'd have a dozen or so visitors at any one time, maybe fifty a day.'

'Please tell me about it before we go in,' Su said.

They stood inside the courtyard, with the four main buildings facing them like an E lying on its side, with a fifth building in the middle on the cross-stroke. Lina had obviously given her lecture before.

'In 1962 this used to be "Ponhea Yat" High School,' Lina told her. 'It was named after a Royal ancestor of King Norodom Sihanouk. During the Lon Nol regime, the name was changed to Tuol Svay Prey High School. Behind the school fence, there were two wooden buildings with thatched roofs. These buildings were constructed before 1970 as a primary school. Today all of these buildings are called "Tuol Sleng" and form part of the museum of genocidal crimes.

'S-21 or Tuol Sleng was the most secret organ of the KR regime. S-21 stands for "Security Office 21." S-21 was Angkar's premier security institution, specifically designed for the interrogation and extermination of anti-Angkar elements.

'S-21, located in Tuol Svay Prey sub-district, south of Phnom Penh, covers an area of six hundred by four hundred metres. During the Khmer Rouge regime it was enclosed by two folds of corrugated iron sheets, all covered with dense barbed wire, which were electrified in an attempt to prevent anyone escaping from the prison. Houses around the four school buildings were used as administration, interrogation and torture offices. They were labelled A, B, C and D. E block was used for administration and archive.'

As she spoke, she indicated the general layout with a sweep of her hand.

Setting off to the left, they visited A block first, stepping carefully on the crumbling paths, then climbing over the threshold into the dim interior of the building.

Lina continued with her explanation. 'All the classrooms of Tuol Sleng High School were converted into prison cells. All the windows were grated with iron bars and covered with tangled barbed wire to prevent possible escape by prisoners. The classrooms on the ground floor were divided into small cells, 0.8 x 2 meters each, designed for single prisoners.'

She paused, allowing Su time to absorb the scene. Fighting back her sense of shock, of outrage, Su peered into the tiny cells. In some of them, the iron shackles were still visible. Blood stained the walls.

As they walked up narrow stairs to the second and third floor, Lina went on: 'The rooms on the top floors of the four buildings, each measuring 8 x 6 meters, were used as mass prison cells. On the middle floors of these buildings, cells were built to hold female prisoners. At first, the interrogations were conducted in the houses around the prison. However, because women taken to the interrogation rooms were often raped by the interrogators, in 1978 the chief of the S-21, a former teacher named Kang Kek Ieu decided to convert Building B for use as an interrogation office, as this made it easier to control the interrogation process.'

'Kang Kek Ieu, that's Duch's real name, isn't it?'

'Exactly. This was Duch's fiefdom. He knew everything that went on here. The Security Office and its branches were under the authority of the Central Committee and the Khmer Rouge Minister of Defence, Comrade Son Sen alias Khieu, who appointed Comrade Duch to head the S-21 system.'

'So Duch ran the place,' Su said. 'But he had helpers, didn't he? How many people did it take to run a torture centre like this?'

'According to the records we found, the number of workers in the S-21 complex totalled 1,720. Within each unit, there were several sub-units composed of male and female children ranging from ten and fifteen years of age. These young children were trained and selected by the KR regime to work as guards at S-21.'

'And the victims?'

'The victims in the prison were taken from everywhere throughout the country and from all walks of life. They were of different nationalities and included Vietnamese, Laotians, Thai, Indians, Pakistanis, British, Americans, Canadians, New Zealanders, and Australians, but the vast majority were Cambodian. The civilian prisoners were composed of workers, farmers, engineers, technicians, intellectuals, professors, teachers, students, and even ministers and diplomats. Moreover, whole families of the prisoners, from the bottom on up, including their newly born babies, were taken there en masse to be exterminated.'

Lina consulted a small notebook before going on with her summary. 'According to the KR reports found at Tuol Sleng Archive, the inflow and outflow of prisoners from 1975 to June 1978 were recorded on lists. Some documents have disappeared. One report estimated the number of prisoners as follows:

    - 1975 154 prisoners
    - 1976 2,250 prisoners
    - 1977 2,330 prisoners
    - 1978 5,765 prisoners

'These figures, totalling 10,499, do not include the number of children killed by the KR regime at S-21, which was estimated by the same report at 2,000.'

'The reports show that in 1977 and 1978, the prison on average held between 1,200 and 1,500 at any time. The duration of imprisonment ranged from two to four months, although some important political prisoners were held between six and seven months.'

'What was it like to be a prisoner here?' Su asked. She felt she needed to know. She felt she owed it to her father – and to the thousands of others who had suffered and died there.

'The prisoners were kept in their respective small cells,' Lina explained, 'and shackled with chains fixed to the walls or the concrete floors. Prisoners held in the large mass cells had one or both of their legs shackled to short or long pieces of iron bar. The short iron bar was about 0.8 meters up to one meter long, and was designed for four prisoners. The longer one was six meters and held twenty to thirty prisoners. Prisoners were fixed to the iron bar on alternating sides, so they had to sleep with their heads in opposite directions.

Before the prisoners were put into the cells they were photographed, and detailed biographies from childhood up to the dates of their arrests were recorded. Then they were stripped to their underwear. Everything was taken away from them. The prisoners slept directly on the floors without any mats, mosquito nets or blankets.'

'My God!' Su exclaimed, still trying to take in the horror of it all.

'Every morning at four thirty a.m.,' Lina continued, 'all prisoners were told to remove their shorts, down to the ankles, for inspection by prison staff. Then they were told to do some physical exercise just by moving their hands and legs up and down for half an hour, even though their legs remained restrained by the iron bars. The prison staff inspected the prisoners four times per day; sometimes the inspection unit from the security office made a special check over the prisoners. During each inspection, the prisoners had to put their arms behind their backs and at the same time raise their legs so that the guards could check whether or not the shackles were loose. If loose, the shackles were replaced. The prisoners had to defecate into small iron buckets and urinate into small plastic buckets kept in their cells. They were required to ask for permission from the prison guards in advance of relieving themselves; otherwise, they were beaten or received twenty to sixty strokes with a whip as punishment. In each cell, the regulations were posted on small pieces of black board.'

They went on into B Block. Just outside the block, a large noticeboard had been erected, headed THE SECURITY REGULA-

TIONS and containing two blocks of text, one in Cambodian, the other in English.

Su read the regulations line by line, trying to comprehend the depths of depravity into which humankind might sink.

1. You must answer accordingly to my questions. Do not turn them away.
2. Do not try to hide the facts by making pretexts of this and that. You are strictly prohibited to contest me.
3. Do not be a fool for you are a chap who dares to thwart the revolution.
4. You must immediately answer my questions without wasting time to reflect.
5. Do not tell me either about your immoralities or the revolution.
6. While getting lashes or electrification you must not cry at all.
7. Do nothing. Sit still and wait for my orders. If there is no orders, keep quiet. When I ask you to do something. You must do it right without protesting.
8. Do not make pretexts about Kampuchea Krom in order to hide your jaw of traitor.
9. If you don't follow all the above rules, you shall get many lashes of electric wire.
10. If you disobey any point of my regulations you shall get either ten lashes or five shocks of electric discharge.

They stood in silence while Su tried to absorb what she had just read. Because in some way it was easier to focus on a detail, rather than allowing oneself to be overwhelmed by the generality. She asked to Lina explain Rule No 8.

'What does it mean?' Su asked. 'Do not make pretexts about Kampuchea Krom in order to hide your jaw of traitor.'

'That's a Vietnamese reference,' Lina explained. 'As you may know, for centuries there has been this intense rivalry, even hatred, between the Cambodians and the Vietnamese. The Vietnamese are probably the largest non-Khmer ethnic group in Cambodia. Rule Number 8 is warning prisoners not to pretend to be anti-Vietnamese when in fact they are ethnically Krom or Vietnamese in origin.'

'What a nightmare!' Su said.

'Much worse than a nightmare. A living hell. The prisoners were required to abide by all the regulations. To do anything, even to move their positions when trying to sleep, the inmates had first to ask permission from the prison guards. Anyone breaching these rules was severely beaten.'

'What about hygiene?' Su asked.

'Primitive in the extreme. Prisoners were bathed by being rounded up into a collective room where a tube of running water was placed through the window to splash water onto them for a short time. Bathing was irregular, allowed only once every two or three days, and sometimes once a fortnight. Unhygienic living conditions caused the prisoners to become infected with diseases like skin rashes and various other diseases, and there was no medicine for treatment.'

They walked slowly on, visiting the different buildings of the Tuol Sleng complex one after another. In almost every room, photographs had been posted. Row after row of mugshots. Row after row of staring, haunted eyes. Su found that she wanted to linger on every face, yet there were thousands of faces to confront.

'This is the base of the photographic archive,' Lina said. 'Any photograph which is posted on the walls here should have been copied into our system.'

Su consulted the piece of paper in her hand. She spoke in a low voice, hardly more than a whisper. 'Block C, ground floor, room three. Can we go there now? I'm not sure I can take much more of this.'

They walked through to the next block. 'Which wall, Su?' Lina asked.

'North wall, top row, eighteen from the right,' Su said.

In fact, they didn't need to count from the right. Whereas the image on the screen in Lina's office had been indistinct, the original photograph as posted on the wall leapt out at them.

'That has to be my father! It couldn't be anyone else.'

'Are you sure?'

'Yes, I'm quite sure.'

She still had The Washingtonian photograph in her pocket, so she took it out and compared the photograph of her father with the picture on the wall.

'There are bruises on his face. One eye seems to be half shut as though he has been beaten up, but look at the hairline, look at the jawline. That has to be the same man.' Su passed her camera over to Lina. 'Please can you take a picture of this wall of photographs, with me standing next to the picture of my father?'

After Lina had obliged, Su took pictures of the room from different angles. Then the two women spent several minutes looking at some of the other faces on the walls. Most were men, but towards the end of one of the rows there were photographs of some women as well. Most were anonymous. In some cases, names as well as numbers appeared in the photo.

Su found herself transfixed. She felt boxed in by the walls of suffering, by the mute piteous gaze of the victims.

They walked out into the courtyard and across to E block.

On the way they passed through the long gallery where Narong Sung's famous portraits were displayed. Prisoners lying in packed rows on the upper floor of S21, prisoners being tortured with electric shocks or whips, or being flayed with whips or having their heads dunked repeatedly in water, women having their throats cut or their babies snatched from them to be dashed against the wall – somehow Narong Sum had captured the unspeakable horror of it all.

'Oh, my God!' Su exclaimed. It was almost harder to endure the paintings than the photographs because they were able to tell a story in a way that the mugshots couldn't.

Most of the canvasses were large, often six foot by four. One or two of them were portrait size, showing prisoners alone and shackled in their cells. There might have been moments, Su reflected, when Narong had been able to talk to them as well as draw them. Had the implacable Duch allowed him, and them, that privilege?

In the end she found the strength to drag herself away. 'Let's go to the archives,' she whispered.

Like the other buildings in the Tuol Sleng complex, E block was a three-storey construction, with the archives on the second floor. The long room was filled with filing cabinets and each cabinet in turn was filled with documents, piles and piles of document.

As she surveyed the scene, Lina sighed. 'One of our priorities now is arranging the documentation room in a proper technical setting. As you can see, this is just a simple room unsuitable for storing all these invaluable documents.'

She gestured with one hand, 'Most of the papers here are under threat of destruction by pests and humidity. Tuol Sleng museum does not have even pesticide.' Lina walked over to one of the nearby shelves and picked up a stack of papers. 'Basically, the material here is exactly what the Vietnamese found when they captured Phnom Penh in 1979 and threw the Khmer Rouge out. The policy of the new regime was to leave Tuol Sleng just as it was, a relic of the past. A propaganda tool. That was the most effective way, they thought, to ensure the crimes committed here were never forgotten. But we're paying a price now.'

She showed Su what she meant. 'As you can see, the papers of the documents are turning yellowish and the typed or handwritten scripts have become increasingly faded to the point that they are hardly legible. If still left without proper care, they will no longer survive in the holdings of the museum for Cambodian generations to come.'

As Lina was speaking a young man wearing dark slacks and a white shirt with the words "Tuol Sleng – Ministry of the Interior" embroidered on the breast pocket emerged from behind one of the stacks.

Lina greeted him warmly. 'I'm glad to see you're on duty today, Sarin.'

She introduced Su to the young bespectacled Cambodian. 'Sarin Bun is a distant cousin of mine. He's training to be an engineer. He works here part-time to earn money for his studies.'

Su shook hands with the young man while Lina explained that they were looking for the file relating to Prisoner No 01746.

'It should be over there,' Sarin said helpfully. 'In theory, the files are arranged in accordance with the file number.'

Lina nodded, 'The Khmer Rouge were very methodical. That is one of the most extraordinary things about the regime. Instead of destroying every trace of their inhuman activities, they recorded every detail.'

'So, we should be grateful for small mercies?' Su said.

'You could put it that way if you want to.'

In the event the search for Su's father's file was not quite as straightforward as they had hoped. It took them the best part of twenty minutes to locate the folder and they would prob- ably not have succeeded without the assistance of the guard who, with his detailed experience of the layout of the room, finally steered them to the right filing cabinet.

The file, when they finally laid their hands on it, consist- ed of a faded crumbling yellow folder with the number 01746 stamped on the outside and a handful of documents inside. At first glance the documents seemed as brittle as the folder itself.

Without a word, Lina handed the file to Su. 'What do you want to do? Do you want to look at the file now? Or else, we could sign for the file and take it away for a day or so while you have a chance to study it. We could do that, Sarin, couldn't we?'

'If you're DC-Cam, you can do anything.' The young guard smiled as he gestured towards his embroidered shirt-pocket. 'Do you think the Ministry of the Interior pays my wages in full? We know DC-Cam makes up the difference.'

'What do you say, Su?' Lina pressed her.

Su hesitated. Faced as she was now by the moment of truth, she felt strangely reluctant to confront it. She also felt strangely troubled. Was she right, she wondered, to push ahead as she had on this personal voyage of discovery? How far could she allow herself to be diverted, for purely personal reasons, from her assigned tasks with SAVE?

'I think we may need the time to absorb all this,' she said at last. 'Let's take the file with us.'

Sarin raised his eyebrows. 'Shouldn't you at least take

a glance inside? Make sure you've got the right file and not someone else's.'

Still Su felt reluctant, almost superstitious. Could the genie ever be put back in the bottle?

Sarin cleared a space on his desk and Su put the file down. Dust spurted from the folder as she opened it. Inside was a thick, manilla document sleeve, with a heavy, black-bordered stamp more or less in the centre. Inside the stamp, there was an inscription in Khmer which Su found it hard to understand. As she had already admitted, she was good at speaking the language, not so good at reading and writing, particularly when the object in question was a crumbling manuscript over a quarter of a century old. Besides her heart was racing and her vision seemed to be blurred.

'What does it say, Lina? You tell me.'

'It's called First Formal Confession,' Lina said, studying the text.

'Name of prisoner? Does it give the name of the prisoner?' Su asked impatiently.

'Not on the sleeve.'

Gingerly, Lina extracted six or seven folded sheets of paper from the sleeve. She glanced at the first page, then quietly passed it over to Su.

Su took the paper in her hand and in a low voice, almost a whisper, began to read: '*My name is Hong Soeung. I live at 14, Street 310, just off Norodom Boulevard. I have been married for ten years to my beloved wife Sita, formerly Keo. We have one daughter, Su, who is seven years old...*'

'Stop there!' Lina interrupted her. She could tell from Su's voice that Su was on the edge. She feared that discovering Hong Soeung's "confession" in the archives as they had done might be too much for her. She had seen it happen before. People had come with her to the archives in a search for relatives. She had seen the brave faces they would put on, fearing the worst but still somehow hoping that the worst had not happened or even now could magically be avoided. Letting in the light was often a painful, too painful process.

But there was more to it than that. She was trained as a professional archivist. There were rules to be respected.

'This file may be introduced as evidence in the trials, who knows?' she warned them. 'We have to do things right.'

She took out a small Dictaphone from her pocket. 'My name is Lina Chan. I am Deputy-Director of the Documentation Centre of Cambodia, DC-Cam. The time is four p.m., the date is November, 2001. I am at present standing in the Archive Room on the second floor of Block E of the Tuol Sleng Prison Museum, Phnom Penh. Also present are Su Soeung, a United States citizen of Cambodian origin, currently working for the international charity SAVE and the guard on duty in the archive collection, Sarin Bun. We have just removed from bookcase number 203, a file numbered 01746. We have opened the file and extracted an envelope from it...'

Lina continued to establish for the record the precise circumstances of the find, the condition of the file and the material it contained. Borrowing Su's camera, Lina photographed the scene in detail, taking both general background shots as well as close-ups of the file.

'I'm sorry to be so formal,' she said, 'but these things can be important.'

In spite of the conflicting emotions which she felt, Su believed she had recovered enough to continue with the reading of Hong Soeung's confession, but Lina counselled otherwise.

'We need to do this properly. We need to get the document back to DC-Cam. We'll scan it into the database this evening, and print off some copies.'

'What are you going to do with the original?' Sarin asked. 'I shall need to explain where it has gone.'

'We're going to keep the original under lock and key for the time being,' Lina replied firmly. 'We'll give you one of the photocopies instead, with a note that the original is being held at DC-Cam for safe keeping.'

'Fine by me. You'll have to sign for it.' Sarin Bun's attention was already beginning to wander. It wasn't the first time since he had worked at Tuol Sleng that he had witnessed a small flurry of excitement as some previously undiscovered text saw the light of day.

Once they had completed the formalities, Su and Lina left Tuol Sleng to return to DC-Cam.

In the car, Su said: 'I'm glad you insisted. Better to do things in good order.'

'You have every right to read it first, Su. I didn't mean to stop you doing that.'

Su put her hand on the other woman's arm. 'I know you didn't. But I'm going to need your help reading it anyway. I could tell that. Some of the words are difficult to make out.'

'Do you think it's your father's writing or do you think they wrote it for him? I hate to say this but sometimes the prisoners were in such a bad way after the interrogations that the prison staff wrote out the confessions for them to sign.'

'I think it's his handwriting,' Su replied slowly. 'My mother has letters from him, written when he was on mission up-country. She showed them to me. I can't be sure though.'

'Perhaps your mother could fax us one or two of those letters. It would be good to have a sample of your father's handwriting to go on. We could get the experts to look at it.'

Su managed a smile, 'My mother wouldn't know one end of a fax machine from another. But perhaps we could find a way to have her send some letters to us. Also, we could try to get a copy of the document to her.'

The car pulled up outside DC-Cam. It was late and most of the staff had already left.

'I see Professor Haq is still here,' Lina said as they walked through the lobby. 'We shall have to tell him about this.'

'Let's wait till we've read it first, Lina.' Su had a terrible sinking feeling in the pit of her stomach.

On their way past the reception desk, they both noticed the curtains in Professor Haq's office twitch. The old boy had clearly noted their arrival.

★★★

Three hours later Su sat at the desk in her sixth-floor room in the Cambodiana Hotel, and contemplated the movements in and out of *Naga*, Phnom Penh's famous floating Casino. A bridge of golden arches connected the hotel to the ship and, as Su watched, parties of late-night revellers made their way on board. What an extraordinary contrast, she thought. Spend the afternoon in Tuol Sleng prison, end the day watching Cambodia's new high-rolling elite visiting one of their favourite haunts. Quite soon, she knew, the band would start playing on the promenade deck of the *Naga*, while the ship's gaming salons would grow increasingly raucous. Indeed, she could hear the noise already, borne by the night breeze towards her across the waters of the Mekong. Gambling, prostitution, drugs, disease – did one thing inevitably lead to another? Was that the price a country like Cambodia had to pay for progress?

She had learned from just a few days what charm the place had. How very different it must be from Hong Kong, Bangkok or even Ho Chi Minh City as Saigon was now known. The broad boulevards the French had constructed were still there, the old, wooden buildings, the pagodas, the famous street markets. Miraculously, these things had survived decades of war. The question was: would they survive the peace?

A sudden blast of sound from the casino opposite caused her to rise to her feet to close the window before returning to her desk. Pulling up her chair, she switched on her laptop, clicked up Outlook Express and started to type offline. (After a good deal of experimentation, she had learned how to dial in to America online in Bangkok which meant that she no longer had to use the hotel's business centre for her email communications.)

> 'Darling,' she began, 'this has probably been the strangest day of my life so far. We found my father's "confession" in the Tuol Sleng prison museum archives...'

Sending Prescott an account of the day's events meant inevitably reliving them. Su found it hard going. More than once she had to stop to gain control of herself. She had been in the very prison where her father had been tortured and died. She – Hong Soeung's own daughter – had been the one to find his "confession" mouldering in a heap of manuscripts untouched for decades. And even now she was still trying to come to terms with what Hong had written. Was it true? What did it all mean? What ought she to do?

If she turned to Prescott at this point, it was not only because she was in love with him, it was because she trusted his judgement.

Forty minutes after she began, Su was still typing. She wanted to be sure that Prescott understood exactly what had happened and how it had happened.

> 'Lina and I stayed at DC-Cam till late in the evening. It's midnight here now and I've only been back an hour or so. We scanned the "confession" into the DC-Cam data-base as well as downloading it to floppies. I'm attaching the original herewith.
>
> Lina and I also made an English translation. Actually, Lina did most of the work. As you can imagine, I was pretty stressed by the whole experience. But I followed what she was doing and I'm sure she was accurate. Lina has had a lot of experience. She has been working at DC-Cam since it started. Anyway, I'm attaching the translation too. Please get in touch as soon as you have had a chance to digest all this. I need your advice. I feel worried and confused but also, in a strange way, elated as though I'm on the track of something...'

Su inserted the floppy disk she had brought back with her from DC-Cam and made sure that the files were correctly attached. Then she dialled the AOL number in Bangkok to get back online.

CHAPTER 6

Prescott read Su Soeung's email in stunned amazement. He had always known, of course, that Su had personal as well as professional motives for accepting the Cambodia assignment. But he had not anticipated that her quest to discover what happened to her father would have borne fruit so soon or in quite such a spectacular manner. He tried to imagine what she must be feeling at this point.

As he sat in front of his computer in *The New York Times'* office in Washington, half-a-dozen blocks from the White House, he printed out Su's email and the attachments.

The scanned-in version of the confession came out as six pages of facsimile, a full-colour copy. Prescott gazed at them curiously, taking in the signs of stains, cracks and blemishes on the original paper. He tried to get his mind round the fact that over a quarter of a century ago, Su's father, under physical and mental hardships which were difficult even to contemplate, had laboured to produce that draft.

Like any trained journalist, Prescott would have preferred to read the basic document, not the translation. Unfortunately, this was impossible. He had an elementary grasp of Chinese as a result of the time he had spent in Beijing with *The New York Times* but that was the full extent of his knowledge of oriental languages. In spite of his enduring association with Su Soeung, the Khmer language remained a mystery.

Putting the facsimile of Hong Soeung's confession to one

side, he turned to the English translation which Su and Lina had sent over. This was altogether more illuminating.

> My name is Hong Soeung, he read. I live at 14, Street 310, just off Norodom Boulevard. I have been married for ten years to my beloved wife Sita, formerly Keo. We have one daughter, Su, who is seven years old…

As Prescott read on, the beaker of coffee on his desk grew cold. His eyes were transfixed by the words on the page in front of him.

> I myself am 46 years old and I am or was a senior official in the Ministry of Culture under the Lon Nol government. I have also been working for the Central Intelligence Agency of the United States, generally known as the CIA. I was recruited first by Thomas Enders when he was Deputy Chief of the US mission in Phnom Penh. Indeed, Thomas Enders and his wife Gaetana on more than one occasion visited my house. After Enders returned to Washington in April 1974, I continued to work for the United States, meeting military and other officials from the US mission on a regular basis and providing information. I also received secret briefings from them.

> My understanding of US policy at this time, from my contacts with Enders and others, can be summarized as follows. Though officially supportive of the Lon Nol regime, the United States was determined to reach a satisfactory accommodation with the advancing Khmer Rouge forces. US Secretary of State, Henry Kissinger, who served both President Richard Nixon and, after Nixon 's resignation in 1974, President Ger-

ald Ford, was especially keen to 'close a deal' with the Khmer Rouge forces ahead of the likely collapse of the Lon Nol regime and the take-over of Phnom Penh and the rest of Cambodia by Pol Pot. Dr Kissinger's key objective by early 1975, when North Vietnam was on the brink of taking over South Vietnam, was to ensure that the forces of Ho Chi Minh did not also gain a victory over Cambodia, thus ensuring a double humiliation for the United States. By the end of 1974 and the beginning of 1975, the victory of Pol Pot and the Khmer Rouge was therefore secretly seen by the Americans, not only as inevitable but as essential.

Prescott scribbled furiously on his legal-size yellow pad, jotting down the key Points. 'Victory of Khmer Rouge seen as essential by US. What can US do?'

Hong Soeung had the answer.

I was aware from conversations held with various US officials at various times that the United States in its objective of doing a deal with the Khmer Rouge faced two main problems.

The first related to the bargain to be struck with the Khmer Rouge. What was it that the US had to offer the Pol Pot regime? The second was of a practical nature. How could secure channels of communication and negotiation be established between the US mission in Phnom Penh and the forces of the Khmer Rouge as they took over increasingly large areas of the country?

Prescott wiped his brow as he continued to devour the document. He could hardly believe his eyes. This was the smoking

gun, he thought! From his years of experience as an Asia correspondent, he had always suspected there was some scandal
like this just waiting to be discovered. He got up from his desk
to shut the door of his office. He didn't want anyone walking
in on him with this kind of material lying around.

Let me take the first point. First: Soeung continued, the
nature of the bargain to be struck. This was a complex matter. My US contacts explained that since Congress had already
since August 1973 put an end to air-borne missions over Cambodia and had also imposed strict limits on other military
assistance, the US was not in a strong position to threaten the
Khmer Rouge with a show of strength, so they would have to
come up with an alternative package: the carrot, not the stick.

In the end, this is what they decided:
Number One – the US would inform Pol Pot that they would
turn a blind eye to Khmer Rouge human rights violations,
past and present. More precisely, they would pretend to be
unaware of such violations, even though there were some US
Foreign Service officers already reporting that KR Forces were
taking over outlying provinces and subjecting the populations
of those provinces to beatings, starvation, rape, forced march-
es, indoctrination and re-education.

Number Two – the US would use its best efforts to ensure that
the KR regime, once it took over in Phnom Penh, received diplomatic recognition by the United Nations.

Number Three – while it would be difficult for US aid to be
supplied directly to the KR regime, such aid would be fur-

nished by proxy through agreement with the Chinese People's Republic.

You may ask where do I, Hong Soeung, fit into all this. I will tell you how. My job was to prepare the fourth element of the United States negotiating package.

I have been, as I explained, a senior official with the Cambodian government for many years. I know — or should I say knew — all the key players in the Lon Nol regime. I was asked by my United States friends to produce a list of up to two hundred key officials in the Lon Nol regime. Names, addresses, occupations, potted biography... that kind of thing. When I asked my contacts why they wanted such a list, they were quite clear about it. I record exactly what they said to me: 'Pol Pot is going to need to know exactly who to hit the day he takes over Phnom Penh. He's going to need a 'death-list' and we are going to make sure he gets one.

Once again, Prescott wrote on his pad: 'US promises Pol Pot death-list'.

The compilation of the famous 'death-list' took me many days. Some names, of course, were obvious candidates: apart from President Lon Nol himself, there was his brother, Lon Non. There was the Prime Minister, Long Boret, Prince Sirik Matak, General Sak Sutsakhan, Saukham Khoy, the President of the Senate, In Tam, Cheng Heng, Sosthene Fernandez — these were the immediate choices. Going beyond the 'shortlist' was more difficult and time consuming but I succeeded. In the end I completed my compilation of what we called the

Judas-List, with a total of 200 names altogether, and handed it over. This was at the end of January 1975, when the Khmer Rouge forces were already beginning to close in on the capital.

Prescott wrote. 'Judas-List of 200 names completed end January 1975.' He read on:

> I come now to the issue of how the communication channel was to be established. As soon as the Americans had all the elements of their negotiating package in place, including the Judas List which they saw as the key sweetener from the Khmer Rouge point of view, the crucial question was how the message was to be delivered to the Khmer Rouge in a timely way. The problem was, of course, that within Cambodia itself there was absolutely no way a US official in Phnom Penh could make contact with a Khmer Rouge leader in the provinces. They might as well have been on opposite sides of the moon.

> I don't pretend to know the full details of the negotiating channels between the US and the Khmer Rouge. Clearly these matters could have been discussed by Dr Kissinger on his frequent visits to Beijing, perhaps using the Chinese as an intermediary. But I do have precise information regarding the mechanism for handing over to Pol Pot the 'death list' or Judas-list which I have mentioned above, together with the associated documentation which I had collected.

> I should explain that, when Thomas Enders left Phnom Penh, he was succeeded by the new US Ambassador, John Gunther Dean, a man with whom I rapidly established good per-

sonal relations, as indeed I had with Enders. On March 29, 1975 Ambassador Dean invited me to dinner at his residence and served some excellent French wine. Dean explained that he would sooner we all drank it than leave it behind for the Khmer Rouge. Given what I knew about secret US dealings with the Khmer Rouge, I found Dean's comment ironic, I must admit.

The true purpose of the dinner was revealed when, in a private discussion in his study, Dean asked my help in responding to a request from Prince Sihanouk which the US mission had received. The facts are these. On March 25, 1975 Sihanouk from his base in Beijing addressed a letter to United States President Ford via the French Ambassador. He asked a special favour: would the Americans try to obtain and send him the copies of the films which he, Sihanouk, had personally produced and directed? These films were apparently stored in Chamcar Mom, Sihanouk's modern Phnom Penh residence. Sihanouk was worried that they might be destroyed in the upcoming battle for control over the capital city. Dean continued by telling me that on March 26 the US Liaison office in Beijing had been instructed to seek a meeting with Sihanouk to inform him that the US was doing its utmost to respond to that request. Dean informed me that at the same time the US mission in Phnom Penh had been instructed by Washington to recover and safeguard the material for onward transmission to Sihanouk.

When Ambassador Dean enlisted my help for this assignment, he observed that if Sihanouk had devoted as much energy and resources to the welfare of his people as he had to the production and direction of inferior films, the situation might not be as desperate as it currently was! He went on to explain that he was unwilling to approach Lon Nol's office with this request because this would reveal that the US was having dealings with Sihanouk and by inference the Khmer Rouge since Sihanouk was not only the titular leader of the Khmer Rouge, but his chief aide in Beijing was Ieng Sary, Pol Pot's principal lieutenant.

To cut a long story short, Dean asked me in my capacity as a senior official in the Cambodian Ministry of Culture to acquire the material Sihanouk had requested and this is precisely what I did the following day, March 27, under the pretext that we needed to make an inventory of the cultural possessions – films, musical recordings, musical instruments etc which Sihanouk had left behind when he was ousted by Lon Nol. Dean was extremely grateful for the trouble I had taken and informed me that the films would be despatched forthwith to Beijing for delivery to Prince Sihanouk.

As Dean was speaking, I suddenly realised that what seemed like a bizarre request by an absentee figurehead was likely to be the absolutely vital means for establishing, at a key moment, a link between the US and the Khmer Rouge. I am convinced that the Judas-List and the other material I had gathered about the criminals of the Lon Nol clique would certainly have been included in the package sent to Beijing.

Prescott scribbled on his pad. 'Query – what delivery mechanism to Sihanouk/KR in Beijing? French Embassy? US Liaison Office? How were meetings set up?'

Turning back to the papers on his desk, he realised that he had almost come to the end of Hong Soeung's confession.

> In the course of interrogation, Comrade Duch has asked me, Hong Soeung wrote, why, if what I say is true, my own name appeared on the 'death-list' as supplied to Khmer Rouge commanders for use on April 17, 1975 when they entered Phnom Penh and carried out the first wave of assassinations and liquidations? I have no explanation for this except to state my belief that my name could have been added in an act of betrayal by my US contacts and so-called friends, in order to ensure that I do not myself reveal the extent of the collusion between the United States and the Khmer Rouge.
>
> However this may be, I hope it will be clearly understood that my actions have in no sense been those of a traitor to Comrade Pol Pot, or to the Khmer Rouge, or our beloved party organisation, Angkar, or to Democratic Kampuchea in a wider sense. On the contrary, particularly through my compilation as mentioned of the key death-list or Judas list which was communicated to Khmer Rouge commanders before they entered Phnom Penh on April 17 1975, it could be argued that I played a significant part in ensuring the rapid elimination of our enemies. On this basis, I would humbly and respectfully ask Comrade Duch to show mercy and to allow me to re-join my family wherever they may be...
>
> Signed Hong Soeung, Tuol Sleng, June 5, 1975.

Su and Lina had also translated the note which appeared on the last page of the confession, after Hong Soeung's final, tragic appeal for clemency.

'Comrade Duch,' he read, 'denied this appeal on June 6, 1975. Comrade Duch stated that Soeung was a CIA agent by his own admission and that was a sufficient warrant for execution. Prisoner 01746 (Hong Soeung) was sent to Choeung Ek on June 7, 1975.'

After he had finished reading Hong Soeung's confession, Prescott stood up and paced round the room, his mind racing. There were many questions to ask. Which one should he ask first? He looked at his watch. It would be almost midnight in Phnom Penh. Su had asked him to call her as soon as he had read her email. He picked up the telephone.

Moments later, he was put through to Su's hotel room.

He didn't beat about the bush. 'I'm so sorry. This must be agony for you.'

'It is. I feel really spaced out. I don't know what to think. Was my father really working for the CIA? Did he really produce a Judas-list for the US to use as a bargaining-chip thereby sending hundreds of people to their death? Or is he just writing whatever he hopes will please the interrogators? What shall I do? I'm out of my depth.'

Ten thousand miles away, Su Soeung sounded increasingly frantic and distraught.

'Take it easy, Su,' he instructed. 'I can probably help but I need some time. I have to check things out. We could make some big mistakes here. And I mean big. Who else has seen this?'

'This end, only Lina so far.'

'What do you mean by "this end?"' Prescott asked.

'I sent an encrypted copy to Jessie Low in Senator Hillary Clinton's office. That was what they wanted if I came across anything of interest.' Su sounded defensive. She hoped Prescott wasn't going to be cross.

'Sure the message was sent?'

As Prescott asked, Su checked the contents of her Sent Mailbox in Outlook Express. 'It has gone all right.'

'How long ago?'

'A couple of hours.'

Hanging up on Su, Prescott dialled Jessica Low's direct number. 'Is that you, Jessie? Prescott Glover here. I've just been talking to Su Soeung in Cambodia. She says she sent an email a couple of hours ago. I've seen a copy of it. Have you read it yet?'

'Haven't had time. It's encrypted and I tend to leave those till later.'

Prescott thought quickly. 'You need to look at it but please don't pass it on to anyone. This could be dynamite. Can we meet in your office later today?'

'Come at four. I'll ask Jack Rosen to join us. Can I show him Su's email or is it too ultrasensitive?'

'Jack can see it. No-one else, though, please.'

'Not even the Senator?'

Prescott shuddered. 'Christ, no! Not yet anyway. If Hillary gets to this before we've had a chance to evaluate it properly, all hell could break loose.'

'Now you really do interest me,' Jessica Lowe said. 'I'm on tenterhooks.'

Almost before the Senator's staffer had time to hang up

her phone, Prescott riffed through his address book and dialled another number.

'Bob, glad I got you. Something's come up I need your advice about. Off the record. You're not by any chance free for lunch today? Oh, you are? Splendid. One o'clock at the Cosmos Club? That's great.'

When Prescott replaced the receiver, he exhaled a small sigh of relief.

★★★

Though he was a long-standing member, Prescott didn't get to the Cosmos Club as often as he would have liked. Whenever he did manage to go, he enjoyed himself. At the height of World War II, it used to be said that the most significant concentration of Washington's public policy intellectuals was to be found at the Cosmos Club, with the exception perhaps of Union Station when the night train from Boston arrived. In many ways the club in its elegant setting at 2121 Massachusetts Avenue had still managed to retain that wartime buzz.

Of course, the Cosmos took itself seriously. It wasn't a place for idle, social chit-chat. On the wall of its Hall of Honours hung portraits of Club members who had received Nobel Prizes, Pulitzer Prizes and Presidential Medals of Freedom. As he walked through the dining room towards the table he had reserved by the window, Prescott reflected that the change in administration in Washington had not so far done much to diminish the self-confidence of Washington's liberal establishment. Many of them had clearly decided that this particular Bush administration, like the previous Bush administration, would have to be endured as a short-term political aberration but it wouldn't put them off their lunch.

Robert Jesson, R.D. Lewis Distinguished Professor of South East Asian Studies at the Johns Hopkins University School of Advanced International Studies, otherwise known as SAIS, was already waiting for him. Aged about fifty, still trim and athletic, Jesson was a former US Foreign Service officer whom Prescott had first met ten years earlier when they had both been in Beijing. Jesson had appreciated the move from diplomacy to academia. He had published three or four books on various aspects of United States foreign policy, including – as Prescott recalled – a well-received monograph on Cambodia.

'I can walk from my office in SAIS to the lunch-table here in less than five minutes,' Jesson said as Prescott took the chair opposite.

Prescott laughed, 'Then you must walk fast. The Cosmos is pretty handy for SAIS, isn't it? A few blocks down Mass Avenue and you're there. Seems a bit like your staff-canteen. I saw Zbig Brzezinski on the way in and there's David Calleo over there.'

Jesson nodded, 'I already said "hi" to David. He's got a new book on Europe coming out.'

'Another!'

'Well, Europe keeps on reinventing itself and David has to keep abreast. Lucky man. Gives him something to write about.'

Prescott ordered a bottle of wine. 'I know you academics don't normally drink at lunch time, but journalists still have their evil ways.'

'I can be tempted,' Jesson laughed.

For a few minutes the two of them reminisced about their days in Beijing. After the waiter had cleared the plates from the first course away, Prescott grew serious.

'I came across something today, Bob,' he began, 'which could interest you. I've brought a couple of documents with me which you might like to take a look at. The first is in Cambodian, the second is an English translation.'

'What do you want me to do with them?'

'I'd like to know what you think.'

Jesson looked at Prescott with a quizzical expression. 'I'm getting the impression you think there's something pretty unusual here.'

Prescott fought hard to keep his tone of voice strictly objective. 'It's your opinion I'm after.'

Jesson looked at the facsimile first, then he looked at the English version, then he went back to the facsimile again. It took him about five minutes to digest the material.

'My Khmer is pretty rusty by now, but I'd say that's a useful translation,' he commented. 'Did Su have a hand in that?'

When Prescott admitted Su Soeung had indeed helped with the translation, Jesson added: 'All this must be pretty painful for her, mustn't it?'

Prescott nodded. 'Knowing your father was locked up and probably tortured in Tuol Sleng is bound to be painful. I've spoken to her on the telephone and I can understand the turmoil she's going through. But, apart from the fact that I sympathize with Su at this point, I'm still a journalist. I've got a journalist's curiosity. What interests me at the moment is the political aspect. Was Hong Soeung simply fabricating his confession? Was his claim that he had been responsible for producing the famous Pol Pot death-list simply a way of trying to ingratiate himself with his captors and buy his way out of trouble? Or are we looking at something that could conceivably have a basis in fact with all the implications *that might have*?'

'You mean: was the US trying to cut a deal with Pol Pot in 1974 and 1975? And could that deal have included the famous Pol Pot death-list?'

Prescott nodded: 'That's what I do mean.'

Jesson reached across the table for the bottle and poured them both some more wine.

'This is background, isn't it?' he said. 'You're not going to quote me?'

'Not unless you want to be quoted.'

'I don't. Let's finish up here and go back to my office then.'

Ten minutes later, they resumed the conversation in Robert Jesson's book-lined and paper strewn office in SAIS.

'In the old days,' Jesson said as he settled down in a chair opposite Prescott, 'I'd take out my pipe after lunch and puff away. Now they make you go and stand on the pavement outside.'

'Even Professors?'

'Particularly Professors. We're meant to set a good example. In the end, I gave up smoking altogether. It was just too much hassle.'

Even without the stimulus of tobacco, Jesson's logic was pretty sharp. He took Prescott through the argument step by step.

'Okay, let's look at the key proposition that Soeung is advancing, namely that the United States at the end of 1974 and at the beginning of 1975 was ready and anxious to cut a deal with Pol Pot and the Khmer Rouge. That's a good question. Don't think the academic community hasn't tried to probe into this. There have been a number of efforts to lift the lid, some of them by people at SAIS, including myself. On the whole we haven't got very far. We tried using the Freedom of Information Act. You can ask for documents under the Act but you have to know what to ask for otherwise they won't give you anything, so it's a Catch-22 situation. You can't just go on a fishing expedition. And if you do hit lucky, you may get a paper back with more black markings than text.

'Redacted is the word they use nowadays.'

'Maybe they're just deleting the expletives?' Prescott was only half-joking.

'I'm not talking tapes. I'm talking embassy airgrams, directives by the Secretary of State, minutes of meetings – things we know exist, but we can't track down, at least in an unexpurgated form.'

'If you don't have, or can't get the documents, what do you have?'

'We have our best judgement,' Jesson replied slowly. 'Our gut instinct based on what we know.'

'And what do we know?'

'For my money we have to see this in the context of what was happening in Indochina as a whole at that time, particularly in Vietnam. Bear in mind that by the end of 1974 and the beginning of 1975, President Thieu's regime in South Vietnam was facing total collapse. The Paris Peace Agreement of 1973 might have provided a cover for US withdrawal, but it couldn't save Thieu. So the US is facing its nightmare scenario. General Dung's armies are rampaging through the south; the fall of Saigon is imminent. Why should the victorious North Vietnamese stop at Saigon? Why shouldn't they sweep on into Cambodia, even Thailand? Ho Chi Minh always maintained that his objective was to take over the whole of Indochina. His party was officially named the "Indochina Communist party?" If you go back a few hundred years, the Vietnamese empire had been more or less coterminous with Indochina. Why wouldn't they wish to recreate it?'

'With Soviet help?' Prescott asked.

'Naturally. Another reason for US concern. Fortunately for the US, Vietnam's historic enemy is just as worried by the idea of a Soviet-aided Vietnamese takeover of the whole of Indochina as the US is.'

'You mean China?'

'Precisely. One thing China fears possibly more than anything else is the resurgence of a strong Vietnamese empire on its southern borders. So if the Russians are supporting Vietnam, the Chinese are going to support in Cambodia the regime most likely to resist Vietnamese expansion. That's why they welcomed Sihanouk to Beijing when he was ousted by Lon Nol in 1970, why they wined and dined him. It's why they sponsored the formation of the Cambodian communist party, or Khmer Rouge, under Pol Pot. China certainly saw the Khmer Rouge as vital players in the game of blocking a Vietnamese – and by proxy a Soviet – takeover of Indochina.'

'And US geopolitical interests were the same as those of the Chinese?' Prescott probed.

'Nixon didn't go to China in February 1972 just so someone could write the musical twenty years later,' Jesson said.

'Kissinger didn't make eight or nine trips to Beijing in the first part of the seventies just to brush up on Chinese cuisine. Whatever grandstanding there might have been over Taiwan, the interests of the United States and China converged far more than they diverged.'

'So the US was predisposed to believe the best, not the worst, about Pol Pot?' Prescott asked.

'Exactly,' Jesson replied. 'Do you remember Kenneth Quinn? Kenneth was a Foreign Service officer who went to Cambodia as US Ambassador in 1995. Before that, he had been Deputy Assistant Secretary of State for East Asian and Pacific Affairs. What people don't remember is that Quinn spent years recovering from an early and almost fatal career setback. In 1973, Quinn was a young, foreign service officer stationed in Can Tho province in South Vietnam near the Cambodian border. Amongst other activities, he made a study of Cambodian refugees entering Vietnam at that time. The study lasted nine months and the end product was a thirty-seven-page report entitled the *Khmer Rouge Program to create a Communist Society in Southern Cambodia*. From the interviews he conducted with the Cambodian refugees, Quinn was able to document every aspect of Khmer Rouge brutality even then, long before they captured Phnom Penh. So if Hong Soeung suggests that continuing to turn a blind eye to Khmer Rouge excesses was part of the deal, I'd say that rings true. To my mind at least.'

'Did you personally see Quinn's report?'

'I did as a matter of fact. He put it out as an airgram which, from the State Department's point of view, was the lowest classification so a lot of people got to see it. I think he did it on purpose. He wanted to be on the record. Anyway, the powers that be were furious. They clawed back all the copies they could. Even today, if you ask to see the 1973 Quinn memorandum inside State, you'll get a negative response and a big black mark against your name into the bargain.'

'Is Quinn still alive?' Prescott asked.

'I believe he is. He left Cambodia in 1999 and went to live in Iowa. He went to college in Iowa, I believe.'

For a moment Prescott allowed his mind's eye to wander towards the Mid-West and its vast plains of corn.

'They have telephones and email even in Iowa,' he said. 'I could try talking to him.'

'Quinn would just confirm what we already know. If you're going to talk to people, talk to the principals. You want to find out whether the US was negotiating with Pol Pot in the mid-seventies, talk to Henry: Henry Kissinger.'

Prescott burst out laughing. 'Come off it, Kissinger's not going to talk to me. Not on this subject anyway. This is dynamite and he knows it. Even today. Anything Henry has to say, he has already said in his memoirs. That's his official line now, and he's sticking to it, whatever the reality may have been.'

As Prescott was speaking, Bob Jesson's eyes lit up with excitement. 'By Christ, you're right,' he exclaimed. 'Why didn't I think of that in the first place?'

From where he sat, Jesson let his eye run over the bookshelves which lined the walls of his office. When he saw what he was looking for, he stood up, walked over to the wall and removed a thick volume.

'This is the final volume of Henry's memoirs,' Jesson said: 'The Years of Renewal. If my memory serves, Henry addresses the issue of US-Pol Pot negotiations in the context of slagging off John Gunther Dean. Dean was the last US Ambassador to serve in Phnom Penh before the Khmer Rouge took over.

There's a tragic photo of a stricken Dean walking to the evacuation helicopter with the Stars and Stripes folded under his arm. Let's look at the index. Here we are. Dean, John Gunther. 509-511, 514, 516, 517-518.'

Jesson riffled through the heavy volume until he found what he was looking for. Then he raised his head with a satisfied expression on his face, 'Listen to this, Prescott, straight from the horse's mouth. Henry Kissinger says – and I quote from page 509:

> Highly intelligent and well informed, Dean understood well enough that congressional restrictions on American funding and advisory activities were certain to doom the country to which he was accredited. And he made it clear that he would not go down with the sinking ship. Like the congressional doves, Dean advocated a "political" way out of the disaster he had been forced to administer. He therefore bent every effort to get a negotiation started usually under his own auspices....'

Jesson paused. 'Here's the significant part. Henry writes:

> Dean's strategy was to urge negotiations now with the Khmer Rouge, now with Sihanouk, at one moment through Indonesian President Suharto, at another via Prime Minister Lee Kuan Yew of Singapore... Dean's basic strategy was to replace the government to which he was accredited with a coalition structure of some kind as prelude to negotiations with the Khmer Rouge.'

'And what does Henry do?' Prescott asked.

'In the memoirs, Henry is fairly circumspect. Remember, he's writing for history and, as far as history is concerned, he tries to distance himself from Dean.'

Jesson once more read out loud from the Gospel according to St. Henry. 'Kissinger quotes his own instruction to the State Department of February 18, 1975:

> *The frenzied approach which Dean seems to have adopted will solve nothing. I want him to adhere to a sober, deliberate policy that neither precludes positive action on our part nor rushes us into it headlong.'*

'It doesn't prove conclusively that the US was negotiating with the Khmer Rouge, does it?' Prescott sounded disappointed. 'Sounds as though this was either a freelance effort by Dean, or else Henry is covering his tracks for the benefit of posterity and letting Dean carry the can.'

'Hold on a moment!' Jesson, still riffling through the vast quarry of Henry Kissinger's memoirs, interrupted Prescott's speculations. 'Remember that reference in Hong Soeung's confession to Sihanouk's request to the US to rescue his films from his Phnom Penh residence? Well, listen to what Henry has to say about that. I'm quoting from page 513:

> *On March 26, 1975, we instructed George Bush to seek a meeting with Sihanouk to inform him that we would do our utmost to respond to his request. On March 28, John Holdridge, our deputy chief of mission in Beijing, met with Phung Peng Chen, Sihanouk 's Chief of Staff, at the French Embassy and delivered an invitation from Bush to Sihanouk for discussion at a mutually agreed venue. On April 1, Holdridge met with Phung Peng Chen.'*

'George H.W. Bush!' Prescott exclaimed. 'President George Bush Senior? Was he there in Beijing then?'

'Of course, he was. Bush Senior succeeded David Bruce in October 1974 as head of the US Liaison Office in Beijing. Remember, those were the early days. We didn't have a full-fledged embassy at that time. Bush Senior stayed there until the end of 1975 when he returned to Washington to become director of the CIA.'

An outlandish, totally unthinkable idea occurred to Prescott. 'Could George Bush *Junior* as well as George Bush Senior by any chance have been implicated in these negotiations with Pol Pot?'

Jesson closed the third volume of Kissinger's memoirs and replaced it on the shelf.

'You might have to do your own research on that one.'

'Give me a clue,' Prescott pleaded.

Jesson relented. 'We hit the jackpot with Henry Kissinger's book. Why not try the Bush memoirs too? Just for a start.'

'Which Bush?'

'The old man, of course. Dubya's still working on his. You may find some circumstantial evidence. You don't necessarily have conclusive proof.'

Prescott knew a hot tip when he heard one. He either didn't hear, or else he deliberately ignored, the note of caution in Jesson's voice.

'If I don't jump to conclusions,' Prescott said, 'I know others who will.'

CHAPTER 7

They seemed to have all the time in the world for him. It was that important.

Jessica Lowe had cleared the conference table in her office. As soon as Prescott arrived, she called Jack Rosen in to join them. The documents were spread out in front of them.

Jessie began by reassuring him, 'We did what you asked, Prescott. No-one else has seen Su's email. We can understand why you wouldn't want it passed around.'

Jack Rosen added on his own account, 'This must be goddam painful, for you as well as Su.'

For the next twenty minutes, Prescott went over the ground he had already covered earlier in the day with Professor Jesson. He didn't pull his punches. He couldn't afford to.

'I'm pretty clear about this in my own mind,' he concluded. 'Really, I knew what I thought even before I talked to Jesson, but what he said makes me even more certain. Hong Soeung didn't write that confession in order to get himself off the hook. He's not inventing some spurious CIA connection as so many of them did because that's what their torturers wanted. He wrote what he wrote because that's what he did.'

There was a long pause. The two senatorial staffers contemplated the papers in front of them.

'We'd have to be careful how we play this,' Rosen said at last. 'I'm not sure Cambodia resonates with the American people the way Vietnam does. We didn't lose fifty thousand servicemen in Cambodia.'

'No, we just bombed the hell out of them for four years,' Jessie said.

'That's right,' Prescott added. 'Do you remember the Neak Long incident in 1973? A B-52 unloaded its bombs on the village by mistake, killed a hundred people and wounded hundreds more. Remember *The Killing Fields*? They showed that episode in the film. They left out the bit where the US Ambassador goes down to the village and hands out one-hundred-dollar bills to some of the survivors! Can you believe it?'

'Was that Dean?' Rosen asked.

'No, that was Swank,' Prescott said. 'Emory Swank. When he left, Enders took over. And when Enders left, Dean came in.'

'Tom Enders would never have tried to do a deal with Pol Pot,' Rosen mused. 'I remember Tom well. He was a can-do kinda guy if ever there was one. They promoted him when he came back from Cambodia, made him Assistant Secretary for Economic Affairs as I recall. We used to see him on the Hill from time to time. Do you really reckon that Hong Soeung was working with Enders as well as Dean?'

'The way I see it,' said Prescott, 'Hong Soeung was working for the United States, or an agency of the United States, namely the CIA. And when the US decided, after Enders left Cambodia, to ally itself with Pol Pot since Lon Nol was clearly going under, Hong Soeung did what we asked him to do.'

'What was in it for him?' Rosen asked. 'It didn't stop him being tortured and killed.'

Prescott shrugged. 'I'm not an expert. There's no telling

why people do these things. It's not always the money, is it?'

For a while they mulled it over. They could see there was something there for them all right, but they were not sure how best to get at it.

'Okay,' Rosen said at last. 'Let's assume that Kissinger was in it up to his neck. Let's assume that this stuff in his book about John Gunther Dean being a loose cannon and trying to talk to the Khmer Rouge off his own bat is just a smokescreen put up ex post to conceal his own involvement at the time. Where does that leave us?'

'It leaves us a hell of a lot further than we are today,' Jessie Low replied.

'Kissinger is still the eminence grise of the Republican Party. Nixon, Ford, Kissinger. And Henry's still around. He's just been in China playing ping-pong with the Chinese vice-premier to celebrate the thirtieth anniversary of his so-called 'ping-pong' diplomacy. We tag Henry, we tag the GOP as a whole.'

'Tag them with what? Helping to send up to two hundred Cambodians to their deaths at the hands of Pol Pot over twenty-five years ago?' Rosen clearly enjoyed playing the devil's advocate. He leaned across the table and wagged his finger at them. 'If we go for this, we've got to be able to make it stick.'

Prescott was becoming increasingly irritated with Rosen's cautious approach. Now he exploded in an emotional outburst.

'Hell, we're talking about sending two million people to their deaths, Jack, not two hundred! We knew all about Pol Pot. Quinn wrote that paper in 1973, two years before the Khmer Rouge captured Phnom Penh. We knew the kind of man he was and the kind of regime he intended to introduce. We could have stopped him. We could have used the Chinese as leverage. They were always in control of Pol Pot and were able to call the shots. But what do we do? Nothing. Absolutely nothing. Worse than nothing. We send George Bush Senior to Peking to cosy up to the Chinese, our new best friends in Asia and incidentally we tell him not to forget to brush up his contacts with Sihanouk and Ieng Sary and the Khmer Rouge crowd in Beijing because quite soon, in fact too darned soon, Saigon and South Vietnam are going to fall to the Communists and the whole damn shooting match is going to go up the spout. Vietnam, Laos, Cambodia, even Thailand – they're all going to blow unless we can stop the rot! That's why the US went for a deal with Pol Pot, as the best bulwark against Vietnamese and Soviet expansionism in Indochina and to hell with human rights! That's what the Senator should expose.'

Jack Rosen banged the table. 'Not the US. *The Republicans!* That's the way to play it. In party political terms, this could be dynamite.'

'You've got my vote,' Jessie Low said decisively. 'Let's go tell the Senator.'

'Hold on,' Rosen held up his hand. He turned to Prescott apologetically, 'You make a pretty good case there, Prescott. I was just probing to see what the weaknesses were. As a matter of fact, dramatic as it is, I think we may have an even stronger case than we think.'

'What do you mean?' Jessie asked.

'The Bush angle, that intrigues me,' Rosen said. 'That could play big for us. Nixon, Ford, Kissinger, Bush. How solid is that? We're sure Bush Senior was in Beijing at the time? We don't want to screw up by making some elementary mistake over the dates.'

'It's cast-iron,' Prescott replied, reaching into his briefcase and pulling out the copy of George Bush's memoirs which he bought en route at Barnes and Noble. 'Jesson suggested I take a deeper look at Bush senior's book of personal recollections *All the Best* and that's what I did in the cab coming over.'

He held up the thick volume. 'Do you know it?'

'Not intimately,' Rosen laughed. 'That one hasn't yet worked its way to the top of the pile.'

'I think we struck gold,' Prescott said. He could see he had their attention now.

'Take a look at the China chapter,' Prescott continued. 'The Bushes arrive in November 1974; they leave in December 1975. George Bush is there for the whole of the crucial period. Phnom Penh falls on April 17, 1975; Saigon falls on April 30. Bush stays on in China until the end of the year. Sihanouk is titular head of the Khmer Rouge and George Bush and the staff of the United States Liaison Office have him firmly in their sights. If you're doing a deal with the Khmer Rouge, you have to go through Sihanouk. That was the case then; it's probably still the case now.'

'We know the US liaison office in Beijing handed the films and stuff to Sihanouk, don't we?' Jessica Lowe said. 'That's clear from the Kissinger memoirs. That gives Bush and co the pretext for a meeting.'

'Not just one. At least two,' Prescott corrected her. 'Kissinger says that they set up a meeting just to tell Sihanouk the reels were on their way and there must have been a further meeting after that when the material recovered from Sihanouk's residence in Phnom Penh was actually delivered to him.'

'Okay, at least two,' Jessie agreed. 'But what if they wanted to establish a system of regular contacts? By the middle of April, Pol Pot is in Phnom Penh. The US have abandoned their embassy in the capital. They've pulled out of Cambodia altogether. Yet, if we believe your hypothesis, we have to believe that US-Khmer Rouge negotiations went on even after the Judas-list had been delivered.' She shuddered involuntarily. 'Christ, it makes you ill just to think about it.'

'It's going to make a lot of people ill, Jessie,' Rosen said. The prospect seemed to appeal to him enormously.

Prescott still had the George Bush memoir in front of him. 'The way I see it, for most of 1975 Bush and the United States Liaison Office in Beijing dealt with the People's Republic of China. They were building common ground there and one of the areas of interest of course was Cambodia. But I think that from time to time they had to have direct contact with Sihanouk and the Khmer Rouge in Beijing. How did they do that? The film business gave a pretext for a couple of meetings as we know. What else?'

Prescott was enjoying himself now. He passed the book over to Jessie.

'Read the second paragraph on page 230. And don't forget the footnote.'

'Aloud?'

'Why not?' Prescott replied. 'Jack ought to hear it too.'

Jessica Low read out the paragraph as requested. 'The letter is dated July 6, 1975:

Today is George's twenty-ninth birthday. He is off to Mid-land – that's Midland, Texas, of course, starting a little later in life than I did, but nevertheless starting out on what I hope will be a challenging new life for him. He is able. If he gets his teeth into something semi-permanent or permanent, he will do just fine...

She paused and looked up inquiringly.

'What does the footnote say?' Prescott asked.

'It says: 'the day before he had to have a tooth drilled in a Chinese hospital.'

Rosen understood what Prescott was getting at.

'We're talking George W. here, aren't we? President Bush Junior?

'The *future* President Bush Junior. Dubya tried to keep quiet about his foreign travels during the election campaign. Liked to pretend he had barely been abroad except to Mexico and possibly Canada. But he spent six weeks in China in 1975. That's a historical fact. And his father's letters bear it out. *The current President – George W. Bush was actually in Beijing in June and July 1975!'*

'Visiting his parents, George and Barbara?'

'Maybe more than that,' Prescott replied. 'Remember, the summer of 1975 would be precisely the time when the US would be firming up its arrangements with Pol Pot. There's no US Embassy in Cambodia. That's finished. Dean and his team pulled out on April 12 that year. The best – and probably the only – way of talking to the Khmer Rouge is via Beijing so the US Liaison Office there is crucial.'

'You think George W. played a role in those contacts? Do you have proof?'

'What kind of proof do you want? Would you go to a Chinese hospital in 1975 to have a tooth pulled? I called my office and they checked with the President's medical records. The Press gets these things nowadays. There's no indication that George W. had a dental intervention in China in 1975.'

'So the dentist story could be a cover for some other kind of meeting between George W., acting on behalf of his father, and the China-Pol Pot axis?'

Rosen rubbed his hands. 'I like it. Now we're getting there. We don't just hang this Pol Pot thing on Nixon, Ford, Kissinger and George Bush Senior, the former President. We bring in George Bush Junior, George W. Bush, the current President too! This could start a prairie fire. We don't just discredit one Republican leader. We discredit them all.'

'Let's go find the Senator,' Jessica Lowe said decisively. She gathered her papers from the table and headed for the door.

***

Senator Hillary Rodham Clinton gave no sign of her former coolness towards Prescott. She shook him warmly by the hand.

'I understand Su may have come up with something important. I want to hear about it.'

'I think so, Senator, but you'll have to make up your own mind about it.'

As the meeting progressed, Prescott found himself impressed by Mrs Clinton's crisp, business-like manner. She wanted the evidence to be presented to her in a clear, orderly way. Paradoxically, the very magnitude of the scandal they had uncovered meant that the Senator probed with almost exaggerated care, testing every hypothesis before moving on.

'This is my foreign affairs debut, and I don't want to blow it,' she told them.

She insisted on putting a call through to Bob Jesson so that he could personally confirm to her what he had earlier said to Prescott. They listened in to the conversation on the speaker phone.

'It's not that I don't trust you, Prescott,' she said when she put the phone down. 'I just can't afford to screw up. Not now. There are a lot of people out there waiting to watch me slip on the banana skin.' She sighed. 'It doesn't make it easier being the ex-President's wife. Not *this* ex-President anyway.'

'No offence taken,' Prescott said. 'I think you're right to be cautious. Remember what Nixon said to Kissinger when he authorised the secret bombing of Cambodia?'

'What did he say? Remind me,' Mrs Clinton said.

'He said: 'It's your ass that's on the line, Henry.'

The Senator laughed. 'Thanks! That's really encouraging.'

After an hour of batting the issue to and fro, they paused to draw breath.

Hillary Clinton turned first to her staffers, 'What do you think? Jessie? Jack?'

Jack Rosen had already made up his mind. 'In the end it's a judgement call. Do we think Hong Soeung is telling the truth or is he making up a story for the benefit of his interrogators in the vain hope of buying himself off? Bob Jesson just told you, Senator, that many victims of Pol Pot who found themselves being tortured in Tuol Sleng admitted to working for the CIA or the KGB when they had done no such thing. However, Bob says that, on the basis of what he knows and the documents he has seen, he believes Hong's confession is genuine. I'll go with that.'

'I will too,' said Jessie Low. She could see the headlines already. Big, bold type, praising her boss for finally pulling back a corner of the rug. God, they needed some good headlines.

Still the Senator wasn't satisfied. 'The involvement of the US Liaison Office in Peking under George Bush Senior, that's clear enough. I'll accept that Bush Senior was the likely conduit for communications between the US administration, Sihanouk and Pol Pot. I'll accept that he probably played a big part in shaping those communications. But can we really pin this on the current President too? Are we really saying that George W. was doing the dirty work during those six weeks he spent in Peking during the summer of 1975? How do we know he wasn't playing golf?'

Jack Rosen sighed. 'There weren't any golf courses in and around Beijing in 1975. Do you think the Gang of Four allowed people to play golf?! No, Dubya had plenty of time to play the spook. For my money, the evidence is circumstantial but it's there. Why did Dubya, in all the campaign literature he put out, never mention his China trip in 1975? Why did he let us all think he's never set foot outside the western hemisphere? Okay, it was good politics. I'm just a hometown boy, that kinda thing. But I think there was more to it than that. He didn't – and he still doesn't – want people to start pouring over the details of his China escapade. He may or may not have had a tooth pulled in China. The point is, what else was he up to?'

'Innuendo, rather than accusation?' The Senator took the point.

'That's all you need, Senator, given how much else you have.'

Before they broke up, Hillary Clinton had one final piece of business to raise.

'Can we verify that Hong Soeung really did write this? Is there anyone still around who could recognise Hong's handwriting? Better still, do we have an authentic sample of Hong's writing and could we get an expert to compare the two?'

'I may be able to help,' Prescott said. 'Su's mother, Hong's widow, is still alive. She lives in Seattle. The original document is still locked up in the Tuol Sleng archives, but I could show her the facsimile. And she may have some old papers in Hong's handwriting. I could take them with me.'

'Take them where?'

Prescott smiled, 'My plan was to stop in Seattle on the way to Phnom Penh. *The Times* is sending me out as an old Asia hand to cover your visit to Cambodia.'

Hillary Rodham Clinton laughed, 'You move fast, don't you?'

'This could be the story of the year, Senator.'

'Make sure you catch my eye when I give my press conference out there. I'll call on you first if you raise your hand. I owe you that. You and Su. I mean it.'

For a moment the Senator seemed to be overcome. 'How could they do that? How cynical can you get? Not just ignoring Pol Pot, but actually sponsoring him! And how many people died? Two million? Two and a half?'

'Who knows? They uncover new mass graves every day,' Prescott replied quietly.

CHAPTER 8

Prescott had to delay his departure for the West Coast and Asia while he waited for his Cambodian visa to come through. In Su's absence, he decided to spend the weekend with friends in Virginia.

Kurt and Anne-Marie Erickson had originally come to Washington over thirty years earlier when Kurt had joined the World Bank as a trainee. The long spell in America had not effaced all traces of the couple's Swedish origins. Now retired, they lived in an old clapboard farmhouse with extensive outbuildings near Harper's Ferry. They had installed a state-of-the art sauna inside the house. As far as outdoor recreation was concerned, both Kurt and Anne-Marie were keen riders. Most days they would exercise their horses in the Virginia countryside. Sometimes, they would make a day of it, hacking up into the foothills of the Blue Ridge Mountains.

'I've asked the Mossmans to lunch on Sunday,' Anne-Marie Erickson told Prescott when he arrived. 'They've got a place a few miles away. They'll probably hack over if the weather's fine. Do you know the Mossmans?'

'Who doesn't,' Prescott replied.

In the end, the Mossmans came by car. The fine November weather had finally broken and a medium-to-heavy drizzle shrouded the landscape. Kurt Erickson lit a log fire in the library and poured pre-lunch drinks for the guests.

Kurt had served for years as an economist in the World Bank's South-East Asia department so when the conversation turned to Cambodia, he didn't hesitate to join in.

'The world needs to make up its mind once and for all,' he said. 'Do we want to go on raking up the past or do we want to draw a line under it and build for the future? I'm a Swede and Swedes are probably as interested in human rights as any other nation. More so, maybe. But we have to realise that what we in the West understand as human rights may seem very different out there in Asia. It's a cultural thing. Cambodia needs a chance to breathe. The UN is still pushing for the Khmer Rouge trials to go ahead. They want to give them a big billing. But whose interest are they trying to serve? Not the Cambodian people's, surely?'

Caroline Mossman was not convinced. 'You've been in the World Bank too long. Too much cost-benefit analysis. But economics is not the whole story. There's a momentum behind the trials now. It's not going to be easy to stop. And I don't think we should try to stop it.' Turning to Prescott, she added: 'I bumped into Jessie Low yesterday. She told me Senator Clinton has finally fixed the timing for her Cambodia trip. She's going next week, focussing on health care – and of course that's of great interest to SAVE. But Jessie hinted that this could also be the Senator's foreign policy debut. Big time. She says Su has been very helpful.'

Prescott didn't know how much Jessie had told Caroline Mossman but he was sure Su wouldn't have wanted him to talk to all and sundry about the latest developments in her attempts to find out what happened to her father. So he contented himself with a noncommittal grunt. Su might work for

SAVE but that didn't mean the Mossmans had to be privy to her inmost thoughts.

'Do you hunt, Caroline?' he asked by way of changing the subject. 'I mean do you ride with hounds out here?'

'We both do,' Caroline replied. 'We go out with the Middleburgh usually.'

As Caroline Mossman spoke, Prescott couldn't help wondering – not for the first time – where they got their money. It cost a lot to keep a horse in the US these days, even more if you went hunting with one of the several socially prestigious packs which operated in the Virginia countryside. It meant having two houses too, one for the town and another for the country, not to speak of staff – cooks, grooms, gardeners and so forth. When he knew Mossman at Princeton, Andrew had not given the impression of having great inherited wealth and you certainly didn't make big bucks working for a charity like SAVE. Maybe Caroline had a family trust fund? Or maybe she just earned a lot. A top-notch lawyer could certainly take home a lot nowadays...

Looking at the pair of them – so sleek and well-groomed – as they went into lunch, Prescott wrote himself a mental memo: Mossman funds – find out where from? He didn't expect to be able to look into the matter in the near future. For the next few days, he was going to be fully stretched. Predictably, the knowledge that the Senator was making her first major foreign trip had been received with considerable excitement. Hillary was local news – after all she was the senator for New York. She was national news. Now she would be international news as well. That said, Prescott promised himself, the time would come when he could pay a bit more attention to

Andrew and Caroline Mossman's finances. He hoped it would come soon.

The Mossmans didn't linger after lunch.

'The Chinese Ambassador's coming over for dinner and we need to get back. He's rather a dear, you know.'

Prescott had heard His Excellency Ting Wei-Ju described in many ways but seldom as "rather a dear". Among the journalistic community, the ambassador had a reputation as a tough negotiator, setting out new parameters for the Washington-Beijing relationship and doing his best to ensure that the US stuck to them. In the recent spat between the US and China over the downed US spy-plane, with hotheads on both sides almost ready to go to war, Ting was widely considered to have played a blinder, having helped to elicit from the US authorities the finely tuned statement of regret or apology (depending which way you read it) that in the end allowed both sides to put the incident behind them. And his reputation had only been enhanced during the United States' War against Terrorism when China's co-operation seemed to have been secured from Day One.

'Do you know Ting well?' he asked curiously.

'Pretty well,' Andrew Mossman replied. 'He's become a loyal supporter of SAVE. He says the Chinese are ready to give a huge, new boost to the de-mining operation in Cambodia but of course it's politically unthinkable. He's not even going to put the idea forward in the current climate. Vietnam put Hun Sen into power in Cambodia. Vietnam keeps him there. Vietnam is China's historical enemy and vice-versa. Can you imagine Hun Sen letting the Chinese in even if it is for humanitarian purposes? How many Chinese sappers and engineers would we see in Cambodia? What uniform would they wear? Who would they report to? If China makes any kind of proposal along these lines Hun Sen will smell a rat at once!'

Mossman paused. 'The sad thing is that Ting Wei-Ju's idea is exactly what Cambodia needs. Every time they clear a province of mines, we save literally thousands of amputees. If the Cambodians could do a deal with the Chinese, they could truly transform the de-mining situation in Cambodia, who else is there to help on the scale that is needed?'

Prescott was intrigued. 'I'd forgotten Ting was a supporter of SAVE. Of course, he was at your reception in the Smithsonian. Saw him talking to Senator Clinton at one stage. They seemed to be getting on like a house on fire. I should do a profile on Ting pretty soon, shouldn't I, before he retires, or they post him somewhere else? Mind you, it's hard to imagine where he could go after Washington.'

'Great idea!' Mossman was enthusiastic. 'If you get a chance to do an interview with Ting, you should jump at it.'

Soon after the Mossmans had departed, Prescott himself said goodbye to his hosts and drove back to Washington. His plan was to collect his visa from the Cambodian embassy first thing in the morning, then catch the lunch time flight to Seattle.

★★★

Sitting next to her on her living room sofa, he showed Sita Soeung the photograph first.

Before he left Washington, he had printed out a couple of copies in his office and now he pulled one from his briefcase.

The grey-haired, old lady flinched when she saw the bruise on the temple, the staring eyes, the ID number across Hong Soeung's chest. She bowed her head and placed her fingertips together, then she rocked herself quietly back and forth, all the while murmuring in her own language a prayer for the soul of her departed husband.

Prescott tiptoed from the room to leave her alone with her grief. As he stood by the window, looking out over the roofs of Seattle's Chinatown, he couldn't help wondering whether he had done the right thing. Maybe it was better sometimes to let the past lie undisturbed.

Twenty minutes later Sita Soeung re-emerged. Her eyes were red with weeping. She held a letter in her hand.

'Here, take this, Prescott. You say Su must have sample of my husband's writing. Here is letter he wrote me on his last trip up-country. He writes date here.' She jabbed with her finger at the paper. 'March 2, 1975. I keep that letter. I hide it with the photograph Su has. Here, you take it now.'

Prescott took it reluctantly, 'I'll look after it, I promise you.'

He knew the hardest part of his task still lay ahead of him. 'Can you look at this too?' he asked her.

Prescott spread out the six facsimile pages of Hong Soeung's confession on the table in the living room of Sita Soeung's Seattle apartment.

'You don't have to read this,' he told her. 'As a matter of fact, I don't think you ought to read this. I think you will find it too upsetting. But at least I would like to know if you think it is Hong's writing. We'll get the experts to compare the letter and the confession but still it would be good to have your opinion.'

In spite of Prescott's admonition, Sita fumbled for her spectacles and began to read the first page of the confession. Prescott felt sorry for her, desperately sorry. What must it be like to be confronted with the incontrovertible proof that your husband has been in the dreaded Tuol Sleng prison and that a confession, true or false, has been forced from him?

After a moment or two, Sita angrily pushed the papers from her. 'Lies, all lies. Hong never worked for the CIA; he was never an American agent. They compel him to say that! Do not believe this rubbish, Prescott!'

'Of course, no-one is going to believe it.' Prescott tried to calm the old lady. 'They forced him to write as he did. If you're sure this is his writing...'

'Sure? How can I be sure?' the old lady was crying now. 'I believe it is Hong's handwriting, it seems so to me... but what he writes, that is not the truth. They tortured him; I know they tortured him.'

He stayed to comfort her, promising her that they would all meet up soon and that they would in any way send her news as soon as they could.

In the end, Sita Soeung dried her eyes and attempted a smile. 'He was a good man. Whatever they made him say, Hong was a good man.'

Prescott patted her on the arm. She seemed frailer and more vulnerable as though this sudden, rude confrontation with the past had taken its toll.

'I'm sure Hong Soeung was a good man,' he said. 'He was your husband and Su's father. Of course, he was a good man. I'm sorry I never met him.'

'Give Su my love,' the old lady said. 'Tell her I miss her.'

'I miss her too.'

Sita clutched the front of Prescott's jacket. 'Why you not marry Su? I have grandchildren then.'

As he stood there, wondering if he still had time to catch his plane on to Hong Kong and Phnom Penh, Prescott felt an overwhelming rush of affection for the old lady.

'She has to say "yes" first,' he said.

'You have to ask her first,' Sita Soeung countered.

★★★

Su came to meet him at Pochentong airport, kissing him passionately as he walked out of the exit with his bag slung over one shoulder and a camera over the other.

'I'm so glad you were able to come, Prescott.'

'So am I.'

Though it was only a few days since they had last seen each other, there was so much to say.

In the car, Prescott told Su about his visit to Seattle.

'I thought your mother was looking well. The confession was a great shock to her. I could tell that. She didn't read it all, but she read enough. She thinks it's your father's handwriting all right, but she's never going to believe that your father wrote that confession as a statement of the truth.'

'I find it hard enough myself,' Su said.

'She has also given me a letter from your father. One she managed to keep, like the photograph, all through the Pol Pot years. We could get the experts in to compare the writing. That should clinch it.'

Su took the creased and travel stained envelope from Prescott, 'Lina will know someone,' she said.

With the Water Festival of Bon Om Tuk now over, the roads were much clearer than they had been the day Su arrived. Prescott looked out of the car window with interest. Some of the road signs were still in French as well as Khmer but it looked as though they hadn't been repainted for decades. Having spent time in both Vietnam and Laos in the past, Prescott could recognise the influence of French colonial architecture. The wide graceful boulevards, the elegant houses that lined the streets – but he could also appreciate how rapidly the place was evolving. New multi-storey concrete buildings were going up, with huge placards in front of them announcing the involvement of Korean, Japanese or even Malaysian construction companies. How soon, he wondered, would it be before McDonalds opened a branch in Phnom Penh? How galling it must be for the French, he thought. It was not just a military defeat they had suffered in Indochina, though Dien Bien Phu had been calamitous enough. It was the lasting damage to French influence, the language, the culture, the way of life. Give it another ten or twenty years he thought, and all traces of Cambodia's Gallic past would be obliterated.

He squeezed Su's hand. 'This must all be very strange for you. Do you recognise any of it?'

'Some of the streets, maybe. It's hard to tell. I certainly remember the bicycles and the oxcarts, the pavement fruit-sellers.'

'Have you seen your old house, the place where you used to live? Your mother asked me to go and visit it. She wants to know whether it's still there.'

Su smiled. 'I knew it. Mother pretends she doesn't want to know, but of course she does. I'm glad she wanted you to see the place. I'd like to see it myself. After all, that's where I began to grow up.'

She found a map of the city in the seat-pocket in front of her, and pointed out her old address to Prescott. 'We're in plenty of time. Our route takes us along Norodom Boulevard, past the end of our street. We could visit my old home now, see what's left of it anyway. Of course, there may be nothing there.'

Ten minutes later, they turned off the thoroughfare into a quiet, tree-lined street. The roadway, like so many in the city, was unpaved. Pools of water from the recent rains lay on the crumbling, potholed surface.

Most of the house numbers either didn't exist or had faded beyond recognition.

'Number 14 should be down on the left,' Su instructed the driver. 'Ah, there it is!' They pulled up in front of a wooden one-storey dwelling, surrounded on three sides by a wide wooden veranda. The house was in need of a coat of paint but otherwise it seemed to be in good order.

It was clear that the house was occupied because two small children were playing on the deck outside the front door. A woman came out of the house to gaze at them curiously for a moment before retreating inside.

'I don't want to bother them,' Su said. For a few moments she sat there without speaking, lost in her thoughts.

'Let me take a picture of you in front of the house,' Prescott said. 'That won't disturb anyone.'

He took two or three photographs, setting Su against the

backdrop of the veranda. 'We'll send some pictures to your mother.'

'At least the place is still standing,' Su said. 'I was afraid they might have pulled it down.'

As they made their way back onto the main boulevard, Prescott noted the increasing number of new brick and concrete buildings which were replacing the graceful wooden houses of the past, even on the side streets.

'It may not be long before they do pull it down,' he said. 'It's in a prime location, isn't it?'

'I suppose it is.'

Su kept silent for most of the rest of the journey, letting the memories flood back. Even now, she could see herself as a child playing on the veranda, while her mother bustled about inside the house. And she could remember the sweet smell of her father's pipe as he sat in his rocking-chair, listening to the sound of gunfire and rockets from beyond Pochentong airport as the Khmer Rouge closed in on the city.

★★★

Lina was happy to be able to bring Professor Haq in on things. As soon as they had found Hong Soeung's confession in Tuol Sleng, she had wanted to make a full report to Haq. After all, the professor was her boss at DC-Cam. But for a time she had hesitated waiting to hear from Su what her mother's reaction to the photo and the confession had been. Now that she had heard from Su that her mother had recognised Hong from the Tuol Sleng photo and now that they had, thanks to Prescott's arrival, an authenticated sample of Hong Soeung's handwriting, it seemed to her that the moment had come to involve her superiors.

'There's an added advantage,' she explained to Su when she proposed her plan. 'Professor Haq is a renowned graphologist in his own right. I can compare one Khmer manuscript with an another with a reasonable certainty of making the correct identification. That's something we have to do all the time at DC-Cam. Sometimes prisoners in Tuol Sleng were forced to write out their confessions not once but several times. Indeed, sometimes they went on writing them until the interrogators were satisfied with what they had got or at least felt, by some twisted logic, that they had enough to sentence them to be executed. Not all the documents are signed and sealed so we are often having to compare one text with another to build up the files correctly.

'But Professor Haq's the real expert. The Interior Ministry's antiquities department even uses him, if he can find the time to get away, to help on the deciphering of ancient Khmer inscriptions. When they find a new temple in the jungle somewhere with some hard-to-read carvings or bas-relief which they think might tell them who built it, when and why, they fly him up to Angkor or wherever to take a look and a week or two later he comes back and tells them all they need to know.'

They met in Haq's office in DC-Cam, the Cambodian Documentation Centre, at six p.m. on the day of Prescott's arrival in Phnom Penh. Apart from Lina Chan, Prescott Glover and Su Soeung, Jules Barron also joined them. In many ways it was a council of war, a time to weigh the evidence, to decide on a course of action.

'Do you need the original document, professor, or will the

photocopy be sufficient?' Lina Chan asked, having briefed the professor in detail before the meeting. 'If you need the original, I can easily get it. I put it in the safe in my office.'

'The photocopy will be sufficient,' the professor replied. With magnifying glass in hand, Haq spread out the thin fragile sheets of the letter which Hong Soeung had sent to his wife in March 1975. As he did so, he turned to Su: 'Have you read the letter?' he asked.

'No. Not yet. I will later. I wanted to give myself time. Prescott only gave it to me today.'

'Very sensible,' Haq murmured. 'Such matters should not be rushed. We do not need to read it ourselves. That is not our business. We are just concerned with the orthography.'

As far as they could tell, Haq's examination of the texts in front of him was totally thorough. He examined the handwriting from every angle, comparing one document with another, word-by-word, sometimes character-by-character. Like Lina, he was quite fluent in English and in deference to Preston and Jules, this was the language he now used.

'Of course, it is easiest,' Haq explained, 'when we find actual words which are the same. Just at a quick glance I see there are several. But even if we don't find similar or identical words, the formation of the Khmer characters by itself is usually enough to tell us everything we need to know. There are so many ways of writing our beautiful language and each one can be subtly different. Each of us develops his or her own way of writing. I am sure that is true for you too, Mr Glover?'

'I am afraid far too many of us in my country are addicted to our computers and word processors. Some of us can barely sign our names!' Prescott said smiling.

'More's the pity,' Haq said.

For the next few minutes, the professor proceeded in silence with his examination. At last he was satisfied. He handed the letter back to Su, who carefully replaced it in the tattered envelope.

'Hong Soeung wrote both documents, the letter and the confession. No doubt about that. I have seldom seen a clearer match. There are certain signs, as far as the confession is concerned, that Hong Soeung was writing – or was being forced to write – under pressure. This is not a copperplate production. But that is to be expected given the circumstances.'

Professor Haq stood up in order – so it seemed – to address them more formally. 'As you must realise, the discovery of the Hong Soeung confession, particularly its reference to US-Pol Pot negotiations and the so-called 'Judas-list' is a matter of great importance not only for DC-Cam but for our country. There are enormous implications here. I shall have to apprise the Minister of the Interior of our findings. That is my clear responsibility as Director of this Centre. The Interior Ministry is after all our sponsoring authority.'

Su had a powerful sensation that matters were being taken out of her hands. 'Do I have some rights in this? This is my father's confession. I'm not sure I want it to become a political football. What will this do to his reputation?'

Haq replied almost fiercely. 'You talk, Miss Soeung, about one man's reputation. A man moreover who is long dead, I'm sorry to say. I have to fight for the truth. And once the truth is known, as it is now, we cannot keep quiet about it. Don't forget, you have already informed Senator Clinton as I understand it. The Cambodian authorities themselves have an equal or greater right to know. It is our people who suffered while the US – how do you say? – played footsy with the Khmer Rouge.' The Professor almost spat out the last sentence, such was his scorn.

'The Professor's right, Su,' Prescott said quietly. 'Painful as it may be, we can't keep the lid on this one.'

Su was on the verge of tears. 'I almost wish I had never started this.'

'Don't say that,' Lina tried to console her. 'Some good may come of this, I feel sure.'

It was Jules Barron who came up with the bright idea. 'Surely, the Senator should talk to Minister Khin Lay as soon as she arrives. This thing has to be handled properly. The two of them could sort it out.'

It was almost as though Haq had been waiting for some such suggestion. 'Excellent idea. I shall ensure that the Minister is fully briefed about the need to see Mrs Clinton as soon as she arrives. I am sure our American friends here,' he nodded at both Prescott and Su, 'will take the necessary steps to inform Mrs Clinton.'

He waited till they had left the room, then picked up the telephone.

★★★

Later that night, Su used her laptop to send an email to Jessica Low, Senator Clinton's legislative aide, summarizing recent developments. Almost by return, Jessie emailed back:

'Your latest email is being studied with great interest here.'

Prescott read the message over her shoulder. 'This thing's moving so fast it's uncanny. It's almost as if it's programmed.'

'I wonder which way the Senator's going to play it,' Su mused, closing the email programme down.

'This is her first big foreign affairs coup, and, in my judgement, she'll milk it for all it's worth.'

'That's a pretty cynical view,' Su bristled. 'I don't think the Senator's just out to score political points to further her own career. What about the issues? Don't you think she cares about the issues? The US doing a deal with Pol Pot? Handing over the death-list? Those were real people on that list. My father was one of them.'

Su was still sitting at the desk in the hotel room. Prescott touched her lightly on the shoulder. 'Don't get me wrong. I'm not saying she doesn't care about the issues. I'm saying she cares just as much, if not more, about how these things play out in the public perception. That's why she's a politician and a damn good one.'

While Prescott went down to the bar, Su – out of curiosity – made a rough translation of her father's letter to her mother.

> *Dearest Sita, Hong Soeung wrote, you may not get this letter before I return to Phnom Penh next week. The Khmer Rouge are now occupying large parts of Siem Reap and Banteay Meanchey provinces. The Angkor Wat complex is now inaccessible, at least to a government official like me. The Khmer Rouge are occupying the area. But I have been able to visit the temple of Ta Keo in the last few days to make arrangements for the conservation of antiquities there. What an amazing place it is!*

In my judgement Ta Keo is certainly the most elegant of the Khmer temples, in particular because of its triangular pediments. They were to be the last of their kind because subsequently all the galleries were vaulted in stone. Ta Keo's ground plan has a linear pattern, on the side of a hill running right up to the natural summit. The site is still covered in jungle but this to my mind adds to the mystery and charm. This morning when I climbed to the top of the temple-mountain, I looked out at the forest which stretched away on all sides as far as the eye could see. How many other great structures I wonder lie hidden there? There is a life-time's work here. What a tragedy it is that this war between the Khmers is destroying so much of our heritage. I have a different vision of how things should be. Perhaps I will one day have a chance to work for it. This would be a good place to start. Please give Su a big kiss from me. I miss her – and you. All my love, Hong.

Su was still dabbing at her eyes with a handkerchief when Prescott returned. She showed him the translation she had made of Hong Soeung's last letter to his wife.

Prescott was fascinated, 'He was a scholar as well as an administrator and, by the look of this, something of a visionary too.'

Earlier that day they had bought a large-scale map of Cambodia which Prescott now consulted.

'There are a couple of sites labelled Ta Keo,' he said, 'but these are in the south of the country. Nothing up north under that name. He must have been a brave man, your father. By March 1975 the Khmer Rouge must have been all over the area. He would have run a tremendous risk.'

'They got him soon enough anyway,' Su paused, then she asked: 'What else did my mother say?'

'She said we ought to get married.'

'And what did you say?'

'I said you hadn't said "yes" yet.'

'You didn't ask yet.'

'I'm asking now. Do you want me to go down on bended knee?'

Su laughed, 'I'd like to see that, but you don't have to. Of course, I'll marry you, Prescott, just as soon as this business is over.'

They stood there, holding onto each other in a passionate embrace. At last, as they drew apart, Prescott joked: 'Hey, do you think this means I get to stay the night? This is Cambodia, I wouldn't want to upset the local customs.'

'I think the Cambodiana can handle it. We've got adjoining rooms anyway. No-one can complain.'

'In that case, why don't we make my room into our office?' Prescott volunteered. 'I have a feeling we're going to need it.'

They raided the minibar and opened a bottle of champagne, then sat together on the hotel room balcony watching the traffic on the river and enjoying the sounds of the night.

CHAPTER 9

Geoff Jackson, the UN Secretary-General's special represent-ative in Cambodia, was in a bouncy mood when he saw Su Soeung and Prescott Glover at breakfast in the Cambodiana Hotel the following morning.

'Can I join you folks?' he asked.

Su introduced Prescott to the Australian. 'This is Prescott Glover of The New York Times. Prescott this is Geoffrey Jackson. Mr Jackson is in charge of the Pol Pot trials.'

'Call me Geoff,' Jackson instructed. And he added, jovially: 'I believe I've mentioned before that the UN is not in charge of the trials. That's Cambodia's business. We're just monitoring the affair. Good news this morning, then?'

As he pulled up a chair, Jackson laid his copy of the Cam-bodia Daily on the table. 'See that headline. That could be a clincher. NEW DOCUMENTS IMPLICATE DUCH.'

Prescott shot Su a warning glance, 'Tell us more.'

Jackson summarized the story for them. 'Don't know how they got hold of this before we did. The UN's meant to have sight of all the papers in the trial before they're introduced into the proceedings. I guess I'll find my copy on my desk this morning. Basically, the prosecution is saying they've found a document which clearly indicates that Kang Kech Ieu – also known as Duch – signed an execution warrant for a Tuol Sleng prisoner.'

'What's so significant about that?' Su asked. 'I thought the prosecution case was that Duch was responsible for hundreds if not thousands of deaths.'

Geoff Jackson nodded. 'That is indeed going to be the prosecution's case. Their problem is going to be making it stick. As you can imagine there aren't any witnesses. All the potential witnesses died, with the exception of the famous seven survivors. And there are evidential problems even there from the point of view of making the charges against Duch stick. Of course, there's the documentary record of what went on in Tuol Sleng, lots of that. Confessions, interrogation notes, that kind of thing. But Duch was clever. He kept his nose clean. Finding his signature on an execution warrant like this could be a breakthrough. Just what we need to pin the bastard down.'

Jackson turned to Prescott. 'You here professionally or just visiting?'

'A bit of both,' Prescott replied. 'Senator Clinton is flying in on Thursday. *The Times* wants me to cover it. I'm going to stay on through next week anyway to cover the trial. Or at least the beginning of it. I guess it may last months.'

'Hell, I hope not. I was hoping to get home by Christmas,' Jackson said. He jabbed with his thumb at the paper. 'If this new document is watertight, we may be able to speed things up a bit.'

The Australian looked at them appraisingly. 'I guess the other reason for being here is Su, am I right?'

Prescott smiled, 'One hundred per cent. The extra bonus as far as I'm concerned is meeting up with Su. Su and I are planning on getting married.'

'Hey, that's great!' Jackson was genuinely delighted for them. 'When's the happy day?'

'We're not sure yet,' Su said. 'Soon, anyway, we hope.'

'Good luck to you both.' Geoff Jackson drained his coffee-cup, picked up the newspaper and strode out of the room.

Seconds later, they saw the UN car with Jackson on board pull away from the lobby, official pennant fluttering in the breeze.

Prescott poured them both a last cup of coffee. 'Professor Haq must have moved fast. He must have called the Minister after we left last night and the Minister must have briefed the press.'

'That's always half the battle, isn't it?' said Su.

'What do you mean?'

'I mean spinning the story so you get the result you want.'

'And what do you think Khin Lay wants?' Prescott asked.

'Well, Duch's conviction, I suppose,' Su replied.

Prescott pushed his cup aside and looked around the room as he did so. 'There may be more to this than that, Su. I'm beginning to get a tingling sensation in the tip of my little finger which tells me something's not quite right around here.'

'Tell me more.'

'I can't pin it down exactly,' Prescott said. 'I just have a feeling that one or two things don't add up. Nothing I can put my finger on. Not now, anyway.'

Su was intrigued and would have pressed him further but just at that moment, one of the hotel bell boys came through the dining room carrying a board on which was inscribed the words: 'Telephone for Miss Soeung.'

'That's me!' Su exclaimed. When she returned to the table a few minutes later, she explained: 'That was Jules Barron. He has just heard that Andrew Mossman is flying in at the same time as the Senator. They may even be on the same plane. He also says that Mark Kelly's arriving for CNN and the BBC is stepping up its coverage.'

'Well, well, well,' Prescott said. 'So, the plot thickens?'

★★★

Prescott left the hotel soon after breakfast to meet *The New York Times* Phnom Penh stringer and to make various practical arrangements for what now looked like being quite an extended assignment in Cambodia.

'Are you sure you don't want me to come with you?' he had asked Su, 'I could probably be back here by mid-morning.'

'I appreciate the offer,' Su had replied. 'Lina Chan is coming to hold my hand. Choeung Ek is one of DC-Cam's responsibilities.'

'Does she think you'll find some trace there, some indication that this is where your father indeed met his end?'

'Hardly that,' Su replied. 'According to Lina, they have lists of the Tuol Sleng prisoners executed at Choeung Ek and my father's name doesn't appear on them. But these are only partial lists. They are known to be incomplete.'

'So, what's the point of going out there? You'll only be upset. More upset.' Prescott wanted to protect Su from yet more turmoil.

'I have to go,' Su replied quietly. 'I have to know how it was.'

★★★

'What intrigues me is the date,' Lina remarked, as – an hour later – they were driven out of Phnom Penh towards the Killing Fields of Choeung Ek. 'Choeung Ek in the seventies was a hamlet with a Chinese graveyard nearby. According to our records, the Khmer Rouge didn't start using it as a "killing field" until some time in 1977 when the burial grounds near and around Tuol Sleng had filled up. Now we have a piece of documentary evidence that people were being transported to, and executed at, Choeung Ek as early as 1975. At least that's what the stamp on your father's confession says. Puzzles me, rather. I'll have to look into that. I'll ask Professor Haq what he thinks.'

Su's mind was elsewhere at that moment. 'I'd prefer you to say 'so-called' confession.'

Sounding as miserable as she felt, she stared out of the window of the vehicle, trying to reconstruct in her mind's eye the circumstances of her father's last journey,

'How did they get them out here?' she asked. 'The people they wished to execute.'

'By truck. Each truck would have three or four guards and twenty to thirty prisoners.'

'Did the prisoners know where they were going?'

'The evidence is that they did. We have recorded interviews with two of the Tuol Sleng guards, Kok Sros and Nhem En. Kok Sros spoke of the prisoners struggling and fighting with the guards as they were "taken away to the west" – in Khmer mythology, the direction of death.'

Su shuddered.

The tarmac barely lasted beyond the city limits. For the last twenty minutes, they had been bumping along a dirt road deep into the Cambodian countryside. For the first time in her life, Su found herself looking out at the viridian green of the rice paddies stretching out on either side of the track. She observed the traditional Khmer houses set among the fields. Built on stilts, some had tin roofs, some thatch; most families, she noted, kept some livestock – cows or pigs or chickens – at ground level below the main dwelling.

A few miles past the turn-off to Pochentong airport, the road forked. One faded sign pointed in one direction towards the 'Agricultural Institute'. The other sign said: 'Choeung Ek Genocidal Centre.' A few minutes later, they saw the gleaming gold roof of the Memorial Stupa soaring above the plain.

A parking area had been cleared a short distance from the entrance to the Centre. Leaving their driver to keep an eye on the car, Su and Lina went inside the gate.

'Take your time,' Lina said. 'You'll want to look around outside first.' She gave a broad sweep of her hand to indicate the extent of the terrain. 'The mapping project I was telling you about has come up with some fairly accurate estimates as far as Choeung Ek is concerned. We think there are 129 mass graves altogether, of which 86 are currently open. Some of them have suffered damage in the recent flooding. There's a risk of greater damage in the future. Will we raise the funds to prevent that? Who knows? How much effort do you put into recording and preserving past atrocities? That's a political decision like so much else in Cambodia.'

Notebook in hand, Su followed her guide around the killing fields. Fragments of bone and bits of cloth were still visible around the disinterred pits.

'How were they killed?' Su whispered.

'They were ordered to kneel at the edge of the pits and ditches that would have been dug earlier by the workers stationed permanently at Choueng Ek. Their hands were tied behind them. They were beaten on the neck with an iron ox-cart axle or some such implement, sometimes with one blow, sometimes with two.'

Besides one of the pits, a placard had been posted with its text written in English as well as Khmer. More confident in English than Khmer, Su painstakingly copied down the English version into her notebook. She wrote down exactly what appeared on the board, including all faults of spelling and punctuation.

THE MOST TRAGIC THING, Su wrote, IS THAT EVEN IN THE TWENTIETH CENTURY, ON KAMPUCHEAN SOIL, THE CLIQUE OF POL POT CRIMINALS HAS COMMITTED A HEINOUS GENOCIDAL ACT, THEY MASSACRED THE POPULATION WITH ATROCITY IN A LARGE SCALE, IT WAS MORE CRUEL THANTHE GENOCIDAL ACT COMMITTED BY HITLER FASCISTS, WHICH THE WORLD HAS NEVER MET.

WITH THE COMMEMORATIVE STUPA IN FRONT OF US, WE IMAGINE THAT WE ARE HEARING THE GRIEVOUS VOICE OF THE VICTMS WHO WERE BEATEN BY POL POT MEN WITH CANES, BAMBOO STUMPS OR HEADS OF HOES, WHO WERE STABBED WITH KNIVES OR SWORDS. WE SEEM TO BE LOOKING AT THE HORRIFYING SCENES

AND THE PANIC-STRICKEN FACES OF THEPEO-
PLE WHO WERE DYING OF STARVATION, FORCED
LABOUR OR TORTURE WITHOUT MERCY UPON
THE SKINNY BODY; THEY DED WITHOUT GIVING
THE LAST WORDS TO KITH AND HOW HURTFUL
THOSE VICTMS WERE WHEN THEY GOT BEATEN
WITH CANES, HEADS OF HOES AND STABBED
WITH KNIVES OR SWORDS BEFORE THEIR LAST
BREATH WENT OUT. HOW BITTER THEY WERE
SEEING THEIR BELOVED CHILDREN, WIVES, HUS-
BANDS, BROTHERS OR SISTERS WERE SEIZED
AND TIGHTLY BOUND BEFORE BEING TAKEN TO
MASS GRAVE!

WHILE THEY WERE WAITING FOR THEIR TURN
TO COME AND SHARE THE SAME TRAGIC LOT.
THE METHOD OF MASSACRE WHICH THE
CLIQUE OF POL POT CRIMINALS WAS CARRIED
UPON THE INNOCENT PEOPLE OF KAMPUCHEA
CANNOT BE DESCRIBED FULLY AND CLEARLY IN
WORDS BECAUSE THE INVENTION OF THIS KILL-
ING NETHOD WAS STRANGELY CRUEL. SO IT IS
DIFFICULT FOR US TO DETERMINE WHICH THEY
ARE FOR. THEY HAVE THE HUMAN FORM BUT
THEIR HEARTS ARE DEMON'S HEARTS, THEY
HAVE GOT THE KHMER FACE BUT THEIR ACTIV-
ITIES ARE PURELY REACTIONARY. THEY WANT-
ED TO TRANSFORM KAMPUCHEAN PEOPLE NTO
A GROUP OF PERSONS WITHOUT REASON OR A
GROUP WHO KNEW AND UNDERSTOOD NOTH-

ING, WHO ALWAYS BENT THEIR HEAD TO CAR-
RY OUT ANGKAR'S ORDERS BLINDLY, THEY HAD
EDUCATED AND TRANSFORMED YOUNG PEOPLE
AND THE ADOLESCENT WHOSE HEARTS ARE
PURE, GENTLE AND HONEST INTO ODIOUS EX-
ECUTIONERS WHO DARED TO KILL THE INNO-
CENT AND EVEN OWN PARENTS, RELATIVES OR
FRIENDS.

Su paused to turn the page. Then, taking care to capture every
last dot and comma, she resumed her task.

THEY HAD BURNT THE MARKET PLACE, ABOL-
ISHED MONETARY SYSTEM, ELIMINATED BOOKS
OF RULES AND PRINCIPLES OF NATIONAL CUL-
TURE, DESTROYED SCHOOLS, HOSPITALS, PA-
GODAS AND BEAUTIFUL MONUMENTS SUCH
AS ANGKOR WATT WHICH IS THE SOURCE OF
PURE NATIONAL PRIDE AND BEARS THE GENI-
US, KNOWLEDGE AND INTELLIGENCE OF OUR
NATION. THEY WERE TRYING HARD TO GET RID
OF THE KHMER CHARACTER AND TRANSFORM
THE SOIL AND WATERS OF KAVIPUCHEA INTO A
SEA OF BLOOD AND TEARS WHICH WAS DEPRIVE
OF CULTURAL INFRASTRUCTURE, CIVILISATION
AND NATIONAL CHARACTER, BECAME A DESERT
OF GREAT DESTRUCTION THAT OVERTURNED
THE KANPUCHEAN SOCIETY AND DROVE IT BACK
INTO THE STONE AGE.

When she had finished transcribing, Su put her notebook away.

'How could anyone ever, ever imagine,' she exclaimed passionately, almost trembling as she spoke, 'that the United States actually backed a regime as evil and as hideous as Pol Pot's? The longer I stay here, Lina, the deeper we dig, the more I realise that we have uncovered a great evil. We must make sure that evil is exposed.'

'That's what we are trying to do,' Lina said. 'Haq will have taken steps, so will Minister Khin Lay. Your Senator Clinton will not allow this scandal to remain hidden.'

The revelation hit Su suddenly. 'It's all so much bigger than my father, isn't it? What he did, what he knew – that's just part of a much wider picture. The real issue here is whether evildoing is to be exposed or not?'

'And what do you think?' Lina asked her quietly as they stood beside one of the open mass graves of Choeung Ek's killing fields.

'Someone said it before me, I believe,' Su answered. 'For evil to triumph, it is enough for good men to stay silent.'

Later, they visited the Memorial Stupa. Here, layer after layer of skulls were arranged by sex and by age – over 8000 altogether. By what logic the categories had been chosen, Su had no idea. One layer contained the skulls of 'adult male Kampucheans twenty to forty years old,' another of 'mature female Kampucheans forty to sixty years old.' Still another, the skulls of infants.

'Many of the skulls have holes, gashes or fractures as you can see,' Lina told her. 'With the children, the damage to the cranium is often massive. The guards would just pick up a child by his or her feet and swing it against a tree.'

If Su lingered longest before the layer of adult male Kampuchean skulls, 20 to 40 years old, it was perhaps understandable. Somewhere in those sinister glass cases which rose, one upon another, for a full seventeen stories inside the Memorial Stupa, might lie the mortal remains of her father, Hong Soeung. Did skulls contain DNA, she wondered? Could she track down her father that way? Then she realised what a laughable idea it was. Even if her father's skull had been correctly classified, how could they sift through hundreds or perhaps thousands of similar specimens?

Still, she asked Lina, 'What about DNA? Could you try to identify some of these remains through DNA?'

As they left the Stupa to walk out into the open air, Lina shook her head, 'Even if it was technically and practically possible, we would still need DNA samples for comparison. Do you know your father's DNA barcode? Do you have a valid sample? Of course, you don't. We're talking about people who died over a quarter of a century ago, whose homes, family and possessions were obliterated in a tidal wave. No wonder, there are no DNA samples we can use.'

'So, there's no way of knowing whether one of those skulls we have just seen is that of my father?'

'No way of knowing for sure,' Lina put her arm round the other woman. 'But the probability your father's remains are somewhere here is high.'

While Lina tactfully went ahead of her to find their driver, Su spent a few minutes on her knees in front of the soaring stupa, saying a prayer for the soul of her father and for all who, like him, had suffered humiliation, torture and death in that hellish place.

★★★

Su spent the rest of the day at the SAVE office. When she returned to her hotel room, she found Prescott sitting in front of his laptop, typing with two-fingered proficiency.

He looked up as she entered. 'Senator Clinton is holding a joint press conference tomorrow morning with Khin Lay, the Minister of the Interior. Officially, no-one is saying why. Unofficially, it looks as though Khin Lay has decided to give her a platform to talk about the Hong Soeung affair.'

'The Hong Soeung affair?' Su sank wearily into a chair, the strain of the long day beginning to tell. 'Is that what they're calling it now, the "Hong Soeung affair?"'

She leaned across and poured herself a glass of iced water from a thermos-jug on the dresser. Her mood brightened. 'I think the Senator's right. It's high time someone went public with this. One day sooner is one day better. If you had seen what I saw today in Choeung Ek's killing fields, you'd be justified in saying this press conference should have been held decades ago.'

Prescott's hand was still poised over the keyboard. He smiled, 'Can I quote you on that? I'm filing a scene-setter right now. Four hundred pithy words to prepare our loyal readers for tomorrow's exclusive!'

'Let's see,' Su said.

She stood up, glass of iced water in hand, and read Prescott's copy over his shoulder:

> For a relative novice in the Foreign Affairs arena, Senator Hillary Clinton who arrives in Phnom Penh early tomorrow on a fact-finding visit, has received an unprecedented compliment by being invited to hold a joint press conference with powerful Interior Minister, Khin Lay. Khin Lay is one of the two FUNCIPEC ministers in the current ruling coalition under Cambodian Prime Minister Hun Sen. Neither side would be drawn this evening on the subject of the topics to be discussed at the press conference. Unofficially, the indications are that in addition to reviewing mutual concerns relating to the progress of de-mining and rehabilitation, new documentation of relevance to the forthcoming Pol Pot trials is likely to be presented...

'You call that "pithy?"' Su teased him.

Prescott laughed. 'Even "pithy" is relative. *The Times* likes to spell things out.'

'Are you expecting to see the Senator before she goes into bat?' Su asked.

'I doubt it. She's being met at the airport by the Minister with an official cavalcade. They are going straight to the new international conference centre where the press will be waiting. This is going to be big, Su. Half the Beijing press corps are flying down; the Bangkok and Hong Kong-based journalists are probably already here. This is a very smooth job, one of the smoothest I've seen.'

'Takes a woman...' Su said.

'It's not just Hillary,' Prescott demurred. 'It's the story as well. Of course, Mrs Clinton's first big speech on foreign affairs in a highly exotic setting is news. But there's more to it. Without giving the game away, the Senator's people are letting it be known that a major rewrite of history may be called for once tomorrow's press conference is over. If you hadn't responded positively to that letter from Mossman when it dropped onto your doormat that morning, none of this might have happened.'

Prescott's mention of Andrew Mossman reminded Su of the message she had received that morning.

'Mossman's arriving. Jules Barron is meeting him at the airport about now. He's staying at this hotel.'

'Then you had better dance attendance too,' Prescott advised. 'That's what loyal employees do when the big boss arrives in town.'

'I'm sure he'll call me when he gets here,' Su said.

She was right about that. An hour later, the telephone rang, and Mossman invited them both for a drink in his suite.

Prescott, who was filing more copy, declined but Su went up to the hotel's top floor to meet SAVE's chief executive officer.

★★★

It wasn't the Cambodiana's finest suite of rooms, but it came close. Andrew Mossman clearly believed that money devoted to keeping up appearances was money well spent, particularly when it was not his own. There were flowers or bowls of fruit on most available surfaces in the huge sitting room with its panoramic view over the river.

Mossman opened the door with a bottle of champagne in

his hand. 'Su, come on in! Good to see you. Jules and I just decided we needed some refreshment before dinner.'

Su joined the two men on the balcony. As the light begin to fade on the Mekong, Mossman raised his glass: 'Congratulations, you've made a splendid start, Su. Apparently, you're already a favourite at SAVE's Phnom Penh clinic. Isn't that so, Jules?'

'It certainly is. The doctors and nurses love her, and the patients think she's Florence Nightingale.' Barron laid it on with a trowel. 'Our next step is to get Su up-country, to visit SAVE's operations in Siem Reap and the surrounding area. We had hoped to leave tomorrow but I think it would be wise to delay. I have a feeling that Senator Clinton may be counting on Su for some moral support.'

Andrew Mossman had clearly been fully briefed by Jules on the extent of Su's extracurricular activities during her brief stay in Phnom Penh. It was also obvious that Mossman was not in the least disturbed by the hornet's nest which Su had stirred up.

'Remember when you came to have a drink at our place?' Mossman reminded her. 'Caroline told you then – and I agreed with her – that this could be a golden opportunity for you to do some digging, find out what happened to your father. Looks like you've turned up an unexploded mine.'

'More like a whole minefield,' Su replied. 'I'm not sure I realised what I was getting into.'

'Don't pull back now,' Mossman said sharply. 'You've got my full support, SAVE's full support. The truth will always make us stronger, however painful it may seem.'

As dusk gathered, the three of them went back inside Mossman's suite.

'Have some fruit. There's loads of it.' Mossman gestured to a cut-glass bowl on the table heaped high with mangoes, oranges, bananas and apples. As she helped herself, Su noted the stiff, embossed card sticking out of the top of the pile bearing the words: 'With warmest personal greetings from the Minister, the Honourable Khin Lay.' How well did Mossman know the Minister, she wondered? Clearly, they were more than casual acquaintances.

The television was, inevitably, still tuned to CNN. Mark Kelly, who was obviously shuttling between Bangkok, Hong Kong and Penh with Kissinger-like rapidity, was informing a worldwide audience that Senator Hillary Rodham had already landed in Hong Kong.

'The Senator is resting now,' Mark Kelly intoned, 'but I shall be accompanying her tomorrow morning on the plane when she flies into Cambodia to give her much-anticipated Press conference. This is Mark Kelly, CNN, Hong Kong...'

Back in CNN's world communication centre in Atlanta, Georgia, the announcer informed them that the network would of course be covering Senator Hillary Rodham Clinton's press conference in Phnom Penh live and unabridged.

'CNN won't be alone, I'm sure,' Mossman commented. 'The airport was full of journalists and camera crew this evening. NBC, Star TV, BBC – you name it. Sharks scenting blood in the water.'

★★★

Prescott Glover finished his work and looked at his watch. Su was still upstairs. He had no idea how long she would be. He decided to leave her a note to say that he had walked along the quay to the Foreign Correspondents' Club of Cambodia and why didn't she join him there when she was through.

It was not the first time Prescott had visited the FCCC. With the Cambodiana Hotel located only a few hundred yards along the quay, it was normal and natural for a man with Prescott's journalistic instincts to pop into the club for a beer or a meal among friends and colleagues. As a former Asia correspondent of *The New York Times*, the Foreign Correspondents' Club of Cambodia held a particular resonance for him. Colleagues on the paper, like Sidney Schanberg, had once made their name in Phnom Penh. They had walked along Phnom Penh's flower-scented streets, smelt the odour of opium; visited the villages along the Mekong; admired the exquisite beauty of Cambodian women and all the while – as the Khmer Rouge closed in on the city – they were sitting on one of the great stories of the twentieth century. He suspected that Sidney Schanberg would have earned his reputation as one of journalism's "greats" even without the immortality accorded him by the film, *The Killing Fields*.

He could tell, as he climbed up the stairs from the street, that this would not be a dull evening. A couple of voices called out to him in greeting as he entered the first floor bar room. 'Hey, Prescott, how are you doing?' 'Good to see you, Prescott!'

Prescott bought himself a drink and went over to join some journalists who were seated at a table by the window.

'Are you guys here for the same reason I'm here?' he asked.

Graham Bender, the cadaverously thin, chain-smoking white-haired doyen of the BBC's Far East correspondents, replied: 'And what reason might that be? Could we be talking about Senator Clinton?'

Prescott laughed, 'We just might be.'

The third man at the table was a distinguished newspaper-man from *Le Monde*. With skin the colour of parchment and close-cropped hair, Henri Le Blanc had reported from South East Asia for well over two decades. Offered major editorial assignments in Paris, he had steadfastly refused, preferring the excitements and uncertainties of the field to a desk-bound existence. During the time he had spent in Asia, he had watched the influence of his own country, France, steadily decline. There were still plenty of players in the game – China, Russia, the United States and Japan for starters – but France was no longer one of them. As if to compensate, he spoke English with the thickest of French accents.

'We are all 'ere for 'illary, *n'est-ce pas?* The US press people 'ere are 'opping mad. They are *furieux!*'

'That's true,' Graham Bender agreed. 'The US mission here is particularly incensed not only because the Senator's people have made all the arrangements without involving the mission but because they've accepted Khin Lay's invitation to hold the joint press conference. I talked to Ben Deakin earlier today. He's the press man with the US mission. He said he didn't know what the Senator was playing at – and I quote.'

'So, what ees she playing at?' Le Blanc asked.

Prescott wondered what to say in answer. At the most basic level, he believed he knew what Senator Hillary Clinton was going to say at her press conference the next morning. On the other hand, he certainly wasn't aware of all the details. The Senator, before going public, would have had a whole team of people working on this. That was for sure. Leaving all that aside, Prescott didn't see why he should lightly surrender to competitors the head-start he had on the story and he knew that the desk back in New York wouldn't expect him too.

He decided to prevaricate without actually lying. 'My office in New York has been talking to the Senator's office in Washington. The word we're getting is that the Senator wants to blow the whistle in a big way.'

The two men gazed at him with a combination of interest and annoyance. They both seemed to believe that Prescott knew more than he was saying.

'What whistle?' Graham Bender asked. 'And why should Hillary Clinton be the one to blow it?'

Prescott smiled enigmatically, 'I think we are all going to have to wait until tomorrow before we know the answer to that.'

Bender shot a quick glance at Le Blanc and they both smiled. Prescott had a momentary sensation that the boot might after all be on the other foot. Maybe it wasn't just a question of him knowing something they didn't know. Maybe they knew something *he* didn't know.

'Things aren't always what they seem. Not in Cambodia,' Henri Le Blanc commented, reaching absentmindedly for a toothpick.

CHAPTER 10

Prescott Glover, well-positioned in the second row of the crowded conference room in the Ministry of the Interior on Phnom Penh's Norodom Boulevard, couldn't help admiring the poise and polish of Senator Hillary Clinton's performance. Sitting on the dais next to Minister Khin Lay, she managed to combine an air of authoritative purpose with an impressive grasp of the political realities.

Her prepared text, as distributed to journalists and media in advance under embargo, dealt with the questions which most concerned her, notably the health situation of the Cambodian population, progress made in fighting aids, the de-mining operation and the spread of waterborne diseases. The Senator promised to devote her full attention to these issues and to do her best to ensure that the Senate Committees on which she served, notably the Health and Budget Committees, took full cognizance of them in their work.

As she came to the end of her prepared remarks, she put her text to one side and turned to her right to address Minister Khin Lay, her platform-companion, directly. 'You can be certain, Mr Minister, that the United States will do everything it can to help you deal effectively with the problems your country faces and that I personally will do everything possible to assist you in your heroic efforts.'

Watching closely, Prescott saw the Senator pause. She seemed for a moment to be gathering her energies together, while making a conscious effort to keep control of her emotions.

'Perhaps you will allow me to conclude on a personal note,' Mrs Clinton said, her voice vibrant with the intensity of her feelings. 'Though I have never visited your beautiful country before, I have studied it over the years – its art and culture, as well as its politics. It seems to me that today Cambodia confronts great challenges, challenges which – if successfully met could allow this country to enjoy a future as glorious as her past. But I do not believe that will happen unless we make a start here and now in coming to terms with the legacy of the past. In this context I want to make it clear how much I welcome the fact that over twenty-five years after the Khmer Rouge came to power in Cambodia, the tribunal is about to begin its work. Better late than never. Much, much better! I also welcome the fact that the United Nations is here to monitor the progress of that tribunal. And it is certainly encouraging to have the personal assurance of the Minister that he will do everything in his power to ensure that the proceedings are expedited.'

Once again, Mrs Clinton paused to draw breath. She sipped from a glass of water in front of her, as Minister Khin Lay nodded his agreement. Then, speaking so softly that those in the back had to strain to catch her words, she launched her thunderbolt.

'The truth cannot be selective,' the Senator continued. 'In the healing process, blame must be fairly apportioned. Many of you in this room will remember that my husband, President Clinton, shortly before he left office, visited Vietnam to help the rebuilding and renewal which is now underway in that country. Though he did not expressly apologise for America's involvement in the Vietnam war, he came as close as he could to saying sorry.

Well, I'm not the President of the United States and perhaps I'm not under the same constraints because – today – I believe I can do a bit better than my husband!'

The Senator waited for the laughter to subside. Judging her moment and still keeping her voice low and dramatic, she continued: 'As we seek to uncover the truth, I think the time has come for the United States to admit – frankly and fearlessly – what some people have long suspected: namely that the United States right from the start aided and abetted the Pol Pot regime and that we will only rebuild a relationship of trust between our two countries if we are ready to admit our historical responsibilities...'

The Senator would have continued but she was interrupted at this point by a burst of applause, led by Minister Khin Lay himself.

Prescott took this as a signal to raise his hand. As he did so, he called out: 'Senator, do you have some hard evidence to back up this assertion?'

Mrs Clinton fielded the question neatly. She looked directly at Prescott as she replied. 'We certainly do have some hard evidence, Mr Glover. With the Minister's permission – indeed with his active encouragement – we are making public today the text of a remarkable document, newly discovered in the archives of Tuol Sleng, which in my judgement and in the judgement of several experts, whom I have consulted, provides incontrovertible evidence of the proposition I have just advanced. I believe the Minister will be calling upon Professor

Haq, the director of the Cambodian Genocide Documentation Centre here in Phnom Penh to introduce the subject.'

Turning the floor over to Khin Lay, Senator Clinton resumed her seat.

If Prescott had admired Mrs Clinton's professionalism, he was equally impressed by Professor Haq's. Invited by Khin Lay to address the press conference, Haq laid out in clear terms the circumstances of the find and his own evaluation. Ten minutes later, he summed matters up for the benefit of his audience.

'It is not up to me,' the Professor chose his words carefully, 'to assess the substance of the document, or the allegations contained therein. I limit myself to the comment that Mr Hong Soeung as a senior official in the Ministry of Culture was certainly in a position to have undertaken the tasks described in the document. I would also point out that the reference to Duch adds to the importance and significance of the document in the sense that it appears to attribute the execution order directly to Duch, though this is of course a matter for the tribunal to establish definitively.

'As to the question – did Hong Soeung write these confessions? I would answer unequivocally, "yes." From everything I know about the art and science of handwriting – and I have spent a lifetime studying it – I am quite confident that this confession was written by Hong Soeung personally. The fact that the confession was most probably written under duress is, of course, another matter entirely and needs to be taken into account when we are evaluating the import of the document.'

While Professor Haq was speaking, three or four of the

Minister's aides moved rapidly up and down the rows of journalists, passing out press packs. Prescott grabbed one and quickly examined the contents. In addition to the text of Senator Clinton's speech, Prescott noticed that the packs contained the full facsimile of the Hong Soeung confessions, as well as translations into French and English. They also contained a 6x4 glossy print of the Hong Soeung ID mugshot as it appeared on the walls of Tuol Sleng prison. They had certainly moved quickly, Prescott thought.

He raised his hand again. 'Professor Haq, would you care to comment on the suggestion that the United States was implicated in the preparation of the so-called "death list" or "Judas list"?'

As chair of the Press Conference, Khin Lay quickly intervened to rule the question out of order.

'Let us be clear,' he commented sternly, 'that the purpose of today's event is not to embarrass our friend and ally, the United States, but to uncover the truth.'

Prescott persisted nonetheless: 'Could the Senator indicate how she believes the "death list" was actually transmitted to Pol Pot by the United States, given the circumstances of the time?'

Again, the Minister sought to intervene, but Hillary Clinton held up her hand. 'I'll take it,' she said.

From her vantage point on the podium, Senator Hillary Rodham Clinton surveyed the now plainly agitated audience. Many of them were still not exactly sure what was happening, but they were all practised reporters. They could walk and chew gum at the same time and, though Prescott Glover of *The New York Times* for reasons they couldn't at that moment fathom clearly had a head start, even a cursory inspection of the material in the press pack was enough to convince them that this was a solid story. Hands shot up on all sides.

The Senator had to raise her voice above the hubbub. 'Ladies and gentlemen, for heaven's sake don't let's speculate at this point. I didn't come to Cambodia to launch an attack on the United States. That's not what US Senators are for. However, as Minister Khin Lay has said, we do all of us have an obligation to try to uncover the truth, however uncomfortable the truth may be. The question is: how was the material – the death list or Judas list – communicated to Pol Pot? I am not prepared at this time to point the finger at any one particular channel of communication. As we all know, the United States had a liaison office in Beijing headed by George Bush Senior,' – and she added helpfully, just in case anyone missed the point – 'that was before Mr Bush left China to become the director of the CIA and, subsequently, the 41st President of the United States. I am certainly not going to suggest' – and here the Senator gave a light, tinkling laugh – 'that the current President George Bush was involved, though we know he was in Beijing at this time. But what I do say is that the current administration owes the American people and, above all, the Cambodian people, the clearest possible statement on this subject and that all the relevant documents should be introduced as evidence before the tribunal. If we are talking about crimes against humanity, we cannot – as I have already said afford to be selective.'

By now, pandemonium had broken out. Cameras whirred; flashbulbs popped. Some pressmen were already heading for the exits to make sure their copy was filed before their deadlines; others tried to press the Senator further.

Seeing that the podium was about to be invaded, the Minister's aides bustled the principals from the room, followed closely by the thundering herd.

Prescott stayed behind as the room emptied. He walked over to the table beside the dais and picked up another copy of the press pack for Su Soeung. Su had wanted to come to the press conference but Prescott had dissuaded her.

'Don't do it,' he had told her. 'You'll find it too painful. There'll be people there who will mark your father down as a traitor. You don't need that.'

As things turned out, Prescott was glad he had advised Su to stay away. Somehow Hong Soeung, the man – his suffering, his anguish, his appalling dilemma – had been swamped by the wider political significance of the "confessions". He pulled out the glossy 6x4 from the press pack and spent a few moments studying Hong Soeung's battered face. There was a dark stripe across the top, left-hand corner of the photo, ending in a kind of curlicue. Prescott hadn't noticed it before, but now he studied it with interest. Had some blemish crept in when they ran off the prints for the press conference, he wondered, or did that dark stripe also exist in the original Tuol Sleng mugshot? He made a mental note to check when he had time. There was something about the photo which puzzled him, something he couldn't quite put his finger on.

Prescott's thoughts were interrupted when a voice behind him said: 'Do you mind if I introduce myself? I'm Ben Deakin, from the US mission in Phnom Penh. They sent me along here this morning because I'm responsible for relations with the Press. The Senator, as you can see, didn't have much need for our assistance.'

Ben Deakin was a young, black American, around thirty years old. He wore a dark suit and tie and looked distinctly disgruntled.

Prescott felt sorry for him. 'There's no stopping her when she gets going, is there? And I don't think she has stopped yet.'

'I don't suppose she has,' Deakin agreed gloomily. 'It's going to take a long time to unscramble this one.'

Prescott looked at him sharply: 'Why try? Isn't it easier to admit we were wrong, time to make a fresh start, that kind of thing?'

If anything, Ben Deakin's despondency deepened. 'That's not the way they're going to see it in Washington. They're going to see that Mrs Clinton has stirred up a hornet's nest with maximum embarrassment to the current administration and to the President personally. All that stuff about China. Was she really saying George W. Bush was involved as a young man in all of this? I mean, for Christ's sake.'

Prescott felt sorry for the fellow. Deakin was probably on his first Foreign Service assignment, keeping his nose clean, and then out of the blue, the hurricane strikes.

'She didn't say George W. was involved,' Prescott said. 'She just said he was there.'

They walked out of the room together onto Norodom Boulevard.

'I've got a car,' Deakin said. 'Can I drop you off?'

Prescott noted that Deakin's Jeep had Phnom Penh rather than CD plates and commented on the fact.

'Embassy policy,' Deakin informed him. 'A lot of us drive ourselves in unmarked cars nowadays. Safer that way. Particularly after the events of September 11, 2001. You don't need to go around flying the flag. Just invites trouble.'

'Today especially,' Prescott commented.

'You can say that again.'

As he wove his way competently through the late morning traffic chaos, Deakin shot a sideways glance at his companion. 'How come you didn't make a dash for the exit like the others to file your story?'

'I already filed a scene-setter,' Prescott told him. 'I'll do a follow-up piece later.'

'Why do you know so much? You fired in with those questions like you had already thought them up.'

Prescott knew the embassy man was fishing but he wasn't about to be hooked.

'You can drop me here,' he said as they turned onto Sisowath Quay. 'I can walk to the Club. Thanks for the ride.'

'Any time,' Ben Deakin, following standard procedures, accelerated away from the kerb. He was not looking forward to having to tell his Ambassador about the morning's press conference. 'Damage limitation,' he muttered to himself, mentally preparing his report. 'That's the name of the game now.'

But a block or two from the embassy, Ben Deakin started to smile. You had to hand it to the Senator, he thought. She had flat-footed the US mission. As a matter of fact, she had left them all standing. She had ensured worldwide press and TV coverage and nailed her colours cleverly to an electorally irresistible issue which positioned her at the forefront of the human rights/foreign affairs agenda. And dammit, wasn't she right? Ben Deakin argued with himself.

He might be the US embassy's press officer, but he was

still an American citizen, and he knew right from wrong when he saw it.

The marine guard at the gate gave him a message when he reached the embassy. 'The Ambassador's asking for you, sir. I said I'd let them know as soon as you're back.'

Ben knew the guard – also an African-American – well. The staff of the US Embassy in Phnom Penh formed a close-knit community.

'Is this a shit-hits-fan situation?'

'I'd say so, sir.' The marine saluted as Ben drove on into the compound.

★★★

Willard Price, a bluff and frequently peppery foreign service officer was nearing retirement age. His Phnom Penh posting was almost certainly his last diplomatic assignment – and he was in a surprisingly equable mood.

'Tell us about it,' he motioned Deakin to a chair. 'Sounds as though the Senator was having a bit of fun there.'

'I'm not sure I'd call it fun, sir.' Deakin hesitated to contradict his superior, but he couldn't see where Price was coming from. Knowing that Price liked brief, punchy reports rather than rambling narratives, he summarized succinctly the events of the morning.

'If the Senator's charges stick,' he concluded, 'we've a major problem on our hands. The US is going to be implicated in one of the most heinous crimes of the twentieth century. And this administration, in particular, is going to appear guilty as hell, if not directly, then at least by association. I believe we should warn the President, sir.'

Price gestured to a television in the corner of the room. It was tuned to CNN and, at that particular moment, was carrying a replay of Hillary Clinton's press conference.

'That went out live at the time. I watched it in the office here,' Price commented. 'The White House probably saw it as soon as I did. They're on the case, don't worry.'

'Do we have a line at this point?' Ben knew that as soon as he returned to his office, the phone would be ringing off the hook with journalists and media types wanting to know the reaction of the US government to the astonishing charges introduced that morning by the junior senator from New York.

'Hell, yes,' the US ambassador smiled benignly. 'Tell 'em that we have the greatest respect for the Senator from New York, as we do for all US Senators. Tell 'em that, as a first step, we're inviting the Cambodian authorities to examine in detail the Hong Soeung confessions, as I believe they're called. We have to establish the bona fides of the documents cited by the Senator. That surely is an elementary precaution, wouldn't you say?'

Deakin was still worried. More than worried. He was deep down scared. He was the embassy's official spokesman and he wanted to get it right.

'What about subsequent steps, sir? Do we have any guidance from State or the NSC after that? I'm not sure stalling is going to get us very far. This story has lift-off already.'

Willard Price walked round the desk and put an arm round the young man's shoulder like an old-fashioned, southern politician. 'The story may have lift-off, Ben, but that doesn't mean it's going into orbit.' Price checked his watch. 'Do you know Andrew Mossman? He's coming in for lunch in a minute. You ought to join us for a drink first. You'll like Mossman. He knows where the bodies are buried.'

Price burst into a loud peal of laughter. 'Forgive me, Ben that's not quite the thing to say in Cambodia, is it?'

With the ambassador still guffawing at his own verbal faux-pas, Ben Deakin pleaded urgent business.

'I'd better be getting back to my desk,' he said. 'Maybe I can meet Mr Mossman another time.'

'Let's hope so.'

Just at that moment, however, the ambassador's PA came into the room. 'Mr Mossman has arrived.'

'Show him in,' the Ambassador said.

Mossman and Price were clearly on the best of terms. The Ambassador greeted his guest warmly and introduced him to Ben Deakin.

'Ben's just come back from Senator Clinton's press conference.' Willard Price announced, while drinks were served. 'Quite a show, wasn't it, Ben?'

Ben found himself, once again, going over the highlights of Mrs Clinton's *coup de théâtre* earlier that day. Andrew Mossman was clearly fascinated.

'Wow!' he exclaimed when Ben finished. 'That's going to put the cat among the pigeons. How the hell did she get that stuff? I mean that's dynamite.'

Leaving the two men together, Ben Deakin made his way back to his office. There was, as he expected there would be, a stack of messages on his desk and his secretary, Dolores, had a bunch more in her hand waiting for him. As he sat down, the phone rang.

'It's been like a madhouse all morning,' Dolores said.

CHAPTER 11

Gathered at the bar of the FCCC, Prescott Glover and most of the rest of the press corps watched Senator Clinton's interview with Cambodian Prime Minister Hun Sen as it went out live on both Cambodian and international TV later that afternoon. All of them professionals, they couldn't help admiring the skill with which Mrs Clinton handled herself and the interview.

The cameras followed the Senator for New York as she made her way through the extensive security cordon to Hun Sen's private office in his fortress-like residence on the outskirts of Phnom Penh. When they had both been served tea, Mrs Clinton opened on a friendly, almost admiring note.

'You've been a leading politician in Cambodia for twenty-two years? That's a long time. What keeps you going?' the Senator asked.

The Prime Minister laughed. 'I'm getting old, my hair is going grey. I'm a grandfather.' He pointed to a picture of his son, West Point graduate Manith, next to a picture of his wife Bounrany. 'There, that's my granddaughter.'

Though not yet a grandmother herself, Mrs Clinton made suitably appreciative noises as she examined the photograph of the baby girl.

Sipping his tea, Hun Sen expounded his personal philosophy. 'To be a leader one has to be firm and strong. No one can remain in power for long if they are not firm. Some people call me a strongman and they seem to think that I am strong because of the barrel of the gun. I believe that the gun barrel cannot solve the problem, the gun barrel cannot keep you in power for a long time.'

The Prime Minister continued in that vein for several minutes more. Prescott, watching the screen carefully, could detect signs of impatience in the Senator from New York. Mrs Clinton was tapping the rim of her cup with the nail of her middle finger. Finally, as Hun Sen was expatiating on the need for 'human resources training' ('when I refer to human resources training, I never forget to train myself'), she managed to interrupt.

'I have said publicly here in Phnom Penh today that the record of the United States must be thoroughly examined as far as our relationship with the Pol Pot regime is concerned and that we must be ready to follow that enquiry wherever it may take us. But I also came here today, Prime Minister, to urge you and your government to make good on your promises to bring to trial the high officials of the Pol Pot regime whom you now hold in custody. Surely Cambodia has waited long enough? Surely the world has waited long enough. When do you expect the special court for trying Khmer Rouge leaders to begin its work?'

The Prime Minister gave a small tight smile. It was not the first time he had been asked such a question by doubtless well-meaning, foreign visitors and he feared it would not be the last. Still, he understood the pressures that people like the Senator were under from the human rights lobby (human rights 'industry' he preferred to call it) in their own countries.

'The arrest of Ta Mok was carried out with the clear goal

of bringing him to trial. In any case, we cannot detain him more than three years without trial, otherwise we would be in difficulty. We would have to amend the law or get permission of the national assembly.'

'What about the others who surrendered? What about Duch? When will proceedings be opened against him? Surely you now have incontrovertible evidence against him?'

Hun Sen took off his spectacles and held them up to the light, as though examining them for spots or blemishes. He took a handkerchief from his pocket and spent a moment or two polishing the lenses. Finally, he replaced the spectacles and beamed at his guest.

'Ah, yes!' he said, 'you are referring to the so-called Hong Soeung confessions. That is certainly a remarkable development in the case against Kang Kech Ieu or Duch as you call him. Of course, you understand that the Special Court is independent and neither I nor anyone else in my government can influence it.'

'I certainly understand that,' Mrs Clinton nodded emphatically. 'In my country we too believe in the separation of powers.'

'That said,' Hun Sen continued, still smiling (like a crocodile, Prescott thought as he watched the screen), 'I am sure the court will be most interested in the evidence you have brought to light.'

The Senator had got what she came for, a clear commitment from the head of government that the Hong Soeung confessions would be admitted into the proceedings against Duch and Ta Mok whenever these began. Nobody, least of all a Cambodian audience, was going to give any credence to Hun Sen's blatantly insincere protestations that the views of the court would need to be taken into account. What Hun Sen wanted was what Hun Sen got. He was not known as the Strongman of Cambodia for nothing.

'She played that pretty well, didn't she?' Prescott commented, turning to his colleagues at the bar. 'Hun Sen's given a commitment on prime-time television. He can't very easily back away from that.'

Prescott drained his glass, almost as though he was drinking a toast to the undoubtedly sparkling performance of the junior senator from New York.

'If you're looking for a foreign policy debut, you can hardly do better than that,' he commented. A low rumble of agreement greeted Prescott's pronouncement. The Phnom Penh press corps, reinforced for the occasion by the big-hitters from out of town, was as cynical as any other group of journalists but for once even the ranks of Tuscany could scarce forbear to cheer.

If Prescott had observed his colleagues closely, he would nonetheless have remarked a certain scepticism in the reaction of Henri Le Blanc, *Le Monde*'s star Asia correspondent, to Mrs Clinton's interview with Hun Sen.

'On verra,' was Le Blanc's muttered comment as he observed the enthusiasm of his colleagues. And then his craggy, weather-beaten face permitted itself a small, almost secret, smile.

Moments later, the cameras were following Mrs Clinton's cavalcade, as it left the Prime Minister's residence for the airport.

Mark Kelly, CNN Asia correspondent, who had stuck to the Senator like a leech throughout the day, had the last word.

'Mrs Hillary Clinton,' he told CNN worldwide viewers, 'has blown in and out of Phnom Penh like a tornado. Like a tornado, she has left a good deal of turbulence, not to say, destruction behind her. Chief among the casualties is the carefully cultivated illusion that the United States has been a consistent opponent of Pol Pot and the Khmer Rouge regime throughout the last several decades when the reality may be far otherwise.'

As he watched Kelly's wrap-up on the day's events, Prescott's mobile uttered its distinctive trill. He could see from the display-screen that it was his New York office on the line, the foreign editor probably making his first call of the day.

Prescott walked away from the bar to avoid the noise and bustle. Harry Schumberg came straight to the point. 'That you, Prescott? Great job! That piece you filed on the Hong Soeung confessions has to be front page. But now we need the follow-up.'

'Such as?' Prescott was cautious. Harry Schumberg's enthusiasms sometimes carried him away.

'What's the China angle in all this? Was George W. Bush – and I mean Dubbya, we know about the old man – really there? Was he implicated? Hell, this could be truly explosive!'

'Dynamite?' Prescott offered. Dynamite was one of Harry's favourite words. He liked stories with what he called dynamite-potential.

'Yeah, that's right. We're ahead on this one, Prescott. We want to stay that way.'

'What do you want me to do? Get up there, I suppose?'

'You bet I do. Use the office there, of course. Use Aster, he's pure gold. As a local, he may have the entrée you need. But you'll have to do some of the legwork yourself. Our people in Beijing don't have the background in the story you have. And, Christ, you know Beijing like the back of your hand. That's where you made your name.'

Schumberg was flattering him now. Prescott knew it but still it felt nice. 'What specifically do you want to know?' he asked.

'Find out whether or not the President had a tooth pulled in Beijing that summer, July 1975. That's what we need to know.'

'Why don't we just ask the White House?' Prescott countered. 'They'll have the President's medical records. If they don't, someone over there can ask the President personally?'

Schumberg guffawed. 'Do you think he'd remember? From what I've heard Dubbya doesn't remember much from back then. Besides, forewarned is forearmed. Let him know what we're after and they'll have time to think up an excuse.'

'And if he didn't have a tooth pulled that summer...?'

'Then he was up to something else. QED,' Harry Schumberg snapped and put the phone down, leaving Prescott with the feeling that Schumberg in particular, and The New York Times in general, would be ready to go to almost any lengths – always within the limits of journalistic propriety of course (of course!) – to prove this particular story.

★★★

Next morning, Prescott caught a China Air flight out of Phnom Penh to Beijing. Su Soeung came out to the airport to see him off. Prescott tried to dissuade her, but she insisted.

'I've got the time,' she told him. 'Nothing much is happening at the office. Nothing that needs me anyway. I'm getting ready to go up-country to see SAVE's northern operation.'

'Siem Reap?'

'Right.'

'Hell, I wish I could come with you. I'd love to visit all those ruins.'

'Maybe we'll be able to when you come back.'

'Let's hope so.'

Su kissed him at the departure gate, then waved him through to the other side.

★★★

It was a clear day. Perfect flying weather. Seated just in front of the starboard wing of the Boeing 737 – how long would it be, he wondered, before China manufactured its own airliners? Prescott had a superb view of almost the whole sweep of the Indochina peninsula, from the jungles of Laos to the coastal plains of Vietnam. What an extraordinary part Indochina had played in twentieth-century history, he reflected. First, there had been that vain attempt by the French to hold on to their colonial possessions in a post-war world which had changed beyond recognition. Dien Bien Phu – there it was, down there somewhere, thirty thousand feet below. In his mind's eye, Prescott could imagine the scene as the last French out-post was ignominiously overrun. How that defeat had seared France's soul! Conversely, what comfort victory had brought to the opposite side. Without Dien Bien Phu, would Ho Chi Minh have had the sheer, brass balls to take on the might of the United States?

And how strange it was that here, in Indochina, some of

the most complicated minuets of the Cold War had been conducted. Each side had used its own proxies. The USSR had used the North Vietnamese, the US had used South Vietnam and Thailand and Lon Nol too in Cambodia (though officially Kissinger and co always denied having a hand in the overthrow of Sihanouk and the installation of Lon Nol). China, motivated by a thousand-year-old rivalry with Vietnam, had its own proxies as well – Pol Pot and the Khmer Rouge. And Sihanouk too? How much, Prescott wondered, was King Norodom Sihanouk still the puppet of China? He had had more than a decade of exile there. When the rest of the world wanted to forget him, Zhou Enlai had offered him sanctuary, espousing Sihanouk's cause at successive international conferences on Cambodia's future. As far as Prescott could assess it, Sihanouk's personal and political debt to China was incalculable.

How did one repay such a debt?

Who was it, Prescott wondered, who had said that a nation should have no permanent friends and no permanent enemies, just permanent interests? Some nineteenth-century statesman, probably, speaking when the British Empire was at its zenith. What was China's permanent interest today? What was the United States' permanent interest? The two countries had had a spat about the EP-3 spy-plane. They were still squabbling about arms to Taiwan. People brought up Tienanmen from time to time, or the fact that the Chinese still executed criminals, and raised their hands in (pretended?) horror at a violation of human rights. But did this, deep down, mean China and the US were going to revert to a pre-Nixon-era stand-off? He doubted it.

President Bush had met President Jiang in Shanghai at the

APEC conference in October 2001. They hadn't just talked about the price of noodles, surely? Not when there were so many other pressing matters to attend to, like the War on Terrorism. That was the real reason, he felt sure, why the President had gone all the way to China in October 2001 to the APEC meeting. No other US President had ever even considered going to APEC. That was something you left to officials. Yet Bush had gone! He'd spent almost four days in Shanghai. What kind of a deal had Bush and Jiang struck, he wondered? The Chinese had come through in a big way as far as the War against Terrorism was concerned. And it wasn't just diplomatic support, though that was important, particularly in the United Nations where things could easily go pear-shaped. No, the Chinese had apparently offered high-grade intelligence, mountain troops, snatch-squads. Even more important, so he understood, was their offer of the use of Chinese territory. Bearing in mind that China shared a land border with Afghanistan up there in the Wakhan corridor, and bearing in mind also that Pakistan and Uzbekistan were looking distinctly flaky because of internal Islamic pressures, this Chinese angle was a very significant consideration.

But what the hell, Prescott thought, did the US have to offer China in return? There wasn't a lot of leeway...

As he mused, he looked down at the ground far below. They were still flying over forest and montane country. He reckoned that they must be in Chinese airspace by now. Yunnan, probably. During World War II, the US had flown nightly relief missions into Kunming, bolstering Chinese resistance to the Japanese. The Allies had sent convoys of trucks up the Stilwell Road. Prescott peered down. Had the jungle swallowed up the old road entirely? Could you bash your way through even today?

Of course, he thought, that might be a double-edged sword. If you could push through the jungle up into China, the Chinese could push back in the other direction as well.

★★★

An hour later, the Air China plane landed smoothly at Beijing's new international airport.

Aster Li, The New York Times' Beijing bureau's totally indispensable factotum, was waiting for him at the exit. Like so many Chinese who had to work on a daily basis with westerners, Aster had chosen a western name as a more manageable alternative to his Chinese name which was in fact Li Ming-Juan. He had joined The New York Times Beijing bureau almost the day it opened. His contacts with the Chinese government were clearly impeccable – the reality was that he could never have taken the job without official approval, certainly not in those early days. But none of the Times team in Beijing, Prescott included, had ever had the sense that Aster Li was a Chinese stooge. Now well over sixty, he seemed to Prescott as youthful as when they had first met, one of those ageless Asians whose years were betrayed, if at all, only by a faint grizzling around the temples and deepening pouches under the eyes. Aster had a wife and son (the latter now of university age) but on the whole he kept his private life to himself. He preferred it that way. But that didn't mean he was reclusive or unfriendly. On the contrary.

'Welcome back, Mr Prescott,' Aster's face lit up with genuine joy. Of all the bureau staff he had known, Prescott Glover had been his favourite. He had seemed to have an understanding of – and sympathy with China which, in Aster's estimation, many of his compatriots lacked.

'It's great to *be* back, Aster.' Prescott shook the man's hand enthusiastically. It was indeed good to be back in China. 'How long since I was last here, Aster?'

'Too long, Mr Prescott. We missed you a lot.'

★★★

As they drove into the city, Prescott tried to work out how long in fact it had been since he had last visited Beijing. Five years? Six years? Whichever it was, the pace of change had not slackened. When he had first come to China, twenty or more years earlier, Beijing had been a different city altogether. You drove in from the airport on a narrow road, competing for space with cyclists and buffalo carts. Crops were spread out to dry on the road surface and peasants, enjoying the first wave of liberalisation, offered vegetables and fruit to the passing traveller.

Now the airport expressway had been built, segregating airport and local traffic. Toll booths had been constructed and, instead of green paddy fields nurtured by the city's nightsoil, high rise blocks were springing up all over.

Prescott gestured out of the window in the direction of one of the new skyscrapers. 'What's the score with those apartment buildings, Aster?' he asked. 'Are the apartments for sale? Can individual people and families buy them?'

Aster laughed, 'You need to have money. To buy an apartment in one of those blocks, you must pay about US $1000 per square metre.'

'Not as bad as New York,' Prescott commented, 'but getting there. Can you get a mortgage?'

'Up to 30%. Pay off in 30 years.'

Prescott knew that Beijing wasn't China. The capital city was the showcase; most of the rest of the country, apart from the great commercial centres like Shanghai, still lagged behind. But there was no doubt that a mighty revolution was in progress. It wasn't like the political revolutions of the past – the Great Leap Forward of the sixties which had turned into a giant step backwards or the Cultural Revolution of the seventies when a senescent and possibly senile Chairman Mao, under the influences of his radical lieutenants, had allowed the whole country to be turned topsy-turvy. No, this was an economic and financial revolution, spurred by the process of liberalisation and privatisation which, if it was allowed to run its course without internal or external disturbance, would in a few more years transform China into a global power-house equal to, and possibly superior to, the United States itself.

'How do you read the latest flare-up in US-China relations?' Prescott asked Aster. 'What's the reaction here been to the US missile defence plan for example?'

'Bad,' Aster replied. 'You have to remember that it comes after the spy-plane incident, after the arms sale to Taiwan, including the submarines with their missile systems. You have President Bush saying he will, "do whatever it takes to defend Taiwan." He's allowed Taiwan President Chen Shui-Ban to make extended transit stops in New York and Houston on his way to Latin America. Then there's Tibet. It's already fifty years since Tibet became fully integrated and yet you insist on Tibet's independence. No wonder the hardliners here, particularly the military, are getting angry.'

Aster passed over a copy of that morning's *China Daily*, the official English-language newspaper which faithfully reflected the views of the Chinese government. 'Take a look.'

As their car left the Shoudujichang expressway and turned onto the second ring-road, Prescott read the lead story in the *China Daily*.

> The Chinese Government today publicly condemned the US proposal for an American missile defence shield, calling it a fruitless step that would endanger global security. At a press briefing on Tuesday, the Foreign Ministry spokesman, Sun Yuri, insisted that China's opposition to the programme is unwavering and said that the proposed defences would harm others without benefiting the United States itself. If the United States continues with the plan, he said, it will, "lift a stone only to drop it on its own toes".
>
> Mr Sun said China hoped to persuade Washington to drop the plan through diplomatic means but also warned: "China will not stand idly by and watch its national interests suffer harm." Mr Sun said that China had extended all possible cooperation to the United States following the events of September 11, 2001 and that it was very disappointed that the United States did not appear to be seeking an appropriate improvement in the US-China relationship as promised when President Jiang Zemin met President Bush in Shanghai in October 2001...

Prescott passed the newspaper back to Aster. 'Pretty strong stuff,' he commented. 'That doesn't sound like idle posturing. And I agree with your assessment, Aster. The trouble is it's not just the US military schemes which irritate or anger the Chinese. We're constantly pushing them on the human rights side, dragging up Tienanmen on every possible occasion even though that's more than a decade ago. Then there's Tibet, as you say. Every time the Dalai Lama makes a speech, we make sure it gets maximum coverage. And we attack China's family planning programme on the grounds that it tolerates abortion, when frankly it's the only truly successful birth control policy in the world and God knows how many Chinese there would be now if they didn't have their one-child policy.'

'Two children if you live in the country and the first child's a girl,' Aster corrected him. 'Just a point of detail.'

'More than a detail if you're a second child hoping not to be aborted,' said Prescott drily.

Later that day, over a drink in the bar of the Beijing Hotel where at Prescott's request the *Times* office had booked him (he preferred the old-style comforts of the Beijing to the glitz of the modern hotels that had sprung up all over the city), Prescott and Aster resumed the conversation.

'Even if the hardliners here in Beijing are rooting for a confrontation,' Prescott said, 'surely there must be some wiser heads around, people who see that the world's two remaining superpowers have to live together, that they really need each other.'

'Yes, of course there are,' Aster pushed a bowl of peanuts across the table. 'I guess the leading light among the moderates is Ting Wei-Ju, who as you know is the current Chinese ambassador to Washington. Everyone here knows that Ting played a crucial role in defusing the spy-plane row and in making sure that China came through with some serious help in the War against Terrorism, though they don't like to talk about it. China has its own Muslim minority to take care of.'

Aster's mention of Ting Wei-Ju reminded Prescott of the conversation he had had with Andrew Mossman. The Chinese Ambassador seemed to be everyone's best friend.

'Tell me a bit more about Ting Wei-Ju,' Prescott said. 'I've met him a couple of times in Washington. I was impressed. But I imagined he was just a career diplomat, not the man who pulled the strings.'

'He's much more than that. He's a political figure in his own right. His powerbase is Hangzhou, in Zhejiang province. He was the equivalent of governor there before he went to Washington. He comes back to Hangzhou frequently, keeping an eye on things. As a matter of fact, I believe he's in China at the moment. He was in Beijing the other day, briefing the Foreign Ministry or being briefed, but I think he's gone down to Zhejiang for the weekend.'

Prescott laughed. 'Some commute – Washington to Hangzhou.' Still, he was intrigued. He scented a story. 'Could you try to set up an interview with Ting? I'd be happy to fly down to Hangzhou if he's still there.'

'I'll try.' Aster replied. 'How many days do you need in Beijing?'

'Give me a couple. If we haven't got what we want in two days, we're not going to get it.'

★★★

The two men had dinner together at Prescott's favourite Beijing restaurant. It wasn't one of the tourist traps, like the Roast Duck on Qianmen Dajie or the Fangshan restaurant in Behai Park. The "One Bowl" restaurant, about ten minutes' drive north from the Zoo, offered Sichuan cuisine to a high standard. Its patrons were almost invariably Chinese. Either foreign tourists didn't know about the place or else its location discouraged them, since most tourists still seemed to feel more comfortable on rather than off the beaten track.

When Prescott entered, the proprietor greeted him like a long-lost friend and the waiters set up a great shout of greeting.

Three hours later, when they had – or so it seemed – tasted every conceivable permutation of fish, flesh, fowl and vegetable – Prescott and Aster staggered heavily out into the night.

Quite apart from the culinary experience, it had been an exceptionally useful evening. Prescott had gone over with Aster the outline of the interview which he proposed to conduct with Ambassador Ting, assuming such an interview was granted. More immediately, they reviewed in detail the arrangements Aster had already made to enable Prescott to discharge his primary assignment.

'I already looked into it when you first filed the story, Prescott,' Aster told him. 'In 1975, the US liaison office was in Xiushui Beije. The Embassy is still there today. That's where most of the embassies are. A quarter of a century ago, medical facilities – particularly for westerners – were much scarcer than they are today. There was only one place you'd go in those days in a dental emergency, which is what we are talking about, or any other medical emergency for that matter, if you were an American diplomat in Beijing.'

Prescott didn't have to be told. 'The Peking Union Medical College Hospital – PUMCH? I remember it well. And it's near the Embassy too, as I recall.'

'It is indeed. Just minutes away. Couldn't have been handier. The US embassy used it then and they still use it today. It's almost like the staff canteen. Professor Wu is going to be waiting for you at nine a.m. tomorrow. If anyone can help, Wu can. He's been at the hospital for decades. He was certainly there in the seventies. He's over eighty now but still bright as a button.'

'Why should he want to help?'

'He will,' Aster answered, 'I'm sure of that. PUMCH has a very special role here. It was founded over eighty years ago by the Americans, the Rockefellers actually, who wanted to bring western medicine to China. There are several Americans on the staff and many of their Chinese counterparts have been to the States as well. If there's one thing they're proud of, it's the US connection. They kept the link going even at the height of the Cultural Revolution.'

'What did you tell him I wanted to talk about?'

'I told him you were a senior journalist on The New York Times researching a story about the famous Beijing Union hospital.'

'Well, I suppose I am in a way,' Prescott commented.

CHAPTER 12

One of the reasons Prescott had chosen to stay in the old Beijing Hotel was that he liked its style. The hotel had originally opened as the Grand Hotel de Pekin in 1917 under French management. For years, it enjoyed a virtual monopoly as far as foreign guests were concerned. You stayed in the Beijing Hotel because, literally, there was nowhere else to go. Though much of the middle section of the hotel had been recently remodelled, Prescott still enjoyed what was left of the old atmosphere: the antique grand piano next to the shopping arcades and the magnificent ornate ballrooms at the top of the lobby staircase. It was a far cry from the glitzy concrete and glass skyscrapers which were springing up all round the city.

The other reason for Prescott's loyalty was convenience. Many of the newer hotels, like the Great Wall Sheraton for example, seemed to be halfway to the airport. To go anywhere, you had to get in a taxi first. With Beijing's growing congestion and air-pollution, Prescott reckoned that the less time you spent stuck in traffic, the better.

Aster had offered to meet him at the hotel, but Prescott had declined. The meeting with Professor Wu had been fixed for ten a.m. and he had told Aster that he would make his own way to the Peking Union Medical Centre Hospital. After an early breakfast, he had plenty of time, so he decided to walk.

Less than a decade earlier, if a foreigner staying in the hotel set off on foot for a stroll through the streets of Beijing, the odds were that somebody somewhere would be keeping an eye on him. At the very least, the hotel reception would know when you left and when you came back if only because you would hand your splendidly tasselled key in at the desk. Nowadays even old-fashioned establishments like the Beijing Hotel had switched over to plastic key cards. You could come and go as you pleased and surveillance seemed to be non-existent.

Avoiding the postcard and trinket-sellers at the door, Prescott walked a block east on Chang'an Avenue, then turned north on Wangfujing.

★★★

During his earlier stints in Beijing, Wangfujing had been a favourite haunt. The newest and the oldest human enterprises in China's capital were grouped together there. All of commercial China seemed to be encapsulated within a few crowded blocks, with old silk shops and open-air markets shoulder-to-shoulder with ultra-modern shopping plazas.

In the past, when he had the time, Prescott would spend hours walking along the narrow hutongs or alleys which gave onto the street and which, in his view, represented the very heart of the old city. If you were lucky, you could catch a glimpse through an open doorway into a broad courtyard. The family's living rooms would be arranged round this central space and the family itself (often three or even four generations) would be going about its business preparing and cooking food, tending to children, fixing things that were broken or whatever.

As he walked along Wangfujing, looking left and right down the alleys, Prescott was shocked to see how much demolition was in train. The one-storey hutong dwellings were being replaced on all sides by tall buildings, commercial or residential. The multi-generational families were being rapidly squeezed out.

'God dammit!' Prescott exclaimed to himself as he walked. 'They don't have to do that, surely!'

But in his heart he knew that this is what the authorities were going to do. It was easy to forget, in this first heady phase of liberalisation, just how much power central government still retained. If you were a foreigner, you might be able to walk along a street without being followed. If you were a native, and you were rich enough, you could buy a car or an apartment. But every relaxation in the rules was a very deliberate affair. Concessions were granted more often than before, but they were still concessions. This was still a tightly controlled, tightly regimented society. You could bring in the bulldozers and virtually overnight reduce a whole neighbourhood to rubble. The Chinese Communist Party might have fewer members nowadays than the Falun Gong (a statistic Aster had imparted the previous evening during their long session in the One Bowl Sichuan restaurant) but that didn't mean the CCP wasn't still firmly in charge.

Progressing through the hutong, Prescott wondered whether the authorities were, for example, aware of the interview which he was about to have with Professor Wu, the interview which Aster had arranged. Had this meeting been endorsed or approved by the hierarchy? The way things were, even in this post-Deng new model China, it was reasonable to suppose that it might have been.

Cutting through to Dongdanbe Dajie and, as he did so, picking his way through the rubble of the ruthlessly demolished family dwellings, Prescott couldn't help feeling that he could be getting into deeper water than he had intended. He recalled Harry Schumberg's almost comical instruction.

'Get up there and find out whether Dubbya had a tooth pulled in 1975!' Harry Schumberg had shouted.

But how much did Harry Schumberg and his colleagues in New York know about how things really worked here in China? Did they think the business of "investigative journalism" – sleuthing, in other words – could be conducted in Beijing in much the same way as it could in Washington, D.C? If they thought that, then – Prescott hissed to himself as he stepped over what seemed to be a live electric cable – they had another think coming.

***

Though there was also a modern extension, the main part of the Peking Union Medical College Hospital on 53, Dongdanbe Dajie, was housed in an imposing former Qing Palace. Prescott walked through a high arch and up some broad steps to find Aster already waiting for him at the top with a piece of paper in his hand.

'I got here a bit early and picked up Wu's C.V. from the faculty office. I thought it might be useful,' Aster said. 'Take a look.'

Standing there at the entrance to the hospital, under the curious gaze of a handful of bystanders, Prescott read the text quickly:

Wu Canping (1917-), native of Changzhou, Jiangsu Province. Vice chairman of 9th NPC Standing Committee; CAS academician; CAE academician; chairman of 10th Central Committee of Jiu San (September 3) Society; expert in dental surgery. A High school student at Huei Wen Academy in Tianjin; settled in Beijing at 16-year-old; then pursued studies in Preparatory Course of Medicine, of Yenching University, and Peking Union Medical College, 1936-1942, acquiring doctorate of medicine; then worked as practitioner, resident and doctor-in-charge; lecturer at Medical Institute of Peking University, 1946-1947; advanced study in dental surgery at Chicago University, 1947-1948; returned to China in November 1948.

Joined Jiu San Society, 1952, and CPC, 1956.

Doctor of Peking Union Hospital; associate professor, professor of Beijing Medical Institute; head of Medical Therapy Group for Premier Zhou Enlai. Sponsored Beijing Medical Institute No. 2, with himself as president, 1960.

From 1970-1993, served as vice president, president, and honorary president of Chinese Academy of Medical Sciences; president of Capital Medical College; president and honorary president of Peking Union Medical University; president and honorary president of Chinese Medical Association...

Prescott skipped a few paragraphs which listed Lu's awards and prizes. The final paragraph indicated that Lu had: *Attended Hong Kong handover ceremony as member of Chinese Governmental*

Delegation in Hong Kong, 1997. Wrote a number of medical books on dental surgery and 150 articles.

'Wow!' Prescott exclaimed. 'Wu's just about done it all, hasn't he? Trained in America but kept his nose clean by joining the Chinese Communist Party. Friend of Zhou Enlai. And still under 85 years old!'

Aster put his finger on the key paragraph in the text. 'Lu was here in 1975; he would have been practising dental surgery in the clinic here.'

'But would there be records going that far back?' Prescott asked. 'That's the key question.'

★★★

The old man received them in his large, airy office on the sixth floor of the modern extension and served them green tea in delicate porcelain cups. He seemed delighted to see them.

'Ah, *The New York Times!*' he reminisced affectionately. 'When I was in Chicago, I tried to read it whenever I could, especially on Sundays when I had time.'

'You couldn't even carry the Sunday edition now, let alone read it!' Prescott joked.

When Prescott took out his notebook (he never liked using tape-recorders), Wu ran through the history of the hospital.

'Peking Union Medical College Hospital (PUMCH) was built in September 1921. It was an affiliated hospital of PIMC established by the China Medical Board which was under the Rockefeller Foundation of the United States of America. After the founding of New China, the People's Government took over the hospital. In 1971, the hospital was renamed

"The Capital Hospital." It restored its original name in March 1985. The Party and Government are deeply concerned with the development of the hospital and have put in tremendous material and financial resources for it. The leaders of the Party and Government met with specialists and leaders of the hospital many times and gave them important instructions on its development and the intellectuals' work. In 1995, the hospital expansion project approved by the State Council was completed and put to use. It marked a new milestone in the development of the hospital...'

Professor Wu, warming to his theme, went on to describe in some detail the hospital's facilities and staff.

'There are more than 2,300 employees,' he concluded, 'including 301 professors and associate professors. Of them, 128 persons have held posts in Chinese Medical Association or in its branches, or in state-level medical journals. Ten professors serve as chairmen and six vice chairmen of specialized branches of Chinese Medical Association. The hospital has 900 beds now. The daily outpatients are over 3,000. There are about 13,000 inpatients every year. In addition, the hospital provides medical service for foreigners and high-ranking cadres.'

Prescott took this as his cue. 'I understand, Professor, you trained here. You also have held a senior position in the hospital since 1970. You must have seen enormous changes since then.'

'Oh, yes,' Wu agreed, 'enormous changes. In those days, the Capital Hospital, as we called it then, was unique. If you were a foreigner, this was the only place to come. And, of course, our strong links with the United States gave us a special relationship with the American community.'

'A lot of US diplomats came to the hospital in the early days?'

Wu laughed. 'There was nowhere else for them to go, particularly in emergencies.'

Prescott took a chance. Who dares, wins. 'I want to get some colourful details into this piece if I can. The United States opened a liaison office in China in the early seventies, after President Nixon's visit. President George Bush, the current President's father, was in charge of that office for a while. Did you ever meet him?'

'Good heavens, yes!' Lu exclaimed, 'I've treated all the US ambassadors in Beijing. Bruce, Bush, Winston Lord.... I certainly looked after George Bush Senior when he was here. As a matter of fact, I even remember having to treat President George W. Bush – *Dubbya* – as I believe you call him.' The old man uttered a high-pitched laugh, which degenerated quickly into a hacking cough.

Perhaps he wasn't as fit as he seemed, Prescott thought. He decided to go for broke. 'Without breaking medical confidentiality,' (*heaven forbid!*) 'do you have the details of that? I could see this piece might get headline treatment if I was able to begin it with the story of our current President's visit here thirty-five years ago. Do you remember exactly when that was?'

Lu sat there in silence for a while, cradling his cup of tea and thinking. Finally, he smiled. 'I am not sure the party would approve, but I am an old man and I have been in charge here for many years. I see many patients in my surgery. Of course, I cannot remember them all. But I definitely remember seeing the young Mr Bush one day. His father called me in person later to thank me.'

'That figures', Prescott said. 'That's the kind of thing George Bush Senior would do.'

Wu nodded. 'His son, as I recall, was most polite too. He had a seriously impacted wisdom tooth and I removed it under anaesthetic. If you want the actual date, we'd have to go to the archives. They probably have it there. Our archives are very efficient. They date from the early days of the Rockefeller Foundation's involvement with the transfer of Western science, medicine and technology to China. Do you have time?'

'Of course, we have time' Prescott said. 'That's what I'm here for.'

As they walked along the corridor, Professor Wu explained: 'The archives of PUMCH go back as far as 1917 when the China Medical Board of the Rockefeller Foundation opened the Peking Union Medical College. The collection may be divided from a conceptual standpoint into discrete sections, based in part on provenance. Records are available documenting central administration, academic and clinical departments, and various other aspects of the PUMCH, such as curriculum and field studies. Records documenting the central administration of PUMCH, for example, constitute a significant portion of the collection and provide a comprehensive view of the programs and politics which helped introduce Western science and technology to China.'

With years of practice, Prescott was able to scribble in his notebook while keeping pace with the Professor.

'And the clinical departments, even the dentistry department, kept records that far back?' he asked.

Wu nodded, 'This is a country of record-keeping. We have

records going back five thousand years. Clinical records are possibly the most interesting records any hospital can have.'

They left the old Qing palace building, walked across a covered footbridge into the modern extension and took a lift down to the basement. Wu opened a door which bore the legend "PUMCH Central Archives." A couple of white-coated technicians, clearly warned of the eminent man's impending arrival, were waiting for him and ushered him towards a section of the room labelled "Dental Records 1917 to Present Time".

'Ah!' Wu gave a grunt of satisfaction. 'It's been some time since I was last down here. What year are we looking for, I wonder? What month, what day?'

'I think I can help there,' Prescott said. He explained the reference in George Bush Senior's diary.

'Very good!' Professor Lu clapped his hands enthusiastically. He turned to one of the technicians. 'Try to find the file for that day, July 5, 1975.'

As far as Prescott was concerned, it was almost too good to be true. They might have been waiting for him. Within seconds, drawers were opened, documents extracted.

Lu sat down at the table to examine the sheaf of papers which was handed to him. 'Yes, indeed,' the old man murmured. 'It all comes back to me now. It was a very badly impacted tooth.' He showed the page to Prescott. 'See what I've written. Lower right molar badly impacted. Needs immediate attention. Patient refused acupuncture as means of anaesthetic.'

Prescott examined the sheet carefully. The patient's name (George Walker Bush) and age (29) as well as the date (July 5,

1975) was shown at the top of the page. Underneath, a contact address had been given c/o US liaison office, Beijing.

'You see your President even spent the night in the hospital. Look, we assigned him a room.'

'A private room?' Prescott was intrigued.

Wu looked at him sharply. 'There were no private rooms in PUMCH at that time, you must understand. Your President would have been our most honoured guest, but he would have had to share a room.'

The technician handed Wu another sheet of paper. Wu glanced at it and continued, 'George W. Bush shared a room on the night of July 5, 1975 with another foreign visitor who also had dental treatment here at that time.'

Prescott, who up to that moment had decided that he had been barking up the wrong tree, pricked up his ears.

'Do we know who that other foreign visitor was?'

Wu had a whispered consultation with the technician. 'He needs to find the appointments schedule, so we can trace the file.'

Minutes later the man came back with another file in his hands. The name on the docket read Ieng Sary.

'Good heavens!' Wu exclaimed. 'How the memory lets you down! I completely forgot that Ieng Sary was here that day, as well as George W. Bush. It seems they both spent the night in the hospital, sharing a room together. It would be interesting to know what they talked about.'

'I think I can guess,' Prescott said quietly.

★★★

Later that day Prescott ran into Robert Jesson in the ornate lobby of the Beijing Hotel.

'Bob! What are you doing here?' he exclaimed. 'I didn't know you were coming to town?'

'I'm a visiting professor at the foreign affairs institute of Beijing university,' Jesson explained. 'I'm here for a month. Staying at the hotel. You still on the scandal trail? How are things?'

Though this was the new China, Prescott didn't want to stand in the busy hotel foyer discussing the events of the day. Nor did he want to go to his room or Jesson's. Though he doubted very much whether they still bugged rooms the way they used to when he was first posted to China, it wasn't worth taking the risk.

'Let's take a stroll around Tienanmen,' he said.

'I'll fetch a coat,' Jesson said. 'It's getting chilly.'

Prescott decided he would manage without a coat. Though it was November, the weather was crisp rather than cold. In another few weeks, Prescott knew, they would all be buttoned up against the wind sweeping in from the steppe. It was easy to forget how far north Beijing was.

When Jesson reappeared, the two men set off at a brisk pace westward along Chang'an avenue. They reached Tien-anmen Gate – the Gate of Heavenly Peace – and paused for a moment. More than half a century had passed since Mao proclaimed the People's Republic from the balcony but still, Prescott reflected, it was hard to walk past without mentally reliving that moment.

'October 1, 1949, Bob? Do you think that's up there among the top half-dozen dates in world history? Like American Independence Day, or the fall of the Bastille?'

'I'd say so,' Jesson replied. 'I think the world is only just beginning to realise now just how significant the birth of the People's Republic of China was. Nixon, Kissinger – that was just the beginning. How the US and China work things out over the next few years is going to define the pattern of world events in ways we can't even begin to guess at. But I would say that, wouldn't I? That's what I'm paid for.'

Prescott laughed. They swung south and headed across the middle of Tienanmen. The square was filling up. The kite-flyers were out in force – some of their creations were unbelievable, Prescott thought. The kites soared and swooped above the crowd, many trailing magnificently embroidered tails forty or fifty feet long. From time to time, they passed groups of people doing their evening Tai Chi and at the Mao mausoleum a squad of PLA soldiers in their dark-green uniforms came smartly to attention as the flag was lowered for the night.

More or less in the middle of the square, they paused to absorb the scene.

'It all looks pretty peaceful, doesn't it?' Jesson said. 'But there's always someone watching even here. If you're Falun Gong, for example, and you start making yourself conspicuous, they'll soon pick you up.'

'Don't tell me,' Prescott said. 'I was here in 1989. I saw it all. Even today, I can see that young man standing in front of the tanks as they rolled into the square as clearly as I can see anything.'

'Did you read the Tienanmen Papers, that book which was published a year or two ago?' Jesson asked. 'There was a hell of a struggle in the Politburo. If the story's true, for a time the leadership didn't know at all what to do. Some of them wanted to send the tanks in. Some of them didn't. The hardliners won in the end, but it was a close thing.'

'Are you sure the book wasn't a forgery? Like the Hitler diaries?'

'No, not sure,' Jesson admitted. He paused: 'Are you sure your Hong Soeung "confessions" are genuine?'

'I get surer by the minute,' Prescott said. He told Jesson about the visit he and Aster Li had paid that morning to the Peking Union Medical College Hospital. 'Sometimes, you play a hunch, and you strike gold,' Prescott said. 'In a sense, I got it wrong. The visit to the Peking Union hospital surprised me. I had been expecting to discover that George W. Bush hadn't been there at all, if you see what I mean. I thought old man Bush was using Junior's supposed visit to the dentist as a cover. Tell the world the boy's gone to have a tooth pulled when in reality he's out there doing a deal with Pol Pot. When Wu found the Bush file showing that Bush junior did indeed have an impacted wisdom tooth treated in the hospital that day, I thought that was the end of the story. Then all of a sudden it comes out that Dubbya has shared a room with none other than Pol Pot's key lieutenant: Ieng Sary! I can't think of a better channel of communication with the Khmer Rouge, if that's what the US wanted to do, than passing through Ieng Sary. Christ, Ieng Sary virtually was the Khmer Rouge! He was with Pol Pot – or Saloth Sar as he was then – in Paris at the beginning of the 1950s. They founded the Cambodian Communist Party together. Pol Pot became Ieng Sary's brother-in-law when he married Ieng Sary's wife's sister. Ieng Sary stuck to Sihanouk like a leech while Sihanouk was in Beijing waiting for the Khmer Rouge victory. He was Pol Pot's man in Beijing, the place which mattered most to the Khmer Rouge. Ieng Sary was Pol Pot's closest ally. They were like that!' Prescott held up his right hand with index and middle finger intertwined.

'I don't believe this!' Jesson exclaimed. 'This is amazing!'

'Not amazing,' Prescott countered. 'Just inspired. Meeting George Bush Junior in the hospital, seemingly by accident, was the perfect strategy from the point of view of both sides. As far as the US is concerned, there has been no official contact with Pol Pot and the same could be said for the Khmer Rouge. The Khmer Rouge might have been in close contact with the Chinese throughout their struggle to gain power in Cambodia, but that didn't mean the Chinese had to know everything they were doing.'

'So what was the purpose of the meeting in your view?' Jesson asked.

Prescott paused. 'You're not going to like this. No-one's going to like this.'

'Try me.'

'Well,' Prescott said, 'I think the purpose of the meeting between George W. Bush and Ieng Sary was so that young George could hand over the Judas-list, the death-list that Hong Soeung had been working on. Maybe it had been micro-filmed. Maybe it had been hidden in a tiny capsule in Bush's supposedly bad tooth. Don't forget Bush's daddy has all kinds of contact with the spooks. Christ, less than six months later he's going to be director of the CIA!'

It was Jesson's turn to laugh. 'Now you're fantasizing!'

'No, I'm not.'

By the time they had reached the northern edge of Tienanmen, the gigantic portrait of Chairman Mao which graced the Gate of Heavenly Peace was lit up by floodlights. The kite flyers and Tai Chi practitioners had gone home. Across the square, the golden arches of the Tienanmen McDonalds beamed across the city centre. (The number of such establishments in Beijing, Prescott had learned that day already, exceeded one hundred and thirty-five and new McDonalds were still being opened, not to speak of Pizza Hut and Kentucky Fried Chicken).

'What are you going to do?' Jesson asked, as they walked back to the hotel.

'What do you think I should do?'

'It's a helluva story. But the Administration's not going to like it one bit. It's going to embarrass the hell out of the United States government and the Bushes in particular.'

If Bob Jesson had tried to think of a way of forcing Prescott's hand, he could not have done better. Prescott felt his professional integrity was being impugned. You don't try to lean on The New York Times. Not if you have any sense.

'I'm going to file a piece,' Prescott said quietly. 'I'm going to tell it the way I heard it today.'

They entered the lobby of the Beijing Hotel. 'I'll write the story,' Prescott repeated. 'If they don't use it, that's their problem.'

'Oh, they'll use it all right,' Jesson said. 'They'll splash it on the front page.'

Prescott wrote the piece as a follow-up to the copy which he had filed from Cambodia. The hospital story was a natural sequel. He reminded his readers of the thrust of the Hong Soeung "confessions" and of the inference that Hong Soeung was working for and with the United States. He recalled the bizarre affair of the Sihanouk films and how exceptional steps had been taken to establish this first contact between the US and the Khmer Rouge, through the US liaison office in Beijing and Norodom Sihanouk. He then went on to document George Bush Junior's visit to the dentist in Beijing on July 5, 1975 and the presence on that occasion of Ieng Sary, long-time deputy to Pol Pot himself.

Prescott's concluding paragraph was a hard-hitting as he could make it:

> It has long been obvious, he wrote, that successive US administrations, confronted with the Vietnamese take-over of Cambodia in 1979 and the prospect of Vietnamese control over the whole of Indochina, opted for a policy of supporting the ousted Khmer Rouge, either directly through secret US forces operating out of Thailand or through proxies such as the Thai military. It is also a matter of historical record that the United States consistently supported Democratic Kampuchea (i.e. Khmer Rouge Cambodia) in its successful attempt to occupy Cambodia 's UN seat as part of the Sihanouk-Son San-Khmer Rouge coalition. But what the recent Hillary Clinton revelations in Phnom Penh, together with the evidence coming out of China, makes absolutely clear is that this policy of tacit or overt US support of the Khmer Rouge was not established as a possibly understandable response to the Vietnamese invasion of 1979. On the contrary, we are talking about a US-Khmer Rouge axis dating from 1975, not 1979. We're talking about a deal which was put together in Year Zero, a deal in which both the current President and his father appear to be deeply implicated.

Prescott stayed up late filing his piece. Next morning, clicking onto *The New York Times* website, he was pleased to see that the paper had run it word for word. What's more, they'd given it front-page billing "above the fold." As a long-time journalist, Prescott knew you couldn't ask for more.

He was still sitting in front of his laptop in his hotel room when the telephone rang. It was Aster Li, offering his congratulations. He too had checked into the NYT website first thing that morning.

'Where are you, Aster? Are you in the office?' Prescott asked. 'I'm planning on stopping by this morning. See how you folks are getting on. Please tell them how sorry I am I didn't make it yesterday. Bad form, I know. Visiting firemen should always check in to base.'

Aster wasn't worried about form, good or bad. He was worried about Prescott's schedule. 'I'm not sure you'll have time to come by the office,' he said. 'I fixed the interview with Ting Wei-Ju. Ambassador Ting will see you tonight in his home.'

'Home in Beijing or home in Hangzhou?'

Aster sounded apologetic. 'Hangzhou, I'm afraid. The Ambassador is not coming back to Beijing. He's flying to Washington from Shanghai.'

Prescott sounded dubious, 'Hangzhou's a bit of a trek, isn't it?'

Aster stood his ground, 'I've made the arrangement. The Ambassador is very keen to see you.'

'What plane can I catch?'

'There's a three p.m. Air China plane which gets to Hangzhou at four forty-five p.m. We've tentatively booked you into the Shangri-La on West Lake. You can fly out from Shanghai the next day if you want.'

'Fly where?'

'You decide.'

Prescott laughed and put down the telephone. What would he do without Aster, he wondered?

What would any of them do? Aster always seemed to have his finger on the pulse.

CHAPTER 13

Hangzhou, the capital of Zhejiang Province, lies around 180 kilometres south-west of Shanghai, has a population of over a million people and is one of China's seven ancient capitals. It is a city of pagodas and temples, set around a lake of astonishing beauty.

Ambassador Ting Wei-Ju had built himself a house, almost a palace, in the hills on the western edge of West Lake. Being that much further south than Beijing, even in mid-November the weather was warm and most evenings, when he was at his home in China rather than *en poste* in Washington DC, Ting Wei-Ju would sit out on the veranda and enjoy the spectacular view. This was exactly what he was doing when the car which he had sent to fetch Prescott Glover at Hangzhou airport turned into the leafy drive.

The Ambassador rose to his feet and went to greet his guest. 'Ah, Mr Glover, welcome to Hangzhou. Is it your first time here? We shall do our best to make you comfortable. Please join me for a drink. Tea or would you prefer something stronger?'

'I wouldn't mind a gin-and-tonic,' Prescott said.

'I think I'll join you. It's that time of day, isn't it?'

Moments later, a butler appeared and took their orders. Prescott noted the respect, the deference with which the servant treated his employer. It was as though the clock had been turned back fifty years. He almost expected the man to kowtow.

Ting Wei-Ju gave a light laugh. 'When you get away from Beijing, you sometimes find the old ways die hard. My family has been around for centuries in Zheijang. Somehow, we survived the Cultural Revolution. I was Mayor here for ten years before I went to Washington. The people know me.'

Prescott had a clear sense as he sat there gently clinking the ice in his gin-and-tonic that the Ambassador had agreed to the interview at that particular time and place for some very specific reasons of his own. He could always have told Aster that he would talk to Prescott when they were both back in Washington. That would have been the obvious thing to do. But, no, he had insisted on Prescott's coming to Hangzhou. What did Ting Wei-Ju want?

'We are at the threshold of a new millennium,' Ting began. 'Since the end of the Cold War, the world has undergone profound changes. The international situation on the whole is moving toward greater relaxation. Peace and development, economic prosperity and social progress, all these have become the common desire of all nations and the imperatives of our times. Don't you agree?'

Prescott nodded. It was hard to disagree with such obvious truths. But he understood the convention. Like Beethoven's Pastoral Symphony, the Ambassador was looking to a quiet lead-in, leaving the rousing stuff for later.

'But there still exist many destabilizing factors in the world. The planet we call home is far from a tranquil and peaceful land. How to bring a peaceful, stable and prosperous world into the twenty-first century is a huge challenge facing all of us.

China and the United States are two great nations. One is the largest developing country and the other is the largest developed country. Both are permanent members of the UN Security Council. The two countries both share common interests in maintaining peace and stability in Asia and the world at large. We share great responsibilities in promoting global economic cooperation, preventing proliferation of weapons of mass destruction, cracking down on international terrorism, drug trafficking and cross-border crimes and many other areas.'

Again Prescott nodded. His gin-and-tonic was getting low and he wondered if it would last the course.

For the next few minutes, the Ambassador continued in similar vein, speaking of the 'huge potential for cooperation' between China and the United States in a number of areas. He smiled benevolently at his guest as he continued:

'The Chinese government attaches great importance to China-U.S. relations and places it on top of its foreign relations agenda. Over the years, China has made tremendous efforts to improve and develop this important relationship because we believe maintaining a sound and stable relationship between the two countries not only serves the interests of our two peoples but also the peace and development of the world.

Admittedly, as we differ in social system, history, cultural background and level of economic development, it is natural that there are differences between us. The key is that these differences should be bridged or narrowed through dialogue on the basis of equality and mutual respect. If we cannot resolve them immediately, we should put them aside and not let them stand in the way of seeking common ground and further strengthening our ties. We should learn to agree to disagree.'

As far as Prescott was concerned, it was all interesting, useful material. The kind of thing you expected highly-skilled ambassadors like Ting to say. Polished. Perceptive. He scribbled dutifully in his notebook but he knew there had to be more. Ting Wei-Ju would not have summoned him to Hangzhou just to mouth platitudes.

At exactly seven p.m. the Ambassador rose to his feet. Ting Wei-Ju nodded again and rose to his feet. 'Come, let's go inside. I have something to show you.'

Ting Wei-Ju led Prescott inside the house to his study. As they entered, Prescott gasped. One wall of the study looked out onto the lake. The other three were covered with the most superb collection of Chinese paintings Prescott had ever seen in a private home. He recognised some of the classic scenes: the soaring mountains and cascading waterfalls, the shimmering lakes, blossoming trees, galloping horses. Others were new to him, the work of modern artists who, while basing themselves on the great tradition of Chinese wall-painting, had managed to inject a new, curiously fantastical flavour.

Ting Wei-Ju pointed to one of his most recent acquisitions. 'See this one,' he waved his hand in the direction of a superb representation of an eagle flying past a mountain peak with a flag in its beak: 'I bought this in Beijing last year. Do you know who the artist is? He's the nephew of Pu Yi, the last emperor. Don't you think the calligraphy is superb?'

'He must be an old man now,' Prescott worked out the dates in his head. Pu Yi had died, as he recalled, in the late sixties. Any surviving nephews or nieces would surely be getting on in years.

'He is an old man, but he can still hold a pen.'

But it wasn't so much the scrolls which grabbed Prescott's attention. It was the statue which stood in the middle of a polished, wood table in front of the plate glass window. In style it was remarkably similar to the one he had seen in Andrew and Caroline Mossman's Georgetown house, though this particular image had four faces rather than one...

Ting Wei-Ju noticed the direction of Prescott's glance. He walked over to the window and placed his right hand, proprietorially, on top of the stone head.

'Magnificent, isn't it? It's a head of Brahma, with four faces, each one facing a different direction. This is how the God Brahma – the Creator – is generally represented, so I'm told. Let me tell you how I came by that piece. It was in late February 1973. I was a young man then, working for the Chinese Foreign Ministry. One of my assignments at that time was to act as a liaison between the Chinese government and Prince Sihanouk. Remember China had welcomed Sihanouk to Beijing after the Lon Nol coup in Phnom Penh in 1970?'

Prescott nodded. 'Of course, I remember that.'

'The dates are important,' Ting Wei-Ju continued. 'By 1973 the tide of battle in Cambodia was swinging decisively in favour of the Khmer Rouge. Pol Pot and his people believed that there would be some propaganda value in having a visit by Sihanouk to the areas they controlled, and I was instructed to be part of the mission. The party consisted of Sihanouk, his wife Monique, Ieng Sary who was always around at that time as Sihanouk's minder, if that's the right word, and around one hundred Vietnamese whose job was to help us negotiate the Ho Chi Minh trail once we left southern China.'

'That sounds like quite a trip!'

'It was. We travelled in Soviet-made jeeps, reaching Cambodian territory after eight days on the road. The first Khmer Rouge we met were Hu Nim and Son Sen, the latter being the Khmer Rouge's leading military strategist. Later on, we were joined by Khieu Samphan and Saloth Sar, alias Pol Pot, and later again by Hou Youn and Sar's wife, Khieu Ponnary, who as you may know was Ieng Sary's wife's sister.

'The Sihanouk party ended its journey at Phnom Kulen, in the Kulen mountains, about 25 miles north-east of the Angkor ruins. The place was particularly symbolic. Phnom Kulen is the place where King Jayavarman II proclaimed himself "universal monarch" or "emperor of the world" in 802 AD around the beginning of the ninth century. Most of Angkor's water supply comes from there, as well as the sandstone they used to construct the monuments.'

'But I digress,' Ting Wei-Ju continued. 'I was telling you how I came to acquire this stone head. It's an intriguing story. Sihanouk was given the head personally by one of the Khmer-Rouge group. It wasn't Pol Pot, it wasn't Khieu Samphan or Ieng Sary or anyone I'd heard of.'

'Do you remember the man' s name?'

'I'm afraid not. I never really had a chance to talk to him. Once or twice, I saw him in conversation with Pol Pot or Ieng Sary. They seemed to treat him with respect. From what I could gather, the man's mission was to save the priceless treasures of Angkor and the other temples in the north of the country from destruction or damage and he seemed to have the approval and even the support of Pol Pot in this effort, surprising as it may seem. The man's qualifications as a custodian of the national heritage were obviously recognised by the Khmer Rouge. The extraordinary thing is that Pol Pot and Ieng Sary and Khieu Samphan and most of the other Khmer Rouge leaders were, if they could be brought to admit it, rather proud of the Cambodian antiquities. American bombing of the Vietnamese bases and supply lines in Cambodia did far more damage to Angkor than the Khmer Rouge ever did.'

Prescott nodded. 'That's a fact.' He couldn't quite see where Ting Wei-Ju was heading but the tale he told was certainly fascinating.

Warming to his subject, the Ambassador continued: 'I remember one evening, when we were sitting round the camp fire, the man I just mentioned came in with a couple of bearers behind him carrying the head which you see in front of you. He bowed low and handed it over to Sihanouk: "This is a token of our esteem, your majesty. An early head of the great god Brahma." That's what he said. The other Khmer Rouge weren't particularly keen on addressing Sihanouk as "your majesty" but this fellow seemed to get away with it.'

'Did he say anything else? Did he say where the head came from?'

'As a matter of fact, he did. He told the King that they had brought the head from a place called Ta Keo. He didn't give details as to the location of Ta Keo, simply describing it as a vast undiscovered archaeological complex three days' journey from Phnom Kulen. He even suggested that Ta Keo might be the site of the lost city of Amarendrapura. Jayavarman II founded Amarendrapura before he came to Phnom Kulen. We know this from the inscriptions. But the site of Amarendrapura has never been discovered.'

'Except by this fellow?'

Ting Wei-Ju nodded. 'Apparently so. Sihanouk realised the significance of what the man was saying and tried to draw him out, but he wasn't saying any more. So Sihanouk accepted the statue very graciously. He knew enough to recognise that it was a fine example of the pre-Angkor or Kulen style. Probably well over a thousand years old. I think Sihanouk would have liked to have hung on to it but he had his own reasons for wanting to keep the Chinese government happy, so he handed it over to me as the senior Chinese official present.' The Ambassador smiled blandly. 'Luckily I got to keep it. The Chinese authorities were too preoccupied with the Cultural Revolution at that time to bother about a piece of old stone!'

'Tell me about this man,' Prescott said. 'How old was he? What did he look like?'

Ting Wei-Ju paused, collecting his thoughts. 'Let me see. It's so long ago now. I have to dig back in my memory. I'd say the fellow was in his thirties. Handsome. Well put together. Held himself well. I've probably got a photograph somewhere. I remember we stayed several days at Phnom Kulen while Sihanouk and Monique took part in a series of photoshoots. Most of us received copies from Sihanouk later. The King was keen on that kind of thing, particularly when the pictures showed Monique and him in a good light.'

Ting Wei-Ju walked over to a shelf and pulled out a leather photo album. He opened it and said to Prescott, 'I've still got my set of photographs from that time. Leaving aside the issue of Sihanouk's vanity, it was a memorable occasion for all of us.'

The ambassador turned over the pages of the album. In one photograph after another, Sihanouk could be observed smiling, surrounded by stern-faced communist chiefs, in front of Ankorian ruins. Behind the leaders could be seen the massed ranks of Khmer Rouge men and women soldiers.

'Look here,' Ting Wei-Ju Pointed to a man standing at the far right in one of the group photographs. 'This is the man who gave the stone head to Sihanouk.'

Prescott looked at the photograph. The man looked curiously familiar. The fact that he was wearing the red Khmer Rouge kerchief around his head was neither here nor there. The eyes were the same, the mouth was the same, the jaw and hairline seemed identical to the picture which, only a few weeks back, had appeared in *The Washingtonian*.

'Good heavens!' Prescott exclaimed, 'that's so like the picture we have of Su Soeung's father.'

'Are you sure?'

'No, not sure. I'd have to set the two pictures side by side and look at them carefully.'

'Perhaps I can help out there,' Ting Wei-Ju said. He walked over to the bookshelf and took out a chunky paperback volume. 'This is my autographed copy of King Sihanouk's autobiography. He describes his trip to Cambodia in March 1973 and his visit to the Angkor ruins and the Kulen mountains. He uses some of the photos I have in my album, including the one with the picture of the man you think may be Su Soeung's father. Look.'

Prescott flipped through the illustrations, recognising immediately that several of the photographs used by Sihanouk in his book were the same as the photographs in the album which Ting Wei-Ju had shown him.

'I can't let you have this,' Ting Wei-Ju said, 'but if you're going back to Phnom Penh, I'm sure you'll find a copy of this book on sale somewhere.'

Ting Wei-Ju smiled at his guest in wide-eyed innocence as he ushered Prescott to the waiting car.

On his way back to Phnom Penh the next day, Prescott changed planes in Hong Kong. With time on his hands, he spent half an hour in a large airport bookstore which, in addition to the usual travellers' fare, offered a wide variety of books about Asia. He quickly located and purchased a copy of King Sihanouk's *Prisonnier du Khmer Rouge*. He was pleased to note that, though it was a later edition than the one which he had seen the previous day in Ting Wei-Ju's house in Hangzhou, the illustrations were the same including the photograph of Sihanouk being greeted by Khmer Rouge leaders, with an unnamed person to the left of the group who bore a striking resemblance to Su Soeung's father.

His thoughts turned to Su herself. How was she getting on, he wondered? He had tried to call her from Hangzhou the previous evening but had failed to make contact. He had wanted to warn her that he had potentially dramatic news. If the man in the picture really was Hong Soeung, they might have to undertake a major rethink and a wholesale re-evaluation of where they were and where they were going.

★★★

Su Soeung was totally stunned to discover a previously unknown picture of Hong Soeung.

'It has to be father,' she exclaimed. 'You're absolutely

right, Prescott. Of course, it's the same man. Just look at the two pictures side-by-side.'

They were sitting on the terrace of Su's room in the Cambodiana Hotel. Prescott had arrived from the airport less than an hour earlier. Using one of the hotel's heavy crystal ashtrays, he held Sihanouk's book open at the right page and laid alongside it, for purposes of comparison, the photograph which a few weeks earlier Su had sent to *The Washingtonian* magazine to illustrate the article on 'Cambodians then and now' and which she had been carrying around with her ever since.

'And you said he talked about Ta Keo to King Sihanouk when he gave him the statue,' Su continued. 'Isn't Ta Keo the place he mentions in his letter to my mother, the one you brought back from Seattle? I'm sure it's the same place. So what does it mean? That's what I don't understand. Why should my father, who worked for the ministry of culture in Lon Nol's government, be having a secret meeting with the Khmer Rouge in March 1973, two years before Pol Pot came to power? Why on earth is he wearing a kerchief? Does that mean he was secretly one of them? If so, why did they capture him? Why did they torture and kill him? Help me, Prescott.'

Prescott put his arm round her. He could well appreciate the agony Su was going through. Every day brought fresh revelations, each one – from Su's Point of view – worse than the last.

'Don't take anything at face value,' he told her. 'Things are never what they seem. I think Ting Wei-Ju wanted me to see that stone head of Brahma, wanted me to see the photograph of Hong Soeung. That's why I had to go to Hangzhou.'

'Why? What is he trying to tell us? Why can't he tell us

straight if there's something he knows which we don't know?'

Prescott shrugged. 'You've got me there.'

Su wouldn't let it go. 'Who set up your meeting with Ting Wei-Ju? Was it your idea or was it his?'

'Mine,' Prescott replied. 'The Times has a brilliant Chinese office manager in Beijing, called Aster Li. Aster has been doing the job ever since we opened for business in Beijing. He is an extraordinary man. Quite frankly, we couldn't operate without him. He told me Ting Wei-Ju was in town and made the arrangements.'

'So it was Aster's idea as much as yours?'

'I suppose you could say that,' Prescott nodded. 'But I'm not sure where that gets us.'

'I'm worried,' Su said. 'It doesn't make sense. Not to me anyway.'

CHAPTER 14

Jules Barron met Henri Le Blanc, *Le Monde*'s Asia correspondent, in the Elephant Bar of the Hotel Le Royal. During the evening 'happy hour' (which usually extended from six to nine p.m.) the bar operated a policy of 'buy one, get one free'. But this wasn't the only reason why Jules selected it. For Barron, French to his fingertips, the Hotel Le Royal was the natural choice. It had style, it had elegance, it had charm. Above all, it had history. If you had been in Phnom Penh during the period 1970 to 1975, those pivotal years in Cambodia's history when the battle between the forces of Lon Nol and Pol Pot was being waged, the Hotel Le Royal was the only place to be. This is where the journalists came when they had filed their stories; this is where they came – often enough – to find out what the story was, meeting their contacts by the pool or downing Pernods in the bar.

Once this spacious building had been the French Officers' Club. French planters, taking a break from the hardships of life up-country, would come in for rest and recreation. French tourists, en route to Angkor, would stay here while the last details of their trips were being seen to. As far as Jules Barron was concerned, the very Frenchness of the Hotel Le Royal was its dominant attraction. When almost every other vestige of France's Indo-Chinese vocation (ever the romantic, Jules had a natural tendency to use words like 'vocation' and 'destiny') had disappeared, Barron took comfort from the continued existence of the landmark hotel which for him at least symbolised all the glory and the dream that was France.

'My father used to stay here,' he told Le Blanc over the first Angkor beer of the evening.

'Was he at Dien Bien Phu?' Le Blanc asked.

'He died in Dien Bien Phu,' Barron replied. 'So did thousands of other Frenchmen. I think that defeat broke France. Up till then we thought we had an imperial role to fulfil. After that, it became clear that even in places like Indochina which we had stamped with what we thought was our own indelible mark, France would always play second fiddle to America.'

'Always?' Le Blanc asked. 'Are you sure?'

Barron smiled. 'Not as sure as I was. From a certain point of view, things are going well. We may make even more progress if we play our cards right.'

If Barron sounded elliptical, it was because that form of speech came naturally to him. With Le Blanc *bien entendu* he spoke in French and that most glorious of languages lent itself far better than English to subtlety and evasion.

'Is that why Jean-Claude Mercier is in town?' Le Blanc asked. 'I saw him in the lobby as I was coming in.'

'Ah, at least Mercier has the good sense not to stay at the Cambodiana.'

'Mercier has a lot of good sense.'

As they sat over their drinks, the two men spent a few minutes reviewing the meteoric career of Jean-Claude Mercier. In the space of a decade he had parlayed a minority stakeholding in a moribund French sewage and waste disposal company into a global media and telecommunication network.

More than anyone, he had demonstrated to the world that the French too could play at the game called 'globalisation' and he did it with a style and impact that often left his rivals gasping.

Mercier's holding company, the node from which he controlled his mighty empire, was known simply and for obvious reasons as JCM investments. JCM was active on every continent. In South-East Asia, in particular, the company seemed determined to stake out a presence to rival, if not outstrip, the American and Asian conglomerates which had so much of a head start.

'What Jean-Claude is trying to do,' Barron ventured, 'is revenge Dien Bien Phu. He wants to re-establish France as the natural power, or at least influence, in the region. There was a time when all the politicians out here, all the civil servants, spoke in French, worked in French, sent their children to France to study. Mercier wants to see that time come again. But he's not just being sentimental. He believes there are enormous commercial opportunities for France, a great reservoir of goodwill ready to be mined by a man with real business acumen.'

'Such as himself.'

'Why not?' Barron nodded. 'Who else is going to take the risk?'

Henri Le Blanc went to the bar and came back with two more beers. 'Are you close to Mercier?' he asked. 'You seem to be.'

'I've known him all my life,' Barron replied. 'His father knew my father.'

Henri Le Blanc nodded. 'It's often like that. The strongest ties are through family and friendship.'

Barron came to a decision. Le Blanc knew so much already. Why shouldn't he know more? 'Jean-Claude has asked me to have dinner with him this evening. Can you join us?'

'Delighted. More than delighted,' Henri Le Blanc replied.

Barron slipped out to make a phone call and when he came back, he said. 'That's all in order. There's a table for three booked for half-past eight.'

'Here, at the hotel?'

'Where else? This is still the finest French food in town,' Barron said.

★★★

In the event, Jean-Claude Mercier was running late. It was almost nine o'clock when he bounded into the restaurant, embraced Jules Barron warmly on both cheeks before extending his hand to Henri Le Blanc.

'Good to see you again, Henri,' he said. 'It has been too long.'

Mercier seemed to possess charm and vitality in equal measure. He wasn't a tall man – not more than five foot ten, Barron judged, which was certainly not tall these days – but he had enormous presence. He had the kind of glow of confidence, of wellbeing about him which so often seems to be achieved by the super-rich. They are different, Barron reflected, not merely because they have more money than the rest of us but because they know they have.

Waiters hurried to the table as soon as Mercier arrived. Barron and Le Blanc had had plenty of time to study the menu. Mercier didn't waste time. He went for a steak and salad and a bottle of 1984 Pomerol to be getting along with.

Once the food had arrived, Mercier quizzed Le Blanc efficiently, some would have said ruthlessly. It was one of his traits. He never missed an opportunity.

'So how do you read things, Henri?' he asked.

Le Blanc was flattered that Mercier had used his first name. Sometimes in France, even now, the old guard would die rather than get on first name terms with someone they might have known for twenty years.

'I'm not an expert on Cambodia,' Le Blanc entered a modest disclaimer.

'Oh, come on!' Mercier scoffed. 'Yours is one of the finest analytical minds writing about world affairs today. And you have a nose too, am I right?'

Thinking about noses, Mercier lifted his glass of claret and sniffed the aroma of fine wine.

Flattered, Le Blanc ventured his own analysis of the situation. 'I have only been here a few days but of course I have visited Cambodia many times in the past. I would say this is a powder-keg waiting to explode. The slightest spark could set it off.'

Mercier nodded. 'I so much agree. That is where the Americans are so crazy. They don't seem to understand that by pushing Hun Sen as they have been to press ahead with the war crimes tribunal, they run the risk of providing precisely the spark that will ignite the conflagration.'

'Surely, the pressures in America are unstoppable,' Le Blanc said, 'particularly after Mrs Clinton's visit. She has dragged the whole thing right out on to the table. The human rights lobby has their teeth into this and are not going to let go, specially not now, with the Democrats having a majority in the US Senate. They're going to use this to score some heavy political points back home and Cambodia is going to pay the price. We may be facing civil war all over again.'

Mercier tapped the table with the middle finger of his right hand to emphasise the point. 'Idiocy, complete and utter idiocy!'

'All is not lost, Jean-Claude,' Barron murmured. 'There are new developments.'

Henri Le Blanc listened attentively. It was almost eleven o'clock before the three men finally left the restaurant.

★★★

The UN building was a short cab-ride from the hotel. Prescott and Su arrived a few minutes before ten. They were shown into a large airy room, with a view of the river on one side and the golden roofs of Wat Phnom on the other. The tables had been arranged in a large horseshoe in front of a raised platform where a long ornate desk had been placed. A single highbacked chair stood behind the desk. A sign indicated that this was where the PRESIDENT would sit. Off to one side of the dais was another smaller desk with a placard saying, CLERK. The room was equipped with a line of interpreters' booths and the usual paraphernalia of headphones and microphones with red and green buttons. Half-a-dozen people had already taken their seats at the table, among whom they recognised both Professor Haq and Lina Chan, as well as Lina's cousin, Sarin Bun, the guard from Tuol Sleng prison who had helped locate the Hong Soeung archive.

Prescott left Su to find a seat at the horseshoe, then made his way to the far end of the room where a section had been roped off for the PRESS. Most of the journalists present were Cambodians, but Prescott was intrigued to note that the international press corps was also represented. As he found a seat, he nodded a greeting to Henri Le Blanc.

'Hello, Henri. Looks like they're setting the stage for something big here, doesn't it?' Prescott said.

'Bigger than big,' Henri smirked, leaving Prescott to wonder – not for the first time – whether the Frenchman's sources weren't sometimes better than his own.

Moments later, two Cambodian officials entered the room and installed themselves at the clerk's table. They were followed in short order by Geoff Jackson. The Australian was wearing a suit and a tie and, in keeping with the solemnity of the occasion, looked totally focussed and serious.

Jackson picked up the gavel and hammered the desk in front of him. There was the usual rustle as journalists present found the right page in their notebooks. The TV cameras began to roll.

'Good morning,' Jackson began. 'I want to make it clear that we are not meeting today as part of the tribunal process itself, but simply as a preliminary to that process. In other words, this is not a court of law but a panel hearing – a one-man panel – which the Cambodian government has asked me to conduct in my role of United Nations' assessor. Any findings which we come to today will of course be available to the tribunal if and when that tribunal is convened.

'The specific purpose of today's session,' Jackson continued, 'is to hear arguments as to the admissibility of the document which has become known as the Hong Soeung confessions. I need not rehearse here the significance of this document. That matter has been widely covered in the press and television, both here in Cambodia as well as internationally. In order to expedite the proceedings, I propose to call various experts and witnesses. I have been asked by the Minister responsible, Mr Khin Lay, the Minister of the Interior, to give a ruling when all interested parties have been heard and I expect to do exactly that.'

Prescott listened in increasing fascination as for the next hour the details of the discovery of the Hong Soeung confessions were rehearsed before the panel. There was no formal witness stand. Participants made their statements from their places at the table, leaning into the microphones in front of them so that their words could be caught and translated by the interpreters. Speakers were not formally on oath but, at least from Prescott's point of view, that didn't make the depositions any less solemn or convincing.

The court – Prescott couldn't help thinking of it as a court, even though he knew it wasn't – had worked out an order of batting.

As the person who had discovered the Hong Soeung archive, Lina Chan went first. Sitting in front of her microphone and speaking English in her clear and precise way, she told the court who she was and what she did as well the circumstances which had led to the discovery of the Soeung confessions.

When she came to describe how she had scanned in the photograph which Su had given her, Geoff Jackson interrupted to ask: 'Would this be standard procedure?'

'Very much so,' Lina replied. 'With the digitalisation of

DC-Cam's photographic archive, computerised search techniques score heavily over manual searches.'

'Let's see this on screen if we can,' Jackson instructed.

Lina was ready for this. She had brought her laptop with the PowerPoint programme already loaded. The lights in the room were dimmed as Lina tapped the keyboard. 'This is the picture which Su Soeung gave me from *The Washingtonian* magazine, the one we scanned in as the basis for the search. What you see is a family scene, involving Hong Soeung and his wife as well as Su Soeung as a seven-year-old child. They are standing on the veranda of their house.'

'You didn't scan in the whole picture, though,' Jackson commented. 'Just Hong Soeung's face and torso, is that so?'

'Exactly so.' Shifting the group photo to the left of the screen, Lina next showed the closeup which she had used as the basis of the scan. 'This is the picture of Hong Soeung which formed the basis of our search.'

Watching from his seat in the press area, Prescott noticed Su Soeung tense as the smiling photograph of her father was projected onto the screen. This must be hard for her, he thought.

Did Geoff Jackson really have to be so thorough, so pernickety, he wondered? Did he have to drag things out? Weren't the bona fides of the Hong Soeung dossier clearly established already?

'Hold it a moment!' the Australian instructed. 'Look at the top right-hand corner of the blow-up. There's a thick black diagonal line behind Hong Soeung's head. What is that?'

Lina examined the two images side-by-side: the photograph of the Soeung family group and the close-up of Hong

Soeung. 'I see what you mean,' she said. 'If you look at the group photograph, you can see that the angle from which the photograph has been taken – with the camera pointing upwards from the road towards the veranda – has had the effect of placing the house's trailing eve more or less behind Hong Soeung. In the close-up, the outline of the trailing eve is blurred, so you get what seems to be the thick dark stripe behind and slightly above the subject's left shoulder.'

There was a longish pause, interrupted when Su Soeung pressed the button on her microphone and asked permission to take the floor.

'I would like to confirm what Lina Chan has suggested,' Su said. 'I was a child when the first photograph was taken but I remember our house as it was then. It was a traditional Cambodian townhouse. The trailing eve was a distinguishing feature. To me, it used to look like the prow of a ship cresting the waves. The house is still there today. I have seen it. The trailing eve is still there. We can go to look at it, if you like.'

Geoff Jackson smiled at her benevolently. 'I don't think that will be necessary. I am quite satisfied with the explanation. Miss Chan, pray continue.'

For the next twenty minutes, Lina Chan continued her presentation, describing how the computer search through the DC-CAM files had led to the identification of the photograph in the archives and how she and Su had visited Tuol Sleng to inspect the original.

Once again, Geoff Jackson had insisted on having a clear understanding of the detail. 'I've visited Tuol Sleng,' he said. 'I know the topography in a general sense. We're talking about one of the ground floor buildings, are we?'

'Block C, ground floor, room three,' Lina confirmed.

'And the precise location of the photograph of Hong Soe-ung in that room?'

Lina consulted her notes. 'North wall, top row, eighteen from the right.'

After Lina had finished giving her evidence, the young Tuol Sleng guard – Sarin Bun – was next to be called on. Not being one of the principals, Sarin had been sitting at the back of the room. On being summoned, he took his seat at the table with a noticeable air of discomfort.

Remembering that Su had told him that Sarin was Lina Chan's cousin, Prescott had expected that some glance of recognition or acknowledgement would pass between them. But Sarin kept his eyes firmly fixed on the microphone in front of him, answering Jackson's queries in a low monotone.

'Mr Bun, can you confirm the narrative of the discovery of the Hong Soeung confession as presented by Lina Chan? Do you wish to add anything to that account?'

'No, sir.'

'Is it possible that Archive No 01746 could have been opened and examined before Ms. Chan's visit on the date specified?'

Sarin Bun shook his head emphatically. 'Not at any time when I have been on duty.'

Jackson spent a few minutes clarifying the procedures in operation at Tuol Sleng regarding the admission of visitors to the prison archives. Bun's answers remained brief; his manner taciturn. When the young guard finally returned to his seat in the hall, he did so with an evident air of relief.

Professor Haq, who gave evidence next, was a marked contrast. The head of DC-Cam spoke with an air of authority befitting someone who was not only the head of a prestigious professional institute but who was acknowledged as a seminal expert on the style and characteristics of the Khmer language.

Just as had been the case with his deputy, Lisa Chan, Professor Haq had prepared a PowerPoint presentation for the benefit of the gathering. With the aid of a series of slides, he took his audience through the finer points of Khmer graphology, comparing the handwriting of the "confessions'" with that of the letter which Hong Soeung had sent to his wife in March 1975.

'Let me use the split screen here and you will be left in no doubt about the fact that both documents were written by the same man,' Haq confidently informed them. With a pointer, he indicated the key factors which had led him to that conclusion.

As Haq spoke, Prescott made notes...: *Khmer language unlike any others...in manuscript form orthography may be highly idiosyncratic....no two people form their letters in the same way.*

The Professor spoke quickly and authoritatively. Prescott found himself hard pressed to keep up. As he scribbled away in his notebook, he observed to his surprise that Henri Le Blanc, *Le Monde*'s diplomatic correspondent, who was sitting in the row ahead of him, had ostentatiously put his own notebook away and was leaning back in his chair with a smug look on his face.

'Tiens!' Prescott asked himself, 'what's Henri got to be so pleased about?'

Around mid-morning, Jackson called a break. Seeing Su

engaged in conversation with Lina Chan, Prescott followed most of the rest of the press corps onto the terrace overlooking the river.

Le Blanc had already lit up a Gauloise and he offered Prescott one.

'You may need it,' Le Blanc said. 'I'd say things are going badly, wouldn't you?'

'Badly for whom?'

'Badly for the proponents.'

'Proponents of what?'

Le Blanc looked him in the eye. 'I'm referring to those who believe in the authenticity of the so-called Hong Soeung confessions.'

Prescott felt a sinking feeling in the pit of his stomach. 'You don't believe they are genuine?'

'Pah!' The Frenchman spat a loose end of tobacco over the low wall in the general direction of the Tonle Sap River. 'It's all garbage. The trouble is you people just swallowed it wholesale. Believe me, you haven't convinced Geoff Jackson. All that technology, the PowerPoint stuff, may look good but you have to make a case as well as show pretty pictures.'

For reasons he couldn't understand, Prescott felt he was being forced onto the defensive. 'I thought they made a pretty good case. What about Haq? I thought his evidence was copper bottomed. What about the photographs? How much more do you want?'

The Frenchman smiled at him pityingly as the bell rang to indicate that the brief interruption was over.

'Just you wait, 'enry 'iggins, just you wait,' Le Blanc mocked.

After the break, Jackson called on the lawyer representing Kang Kek Ieu, alias Duch, to take the stand. As he did so, Jackson once again made it clear that these were not formal proceedings, but preliminary hearings designed to allow both sides to argue the admissibility of the Hong Soeung confessions in the event the tribunal finally began its work.

In response to Jackson's invitation, a tall, white-haired man took the stand, exuding a powerful sense of indignation on behalf of his client. He spoke rapidly in Khmer, so rapidly in fact that Geoff Jackson, listening through earphones to the simultaneous translation, had to instruct him to slow down.

'We are having difficulty in following you, Mr Hu,' Jackson barked. 'Please repeat your last statement. Did I understand you to say that Duch denies ever meeting, let alone interrogating or torturing Hong Soeung and therefore any statement which alleges this must be false?'

The defence lawyer bristled. 'With respect, as I believe I have already indicated, my client wishes to be known as Keng Kach Ieu, not Duch.'

'My apologies,' Jackson sounded contrite. 'Keng Kach Ieu it will be from now on. That said, did I interpret you correctly?'

Hu Phen nodded. 'Quite correctly. My client further wishes to point out that he is supposed to have authorised the removal of Hong Soeung to Choeung Ek for execution on June 5, 1975. Without accepting in any way his involvement in those events, my client draws the attention of the panel to the fact that no executions are thought to have taken place at Choeung Ek until some time in 1977 when the burial grounds in the vicinity of S-21 had reached the limit of their capacity.'

'By S-21, you mean the code name for Tuol Sleng?' Jackson interjected.

Once again, Hu Phen nodded. 'I believe the term is well-understood as a synonym for Tuol Sleng.'

'Thank you for that elucidation,' Jackson commented frostily. Then he turned his head to the right to address the small delegation from DC-Cam who were still occupying their seats at the horse-shoe shaped table.

'Professor Haq, Miss Chan. You're the experts here on the history of genocide in Cambodia. What do you say to the point at issue here? Is it true that Choeung Ek was not used as a killing field until 1977 and certainly not as early as 1975?'

It took ten minutes to clarify the point. Both Professor Haq and Lina Chan were clearly taken aback by the thrust of the lawyer's attack. Haq admitted that the discrepancy had escaped him. He had been concentrating on the handwriting rather than the internal evidence. But, yes, it was an established fact that executions (and mass burials) at Choeung Ek did not start before 1977. Lina Chan was even more shamefaced. She admitted that the dating of Hong Soeung's execution had puzzled her and that she had actually mentioned this to Su Soeung at the time of their visit to the killing fields, but such was the force of Hong Soeung's testimony that she had, possibly unconsciously, pushed the problem of chronology onto the back burner as it were.

'I always had it in mind,' she told the panel in a faltering tone of voice, 'to look into this matter further at some point but...'

Hu Phen seized his opportunity. 'It is our contention,' he thundered, 'that the Hong Soeung confessions are false in every respect. Not only did my client never meet Hong Soe-ung. We do not believe that Hong Soeung was ever at Tuol Sleng.'

There was a rustle of excitement in the body of the hall as the implications of what Duch's lawyer was suggesting sank in. The journalists started writing furiously in their note-books. The television cameras whirred into action.

'You had better explain yourself,' Jackson instructed with more than a hint of menace in his voice.

CHAPTER 15

The defence lawyer ostentatiously poured himself a glass of water from the jug in front of him.

'Since technology seems to be the flavour of the month' – Hu Phen nodded towards the DC-Cam team – 'the defence would like to take a few moments to make its case to the panel with our own PowerPoint presentation.' He motioned to a young man sitting behind him to bring up his laptop. 'Thank you. And the scanner too, please. We're going to need the scanner.'

'Is this leading anywhere in particular?' From his querulous tone of voice, it seemed that Geoff Jackson's patience was wearing thin.

'I believe it is,' Hu Phen replied. Gesturing with one hand in the direction of Lisa Chan, he continued: 'In her statement this morning, Miss Chan indicated that on the occasion she and Miss Soeung visited Tuol Sleng, several photographs were taken including one of Miss Soeung standing in front of the north wall of room 3, ground floor, Block C. We understand the prosecution team may have that photograph with them at the present time and, if that is the case, we would ask the permission of the panel to scan the photograph and to project it onto the screen.'

Jackson considered the request for a moment, then he nodded. 'Fair enough,' he said.

Moments later, the photograph had been located, scanned and displayed. Su Soeung stood in the foreground, looking solemn and strained. Behind stretched the rows of mugshots of the Tuol Sleng victims, including the face of Hong Soeung himself.

'Remember the position of the Hong Soeung mug-shot,' Hu Phen admonished, 'third row down, fourth from the right.' He pointed with the mouse. 'You can see Hong Soeung clearly just behind Su Soeung's left shoulder.' The aggression which had characterized the lawyer's earlier performance seemed to have disappeared to be replaced by an almost avuncular courtesy. 'I realise, Miss Soeung, that this must be painful for you. I assure you the demonstration is necessary.'

Leaving the first slide up on the screen, Hu Phen bent over to rummage in what looked like a Gladstone bag placed on a chair beside him, before resurfacing to flourish a well-thumbed paperback in the direction of the bench.

'I am sure Professor Haq will recognise this book,' Phen said. 'After all, he is the author. The book is well-known in Cambodia and indeed worldwide. This is the English translation.'

Hu Phen read out the title 'S-21: *The history of Tuol Sleng prison.*'

'With your permission, President,' Hu Phen addressed the bench, 'I would like to invite Professor Haq to examine the photograph printed on page 77.'

'Granted.' Jackson nodded.

Haq took the book which the defence lawyer passed over. 'Page 77?' he repeated.

'Exactly.' Hu Phen said, 'Could you please read out the caption to the photograph? Be very precise please.'

Professor Haq did what he was told. He sounded both puzzled and alarmed, as though he could sense that a trap was being prepared for him, but he couldn't quite see what it was. 'The caption says: *Nhem En at the Tuol Sleng Genocide Museum, 1997. En was the first Khmer Rouge photographer to take mugshots of S-21 prisoners. Photograph by Douglas Niven.*'

'Thank you.' Hu Phen took the book back and passed it over to his technician. 'We are going to scan in this 1997 photograph and project it alongside the other one.'

Moments later, the second photograph joined the first on the screen. 'I was looking at Professor Haq's esteemed book,' Hu Phen told them, 'as I was preparing for this case. Would I not be right, Professor, in believing that this is also a photograph of the north wall of room 3, Block C. If we look at the rows of faces to the left of Nhem En's right shoulder, we can see that they are exactly the same as the faces behind Su Soeung's right shoulder. Let's zoom in on one or two of them to make sure.'

As the technician manipulated the laptop, Professor Haq nodded. 'There is no doubt at all. This is the same room, the same wall, the same group of mugshots.' Hu Phen pounced, 'Except for one omission, Professor! Where is the photograph of Hong Soeung? There is a mugshot behind Nhem En's left shoulder, just as there is behind Su Soeung's left shoulder, but it is not the face of Hong Soeung. Both Nhem En and Su Soeung appear to be standing in the same position with regard to the wall. So why does Hong Soeung not appear in the 1997 photograph? Why does he only appear in the later photograph? I will tell you why, professor. Because the Hong Soeung mugshot has been inserted into the display on the wall some time after Douglas Niven took the photograph which you have included in your book! How do you explain that?'

'I…I'm not sure I can explain it,' Professor Haq floundered.

'Well, I can,' Hu Phen savoured his moment of triumph. Once more he rummaged in the bag to produce for the court a six by eight photograph which was at once scanned and projected. 'We can all agree, can we not,' Hu Phen said, 'that this is the same man as appears in the line-up in Professor Haq's book. On the wall, he occupies the position three down, second from right. We have no name for this prisoner, but we have an ID number.'

Again he pointed with the mouse. 'Today we are looking at prisoner 259.'

'How did you acquire this photograph, Mr Hu?' Geoff Jackson asked sharply. 'Will you pass it up? I'd like to take a look at it.'

As the photograph was passed up to the bench, Hu Phen explained: 'It occurred to me that whoever had substituted the picture of prisoner 259 with the picture of Hong Soeung probably intended at some later date to reverse the substitution. In that case he or she would not have destroyed the original. I decided to look for it.'

'Where did you look?' Jackson asked.

'In the obvious place.'

'Which was?'

'In the Tuol Sleng archive itself. In the file for prisoner 259. We followed all the correct procedures. We have not stolen the photograph from the archive. We have signed for it and our intervention has been correctly recorded. If you examine the back of the photograph carefully, you will see rust marks made by the metal staples which fastened it to the wall.'

Jackson turned the eight by ten photograph over and examined the reverse side, running his finger over the rough and rusty indentations. Then, briefly, he put his head in his hands: 'Where the hell is all this getting us?'

'I'm coming to that,' Hu Phen explained patiently. 'Let's forget for the time being about Prisoner 259. Let us examine closely the picture of Hong Soeung which was displayed on the wall of Room 3, Block C in Tuol Sleng.' Hu Phen paused to give the technician time to project the Hong Soeung mugshot onto the screen.

For most of those in the room, it was the first time they had seen that shocking image – the vacant staring eyes, the visible bruise on the forehead, the lank unkempt hair. It was hard not to be moved and, hardened though they were to tales of atrocity (you couldn't live in Cambodia without being exposed on an almost daily basis to the horror of the past), some of them reacted with an audible intake of breath or suddenly averted gaze. Though this was but one of hundreds, even thousands, of such mugshots, Hong Soeung could not be seen just as a face amid a multitude of faces of Pol Pot's victims. Day after day, the media had been writing about this man known as Hong Soeung whose daughter had come to Cambodia on a 'personal quest track to down her father'. The name 'Hong Soeung' had become almost a household word on the streets of Phnom Penh. The big-screen projection brought him into the room, into their very lives, in a direct, almost confrontational, manner.

Hu Phen gave them plenty of time to absorb the picture. Then he nodded to the technician. 'Go back to The Washingtonian photograph,' he instructed.

Once again, they had a chance to look at the happy family snapshot which Gaetana Enders had taken on the steps of the veranda of the Soeung family home.

'Now let's have the close-up of Hong Soeung's face and torso,' Hu Phen continued, 'the one DC-CAM used when they ran the search-programme. Let's have it side-by-side with the Tuol Sleng image of Hong Soeung.'

The tall lawyer paused. This time he didn't bother about the mouse. He strode to the screen and stood in front of it, pointing with a ruler. 'Look at the tell-tale stripe. See how the trailing eve appears not just in the family shot, not just in the blow-up of Hong Soeung on the veranda but even in the Tuol Sleng mug-shot!'

Hu Phen swivelled suddenly and barked an instruction at his technician. 'Show them how it was done. Run the programme!'

Watching the lawyer's polished performance, Prescott realised that it had all been carefully scripted in advance. Hu Phen knew how to milk a situation so as to achieve maximum dramatic effect. Prescott's heart sank to his boots as the series of pictures came up on the screen. Six clicks was all it took, he thought. Six clicks which showed how the veranda photograph of Hong Soeung had been electronically manipulated so as to produce the Tuol Sleng mugshot.

Prescott was too good a journalist not to put pen to paper even when in practice he was recording his own total humiliation.

> Click number 1 – for the bruising, he wrote.
> Click number 2 – the hair
> Click number 3 – change the expression from family snapshot smile to vacant staring look

Click number 4 – angle of jaw
Click number 5 – gap in teeth as though some knocked out
Click number 6 – tidy whole and rearrange.

And all the time, in each successive shot, they could all see the tell-tale black smudge of the trailing eve running down from left to right behind Hong Soeung's left shoulder.

To make assurance doubly sure, Hu Phen asked the technician to run the programme backwards as well. With the same six clicks, the Tuol Sleng mugshot was retransformed into husband and father posing with his loved ones.

'Jesus!' Prescott muttered to himself. 'What a fiasco!'

Hu Phen hadn't finished. During the following fifteen minutes he completed his hatchet job. Having comprehensively demolished the Hong Soeung mugshot, he turned his attentions to the "confessions" calling up two forensic experts of unimpeachable qualifications to testify on the basis of their minute scientific examination of the documents that the "confessions" had been written within the last six months, probably within the last three, and certainly not more than twenty-five years ago.

Hu Phen was clearly enjoying his triumph. When his experts had finished giving evidence, he summed things up for the benefit of the panel. 'As I understand it,' he told them, 'the key question is the insult to the surface of the paper which any writing implement inflicts, an insult which can of course be examined and measured microscopically. Over a period of time, the natural contours of the surface will reassert themselves, as the molecules of the fibres which make up the paper regroup. The wound heals in other words. With the Hong

Soeung confessions, that phenomenon is absent. The indentations, the scratches made by the nib of the pen are new. The tears in the paper – invisible of course to the naked eye, but present nonetheless – are still fresh.

'The further – and to my mind crucial – point is the result of the chemical analysis to which the Hong Soeung confessions have been subjected. Modern ink, ladies and gentlemen, differs in its chemical composition from the inks which were in use in the mid-seventies. You have heard expert testimony as to the precise discrepancies and I need not repeat that testimony now. The nub of the matter is that chemicals appear in the ink which have been used to write the Hong Soeung confessions which could not possibly have been available in 1975 or 1977. We have made a random check on dozens of other documents contained in the Tuol Sleng archive and not one of them has been written using the ink or inks which we find in the Hong Soeung confessions.'

'I take it, Mr Hu, that you are giving us your summing-up at this point. We would welcome that.' Geoffrey Jackson looked pointedly at his watch.

'Gladly,' Hu replied. 'It is our contention, sir, that the Hong Soeung confessions should play no part at all in the forthcoming tribunal on the grounds that they are fatally flawed, as this morning's proceedings have amply demonstrated. We are in other words dealing here with a blatant forgery, a forgery which could perhaps take its place alongside the Zinoviev letter, the Hitler diaries or – dare I say it? – the so-called Tienanmen papers...'

'Spare us the historical analogies,' Jackson barked.

Hu Phen wasted no more time. He completed his summing-up within the next five minutes and, as he sat down, confidently called for an immediate ruling from the one-man panel.

Watching Geoff Jackson from his vantage-point in the press gallery, Prescott Glover could well understand the Australian's dilemma. Jackson's mission in Cambodia was to help the government by all means to get the long-delayed Pol Pot tribunal under way. That was his *raison d'être*. Jackson represented in his person, as well as symbolically, the will of the international community to see war criminals prosecuted. If they could not be brought, like Yugoslavia's Slobodan Milosevic, to the international court of justice in the Hague, then at least they should be brought to trial within their own countries with as many safeguards built in as might be humanly possible to ensure that the processes of justice were not compromised.

The whole Hong Soeung affair, Prescott knew, had erupted at a crucial moment. So much hung on the outcome of the morning's enquiry. At a time when it looked as though, little by little, the political situation was edging its way towards a final decision on staging the tribunal which could indict Duch and Ta Mok for crimes against humanity, a decision to admit the Hong Soeung confessions in evidence could be crucially important. That certainly was the way the media, national and international had seen it when Senator Clinton gave her press conference a few days earlier.

Of course, the media had presented it as a done deal. The media always saw things in black and white. But what if it all went wrong now? So many expectations had been raised. If the Hong Soeung confessions were exposed as a blatant forgery, the whole climate of opinion in Cambodia could rapidly swing the other way.

Geoff Jackson, Prescott firmly believed, was dedicated to

his job. Under that bluff Australian exterior beat the heart of a man who desperately believed in what he was doing. No doubt about it, Prescott reflected, Geoff Jackson had been keen to hold the enquiry. He had wanted for his own perfectly valid reasons to see the Hong Soeung confessions form part of the proceedings, perhaps a vital part. But had he allowed his heart to overrule his head? Had he staked too much on the outcome? Should he have been more cautious?

Jesus, Prescott thought, why blame Jackson? What about his own part in the fiasco? Who had first floated the story about the Hong Soeung confessions, who had persuaded *The New York Times* to run with it, give it top billing? Prescott discovered he was blushing to the roots of his hair. They had set an elephant trap in his path and he had fallen straight into it.

The sound of Geoff Jackson's gavel brought him back to reality. He got out his notebook. Eschewing further interruptions or recesses, Jackson had obviously decided to give his ruling straightaway.

★★★

Later that day, Prescott had a quiet dinner alone with Su.

Su was bewildered, almost distraught. She begged him to explain.

'What the hell is going on, Prescott? Why did Jackson rule against my father's confessions? Why didn't they use them against Duch?'

'You still don't get it, Su, do you?' Prescott knew he had to be gentle with her. She was near breaking-point. But he couldn't allow her to nurture any further illusions. 'Don't you see, they used you right from the start? They brought you here to Cambodia in the first place. They made sure you found the Hong Soeung archive. They knew about me too. That helped. They read me right. They knew I'd try to splash the story and of course I did. Damn fool, that I was. As a result, of this morning's events the tribunal process has been almost totally discredited. Those who oppose the tribunal have been able to argue that the Hong Soeung forgery shows to what despicable depths the proponents of the tribunal will sink. The Prime Minister, Hun Sen, has certainly been wounded politically today by the turn-around in the Hong Soeung affair. The newspapers, the radio, the TV have been full of it. There are more people out there than you can possibly imagine who have a vested interest in keeping the lid on the Pol Pot years. Someone, somewhere, saw a golden opportunity. Run a story which looks plausible, appear to implicate the US in a secret bid to support Pol Pot. Push the publicity to the limits and then, when the story is discredited and dead in the water, as it is now, a lot of people are left grinning from ear to ear.'

'When did you see all this, Prescott?' Su asked quietly. 'If you could see this was the way things were, why did you write the stories you did?'

'Mea culpa,' Prescott replied. 'I allowed myself to be carried along. I think I lost my objectivity. There were signs and I failed to read them.'

'Such as?'

'Such as when you told me that Lina had said no executions took place at Choeung Ek until 1977. I should have picked up on that and I didn't.'

'You wanted to believe in it for my sake too, didn't you?' Su's hand searched out Prescott's across the table.

'That too,' Prescott said.

They sat in silence for a while. The hotel waiters, sensing a lovers' tiff perhaps, left them in peace.

'Who's behind this? We don't really know, do we?' Su said at last.

'No, but I'm damn well going to find out,' Prescott replied. 'I sold *The Times* a pup and I'm going to make amends. It's not just a question of my professional reputation. My personal pride is at stake. They made a fool of me and they're not going to get away with it.'

'Hold on a minute, Prescott,' Su said. 'Don't go so fast. Aren't we forgetting about Professor Haq?'

'What do you mean?'

'Haq gave evidence that the Hong Soeung confessions and the Hong Soeung letter were written by one and the same person. The Hong Soeung confessions were revealed as a forgery. But Haq never retracted his statement.'

'Nobody asked him to,' Prescott said. 'Come on, Su, let it go,' he pleaded. 'Your father's dead. He was never in Tuol Sleng. He probably died or was killed on the road somewhere. He's buried out there in the fields, with all the rest. They used his name, they used his story, because they wanted to involve you – and me – in their sting.'

He had known her for so long, but he had never realised how determined she could be.

'I want to talk to Professor Haq,' she hissed, angry that he was trying to block her. 'I don't care, Prescott, about the games people play. I'm sorry they took us for a ride but that's not the main thing.'

'What is the main thing, then?'

'I still want to find my father.'

CHAPTER 16

Su found Professor Haq sitting alone at a corner table in a small restaurant not far from the DC-Cam office. The old man had almost finished his meal when she approached. Laying his chopsticks aside, he motioned to her to sit down, almost as though he had been expecting her.

'I'm so sorry, Miss Soeung,' he said. 'It must be very hard for you. Have you eaten? Let us order something for you?'

Haq called a waiter over. When Su had given her order, he said: 'All my people know where to find me if they want to talk. I expect Lina Chan told you to come here, didn't she?'

When Su nodded, the Professor continued. 'I'm so glad she did. I suppose you just think I am discredited, a disgrace to my profession. What's more, you think I have let you down personally. My evaluation of the document was shown to be worthless. The Soeung confessions are a fraud. So why are you here, Miss Soeung?'

'Because I want to understand,' Su replied. 'How could you, probably the world's leading authority when it comes to Khmer orthography, have been one hundred per cent convinced the Soeung confessions were written by my father and yet you now agree that they were faked?' She rounded on him then, accusingly. 'You made no effort to contradict that odious lawyer, Hu Phen. You didn't intervene! You could have challenged him, why didn't you?' Su's eyes flashed. Angrily she thrust her plate away and leaned across the table towards Haq.

'Nobody called on me,' the Professor protested, echoing Prescott's earlier comment. 'This was a quasi-judicial proceeding. You can't just get to your feet and spout away when you feel like it. You have to be called. Besides Hu Phen was right. The confessions clearly were not authentic. The chemical evidence alone proved that beyond doubt.'

'So you have retracted your earlier view that my father wrote the Soeung confessions, in spite of what you called the incontrovertible orthographic evidence?' The note of accusation was still there but there was now a plaintive, almost despairing tone in Su's voice.

For a moment Haq looked away. Beyond the bead curtain, there was the usual noise and bustle from the street but inside the restaurant it was quiet. Su Soeung and Professor Haq were almost the only clients left.

The Professor turned back to the young woman who sat, consumed with misery, across the table from him. 'Think about it, Su,' he said. 'That's what I've been doing ever since the panel hearing. How do you square the circle? How do you reconcile the contradictions? I'm still convinced that your father wrote the Soeung confessions and yet, yes, I am also convinced that those confessions are fraudulent. How can both propositions be true at one and the same time?'

Professor Haq paused to refill his cup from the delicately painted porcelain teapot. 'Believe me, Miss Soeung, I have been wracking my brains. I can only think of one thing.'

'What is that?'

'It may sound absurd to you,' Haq continued, 'and almost unthinkable. But at least you should consider the possibility that I was indeed correct in my analysis of the handwriting and that your father did actually write those confessions – not in S21, not in Tuol Sleng, but much much later, maybe even in the last few weeks. Could your father somehow, somewhere still be alive? Could he have participated in the fabrication of the Hong Soeung confessions by actually writing in his own inimitable hand the text which we all have studied? I cannot say definitively that this is what happened. I advance it merely as a hypothesis, an explanation which would fit the facts.'

As Haq was speaking, Su experienced a wave of almost indescribable joy. 'I don't believe it. It can't be true. How can it be true?'

Haq leaned across and laid a hand on her arm. 'Don't go too fast,' he cautioned. 'I said it was one possible explanation to resolve the contradictions. We know the Soeung confessions are fraudulent because they are not an original document from the Tuol Sleng prison at the time of the Pol Pot tyranny. But if the document is indeed, as I believe, in your father's hand, then he could have, must have, written it quite recently since it has been demonstrated conclusively that the document is of recent origin. When, how, where and, above all, why your father participated in what seems to be a gigantic political manipulation remains to be seen.'

As far as Su was concerned, the detail was irrelevant. Whatever chicanery might have been involved, seemed to her to be utterly secondary.

'So, he may be alive,' she whispered. 'My father may be alive. I can't believe it. I think I'm going to cry.' The tears poured down her face, but they were tears not of grief but of joy.

'I didn't say he is alive. I say he may be alive.' Haq again sounded a note of caution. 'If he is alive, he can be found.'

'Oh my God!' Su exclaimed. 'I can't believe this.'

For a few moments she sat there, overwhelmed. How could she be sure that Haq's conclusions were correct? What if she went tearing off on a wild goose chase? 'Are you saying that my father was never in Tuol Sleng?' she asked.

'No, I'm not saying that. I don't know for sure whether Hong Soeung was in Tuol Sleng or not. But if my hypothesis is correct, then he did not die there or at Choeung Ek.'

'How do I look for him? Where do I start?'

'Are you sure you want to start?' Haq asked. 'Are you ready for what you may find? These are tense times, Miss Soeung. The political scene in Cambodia as you know is very fluid.'

'Do you think someone is using my father?'

'Quite possibly.' The Professor paused and then added, cryptically: 'Or else he is using them.'

A frown crossed the Professor's face as the bead curtain at the door was thrust aside and two young men in police uniform entered the restaurant. They sat down at a table on the far side of the room. Even though they seemed to be out of earshot, Haq lowered his voice.

'Don't underestimate the difficulties or the dangers,' he told her. 'The cauldron is still seething in this country. Some day it may explode, blowing the lid off. You may be caught up in something much bigger than you know.'

As Haq stood up to go, Su felt increasingly desperate. 'Help me, Professor,' she pleaded. 'I don't know where else to turn.'

The older man took pity on her. She was so young, so naive. She had so much to learn. He sat down again. 'I'll tell you what I think, Miss Soeung.' He still kept his voice low even though the two policemen seemed to be totally engrossed in their meal. 'I think your father may have been in Tuol Sleng very early on, right at the beginning, back in April 1975, at the time Phnom Penh fell to the Khmer Rouge. But I think he may have survived or escaped.'

'I thought only seven people survived Tuol Sleng. As far as I know, the name Hong Soeung doesn't feature on the list.'

'Only seven people are known to have survived,' Haq corrected her. 'That is what the documentation indicates. But at DC-Cam, we have long wondered whether there might have been others.'

'How many others?'

'One or two. Two or three. Not more than that.'

'And my father could have been one of them?'

'It's possible.'

Su had the strong impression that Haq wanted to tell her more but something was holding him back.

'If you cannot tell me,' she said, 'how can I find out?'

For a moment she thought Haq was going to walk out on her. Once again, he half rose from his seat and then appeared to think better of it. 'You've met Narong Sum, haven't you?' he asked abruptly.

'You mean the man who painted the pictures in Tuol Sleng? One of the survivors. Yes, I met him at Lina's place. Jules Barron was there too, I remember.'

'Talk to Narong,' Haq urged. 'Talk to him soon. Narong is getting a set of his drawings together for a possible exhibition at DC-Cam. He has been telling us more about his time in Tuol Sleng. That's one of the reasons we believe there may be other survivors.' And with that Professor Haq strode out into the sunlight, leaving Su to finish her lunch alone.

She went to Narong's home later that day, having telephoned earlier to make an appointment.

'Do come over,' he had urged her. 'I will be so pleased to see you again.'

When she arrived, he introduced her to his wife, an attractive woman perhaps ten years younger. 'The children have left home,' Mrs Narong smiled at her. 'Sum and I have just ourselves now. But it is a busy time anyway. Sum is preparing his evidence for the tribunal and I am helping him.'

They went into the office, a largish room piled high with papers.

'We are working with DC-CAM,' Narong explained. 'They have given us a small grant to help get things ready. They say some of my material may be useful for the tribunal.'

'If there ever is a tribunal,' Mrs Narong added. She looked disappointed, Su thought. It was clear that the episode of the Hong Soeung "confessions" had changed the political climate dramatically. Nothing was certain anymore.

★★★

Earlier that evening, watching television with Prescott at the hotel, she had heard Hun Sen, Cambodia's Prime Minister, in what was clearly a defensive gesture declare that he had terminated the UN's mandate, sending Geoff Jackson packing. Hun Sen indicated that if there was to be a tribunal at all (which wasn't sure) this would be a purely Cambodian affair with no input from the international community.

'We must dig a hole and bury the past,' Hun Sen had announced solemnly.

'The knives are out for him now all right,' Prescott had commented. 'This is a major climbdown. He has lost face in a big way. I don't think he's going to last.'

Su had been less concerned than Prescott with the political ramifications. All she wanted to do now was to find out whether her father was still alive.

'You're one of the Tuol Sleng survivors,' she said to Narong as they stood among the clutter. 'We know there were six others. Today, Professor Haq told me you thought there might possibly be more. Why is that?'

Narong exchanged a quick look with his wife.

'It's all right,' she reassured him. 'The Professor has sent Miss Soeung to talk to us. He wants her to know. She needs to know.'

Narong sighed. He wondered if he would ever be free of the burden of the past or whether it would follow him to his grave.

'Look at these drawings.' He drew Su over to a long bench which ran down one side of the room. She saw that twenty or thirty charcoal sketches had been laid out side by side.

'If you were a prisoner in Tuol Sleng, you had to write a personal history. They used that as a basis for the interrogation. As I already told you when we last met, I wrote in my confession that I knew how to draw and to paint. I took a risk. It could have killed me. It marked me as one of the educated classes. Like wearing glasses. But Duch was intrigued. He realised he could use my skills. Sometimes, when there was a new batch of prisoners, he forced me to draw them. Later I painted some of them too. These are some of my early drawings. They have never been seen before.'

'Did all these men die?' Su stared at the series of images with a mixture of horror and fascination. She had seen the rows of blank-eyed mugshots on the walls of the prison, but the rough charcoal drawings had somehow caught the anguish in quite a different way.

'I can't be sure,' Narong replied. 'Sometimes I would talk to the prisoners as I drew them. They could be there one day, then next day they could be gone. The graveyards around the prison were quickly full.'

Suddenly, Narong swung round to face her. 'I'm sure I met your father in Tuol Sleng. As soon as they showed his face on television the other day, I knew I recognised him. He was one of the first prisoners I drew. I could never forget that face.'

He led Su along the bench and pointed out a frayed piece of paper. 'I never knew his name, of course. I don't think he ever told me. But even if he had, "Hong Soeung" would not have meant much to me. I was the son of a farmer, a peasant really. Hong Soeung might have been a high official of the government, but I couldn't have known. It was a different world.'

Su gazed at the drawing, recognising immediately the unmistakable characteristics of her father's face.

'Why do you think this man may have escaped,' she asked, 'when so many others perished?'

Again, Narong looked enquiringly at his wife and again Mrs Narong gave an affirmatory nod. 'I remember it so clearly,' Narong resumed. 'Your father was shackled to the bar in one of the cells. That was where I drew him one day. You can see the sketch isn't complete. I haven't shaded the torso, for example.'

Su understood what Narong meant. Whereas almost all

the other sketches had a finished look, the drawing of Hong Soeung was clearly embryonic, at least in certain aspects.

'Why didn't you finish the drawing?' Su asked.

'I was interrupted. Duch came into Hong Soeung's cell while I was there. He had some guards with him. He was shouting furiously that there had been a mistake, a terrible mix-up. He was trembling and swearing, as though he feared for his own life. I tell you, that was something seeing Duch in a panic like that. He was always the hard man. The man they all feared. Now the boot was on the other foot.'

'What was the mistake?'

'The mistake – apparently – was locking Hong Soeung up at all. Duch had some papers in his hand and he was waving them around like a maniac. "Orders from Angka!" he shouted.

"Release that man at once!" The guards hammered off Hong Soeung's shackles then and there and your father stood up a free man. He walked out of the room and, as far as I know, out of the prison for good.'

Su felt a tremor come over her as she tried to comprehend the implications of what Narong was saying. 'No wonder Duch was so confident that my father hadn't died in Tuol Sleng. Not if he was released on Duch's orders.'

'Not on Duch's orders,' Narong corrected her. 'Angka's orders. This came from the highest level. Duch was shouting about Brother Number One. I remember it clearly. The release order came from the top.'

'Pol Pot himself?'

'The same.'

'Why didn't any of this come out before?' Su still found it hard to believe Narong's story.

Narong looked away. 'Sometimes we do not wish to dwell too much on the past. Of course, I remembered the incident when Duch came to the cell. I even told Professor Haq about it one day. But I was never able to put a name to the face. Not till now at least. Now I am sure. If Hong Soeung escaped from Tuol Sleng, this was definitely on Pol Pot's express orders. I remember Duch yelling at the guards: "He's one of ours, you idiots! One of ours! Let him go!"'

'Sweet Jesus!' Su buried her face in her hands.

★★★

Later that evening, Prescott and Su sat on the balcony outside their room at the Cambodiana Hotel gazing, as they had so often before, at the wide sweep of the river in front of them. With the current in the Tonle Sap now flowing strongly to-wards the sea, the tide had turned Prescott thought – in more senses than one.

'Do you think Narong was telling the truth?' Su asked him. 'That's the key thing, isn't it?'

'Ah, that's the sixty-four-thousand-dollar question, isn't it?' Prescott took a long pull at his beer. 'Are they still playing games with you, whoever "they" are? Is this yet another set-up? Or is this, for once, the real McCoy?' He ran his finger around the rim of the glass. 'My gut instinct,' he said at last. 'is that Narong is telling the truth. He did meet your father in Tuol Sleng. Or he believes he did. And he did witness the event he described, namely Duch's bizarre intervention to save a prisoner who, in other circumstances, he probably would have tortured to death. Where does that leave us? It leaves us,

I submit, having to confront the reality that your father was a Pol Pot supporter all along.'

Prescott stretched out a long arm to comfort her. 'I know it's tough to contemplate from today's vantage-point all that we know about the Pol Pot regime. But cast your mind back to the circumstances of the time. You're Hong Soeung, an honest decent man trying to do your best for your family and country. You're a high-level official in Lon Nol's government, a government which you know is by and large a stinking corrupt sewer. You genuinely believe that out there in the field, Pol Pot and his people offer a better alternative. All right, it's a Marxist, Maoist alternative, but you believe it's right in the sense of offering a better deal for the vast masses of your countrymen. But you're a key man in government, so instead of joining the red kerchief brigades in the field, fighting their way towards Phnom Penh and final victory, you become their agent in the capital, the eyes and ears if you like, of the advancing army.'

Su took some comfort from Prescott's words. As much as she wished to believe that her father was still alive, she wanted also to know that he was a man of honour.

As she sat there on the balcony, she found herself recalling with almost total clarity the last time she had seen her father, the way she had flung her arms around his legs to keep him from being dragged away.

'Then why didn't he tell them he was on their side?' she protested. 'Why did he let my mother and I be taken off into the countryside with all the rest? Why didn't he try to contact us, find out what happened to us?'

'I don't have the answers to any of these questions,' Prescott told her gently, 'though I can imagine some of them. For example, if your father had protested his innocence too much when they arrested him, they might have killed him on the spot. And your mother and you as well. If he was a Pol Pot spy, he was in deepest cover. Maybe he had orders not to admit it, not to anyone. As for why he never tried to contact you, maybe he did try and failed. Or maybe he never realised you and your mother survived. Most people didn't. Hundreds of thousands, millions in fact, died. Why shouldn't you have been among them? That was the reasonable supposition. But all that's just for starters. I might be right. Or again I might not.'

'How will I ever know for sure?'

Prescott looked at her in the darkness. How much he loved her, he thought. He would go to the ends of the earth for her. Damn it, he thought, that's just what he had done!

'You've got to find him, Su. It's as simple as that. That's the only way you'll get the answers you need.'

'And where do I start looking?'

★★★

They spent the next hour reviewing everything they knew or thought they knew.

'If what Professor Haq suggests is true,' Prescott says at one point, 'namely that Hong Soeung quite recently wrote out the so-called confessions in his own fair hand, then some-one knows about it. Someone has made contact with him, wherever he is. Someone knows where he is. Even if Soeung just mailed the manuscript to Phnom Penh, which I seriously doubt, someone has been in touch with him. What's more, someone planted the confession in the Tuol Sleng archive.

Otherwise, you wouldn't have found it. Are we to believe that your father came out of hiding, wherever he is, and visited the former prison with the document in his hand, then just waited until the guard's back was turned before conveniently finding the right drawer and the right folder to put his document in?'

'We can't rule it out,' Su said. 'We can't rule anything out.'

'No, we can't,' Prescott agreed. 'The problem is, as you say, we don't know where to begin. As far as the official world is concerned, the Hong Soeung affair is closed. The confessions have been proved to be a forgery from a practical point of view and no-one is out there looking for Hong Soeung himself. He disappeared over a quarter of a century ago and no-one is going to bring him back. But, as I said, someone knows where he is. It doesn't make sense otherwise.'

They went round the course again and again.

'If it's true,' Prescott mused, 'that your father was somehow sprung from Tuol Sleng because he was working for Pol Pot as a secret agent inside the Lon Nol government, then I think it's fair to assume that Hong Soeung held a very high rank indeed in the party. So where does he go when he escapes from Tuol Sleng? Does he join the leadership in Phnom Penh, even under a changed name? Or does he go up-country somewhere on a new assignment? And assuming he did survive, what happens in 1979 when the Vietnamese take over? We know the Pol Pot leadership made for the refuge of their camps at Anlong Veng on the Cambodia-Thailand border. Is that where your father went? Is he still there?'

Su shook her head decisively. 'I don't believe my father went to Anlong Veng. I don't believe he is there now. The word would have got out. And, frankly, I don't know if he was working for Pol Pot and that was the reason he was able to escape from prison. That's one supposition and I admit it sounds plausible. It fits the bill. As you yourself said, Prescott, we'll probably never know for sure until we talk to my father, if we ever do. But from everything I remember about my father, from everything I've heard about him since, one thing stands out.'

'What's that?'

'His dedication to conserving Cambodia's past, particularly the cultural and architectural legacy of the Khmer empire. I believe that this was his lifework and that it was far more important to him than the regime he worked for. Everyone thinks the Khmer Rouge ravaged the great temples up north. But that's not true. American bombing of Cambodia in the early seventies did far more damage to the temples than the Khmer Rouge ever did. Surprising as it may seem, the Khmer Rouge cared about the monuments.'

Prescott listened fascinated. 'So you think Hong Soeung went back to the jungle when he escaped, went back to one of the great historic sites and has been working there ever since?'

'I just feel it,' Su said. 'I can't see my father spending twenty-five years of his life in Anlong Veng or some other Khmer Rouge camp on the border. I can see him pursuing his lifework somewhere, painstakingly studying some great temple complex, rebuilding it perhaps, conserving it certainly, until one day in the fullness of time, some archaeological complex rivalling even Angkor itself will rise from the jungle.'

Prescott's heart went out to her. She so much wanted to believe the best about her father, even now. 'Perhaps you're right,' he said. 'I so much hope you are.'

Su rose to her feet, went into the room and returned to the balcony. She switched on the outside light so that she could see to read. 'Remember what my father wrote in his letter to my mother, Prescott. See the kind of man he is!' She found the passage and read it out. Truth to tell, she could have recited it by heart, so often had she gone over the words since Prescott first brought her the letter from Seattle.

> '...There is a life-time's work here. What a tragedy it is that this war between the Khmers is destroying so much of our heritage. I have a different vision of how things should be. Perhaps I will one day have a chance to work for it. Ta Keo would be a good place to start.'

She looked at him triumphantly. 'Ta Keo! That's the key to it, I'm sure. Father could have gone back there. He could still be there. He says himself there's a lifetime's work among the ruins. And remember what Ting Wei-Ju said? You told me yourself. He said father found the stone head at Ta Keo, the head he presented to King Sihanouk. Doesn't it all add up? It's worth a try, isn't it?'

'You have to find Ta Keo first,' Prescott said, 'before you find your father. That may not be so easy.'

As it turned out, Prescott was right. The following morning, they bought a detailed map of Cambodia which marked amongst other things the known archaeological sites. They were encouraged at first to see several ruins labelled Ta Keo but their hopes were immediately dashed when they realised that none of these sites appeared to be in the area indicated by Hong Soeung in his letter to his wife, Sita. Nor did they correspond with the indications as to location given by Ting Wei-Ju in his account of Hong Soeung's visit to Sihanouk's camp in the Khulen mountains.

'We had better go and consult the experts,' Prescott advised.

Four hours and several false starts later, they had an appointment with the former co-director of the École Française d'Extrême-Orient. By now in his late seventies Arn Bou received them courteously at his home in the suburbs of Phnom Penh. When Su introduced herself, his curiosity was immediately aroused.

'So you are Hong Soeung's daughter,' he said. 'I knew your father well. He was a good man. I am sorry his memory has been traduced in this way. Someone has an axe to grind. That is always the way it is in this country.'

'I believe my father may still be alive,' Su said. 'I'm trying to find him.'

For the next few minutes, without in any way hinting at Hong Soeung's possible connection with the Khmer Rouge, Su explained the problems they were having finding the historic site they were looking for.

'There appear to be several Ta Keo's,' she said.

'That's not surprising,' Arn Bou explained. 'In the Khmer language the words simply mean 'tree temple', denoting ruins found in the jungle. Most often archaeologists and explorers would simply repeat the name the local people used, so of course the name Ta Keo can apply to more than one location...'

'What we are looking for,' Prescott interrupted, 'is a Ta Keo somewhere near the Kulen mountains, north-east of Angkor.

We believe Hong Soeung once found a stone head of Brahma there, a splendid piece which is now in a private collection in China.'

'Do you have a photograph?' Arn Bou asked.

'I'm afraid not.'

'Can you draw it?'

'I doubt it, but I'll try.'

Prescott's draughtsmanship left much to be desired. After a few minutes, Arn Bou interrupted his efforts.

'I'm sorry, I can't tell much from this. If I had a clearer idea of the piece or pieces you are talking about, I might have been of more help. I don't doubt what you're saying, but what you have to remember is that there are hundreds of archaeological sites in this country, many of them still unknown and certainly not excavated, uncovered or restored in any way. Even the great temples of Angkor near Siem Reap disappeared under the jungles for hundreds of years. That's why the work of the École Française was amazing, superb. As a Cambodian I am the first to acknowledge it. For France it was a matter of national pride. I worked with some great men at the École. Jean Laur, Rénée Dumont, Bernard-Philippe Groslier. They had connections, sometimes at the highest level. They had *piston*. The École enjoyed enormous prestige and had considerable resources, including large grants from the French government itself.

If this country had enjoyed a generation of peace maybe the École would have found Ta Keo. But we did not enjoy that luxury. When the civil war broke out in March 1970 following the overthrow of Sihanouk, Groslier – he was the last French curator at Angkor – tried to close the work down in an orderly fashion. Some works were transferred to the National Museum in Phnom Penh. Many, many more were stored in the Depository in Siem Reap. But the task was too enormous. In the end, the French had to leave in a hurry. They were lucky to escape with their lives.

'The Ta Keo you are talking about may or may not have existed,' Arn Bou concluded, 'but one thing is sure. If it does exist, it will still be covered in deepest jungle. Even at Angkor, the jungle has taken back many of the temples which were brought to light by the École.'

★★★

When later that afternoon they returned disappointed to the hotel, the telephone in Prescott's room was ringing. It was Harry Schumberg, the foreign editor of *The New York Times*. He was clearly in a bad mood.

'Where the hell have you been, Prescott? I've been trying to get you all day.'

Prescott's heart sank. The previous day, he had had a very sticky conversation with Schumberg. He had told him that he was still pursuing the Hong Soeung affair and immediately regretted it.

As far as *The New York Times* was concerned, Prescott had not exactly covered himself with glory during his Phnom Penh assignment. 'For Christ's sake, Prescott!' Schumberg had berated him over the telephone, 'you led us by the nose on this one. You lost your objectivity there for a while and we all ended up with egg on our face.'

Prescott had found himself agreeing, willy-nilly, with his

boss. 'Not just egg,' he had muttered into the phone: 'The whole fucking omelette!'

Of course, they had tried to make the best of a bad job. Newspapers were a bit like the stock market. You could make money when the Dow was going up and you could make it when it was going down. You needed the movement. That was all. In much the same way, the recent events in Cambodia had probably sold a fair number of papers around the globe. First, you built up the story, then you knocked it down. The head-lines were what counted.

Following that line of thought, Prescott had tried to talk The Times into allowing him to stay, arguing that he was well-placed to find out the truth behind the Hong Soeung affair.

'It was a put-up job from start to finish,' he had protested over the line to New York. 'They knew Su would fall for it and she did. They made sure of that. And they knew enough about her to know that I would get involved too. And The Times. The whole damn caboodle. Come on, Harry, we need to find out what's behind all this, who "they" are. Why don't I stay put for a while instead of running out of here like a scalded cat with my tail between my legs?'

For a moment, ten thousand miles away in New York, Schumberg had sounded tempted. 'I'll get back to you,' he had said.

Twenty-four hours later, he had obviously thought better of it. No point in sending good money after bad. 'You're going to have to pass on this one, Prescott,' Schumberg instructed. 'We've devoted enough column inches to Cambodia for the time being. If anything else crops up, we'll get it off the wire. Or we'll send a man down from Beijing.'

In the end, if you were a reporter, no matter how senior you were, you had to do what the desk told you to do. After he put the phone down, Prescott walked through to the other room. 'They want me to cover the G8 meeting in Paris,' he told Su. 'The Japan bail-out is high on the agenda and China is knocking at the door. They say they need the Asian perspective and I'm a natural. I'm sorry, Su. I'm going to have to do it. It was time for me to leave anyway. Harry Schumberg is right. I haven't exactly covered myself with glory out here. I probably did lose my objectivity for a while there.'

Su was devastated. 'How am I going to manage without you?'

'I'm afraid you're going to have to.'

CHAPTER 17

Prescott's departure only served to heighten the feeling Su already had that she had been hanging round in Phnom Penh long enough. Sympathetic glances from colleagues were small consolation for her sense that she had been deliberately used, manipulated, played like a musical instrument – she could think of a hundred suitable expressions – and that her own feelings and emotions had featured precisely nowhere in the larger schemes of those, whoever they were, who had devised what had by now become widely known as the Hong Soeung affair. Though she clung fiercely to the belief that her father was still alive, it was clear to her that no-one else in her immediate vicinity shared that view. Even Professor Haq, whom she met on the street one day when she was shopping for food (her hotel room had a small kitchen and, tired of the restaurant, she was beginning to use it), now looked at her blankly when she reminded him of what she thought of as the "Haq hypothesis": namely that the "confessions" were indeed written by Hong Soeung but were of recent origin.

'Drop it, Miss Soeung,' Haq had advised her sharply, glancing nervously over his shoulder as though he himself had already been rapped over the knuckles for talking too much. 'Drop it. No good will come of it. I don't think you will ever know for certain what happened to your father. I know it may sound harsh, but you are not alone in your suffering. Even today, hundreds of thousands of Cambodian families have no idea what happened to their loved ones during the years of terror.'

Prescott's departure only served to increase her sense of isolation. He had sent her a message to say that he had arrived safely in Paris but after that, there had been nothing from him. The time difference between Paris and Phnom Penh made personal communication difficult and she realised he must be busy with the G8 summit. But still she was disappointed. She realised, now that he had left, just how much she had relied on Prescott's solid support. He had been much more than a stout shoulder to lean on in time of stress. He had a strategic vision, could grasp the big picture, discern motives and inter-pret events with far greater lucidity than she was capable of herself. She had known she was too close to the Hong Soeung business to see it clearly. With Prescott gone, she was floun-dering.

She had spoken to her mother once or twice in recent days but Sita Soeung's counsel was erratic. Sita had, up to a point, followed the progress of events. She had learned from the media, from the Cambodian community in Seattle and from Su herself about the re-emergence of Hong Soeung as a key figure in a political drama which was being played out on the other side of the world. But she felt too old, too battered, too fragile to take it all in.

'Of course, you must look for him, darling, if that is what you think is right,' Sita had told her. 'It would be wonderful if you could find him.'

But from Sita's tone, Su knew that her mother was hu-mouring her. She suspected that Sita's lack of conviction was mostly a gesture of self-protection. Sita had missed her husband so much and for so long that she was refusing to allow her hopes to be built up now lest they be dashed to pieces later. No, Su reluctantly admitted to herself, her mother was not much help in her current dilemma.

So when word at last came through from Washington that her long-delayed trip to visit SAVE's Siem Reap facilities was confirmed, Su could not have been more pleased. Andrew Mossman, back at his desk in Washington, had come on the line in person.

'You've been doing a fine job in Phnom Penh under difficult circumstances, Su,' he had told her. 'Now we want to be sure that you're fully briefed on SAVE's northern operations. Go up to Siem Reap. Look at our clinic there. And you may have a chance to get out into the field. We're hoping to see a major breakthrough in the de-mining operations in the next few weeks. Can't tell you much more at the moment. But watch this space.'

When Mossman had rung off, Su had sat staring at the telephone. Was Mossman playing games with her? Her mind went back to that first afternoon when she got back to her apartment to find the letter from SAVE lying on the mat in the hall waiting for her. How nicely judged that particular approach had been! If she had been set up from the start, then surely Mossman had to have been involved.

Before Prescott left for Paris, she had sought his opinion as to whether she should challenge Mossman to his face, but Prescott had strongly advised her against it.

'You won't get anywhere,' Prescott had said, 'and you'll probably find yourself out of a job. These people cover their tracks better than you'll ever know. Frankly, I've no idea at this point what role Mossman has been playing and, if you ask him, he's certainly not going to tell you. He's going to look you straight in the eye and tell you that SAVE's offer of a job was one hundred per cent kosher.'

'Then how come SAVE made that offer at precisely that moment, with the Hong Soeung "confessions" just waiting there in the archive for me to discover?' Su still blushed when she thought of it.

'Don't go so fast,' Prescott had cautioned. 'Maybe the confessions weren't planted in the archive until it was known you were on your way. What about Sarin Bun, the guard in Tuol Sleng? He works for the Interior Ministry, doesn't he? That means he comes under Khin Lay's responsibility ultimately and Khin Lay is the one man whose stature had been enormously increased as a result of the Hong Soeung affair. I'd say the Hun Sen government is on its last legs. Soon we are going to witness a small earthquake in Cambodia.'

'Sarin Bun is Lina Chan's cousin,' Su protested. 'I don't believe he's corrupt.'

'How can you possibly know?' Prescott exploded. 'Maybe he has a wife and three kids to support. Maybe someone offers him a large bribe to look the other way. Maybe someone hints that the Minister himself could be pleased if Bun could find a way of being absent from his post in the archive one afternoon. This is Cambodia, Su. This is Asia. We can't begin to understand how things work here.'

Su had salvaged what she could from this defeat. 'Please don't try to tell me Lina Chan is corrupt, too. I simply won't believe it. I believe Lina is honest as the day is long. Do you know one evening we were sitting together, and she told me straight out that she had once been a member of the Khmer Rouge youth brigade? She didn't have to tell me that. She could have disguised or concealed her past. That's what most people do around here, I've discovered.'

Prescott had backed off at this point, conscious that the professional journalist's almost daily exposure to the worst side of human nature had perhaps made him too callous and cynical. Better once in a while to believe the best about somebody, at least till the evidence clearly pointed in the other direction.

'I'm sure you're right about Lina Chan,' he tried to mollify her. 'Anyway, we're getting off the point which is that Andrew Mossman could be simon-pure in this whole business. As a matter of fact, one might ask why Mossman should be implicated in the Hong Soeung affair when one of the consequences of that affair has been the total humiliation – at least for the time being – of Senator Hillary Rodham Clinton. The Mossmans are meant to be close to Hillary. Caroline in particular is. Why should they want to derail Hillary's Presidential ambitions in 2004 or 2008 for that matter? If you look at it from that point of view, pointing the finger at Mossman doesn't make sense.'

Grudgingly, Su had conceded that Prescott was probably right. Ten minutes after concluding her call with Andrew Mossman, she left SAVE's Phnom Penh office to clear out her room at the Cambodiana.

★★★

Su flew from Phnom Penh to Siem Reap the next morning. She would have preferred to have gone up the Tonle Sap by boat but her colleagues in the SAVE office dissuaded her pointing out that the deteriorating political situation in Cambodia would be likely to exacerbate the already high risks associated with travel up-country.

'Don't do it, Su,' Dr Borei Pen warned her. The young doctor whose skill in rebuilding shattered limbs Su had so much admired during her time in the Phnom Penh clinic went on to explain: 'Armed bandits have a habit of intercepting the boats. If you're lucky, they just rob the passengers of their valuables. If you're not lucky, you can get caught up in a gunfight. They've even been known to take hostages and with an American passport you're a likely candidate.'

An hour after leaving Phnom Penh, the plane touched down in Siem Reap. Su was met by a young man who introduced himself as Koy Chea.

'I'm going to look after you during your time here,' Koy explained. He waved a hand and a four-wheel drive vehicle with the SAVE logo stencilled on the side-doors nosed forward out of the parking lot.

'Air-conditioned, I'm glad to say,' he laughed. 'You need air-conditioning up here. It can be very hot.'

He held the Jeep door for her, and she sank back into the seat welcoming the blast of cool air which greeted her. 'We thought you'd like to go to the hotel first to freshen up,' Koy said. 'After that, they'll be waiting for us at the clinic.'

The Siem Reap hotel where Su was to lodge was a much more modest place than the Cambodiana. The town's main street, as far as Su could see, seemed to consist of an unpaved dirt road with her hotel – the Borei Angkor – being situated about halfway down on the left. The lobby was empty and, judging by the number of keys hanging next to the pigeon-holes, there seemed to be very few other guests besides her-self. The manager, understandably, seemed delighted to see her.

'What happened to all the tourists?' Su asked him in Khmer as she checked in. She had imagined that the temples at Ang-kor Wat would be a popular destination.

'The U.S. State Department is a big problem,' the hotel manager frowned. 'They're telling people not to come to Cam-bodia. Particularly not the north. They seem to be expecting trouble. They've put out a travel advisory. Stay away from the Siem Reap area, they say. But that's unnecessary. Everything's fine here.'

Su nodded in sympathy. 'Washington's running scared nowadays. Ever since the World Trade Centre disaster. It's hard on you people, I know, but I don't blame them.'

The good news, Su reflected as she followed the bellboy to her room, was that there would be no crowds at the temples. She would have the place to herself when she got there.

★★★

In the event, Su didn't pay her first visit to the ruins at Angkor until several days after reaching Siem Reap. The local SAVE office manager had fallen sick on the day of her arrival and Su discovered that she was needed to help organise and direct the steady flow of the sick and injured through the clinic. In some ways the work was a relief. Su realised that her own preoccupations, intense though they seemed, were in reality fairly secondary now that she was being confronted on a day-to-day basis with some of the extremes of human suffering (getting one or more limbs blown off certainly fell into that category from Su's point of view).

SAVE's Siem Reap clinic was much less well-equipped than the Phnom Penh one. The building in which the SAVE team operated was a cramped shed situated down a side street half a mile from the hotel. The facility was crudely partitioned into two rooms, a waiting room and an operating-room. There was a third room to the side, labelled STORES and, during a pause in the proceedings on her first afternoon in Siem Reap, Su cast a curious eye inside.

The place seemed to be filled with wooden crates, stamped with the SAVE logo and with the word FRAGILE stencilled in large black letters on the sides and lid.

Koy Chea, who still seemed to be acting as her minder, followed her in and, when Su enquired what was in the crates, explained: 'All these boxes contain damaged or broken prostheses. They are being shipped over the border into Thailand and then taken down to a repair factory in Bangkok. Once they have been rehabilitated, the prostheses are returned to us. As you may know, the Minister of the Interior has waived customs formalities for us, otherwise we would be drowning in a sea of red tape.'

Su pricked up her ears at the mention of Khin Lay's name. The Minister of the Interior seemed to have his finger in an inordinate number of pies.

'Have you ever met Khin Lay?' she asked curiously.

'Not personally,' Koy replied. 'But he came to Siem Reap

a few weeks ago and I saw him as he drove in from the airport. He has a lot of support in this region. The people were lining the street in the town. They gave the school children the afternoon off and they all turned out with flags and balloons. Khin Lay comes originally from Preah Vihear province but Siem Reap is like his adopted town. We are lucky to have a man like Khin Lay with such an interest in the place. If anyone has stopped the indiscriminate looting of Angkor Wat, that man is Khin Lay. He can bring the army in if he has to and sometimes, he does!'

'Has he ever visited the SAVE clinic here in Siem Reap?'

Koy nodded. 'Yes. But not the last time he was in Siem Reap. The time before. Mr Mossman came specially to greet the Minister.'

Su was surprised. 'All the way from Washington?'

'I believe so. That was when they made the arrangements about the prostheses being shipped to Bangkok. Mr Mossman and the Minister signed an M.O.U.'

'An M.O.U? What's that?' Su asked.

'A Memorandum of Understanding,' Koy explained.

'Ah!' Su nodded. She imagined Mossman would have arranged a special ceremony so that in due course another framed and signed photograph could go up on the glory wall in his Washington office, next to the picture of him greeting Princess Diana. Still, it seemed a long way to come from Washington to Siem Reap just to agree on a system for getting artificial limbs repaired.

As they left the room, Su noted straw sticking out of the sides of one of the wooden boxes where a panel had split. She idly prodded at the crate with her finger and more straw spilled out, some of it mouldy and discoloured. Su was momentarily puzzled. Why were they packing up damaged limbs in mouldy straw? Didn't they have anything better, like plastic bubble-wrap? Before she had time to pursue that line of thought, the gong sounded.

'Tea break's over,' Koy said. 'We had better be getting back.'

'Yes, indeed,' Su nodded. As they left the storeroom, Su noticed that Koy took a key from his pocket and locked the door. 'Worried about burglars?' she asked.

Koy laughed. 'You can't be too careful in Siem Reap. People will steal the tyres off your car if you let them.'

'Why not the wheels too?' Su joked.

The young man laughed again. 'Those too if they can.'

After three days hard work at the clinic, Su was only too glad that the SAVE facility was going to be closed for the whole weekend.

'Normally, we're open on Saturday,' Koy explained. 'But this Saturday we're going to shut for the day. We've got the army in.'

'Whatever for?'

'The crates and boxes, the ones you saw in the store-room. They're being shipped out. The army is sending trucks.'

'I didn't know,' Su said. 'Am I needed?'

Koy shook his head emphatically. 'No, we can handle it. We know what to do. All we need is a skeleton staff. The army has fork-lift trucks and other necessary gear.'

'This isn't the first time?'

'No, and it won't be the last.'

'I'll take your word for it,' Su said. There was something

about the whole business which puzzled her. Why were the damaged artificial limbs being shipped out to Thailand for repair? Why couldn't they repair the prostheses in Siem Reap? Weren't there skilled people available to do the job locally?

Mossman obviously thought not, otherwise he wouldn't have done the deal with the Minister.

★★★

Su hired a guide in the hotel for her first visit to Angkor Wat. The hotel manager recommended a local firm run by his brother.

'My brother will find the best guide for you, I guarantee you,' the manager said. Su had been happy to take his word for it.

At eight a.m. sharp on the Saturday morning, a Cambodian of about her own age, smartly dressed in a white shirt and dark slacks, was waiting for her in the lobby as she came out from breakfast. He seemed disappointed when she addressed him in Khmer.

'I hoped to practise my English,' he said.

Su laughed. 'I need to practise my Cambodian.'

The man's name was Heng Nim. He said he had a car and driver waiting outside for her. Su went to her room to pick up her camera and water-bottle (she knew how quickly you could become dehydrated when you were walking around the ruins with the sun beating down). A few minutes later they were on their way.

Their route took them down the side street where the SAVE office was located. As they passed the clinic, Su saw a couple of army trucks parked in the street outside. Koy had been perfectly well informed, she thought. This *was* the day the army was going to move the crates over the border.

Heng Nim caught the direction of her glance. 'Do you know SAVE?' he asked.

'I work for them.' Su replied. 'What do you think of them? Are they doing a good job?'

'Good job? Oh yes! Very good job!'

The man spoke quickly. Too quickly, Su thought.

Though they had started early, the bumpy, potholed, dirt road leading to Angkor was already crowded with the usual throng of pedestrians, bicyclists, motorcyclists, oxcarts and so on. Garish advertisements lined the sidewalks where a multitude of booths offering every conceivable service (including nail-cutting and hair-shampooing, Su noted) were open for business. Su gazed out of the window, fascinated. It didn't matter if you were the President of the United States or the Queen of England, she thought. If you wanted to visit the great temples of Angkor, this was the route you had to take. She imagined what it would be like to be a bigshot, sitting in the back seat of a limousine being driven through the grubby streets where children could press their sticky hands and faces right up against the window of the car, while they waited for their life to change.

She was tempted to roll her window down and throw out some notes or coins but changed her mind when Heng said: 'Don't. They'll pester you unmercifully if you let them. We'll never get there.'

So they moved on at a snail's pace through the outskirts of Siem Reap, across the river, out past the Grand Hotel d'Angkor and onto the main road to the ruins. On the way Su learned that Heng had been working for the last four years as a tourist guide. Before that he had been a teacher.

'Why did you leave the teaching profession?' Su asked.

'Money,' Heng replied frankly. 'I have a family to support. I earn much more now than I could ever earn teaching. I have a passion for Angkor and all the sites that surround it. There is so much to learn, so much to know. I could be a guide here for fifty years and still there would be so much more for me to learn.'

Over the next two days (she had hired him for the whole weekend), Su came to realise just how lucky she was to have a guide as good as Heng Nim.

'You only have two days, is that right?'

Su nodded. 'I have to work on Monday.'

'Well, it's not much but it's enough to make a start. We shall do Angkor Tom and the Bayon this morning and Angkor Wat this afternoon when the sun is in the West. At dusk we will watch the sun set over the forest and the temples.'

That first Saturday at Angkor was, for Su, one of the most extraordinary days of her life. Though her guide kept up a running commentary as they walked from temple to temple, giving her precise explanations as to the meaning of this or that carving or bas-relief, she listened to what he said with only half her attention. She knew she could always come back to the detail later by consulting the textbooks. What she would never be able to do again – at least without revisiting Angkor – was to absorb the atmosphere of the place, its majesty and mystery.

Having lived most of her life in the United States and being the proud possessor of an American passport and green card, Su certainly considered herself as much an American as a Cambodian. The United States had provided a refuge, a safe haven, when she and her mother had escaped from the horrors of Pol Pot. She had gone to American schools, had a job and an apartment in the nation's capital, had in every sense been integrated into the American way of life – all this she was proud of. Yet now she suddenly felt crudely nationalistic – as a Cambodian.

Centuries before America had been "discovered" the great Khmer empire had been built in Indochina. A series of mighty rulers had over hundreds of years constructed possibly the most spectacular series of monuments the world had ever known. Admittedly, these vast and intricate constructions had been built with sweated labour. Thousands, hundreds of thousands, had died as they dug the ditches and heaved the stones. And the craftsmen who had produced the superb work which she saw at every turn had probably not fared much better than the labouring masses. When their work was done, they would have been ruthlessly cast aside.

Su knew enough history to know that the Khmer civilisation, like most other "great" civilisations of the world, probably came in with a zero on the scorecard of political correctness. Nonetheless, she found it quite possible, in the extraordinary, eery calm of these jungle ruins, to ignore the historical facts, concentrating instead on the superb artistry and sheer scale of the achievements.

From time-to-time, she paused to take photographs but mostly she walked behind the guide, lost in her thoughts. She wondered what it might be like to come back to Cambodia for good, to build up a new life here. After all, but for a twist of fate, this is where she would have been anyway. How would Prescott take it, she asked herself, if she suddenly announced that she was heading east for good? Would that change their plans to get married? Would The New York Times open up a Phnom Penh office?

Around midday, when the heat of the sun was beginning to be uncomfortable, Heng suggested it was time to take a break. They had as planned visited Angkor Tom and the Bayon as well as a couple of the smaller temples. It was time for lunch. The hotel had provided a picnic hamper which they retrieved from the car.

'Let's go over to the trees,' Su said, pointing towards the dense fringe of jungle behind the Bayon. She set off with determined strides carrying the cool box while the guide lugged the hamper.

'Don't go far into the forest,' Heng called out to her as she forged ahead. 'There may be mines!'

Mines! The guide's warning brought Su up short. She waited for Heng to catch up and was happy to let him reconnoitre the area before settling on a likely spot.

'If you keep to the beaten track, you'll generally be safe', Heng told her. 'The problem is so many of the sites are still deep in the jungle. If you try to visit them, you can run into mines. It's not worth the risk.'

★★★

The meal was excellent. As she leaned back against a fallen lintel, contemplating the giant figure of a reclining Buddha which occupied the whole of the northern side of the Bayon, Su found that some of the anxieties of recent days were diminished. The intrinsic peace of the place and the absence of crowds (there was hardly another visitor in sight), together with the sheer splendour of the monuments, had a calming effect on her. Sitting quietly amid the ruins of a great empire was a good way to gain a sense of perspective.

The hotel had included a thermos of tea in the hamper to complete the meal and as she sipped a mug of the fragrant, green liquid, Su found herself wondering what it must have been like to have stumbled across these jungle ruins for the first time.

'The Angkor temples were lost for centuries in the jungle, weren't they?'

Heng nodded. 'That's true. Many of them still are. Even the local tribesmen probably don't know where all the ruins were. What you see here is only the tip of the iceberg. There are hundreds of sites still unexplored. We don't even know where Jayavarman II's first capital city – Amararendrapura – is located. We believe it is somewhere up in the Kulen mountains, but we do not know for sure. To find Amarendrapura would, in my view, rival even the discovery of Angkor in significance. After all, Jayavarman II was the first great ruler of the Angkor era. Without him, there would have been no Angkorian empire.'

Listening to Heng talk, Su realised that he was much more than a run-of-the-mill tourist guide. He was a man deeply versed in all aspects of his trade. He knew the history, he knew the art, he knew the geography.

'How do you know so much?' she asked him.

'I read all the books I can. And then you learn as you go along. Every day you learn something new.'

'Did you ever hear of a site in this region called Ta Keo?' Su asked. 'I know there are other Ta Keo's in different parts of Cambodia and that it is a common enough name. Might there be a Ta Keo up here? In the Kulen mountains, perhaps. You were talking about the Kulen mountains a moment ago.'

Heng shook his head. 'I've not heard of such a site up here, but that doesn't mean there isn't one. What you have to re-member is that the local people almost always had their own name for some jungle-covered ruin. It was only "undiscov-ered" in the sense that no-one from the West had discovered it.'

Su laughed. 'Cultural imperialism? The locals didn't count.'

Heng laughed too. 'You could call it that if you like. But I'm not going to knock all the foreign explorers who came here. Okay, there were some like André Malraux who were basical-ly rip-off artists. He came to this country and tried to pillage some of finest treasures before he was caught. But there were others who were truly dedicated to the conservation of this country's heritage.'

'Who for example?'

'Well, take Bernard-Philippe Groslier. With the onset of civil war in Cambodia in the earlier seventies, he and his team at the École Francaise d'Extrême-Orient worked round the clock to protect Angkor's treasures. Hundreds of objects were stored away for safe keeping, priceless carvings and statues and ornaments, all of which in the fullness of time can be restored to their rightful place. That is the debt we owe to the foreigner too.'

Su was intrigued. She remembered the conversation she and Prescott had had with Arn Bou, the former co-director of the École Française d'Extrême-Orient. 'You say hundreds of the objects which the French team removed are still in storage. Can they be visited? Can they be inspected?'

Heng shook his head. 'Apart from what was sent to Phnom Penh, all the pieces are in the Depository, a warehouse in Siem Reap. It is not open to the public. It never has been. The Ministry of the Interior guards it very closely. No-one is allowed in. Even I have never been there.'

'I suppose one day, when stability has returned to this country, the warehouse will be opened, and the treasures brought out again into the light of day?'

Heng looked dubious. 'I'm not so sure.'

'Not sure about what? About the return of stability or the return of the treasures?'

'Both. Will peace ever truly return to Cambodia? And are the treasures still there? Are all of them still there? I doubt it. The temptations are too great.'

Su wanted to press him to talk further but Heng briskly gathered up the picnic things.

'Come,' he said. 'We have so much to do this afternoon. We must not delay.'

CHAPTER 18

They spent the whole afternoon at Angkor Wat itself. Even though there were more visitors at this, the crown jewel in Cambodia's archaeological diadem, than there had been at the sites they had visited earlier in the day, so vast was the scale of the place that Su had no sense of being crowded. She walked with her guide around the water-filled moat, she marvelled at the great bas-reliefs, she climbed up the steps to the upper levels of the sanctuaries.

On several occasions, Heng Pointed out to her a niche, plinth or pedestal where a statue would once have stood. 'Still in the Depository,' he commented. 'Next year, they may bring it back. Maybe.'

Seeing the empty places with her own eyes made Su appreciate as nothing else could have done the sheer immensity of the effort Groslier and his colleagues at the École Française had made to safeguard the most precious items at Angkor Wat. How tragic it was that it had taken so long for the pieces to be brought back out of safe keeping!

At the end of the day, they left Angkor Wat to drive some ten miles along a jungle road. They parked the car in a rough clearing at the foot of a pyramid-shaped hill and, declining the offer of a ride on the back of an elephant, climbed up on foot to the summit. Here, amid the ruins of yet another temple, they sat in silence watching the sun go down. The jungle stretched out all around and, in the distance, Su saw the shimmer of the great Tonle Sap lake and, nearer at hand, the glint of the river connecting the lake to Siem Reap and Angkor itself.

Sitting next to her, Heng Pointed out a distant line of mountains. 'Those are the Kulen mountains. It is believed the Khmer emperors quarried the stone for the temples there, then brought them via the lake and the river to Angkor.'

Could we do that today, Su wondered? Would we know how to cut and carry the stone? We might be able to fly to the moon, but would we be able to harness the region's hydraulic energy in the way those ancient civilisations managed? She doubted it very much.

Just before sunset, a hush descended on the waiting crowd. They watched the dark shadows fall across the jungle until at last they engulfed the great ruins of Angkor Wat. Minutes later, all that was left of the day was a distant red glow in the sky.

★★★

The following day, Sunday, they again made an early start. Su was waiting in the hotel lobby at eight a.m. Heng arrived promptly. After a few minutes' delay while the lunch-hamper was being prepared, they headed out of Siem Reap towards the south-west. After a short stretch of tarmac, the road deteriorated sharply into a series of fissures and potholes.

'Banteay Srei is only twenty miles from Angkor,' Heng told her, 'but it may take us two hours to get there.'

'How long has the road been open? Are you sure it's safe?' Su asked.

Heng had told her the previous evening that he planned to take her to Banteay Srei so Su had had time to do her homework. Both the guidebooks she consulted warned that Banteay Srei, though one of the outstanding sites of the Angkor era, should be considered off-limits owing to the presence of Khmer Rouge remnants operating in the region. Not many months before a Briton travelling to Banteay Srei had been intercepted and taken hostage. Though negotiations had been begun for his release, he had been summarily executed before they could bear fruit. Su was keen as mustard to see the temple but even so there were some practical limits to her enthusiasm, like not wanting to end up dead.

'No, I'm not absolutely sure it's safe,' Heng admitted, 'but the information I have is that in recent months the Khmer Rouge has pulled out of the area. The government has been stepping up the pressure. The safety of tourists has become a national priority.'

'Not surprising, given the amount of money they bring in,' Su commented. 'So where have the Khmer Rouge disappeared to?'

Heng paused while the driver negotiated a particularly hazardous pothole, then replied. 'Now, that's the interesting thing. Normally, after a foray to show they're still in business, the Khmer Rouge tend to pull back and regroup on Anlong Veng which is their historic stronghold. That's where Pol Pot held out until his death and it's where Ieng Sary and Khieu Samphan are to be found now under the terms of the deal they struck with the government. But there are rumours that – besides An Veng – the Khmer Rouge have a new redoubt, somewhere in the Kulen mountains, north-east of Angkor.'

'What kind of rumours?' Su asked sharply. Mention of the Kulen mountains in this context pricked her interest.

Heng shrugged. 'Bazaar talk. Nothing concrete.'

The guide clearly didn't want to be drawn further so Su concentrated on the scenery instead. What a relief it was, she thought, finally to be deep in the countryside. There might be bandits out here but, as a compensation, there was that marvellous sense of having left the clamour and fumes of the city behind. There was a magic and a purity about the vast expanse of paddy fields stretching out on either side. Every mile or so, they would pass a typical Cambodian farmhouse built on stilts with room for animals and implements underneath. People stared at them curiously as they passed. A child waved.

'I don't think they've seen much traffic on this road recently,' Su said.

Heng nodded. 'I should think we are the first of the morning.'

Whatever misgivings Su might have had about the wisdom of the enterprise, they reached Banteay Srei without incident and spent the whole morning at the temple. Su was completely staggered by the place. Banteay Srei was possibly the most beautiful building or group of buildings that she had ever seen. In scale, it was a miniature Angkor Wat, delicate and intricate where Angkor Wat was stupendous and overwhelming. And the colour was out of this world, a rose-red sandstone which blended magically with the surrounding jungle.

'What makes Banteay Srei unique among all the sites in the Kingdom,' Heng informed her, 'is that the bas-reliefs here are exceptionally deep, almost fully-rounded carvings. The special sandstone they used here is so firm they could do that without the rock crumbling.'

As they walked round the complex, Heng once more had the opportunity to point out the empty places where key objects had been removed.

'Malraux?' Su asked.

'No, not Malraux. Because the authorities intercepted Malraux before he could take the pieces out of the country, he was forced to bring back what he stole. Even though Malraux's men used saws to remove some of the carvings, our experts managed to repair most of the damage. So we can't really blame Malraux for the state of Banteay Srei. But there have been other later thefts where we have not been so lucky in catching the culprit. And worst of all, of course, is the fact that so much is still in the Depository.'

'With bandits still operating in the region, maybe this isn't the time to open up the Depository and bring the pieces back,' Su suggested.

Heng nodded. 'You could be right.'

They broke for lunch, just as they had the previous day. Over the picnic which the hotel had provided, Su once again found herself being drawn into deep conversation with her guide. She learned far more about him on the second day than she had on the first. She heard about his wife and children, about his own dreams and ambitions.

'I don't want to be a guide for ever,' he told her towards the end of their meal. 'I would like to be a poet too.'

'A poet?'

'Why not? The land has suffered so much. The time for poetry is now. These ruins sing to me.' He waved his hand at the fallen stones on which they were sitting to have their picnic. 'We should all sing in our different ways. My way would be through poetry.'

'Can you recite some now?'

'If you like.'

Heng didn't make a big performance of it. He didn't puff out his chest and close his eyes. He simply sat there and re-cited, in an almost matter-of-fact way, two or three short lyric poems. Su was deeply moved. Most poignant of all were the memories of her father that came to her at that moment. For the first time in years, she felt she was remembering the actual sound of her father's voice.

'My father loved poetry,' she told Heng. 'He would recite poems to us in the evening instead of reading stories. I wish you could have met my father.'

'I wish so too.'

As they sat there in the shadows of the temple, Su sudden-ly felt that she both needed and wanted to talk about her fa-ther. In recent days, she had tried to put Hong Soeung out of her mind. The trail seemed to have gone cold. Nobody else seemed to be interested. Now, with a sympathetic listener, she found herself in full flow.

'It would mean so much to me, so much to my mother, to know if he is still alive. Or at least to know, definitely, that he is dead.'

'I would like to help you if I can,' Heng said.

He sounded so earnest, so sincere that Su could have hugged him.

★★★

Immensely refreshed and invigorated by her weekend among the ruins, Su arrived at SAVE's Siem Reap clinic bright and early on Monday morning. She noticed straightaway that the door to the storeroom was open and that the crates had disappeared. After consulting rapidly with colleagues, Su decided to use the extra space now available to create an extension to the waiting-area, thus relieving some of the pressure on the outer office.

'I'm afraid you can only use this room temporarily,' the office manager warned her sternly. 'In a few weeks' time we shall be preparing another shipment of damaged prostheses for Bangkok and we will need the storage space.'

On her first day at work in Siem Reap, Su had taken an instant dislike to the man. He was an officious individual who, from the moment she arrived, had seemed to resent Su's presence as though he suspected that Su might, accidentally or on purpose, upset some favourite applecart.

'I quite understand, Mr Tran,' Su replied coldly. 'But let's use the place while we can, shall we?'

For the next three days Su worked at full stretch. One of the areas she specially concentrated on was record keeping. It seemed to her that the clinic was almost totally focussed on the curative and palliative side of its role, namely prescribing and fitting prostheses, rather than the preventative side.

'Surely,' Su argued vehemently at a mid-week staff meeting, 'we should be able to use the data we have to pinpoint the landmine clearance priorities. We help rebuild people's shattered limbs and I know SAVE does a magnificent job in that respect, but shouldn't we be developing a much more sophisticated database? Where have these people received their injuries? What kind of injuries are they? As I understand it, different types of landmine produce different types of injury.

If we did in-depth interviews with the people who come to the clinic and passed the information on to the proper authorities, we might be able to avoid some of these injuries and save lives as well.'

Tran, the office manager, rolled his eyes as Su was talking as though to indicate that the last thing a landmine victim would want was a catechism by some social worker. But others around the table supported her. The staff meeting broke up after authorising Su to establish a system of recording, wherever practicable, the place where landmine injuries had occurred and the nature of those injuries.

'You'll have to do the interviewing yourself,' Heng informed her as he gave his grudging consent. 'We really don't have spare staff for that.'

So Su had moved a table and some chairs into the ex-storeroom and reorganised the flow of patients from the waiting room to the operating room so as to include a neat loop past her desk. She found a large-scale map of the northern provinces of Cambodia and pinned it on the wall.

'If I can get the name of the place where they were injured from the victims,' Su explained to her co-workers, 'then I have a chance of pinpointing that place on the map.'

Overhearing the remark, the office manager scoffed. 'Maps? They're mainly fiction. Local people have their own names for most places. You won't find them on the map.'

Undeterred, Su set to work. By close of business that day, several dozen coloured pins had sprouted on the wall map behind her. 'Blue for one leg injury,' she announced to curious staff. 'Red for both legs. Yellow pins indicate arm injuries.' She pointed with her pencil. 'Already you can see the first clusters emerging. That's where they should be sending in the de-mining teams.'

This was the point at which Tran exploded. 'De-mining teams! What de-mining teams? Do you see any de-mining teams in Siem Reap or anywhere around? The government has no resources for de-mining, no equipment, no sniffer dogs. This is all fantasy. A pure waste of time!' With that he had stormed off.

Su had been distressed by the man's outburst. 'Is it true what Tran says?' she asked Koy Chea whose all-purpose role as minder-come-assistant now included the tasks of notetaker. 'Is de-mining actually a fiction? Will we never be able to prevent as opposed to palliate these terrible injuries?'

'We certainly appreciate what you are doing,' said Koy, 'and we believe the data gathered will be valuable. But it is unfortunately true that at the moment, de-mining operations have come to a halt in almost the whole of the northern part of the country. Of course, that may change in the future. But massive resources will be needed.'

It wasn't clear to Su whether Koy spoke for all his colleagues but from the nods of assent which greeted his remarks he certainly appeared to speak for some of them.

Back in her hotel room that evening, Su had found herself consumed with doubt. She had, she knew, been carried away by the force of her own enthusiasm. Typical bloody American do-gooder she told herself harshly. You come in. You think you know all the answers. You clap your hands and expect people to snap to... and it's all probably futile.

It had been a long and thirst-making day. She went down to the hotel restaurant for dinner and had a beer with her meal, then another. At last, her mood lightened. As Koy said, things could change. The information she was gathering might not be of any value now, but one day it could be. She decided that for the time being, at least, she would press on with her interviews and her little coloured pins. There was also a question of face. She was enough of a Cambodian to know that losing face was one thing. Being seen to lose face was something else altogether.

The following morning Su was at her table interviewing amputees with a bright, cheery smile on her face as though the previous night's anxieties had been a mere mirage. By eleven a.m., six more coloured pins, four blue, one red and one yellow, had appeared on the wall-map.

Around half past eleven, a forty-year-old man with one missing leg hopped across the room with the aid of a crutch and sat at the table opposite her. Su asked him some preliminary questions – age, family status, occupation, income. This was standard SAVE procedure. You asked the questions, even if the answers were sometimes less than illuminating. Then she came to the part of the questionnaire which she herself had devised.

'Where did you sustain your injuries?' she asked.

'In the leg, of course.' The man looked at her as though she was a raving lunatic.

'No, I mean, in what part of the country?'

'In Ta Keo,' the man replied.

Su wasn't sure she had heard him correctly. 'Please can you repeat that?'

'Ta Keo,' the man said again.

'Where is this Ta Keo?' Su was trying not to betray the excitement she felt.

The man shrugged. 'Far away. They carried me over the mountains and through the forest to bring me here.'

'Who is "they?"'

A shutter seemed to come down across the man's eyes. He said nothing. It was as though he had not heard the question.

Su tried another tack. 'Could you point Ta Keo out to me?' She indicated the map on the wall behind her.

The man looked vaguely in the direction Su was pointing and again shook his head. Either he didn't understand about maps, Su thought, or else he didn't know where Ta Keo was in cartographical terns.

She made one last effort. 'Do you live in Ta Keo?'

The man nodded. 'Near Ta Keo.'

'What kind of place is it?'

The man's reply was suddenly surprisingly explicit. 'A temple covered in jungle. Many temples. Much jungle.'

She shivered involuntarily. 'When we have fitted you with a new leg, how will you return to Ta Keo?'

'I will walk, of course,' the man said simply. 'That's why I am here. To walk again.'

Su made a sudden decision. She didn't know whether SAVE would authorise it. She suspected not. The organisation had a clear policy that transport both to and from the clinic was the responsibility of the amputee and/or his family. But she didn't care. Somehow, she would find a way.

'We could help you return to Ta Keo,' she said. 'We could arrange transport: jeeps, mules, boats – that kind of thing. Would you agree to that?'

For the first time the man's face lit up. For all his stoicism, he couldn't have been relishing the prospect of a lonely trek across the mountains with a new, artificial limb.

'Yes, I would agree to that.' And then he added, almost craftily. 'The risks must be your responsibility.'

'What risks? What do you know?' Su pressed him.

For the next few minutes, Su tried to establish without success where Ta Keo was, who lived there and how they would get there. But the man refused to talk further.

'If you come with me, you will see for yourself,' was all he would say.

'And you know the way?' Su wanted to be sure they would not be chasing some will-o'-the-wisp.

The man looked at her scornfully. 'I have lived there all my life. Of course, I know the way.'

CHAPTER 19

On the whole, Prescott hated having to cover the annual gathering of the G8, or Group of Eight, top-dog nations. He had been to over a dozen such meetings in his time. Most often they were formal affairs with the final "summit" communiqué pre-cooked by the "sherpas", the only drama being whether some last 'i' would be dotted or 't' crossed in an otherwise bland and unrevealing text.

But the G8 meeting which took place in Paris in early December 2001 was another story. The anti-globalisation protesters had first been heard at the World Trade Organisation's conference in Seattle in December 1999. There the local Police had at first appeared stunned by the appearance of balaclava-helmeted rioters, burning barricades and trashing McDonalds. Not until the third day had they decided to replace their "softly, softly" approach with a more vigorous policy of retaliation and by then, the meeting had degenerated into chaos with delegates unable to reach the conference venue without risk to life and limb.

After Seattle, the protesters had gone from strength to strength. Prague, Washington, London, Genoa – all these were cities where, welded into a new powerful force through the opportunistic use of the internet and email, the anti-globalisation protesters had gathered in their thousands to cause trouble. Even the World Trade Center tragedy had not held them back for long. After a period of relative inactivity when they had obviously been considering their options, the anti-globalisation protesters had returned with a vengeance. There were those who suspected that some of the AGPs might actually have links with the terrorist networks targeted by the United States and its allies, but proof was, as always, hard to come by.

As the protests continued, lessons were learned on both sides. The demonstrators perfected their attacking techniques – the jeers, the taunts, the banner-waving, the dramatic abseiling from high buildings, the hit-and-run tactics; the authorities in their turn developed increasingly effective counter-measures, including sealing-off the conference centres with solid walls of police or, in the case of the Genoa meeting, ensuring that the participants were screened from trouble by incarcerating them on board a commandeered cruise-liner anchored off-shore in the Mediterranean.

When France's turn to host the meeting came round, President Chirac indicated that he was going to hang tough. Though some of his advisers urged him to shift the event to another location (to a site high in the French Alps, for example which could only be reached by helicopter), Chirac scorned all such suggestions. He had made his name as the Mayor of Paris. Paris was the rock on which he had built his political career. To hold the G8 meeting anywhere other than Paris was unthinkable. *Impensable*, Chirac intoned, addressing the nation on television. With a solemnity worthy of President de Gaulle, he promised that France would never yield to violence. *La France ne cédera jamais à la violence.*

Well, Prescott reflected, as the tear-gas bombs exploded in

front of the Louvre (where the "summit" was being held) for the second day running, France was certainly paying a high price for Chirac's obstinacy. Even the famous CRS riot police were having trouble containing and controlling the protesters who at one stage actually launched a sortie across the river Seine itself, using rubber-boats and full commando gear. This is insane, Prescott thought. It's war by another name.

In this atmosphere of crisis, even the journalists were excluded from the building. The doors of the Louvre were firmly closed to all but the selected few. Tanks ringed the whole complex. Food was taken in and occasional messengers emerged with crumbs of news as to the progress of the deliberations, but they weren't the kind of crumbs, Prescott thought, you could bake a cake with.

As he twiddled his thumbs waiting for something to happen, Prescott found his mind constantly wandering in the direction of Cambodia, the other side of the world. Above all, he wondered what Su was doing. He had tried to contact her on several occasions but without success. She had checked out of the Cambodiana. SAVE's office in Phnom Penh had given him a number for their Siem Reap branch but so far, he had been unable to get through. Was she, he asked himself, still pursuing the chimera of her father's disappearance? If so, what progress had she made? What were her plans? What were her next steps?

With time on his hands, Prescott's thoughts moved down strange speculative paths. He found himself focussing increasingly on the key question of Hong Soeung's identity. Surely, he said to himself, if Hong Soeung had indeed been Khmer Rouge cadre, a senior figure in the Cambodian Communist Party, there should be some trace of him somewhere in the archives?

One evening, during a more than usually protracted lull in the proceedings – the G8 participants were at a "working lunch" in the Élysée Palace, but the Press corps was still on stand-by – he put a call through to Professor Robert Jesson at the Johns Hopkins School of Advanced International Studies in Washington, DC.

'Hi, Bob, how are you doing?' Prescott had greeted him. 'Did you get back from Beijing all right? Great to see you there!'

After some banter about how the protesters in Paris seemed to have got the better even of President Chirac's much-vaunted anti-riot squads, Prescott came to the point.

'Bob, I'm still hung up on this Hong Soeung business. There seems to be a possibility that Soeung might at one stage have been a high-level official in the Khmer Rouge. Might there be a record of that somewhere?'

There was a pause at the other end. Then Jesson said, 'Hell, Prescott, you don't give up, do you? Let me get back to you on that. I'm off to the Club for lunch. It's that time of day, you know, over here. But I'll give it some thought and call you as soon as I'm back in the office.'

A twinge of regret came over Prescott as he replaced the receiver. He envied the quiet certainties of Bob Jesson's life. Unless he was out of town, there were few days, he knew, when Bob wouldn't step over to the Cosmos Club for lunch.

He had given Jesson his cell phone number and a couple of hours later, when the assembled international press corps had been able to report nothing more significant than the fact that the world leaders had moved on from cheese to dessert ('that's the way it is in Paris, France, as opposed to Paris, Texas,' Prescott wrote, 'cheese first, dessert later'), the call from Washington came through.

'Do you think Hong Soeung was a KR cadre right from the start?' Jesson asked by way of a preliminary. 'I mean: was he in on the ground-floor, if you see what I mean?'

'Might well have been,' Prescott said. 'We can't exclude that possibility.'

'In that case,' Jesson told him, 'you'll need to look at the first official history of the Cambodian Communist Party. That came out in 1972. As a matter of fact, until that document appeared, Pol Pot and entourage kept totally quiet about the fact that the Khmer Rouge was a communist party and part of the Communist International. This was the first time they acknowledged the matter publicly.'

'Will the history give the names of the key people?'

'Bound to,' Jesson replied. 'One of the distinguishing features of those early communist regimes – China, Vietnam, Korea, Cambodia, you name it – is that they were meticulous record keepers. Someone goes to the bathroom, someone else makes a note of it.' Jesson laughed at his own joke. He had clearly had a good lunch, Prescott reflected. Usually, academics tended to be a bit more buttoned-up in their use of language.

'Where will I find it, this official history?' Prescott asked.

'Well, since you're in Paris, you could try the Bibliothèque Nationale. The official history of the Cambodian Communist Party was originally published in Khmer but there would almost certainly have been a French version. The intellectual hinterland of all those early Communist regimes was France. Zhou Enlai, as you will remember, studied in Paris. So did the Khmer Rouge leaders. I'm sure you'll find what you're looking for in the BN. They'll have a section on Cambodia. Look for Cambodge. They'll probably have a whole roomful of documents. Dammit, France ruled Indochina for the best part of a century and they're proud of it. The French don't have the hang-ups about colonialism that we have.'

It was as a direct result of this conversation with Bob Jesson that Prescott found himself in a taxi, bound for Neuilly, the Paris suburb where thanks to measures of decentralisation introduced by former President Francois Mitterrand, the Asian archives of the Bibliothèque Nationale had been relocated.

As the vehicle sped north up the quai from the Louvre, Prescott smiled to himself. Under normal circumstances he would have been waiting with an increasingly jaded press corps for the final "wrap-up" from the G8 meeting. As it was, he had delegated that chore to a new young colleague from the Paris office of *The New York Times*. What was the point of being a veteran reporter, if you couldn't occasionally behave like one?

An hour later, Prescott was sitting in front of a keyboard consulting the Bibliothèque Nationale's computerised catalogue. As Bob Jesson had surmised, the French national library's Asian collection was both extensive and well-arranged. It took Prescott only a minute or two to locate the text he was looking for and less than thirty minutes after that it was delivered on the conveyor belt to his cubicle.

The book looked fragile. The paper had yellowed, and the spine was beginning to crumble. Prescott opened the volume carefully and began to read. His command of French was not brilliant, but it was adequate. From time to time he made notes.

> *Saloth Sar comes to France in September 1949, he wrote. Takes courses in radio-electricity. Shares lodgings with Ieng Sary in Cite Universitaire. Adopts pseudonym Pol Pot as cover. April 1950 moves into new lodgings at 31 Rue Letellier, sharing with another Cambodian student who is studying archaeology. No name given. Summer 1952 Saloth Sar (Pol Pot) marries Khieu Ponnary, sister of Khieu Thirith (Khieu Thirith was already married to Ieng Sary). Returns to Cambodia Jan 1953. Joins Viet Minh...*

Prescott paused. Slow down, he told himself. Don't rush this.

For the next hour, Prescott worked his way laboriously through the rest of the document. Though he studied every paragraph carefully, there was, as far as he could ascertain, no further reference to the mysterious student of archaeology who shared lodgings with Pol Pot in Rue Letellier at the beginning of the 1950s. The official history covered in great detail Pol Pot's return to Cambodia, the support given to the CPC by the Chinese Communist Party, the negotiations in Beijing between Ieng Sary and Zhou Enlai and so on and so forth. But of the enigmatic scholar, there was not one single further mention. It was almost as though, through some act of historical revisionism, he had been air-brushed out of the record, with no trace beyond that first tantalising reference to some salad days in Paris.

When he had reached the end of the document, Prescott

went back – yet again – to the key passage. Re-examining the text with special care, he noticed that a previous reader had scribbled a pencilled annotation in the margin beside the paragraph describing Pol Pot's stay in 31, Rue Letellier. The note had been partially erased which was the reason Prescott had missed it on first reading. He held the book up to the light, trying to make out what had been written. Finally, he thought he had it.

'Père no. 4?' he read. What could that mean? He peered again. This time he made out the "r" after the letter. Not 'père,' he thought, but 'frère.' Frère no. 4? Brother no. 4?

Jesus! Prescott thought. Brother Number Four! The whole world knew that Pol Pot was Brother Number One, Ieng Sary was Brother Number Two and Khieu Sampham was Brother Number Three. This was the famous triumvirate which had brought the Khmer Rouge to power in Cambodia and guided its fortunes over so many years. Was there a fourth man too? A Brother Number Four? And was Pol Pot's anonymous fellow-lodger that very man?

If the rules of the Bibilothèque Nationale had permitted smoking, Prescott would at this point have lit a cigarette, left his cubicle and paced up and down some convenient corridor. As it was, confined to his reader's cubby-hole, he had to content himself with staring intently at the greenly luminous screen of the monitor in front of him. Who had made that marginal annotation, he wondered? And when had it been made?

For a minute or two Prescott fiddled with the keyboard in front of him. Maybe if he pressed the right button the screen would light up and tell him all he needed to know. Who took the book out and when? Names, dates and telephone numbers. In the movies, at least, that's what might happen.

But real life, as he knew, wasn't like the movies. After a while he gave up on his attempts to manipulate the keyboard. He gathered up his notes and made ready to leave. As he did so, he noticed an instruction which said: 'On leaving the reader's cubicle, please replace borrowed books on the conveyor belt.'

'Dammit,' Prescott inwardly exploded. 'I'll do no such thing! This is a god-darn library and libraries should have librarians. I'm going to talk to a real live human being before I go.'

Carrying the book in his hand, he went in search of a human face. He had walked about ten steps towards the exit when a buzzer sounded and a young woman, emerging from nowhere, hurried up to him.

'It is not permitted to leave the cubicle with a book,' she warned him in French.

'So sorry!' Prescott apologised. In his haste to comply with the woman's instructions, he managed to drop his notes. The librarian graciously helped him to pick them up and escorted him back to the cubicle. She hovered by the door, waiting for him to place the book on the belt. Prescott decided to seize his opportunity.

'This book here,' he said (in French) pointing to the history in his hand, 'was published in 1972. It has probably been in the Bibliothèque Nationale since then. Is it possible to know how often it has been asked for by a reader?'

The young woman seemed intrigued by the general air of disorder which Prescott managed to convey at this point.

'Why do you want to know?' she asked.

'Just curiosity,' Prescott smiled. 'Can your computer system tell you that kind of thing?'

'Pah!' the young woman exclaimed with true Gallic scorn. 'This is the most advanced library system in the world. Of course, we can tell you who asked for the book and when. Every reader has an ID number, even a temporary visitor like you. You had to fill in a form when you arrived, didn't you? And they gave you a magnetic card for the console? Yes? Well, that card is your unique ID. Every time, you ask for a book, the information is recorded.'

'How long have you been doing this?' Prescott asked.

'Since 1995,' the young woman replied. 'When we moved to the current site, we installed the new systems.'

'1995 is good enough for me. Would you mind taking a look?'

The young woman seemed to relish the challenge of meeting Prescott's request. Computerising the system had, Prescott suspected, in some respects made the librarian's life duller. There was certainly less opportunity for personal contact.

'We'll soon see.' She smiled as she sat down at the keyboard and tapped away.

Moments later, the answer flashed up on the screen. Since the mechanisation of the archives, only one request had been made by a reader for the first Official History of the Cambodian Communist Party. The ID number of the borrower was shown, as well as the date and time of the request which, Prescott noted, was two days previously.

The librarian pointed at the screen. 'There is the answer to your question. The book was borrowed just once since 1995.

Very recently, in fact, as you can see.'

Prescott wondered how far he could push it. 'Any way of finding out the name of the borrower?'

If he had been in Cambodia, he might have palmed a twenty-dollar bill at this point, but he sensed that option was not available. He tried charm instead. 'I'm a journalist as a matter of fact,' he told her. 'I was thinking of doing a piece about the brilliant new system you have at the Bibliothèque Nationale.'

The young woman had already made up her mind. 'We have no reason to keep the ID of borrowers secret. It's only a matter of convenience.'

Moments later, she brought a name up on the screen: Mercier, Jean-Claude.

'Tiens!' Prescott exclaimed. 'I wonder if that could possibly be the great man himself? How many others could there be?'

'You mean the boss of JCM?' The young woman was impressed. 'If Mr Mercier came here a couple of days ago, I'm sorry I missed him. I'm a big fan. Strange, though. You don't imagine a big cheese, le grand fromage, like Jean-Claude Mercier coming to the library in person and doing his own research.'

Prescott couldn't let it go now. There was too much at stake. If Mercier himself had been ferreting around in the Cambodian archive at the BN, there had to be a good reason.

He remembered he had filled in his own address on the form when he had entered the library that afternoon. 'Does your system show the address of the borrower as well as the name?' he asked.

'Certainly,' the librarian replied. 'In spite of our best efforts to prevent it, readers sometimes go off with books and we have to track them down. There's another reason too. Even the BN has to raise funds for special projects. The government won't pay for all the improvements we need. Not in these days of financial austerity. Knowing the addresses of our readers means we can target them with appropriate literature.'

Prescott didn't want to be drawn into a discussion of the privatisation of public services or the ethics of direct mail. Not at this point anyway. 'Just as a matter of interest,' he pleaded, 'just to satisfy my curiosity, shall we see what address you have for this Mr Mercier?'

'My curiosity too,' the young woman said. She read out the address from the screen. 'JCM headquarters. 146 Boulevard Haussmann, Paris. There you have your answer, do you not?'

'Indeed, I do,' Prescott replied, 'though quite what it means is another matter. Thank you so much.' He took the woman's hand and shook it warmly. 'You've no idea how helpful you've been.'

Blushing, the young woman stayed behind for a moment after Prescott left, making sure that the belt carried the book safely back to the stacks.

***

As it turned out, Prescott returned to the temporary Press Centre which had been erected in the Tuileries in time to file a piece after all. The G8 participants had lingered over their working lunch until well into the afternoon and the official summit communique did not finally emerge until some minutes after Prescott reached his desk.

He felt in an optimistic, bullish mood. Hounds were running. The scent was hot.

'Thanks, Bill,' he said, taking the communiqué from the hands of the younger man. 'I think I'll bash this one out if you don't mind, otherwise they may start wondering back in New York why they're paying my hotel expenses in Paris.'

'They may have a point,' his colleague snapped, irritated that his own name would not, after all, be on the story.

Prescott glanced sharply at him. Cocky, young bastard, he thought. Reminds me of myself once upon a time. Rolling up his sleeves, he began to hit the keys. 'G8 leaders meeting in Paris,' he wrote, 'late this afternoon, concluded possibly the most turbulent summit ever held...'

For the next hour he typed away. When he finished, he read through what he had written. He belonged to the old-fashioned school of journalists who believed that it was worth checking a piece before you pressed the button. He made one or two minor alterations, then – satisfied – he clicked SEND.

Leaning back in his chair, he watched his colleagues going about their task. God knows how many different newspaper and television stations from all over the world had people in Paris. The huge Press tent was full of men and women, typing and telephoning, as they met their various deadlines. How many reporters were present, he wondered? Hundreds, certainly. Maybe thousands. But were they covering the right story, he wondered? Somehow, he doubted it. He was beginning to believe there was an altogether bigger story out there somewhere.

★★★

Later that evening, Prescott ran into Larry Steinbeck, the White House Press Secretary, in the bar of the Hotel Crillon. Prescott was surprised to see him.

'I thought you'd all gone back on Air Force One after the meeting,' he said.

'Hell, no,' Larry smiled. 'Air Force One is still here. The President reckons he's earned some time off for good behaviour this week and France is a good place to take it. Mrs Bush was pleased about that, I can tell you. So were the girls. No ID checks in the bars and bistros here!'

Prescott's journalistic instincts were aroused. 'Where has the First Family gone? Or is it a State secret?'

'No secret as far as I'm concerned,' Steinbeck replied. 'The President has accepted a longstanding invitation from Mr Mercier to spend the weekend at his chateau in the south of France.

'Mercier's quite the up-and-coming man, isn't he?' Prescott commented thoughtfully.

'The President and Jean-Claude go way back,' Steinbeck's reply was judicious. 'They were at Yale Business School together and they've kept in touch ever since. Besides, you know how the President likes to keep close to the business community.'

'The business of America is business,' Prescott said.

'You can say that again.'

The two men carried their drinks over to a quiet corner of the room to continue their conversation. At a certain point, Steinbeck leaned towards Prescott and said in a confidential tone of voice: 'You've been doing some very good work recently, Prescott. The President is pleased. Very pleased. He was tickled pink about the way you managed to track down that visit to the dentist in Beijing all those years ago. He'd clean forgotten about it! And all that Cambodia stuff you wrote. Right on the nail! She's dead in the water, isn't she?'

'Who?'

Steinbeck looked at him in surprise. 'Senator Clinton, of course. No way is she going to run in 2004. 2008 could be a different matter, but that's a lifetime away and the President will be gone by then anyway. Someone else's problem.'

Moments later, chuckling to himself at the thought of Senator Hillary Rodham Clinton's discomfiture, Larry Steinbeck had moved on with drink in hand.

Still sitting in the corner of the room, Prescott watched him go. He felt stunned, shellshocked. What the hell had Larry meant, Prescott asked himself, by those last remarks about Beijing and Cambodia and Mrs Clinton? And what the hell did he mean by giving him that pat on the back and saying the President was mighty pleased? Of course, the Hong Soeung affair had panned out pretty well for the administration in the end. No doubt about that. The pendulum of public opinion had swung one way for a time but after the revelation that the Hong Soeung confessions were fraudulent it had rapidly swung back again – even further – the other way. It was certainly true that Mrs Clinton had been cosmically humiliated. But surely that was all happpenstance, wasn't it? Was Steinbeck implying that someone somewhere had planned it that way? Was there some play going on which he hadn't cottoned on to yet?

If Su had been used, was he being used too? He felt the hot flush of embarrassment on his cheeks. He thought about running after Steinbeck and having it out with the man, but he discarded the idea immediately. Steinbeck wouldn't have the faintest idea what he was talking about, he felt sure of that. Larry was just another hack doing a job. He didn't know where the bodies were buried.

So, who did know? Prescott drained his glass and made his way to the bar for a refill. It was pointless to hypothesize at this stage, he thought. He needed facts. More facts. Better facts. If you wanted to find buried bodies, you had to start digging.

CHAPTER 20

Prescott had breakfast delivered to his room at the Crillon early the next morning. He knew he had a lot to do and he wanted to get started. He briefly considered hiring a car but then decided against it. It was a Saturday. There would be lots of traffic and parking would be a nightmare. Given the present somewhat delicate state of their relationship, he didn't imagine that The New York Times would be amused if he included a number of parking tickets among his expenses.

As he munched his croissant, he tried to imagine what Paris must have been like at the beginning of the 1950s. What a mind-blowing experience it must have been for young Cambodian students who had stepped off the boat at Marseilles and caught the overnight train to the capital! This was the time and the place where intellectual winds blew at almost hurricane force. The French Revolution had occurred one hundred and seventy years previously, but Paris was still the spiritual home of those who believed that the world could and should be changed.

What had they been like, he wondered, these young men who had gone on to found the Khmer Rouge, the Cambodian Communist Party? Could they have ever imagined, as they gathered in each other's rooms, or met in Left Bank bars and cafés, that they would take on the leadership of a movement which would a quarter of a century later become the by-word for terror?

The concierge at the Hotel Crillon hailed a taxi for him as he stepped out into a sunlit Place de la Concorde.

'31 Rue Letellier, please,' Prescott instructed the driver as he got in.

The man nodded and pulled away from the kerb without hesitation. Paris differed from Washington in so many ways, Prescott thought. One of them was that taxi drivers on the whole seemed to know where they were going.

They drove across the Seine and down the Boulevard St Germain. Ten minutes later the car pulled up in front of a two-storey building. The ground floor was occupied by a bar-come-restaurant. A bronze awning bore the legend Café Letellier. The paintwork of the upper storey was crumbling and the shutters in the windows were in need of repair. As he got out of the taxi to stand on the pavement, Prescott saw a lace curtain twitch behind one of the windows on the first floor. An old woman thrust her head over the sill to peer down at him, then drew back closing the window behind her.

Asking the driver to wait, Prescott went into the bar and ordered a coffee. When he had finished, he carried the empty cup back to the counter.

Business was quiet that morning. The barman, a large, florid individual, was obviously pleased to have someone to talk to.

'So, what are you doing in Paris? You're an American, n'est-ce pas?'

When Prescott acknowledged that fact and mentioned that he was in Paris for the G8 meeting, the man grimaced.

'We should send them all packing,' he said, referring to the protesters. 'As a matter of fact, we should never have let them in. That's the trouble with the Common Market. We've lost control over our own frontiers.'

Prescott realised that he could be in for a long morning if they started talking about the European Common Market and all its faults, so he gently steered the conversation in another direction, explaining that he was engaged in some historical research of an intriguing nature having to do with Cambodia.

'It seems possible that Pol Pot once lived at this address,' he said. 'Would you know anything about that?'

The barman looked at him curiously. 'Another man came in here a day or two ago and asked that same question. I told him to get lost.'

'Why did you do that?'

'Because I didn't like the look of him. Have some more coffee. On the house. Pol Pot!' The man turned round and spat into the sink behind him. 'That's sick. Totally sick. Who would be interested in Pol Pot?'

Realising that the barman was unlikely to be a fruitful source of information, Prescott asked: 'Is it possible to talk to the woman who lives upstairs? Has she lived here a long time?'

'You mean Madame Lefarge? Yes, I'm sure you can talk to her. She actually owns the whole building. She's our landlord. The Lefarge family have lived in this building for years. Generations, actually. Tell her Gerard sent you. Gerard, that's my name. Turn right. Just ring at the side-door and walk up the stairs when you go in.'

Prescott laid a fifty franc note on the counter to pay for his coffee, then went out into the street and turned right as instructed. The side-door to 31, Rue Letellier had two bell-buttons. One was unlabelled. The other bore the name Lefarge.

Prescott rang the bell. 'Madame Lefarge?' he enquired when the old woman answered.

For a moment, Prescott supposed that she wasn't going to let him in but when he mentioned the magic words, 'Gerard sent me,' the buzzer sounded, and he was able to push the door open.

★★★

When he first rang the doorbell, Prescott had imagined that he would be meeting some hunched and withered, old soul living out her old age in virtual seclusion. He could not have been more wrong. Madame Lefarge was a handsome and well-preserved seventy-year-old. Though she could not have been expecting visitors at that hour of the morning, she was beautifully turned out in a stylishly cut suit and pearl necklace. Her eyes sparkled and her step was light and full of vigour.

She showed him into the sitting room, then bustled off to make coffee, explaining that the maid was off for the weekend.

When she came back and had poured the coffee, she started to talk. 'I like to talk about those days,' she told Prescott. 'I was young then, barely twenty years old. For me, it was an education, having these young men in the house, talking politics, smoking, staying up till all hours of the night. I had barely heard of Cambodia then. And I knew nothing of Cambodian politics. I learned just by listening.'

'How many of them were lodgers?' Prescott asked. 'How many actually lived here? I know Saloth Sar did. I found that out from the official history. But were there others? Where did they stay?'

Colette Lefarge took a sip of coffee before replying. 'We never really thought of them as lodgers. At least, if they were lodgers, they were our friends as well. Both my parents were intellectuals. You know, in France in the 1950's, it meant something to be an intellectual. Nowadays, it may be – how do you say, a dirty word? – but that wasn't the case then. I don't know for sure, but I think that my father at least was a member of the French Communist Party. Certainly, he was a good friend of Maurice Thorez, who was the leader of the party then. Thorez came here often.

'My parents were rich. We owned the whole building then. And this one wasn't the only one. We had other property in Paris and an estate in the country. But father and mother were never comfortable with their wealth. If they befriended the Cambodians, they did so out of political conviction – they believed France's days as a colonial power were over – but they also genuinely wanted to help people who needed help. We hardly charged them any rent, you know. And those young men had the run of the whole house. That's why I say, they weren't really lodgers in the usual sense.'

'Do you remember them well? Saloth Sar, for example? What was he like? And Ieng Sary? Did he come here too?'

Colette smiled. 'Oh, they all came here. This was like a second home for them. Of course, I remember them. How could I forget?'

For a moment Colette Lefarge paused, allowing her mind to run back over the years. She could see herself, standing by an open door, almost eavesdropping, while inside these brilliant, young men set the world to rights.

'Yes, I can see them now,' she continued. 'Ieng Sary had a bright face and easy smile while Saloth Sar, the man they call Pol Pot, was – it seemed to me – quiet, more calculating.'

'Who else do you remember?' Prescott didn't want to push the old woman too hard but he felt sure he was on the verge of finding out what he needed to know.

'Well, there were the girls, of course. There was Khieu Thirith. Her father, as I remember, was a well-respected judge in Cambodia. The family sent her to study in France and, when she arrived, she took the place by storm. She was a real beauty. She married Ieng Sary soon after she arrived. I think they had known each other in Cambodia. Saloth Sar married her sister, Ponnary, but that was later.'

'Who else do you remember?'

'I remember Thioun Mumm,' Colette continued. 'He was a scion of one of Cambodia's most aristocratic families. Unquestionably brilliant and handsome. I remember him telling me once that King Sihanouk had wanted to marry his sister but she had turned him down.'

'Was there a fourth man?' Prescott pressed her. 'An archaeological student, I believe. The official history of the Cambodian Communist Party says such a man lived at 31 Rue Letellier at the same time as Saloth Sar and then when he went back to Phnom Penh, Saloth Sar stayed on.'

Colette Lefarge wrinkled her brow as she tried to remember. 'Let me see. As far as I remember, Saloth Sar's fellow-lodger was a young man called...er... Soeung... Hong Soeung. Yes, that's it. And I do believe that Soeung was a student of archaeology. I can see him even now. A handsome fellow. I quite fancied him. I remember we took at taxi together to Khieu Thirith's wedding to Ieng Sary. She and Sary had rented a ballroom and asked all the students, all the Marxists they could think of. We each had to contribute two hundred francs towards the cost of the event. And I ended up paying for Hong Soeung as well, since he didn't have any money with him. I didn't mind. He was such a charmer.'

Prescott knew he had to be sure. Absolutely sure. 'What about the wedding photographs?' he asked. 'Were there any? Do you still have them? I am curious to see what that Hong Soeung looked like in those days?'

Madame Lefarge looked at him sharply. 'Is Hong Soeung still alive? I never heard any more about him. He went back to Cambodia and that was that.'

She went over to an antique chest of drawers and pulled out an album of photographs.

'As I told you,' she said, 'the wedding between Ieng Sary and Khieu Thirith was a great occasion.' She cleared the coffee cups from the table and opened the album. 'Here's the happy couple.' She pointed to a photograph of Ieng Sary and his bride emerging from the *mairie* in St Germain des Pres. 'And here I am. Do you recognise me?'

'Of course, I recognise you,' Prescott said tactfully, gazing at the dark-haired beauty smiling at the camera. 'Who is that with you?' Prescott knew the face was familiar, but he couldn't place it.

Once again, Colette Lefarge screwed up her eyes as she tried to remember. 'It's so long ago. I think he was called Khin... Khin Lay, if I recall correctly. He was a friend of Ieng Sary and Khieu Thirith, I suppose. At least they invited him to the wedding as you can see.'

Prescott sat for a moment in stunned silence, trying to comprehend the meaning of this latest piece of information. What was Khin Lay doing in Paris in the early fifties? Had he been part of the Khmer Rouge too?

'And Hong Soeung?' he asked quietly. 'Do you have a picture of him somewhere. A group photo perhaps? They must have taken a picture at the reception?'

'There's certainly a group photo, but I'm not sure I could pick Hong Soeung out, not after all these years. There were so many Cambodians there that day, and Vietnamese, as well as Tunisians, Algerians and Moroccans. All the anti-colonialist movements were represented. It was quite a gathering I can tell you.'

When she found the page in the album with the group photos, Prescott saw what she meant. There must have been a hundred people in the picture.

'We'll need a magnifying glass,' Colette said.

'No, we don't.'

Prescott was looking intently at the line-up in the front row. The happy couple – Ieng Sary and Khieu Thirith – were sitting in the front row. Saloth Sar was sitting on Khieu Thirith's right and Thiounn Mumm on Ieng Sary's left. Khieu Ponnary, Thirith's older sister, was sitting next to Saloth Sar and next to her, Prescott recognised Khin Lay.

'Who's that sitting next to Khieu Ponnary?' Prescott asked. 'That's Hong Soeung, isn't it?' He stared at the man's face. He felt sure that he was not mistaken but he needed to have Colette's confirmation.

'You may not need the magnifying glass, but I do!' Colette Lefarge found one and peered intently at the photograph. 'You may be right. It's so long ago I can't be sure. But that could well be Hong Soeung, the student who lived with Saloth Sar.'

Colette Lefarge dabbed at her eye with a handkerchief. 'It seems just like yesterday.'

Prescott's heart went out to the old woman. Though she clearly kept up appearances, Prescott wondered momentarily how easy life was for her. Did she have friends? Did she have family? Maybe the reason she had been talking with such animation about the past was because the past was somehow more vivid, more real than the present.

'If we ever track Hong Soeung down, I'll tell him I met you,' Prescott promised. 'I'll tell him you are well and that you remember him fondly.'

'Please do that! Tell him he still owes me two hundred francs!'

Twenty minutes later, Colette Lefarge insisted on coming downstairs with him to see him into his taxi.

'It has been such a pleasure,' Prescott said. 'I really mean that. I'll keep in touch'.

'The pleasure has been mine, I assure you.' Colette Lefarge waved him on his way.

As Prescott walked past the open door of the Café Brazza, he saw the barman setting the tables for lunch.

'Merci, Gerard,' he called. 'Grand merci.'

The man looked up and gave a nod of acknowledgement. 'Pas de quoi.'

★★★

The taxi driver was still waiting for him, the metre ticking.

As he got into the car, Prescott looked at his watch. It was already half-past eleven. His visit to Madame Lefarge had proved to be so absorbing that he had hardly noticed the passage of time.

'Where to, monsieur?' the driver asked.

Prescott hesitated. At this precise juncture, he wasn't entirely sure where he wanted to go. He knew he needed to talk – and very soon – to Jean-Claude Mercier. Mercier, he suspected, was as anxious to track down Hong Soeung as he was, though why this should be so, Prescott didn't know. Mercier had followed the trail to the Bibliothèque Nationale. It could well have been Mercier, or someone sent by him, who had visited the Café Letellier two days previously.

He knew he definitely had to see the man and find out, if he could, what was going on. The problem was: Mercier was out of town, down at his chateau in the south of France entertaining none other than the President of the United States. Larry Steinbeck had told him about the visit the previous evening in the bar of the Crillon and that morning, as he read the newspapers over breakfast, there had been front-page pictures of Mercier greeting the First Family at the entrance to his chateau.

He could catch a flight down to Nice that afternoon, Prescott supposed, and hire a car at the airport but he knew he wouldn't get close to the Mercier establishment. The roads would be shut off for miles around. Even a distinguished correspondent from *The New York Times* wouldn't get past the barricades.

'Just keep going for the time being,' he instructed the taxi driver. 'Back across the river. I've got to make a telephone call.'

Prescott took out his cell phone and tapped in the number of Su's mobile. He doubted it would work. You were lucky if you got a signal even in Phnom Penh and he felt sure Su was way upcountry by now.

Amazingly, he heard a ringing tone. Then the answer message came on. 'The person you are calling is not available. If you wish to leave a message, please speak after the tone.'

'Su, call me as soon as you get this. We need to speak. Where are you? What are you doing? For Christ's sake don't do anything rash! Love you, Prescott.'

He was about to ring off when he realised he hadn't said why he needed to speak to her so urgently. It went against the grain to say too much over a cell phone, which was probably the most insecure form of communication known to man, but he knew that if he didn't add something reassuring, she would be alarmed when she got his 'call me at once' message.

'It's about your father,' he went on. 'I think I'm on to something. Do you know if he was ever in Paris, as a young man? I'll try to call your mother now, but it's after midnight in Seattle and she may not pick up... Damn!'

Prescott swore as the line broke up. He leaned forward and tapped the driver on the shoulder. 'Do you think you could pull over? I'm having trouble with the reception.'

The man found a gap in the traffic and drew up beside the kerb, next to one of those old-fashioned circular billboards announcing various spectacles, actual or forthcoming.

'That's better,' Prescott dug out his pocket diary, looked up the number and dialled Sita Soeung's number in Seattle.

It took more than a dozen rings before Sita picked up. When at last she did so, she sounded worried and confused. 'Who is it? What do you want?'

'Sita, this is me, Prescott. Can you hear me all right?'

The reception was better now but it still wasn't perfect, and he had to raise his voice to be heard. He tried to explain that he had had to leave Cambodia but Su was still there.

'She's gone up-country. She'll be fine,' he shouted.

'I'm so worried for her, Prescott.'

'She'll be fine,' he repeated. 'I'll call you again as soon as I speak to her. Sita, Sita? Can you still hear me? We're trying to find out more about your husband, Hong Soeung. We think he may still be alive. I need to find out if he was ever in France, in Paris. In the early fifties? Did he come here as a young man, as a student?'

Mercifully the line cleared, and Prescott was able to hear Sita Soeung's reply as clear as a bell. 'Paris? Yes, of course he was in Paris. That's where he studied archaeology. That's where he learned French. That's how he got a top job in the Ministry of Culture. Why do you ask?'

The line was breaking up again. 'Sita, I can't talk now. You've been a great help. We'll speak again soon. Very soon. I'll have Su with me. I'm going to go and look for her.'

The line suddenly went dead. Prescott sat back in the seat, the cell phone still in his hand, trying to take in the implications of the information.

So Hong Soeung had definitely been in Paris in the fifties! He had been part of a close-knit group which included the young Cambodians who were later to be the key leaders of the

Khmer Rouge: Pol Pot, Ieng Sary, Thioun Mumm. And Khin Lay too? What did that mean? Was Khin Lay once a member of the Khmer Rouge? Or at least a sympathiser?

The minutes passed. Prescott's sharp, analytical mind was in overdrive. Hong Soeung leaves Paris, he hypothesised, and goes back to Phnom Penh as a Khmer Rouge "sleeper." He takes a job in the Ministry of Culture, ultimately rising to the rank of senior civil servant in that Ministry. In the chaos of the Khmer Rouge takeover of Phnom Penh on April 15, 1975, Hong Soeung is mistakenly arrested and imprisoned in Tuol Sleng. The mistake is rectified on orders of the Pol Pot hierarchy (Pol Pot? Ieng Sary?) and Hong Soeung is released. He disappears up-country, somewhere in the north of Cambodia, and is not seen or heard of again.

'Time to move on, sir? This is not a good place to wait.' The taxi driver sounded impatient.

As he came out of his reverie, Prescott found himself staring at one of the posters on the circular billboard three feet in front of his nose.

'Musée Guimet,' the poster said. 'Muséee Nationale des Arts Asiatiques.'

'Oh, my God!' Prescott exclaimed. 'The damn thing has been under my eyes all this time! Look at that!'

'Look at what, sir?'

'The poster!'

Prescott wound the window down so as to get a better look. He knew immediately that his first supposition had been correct. The photograph being used to promote the collection of antiquities at the Musée Guimet was of a stone head of a Hindu God, so similar in style and appearance to the pieces which Prescott had seen in Washington and Hangzhou that for a moment he imagined that one or other of those items had somehow found its way to Paris on temporary loan.

But when he examined the photograph further, he realised that, though similar to the other two pieces, this third head was also different. Same style, same period, Prescott thought, maybe even the same craftsman. But a different God. Or maybe a different aspect of the same God. He had seen Vishnu; he had seen Brahma. Could this be the third God in the Hindu Trinity: Shiva the destroyer?

'Where's the Musée Guimet?' he rasped.

'Avenue d'Iena.'

'Will it be open?'

'On Saturdays, till five p.m. probably.'

'Take me there,' Prescott sounded decisive. He felt decisive.

The taxi-driver swung out into the traffic.

'Step on it!' Prescott instructed.

CHAPTER 21

When they reached the Musée Guimet, twenty minutes later, Prescott paid off the taxi, hurried up the steps and bought an entrance ticket. Included in the price of the ticket was an audio phone, enabling visitors to walk round the exhibition while listening to a commentary in the language of their choice.

'Why the hell not?' thought Prescott. He had spoken enough French that morning. He felt in need of a break.

He fast-forwarded through the first few items. Not that he wasn't interested. He just didn't have the time. Halfway down the right-hand wall, where works of art from South East Asia were arranged, his eye fell on the stone head which appeared on the poster.

'Good God!' he muttered, threading his way through the afternoon crowd and positioning himself in front of the piece. The similarity in style between this particular object and the two images which he had seen earlier was uncanny. They could almost have been carved by the same hand, Prescott thought.

An engraved notice beside the statue read: *Shiva – Cambodia. Late 9th-Early 10th Century.*

A headset symbol indicated that an oral guide was available for those who wanted to know more. Prescott found the right place on the tape, pressed the button and began to listen. Whoever had recorded the commentary managed to convey brilliantly the drama behind the discovery of the piece.

Prescott listened with rapt attention to an agreeable female voice speaking English with a slight French accent. From time to time he scribbled some notes on the cover of the catalogue which he had bought as he came in.

'In his book *Voyage to Cambodia – Voyage au Cambodge –* first published in 1880,' the anonymous commentator informed him, 'Louis Delaporte describes his discovery – nine years earlier – of this extraordinarily beautiful statue of Shiva. Listen to what Delaporte wrote:

> *A priceless discovery awaited us among the ruins. We noticed the remains of candles, cleared the ground, and soon unearthed a limestone cylinder with a very smooth grain, then a skullcap decorated with braid, then a face and finally the remains of a head. There could be no mistake: these were the heads of the major Brahminic divinities, and each of them must have occupied one of the three sanctuaries.*

Prescott pressed the rewind button, then replayed the commentary, scribbling furiously. He paused for a moment, then pressed Play.

> *It is believed that the three images described by Delaporte represent the Trimurti, the triad of the three great Hindu gods – Shiva in the middle, Brahma on the left, Vishnu on the right or the three aspects of holiness in the Brahministic conception inherited from India.*

> *The statue of Shiva which confronts us in the Musée Guimet was part of the collection of Cambodian antiquities which Delaporte brought back to France...*

Prescott turned off the machine. He went over to a bench by the wall. He needed to take a break. To think things through. As he sat there, amid the all the monumental splendour of the past, an idea suddenly occurred to him. Could he somehow track down Louis Delaporte's original text? He looked at his watch. It was one o'clock already. He knew the Bibliothèque Nationale opened on Saturday mornings but it would probably be closed by now. In any case, he didn't fancy another trip out to the suburbs. Where else to look?

Prescott had been coming to Paris over the years. You couldn't be a top-flight international correspondent without coming at fairly regular intervals to the City of Light. If you didn't have a reason, you invented one. Some of those visits had, in the past, been fairly leisurely affairs. He had had time to walk the streets, to take the bateau mouche along the river, to amble along the banks of the Seine. There were so many marvellous old bookshops, he recalled, along the Left Bank.

He stopped at the museum shop by the entrance to buy a copy of the Shiva poster. At least he wouldn't have to try to draw the damn thing again, he thought. The sales assistant rolled it up for him and gave him a plastic bag to carry it in.

***

Prescott found what he was looking for in the third place he visited. It was a small, crowded bookshop where almost every volume was covered in a layer of dust.

An old man, almost as old – it seemed to Prescott – as some of the books, sat in a corner hunched behind a desk. When Prescott asked whether he had a copy of *Voyage au Cambodge* by Louis Delaporte, he levered himself upright to return five minutes later with a yellowing cloth-bound book in his hand.

'You're in luck,' the bookseller said.

The book was a rare antique. Prescott wasn't inclined to bargain but shelling out two thousand Francs (the equivalent of US $280) made a hole in his loose change. After buying the book, he realised he didn't have enough cash on him to pay for a taxi back to the hotel so he strode out along the river and crossed the bridge into the Place de la Concorde.

As a matter of fact, he was glad of the exercise. Glad, too, to be able to enjoy – as any tourist would – the majestic beauty of Paris, loveliest of cities. If he wasn't American, Prescott thought, he would be happy to be French. The scale and harmony of the buildings which lined the river on both sides could be seen as the reflection of the extraordinary self-confidence of the French people. Words like *patrie* and *nation* had a special meaning over here.

As he walked, his eye fell on the great stone needle covered in hieroglyphs in the middle of the Place de la Concorde. Cleopatra's needle. Why was Paris littered with obelisks? Because Napoleon had shipped them back from Egypt. With that kind of example in front of them, no wonder men like Louis Delaporte hadn't thought twice before removing priceless artefacts from Cambodian temples and shipping them back to enrich the collection of the great museums. They would have seen this as a normal and natural endeavour. This was what you did when you were a French explorer. You brought the goodies back to base.

Back in his hotel room, Prescott unwrapped the parcel, laid the book on the desk and settled down to study Louis Delaporte's account of his journey to Cambodia.

Once again, he made notes of the key facts:

> Delaporte is French sailor stationed in Far East. Is part of Commandant de Lagrée's expedition to explore the Mekong (1866-67-68). Returns as leader of his own expedition in 1873. Delaporte and colleagues leave Saigon (now Ho Chi Minh City!) 23 July 1873 by steamer. A few days later boat arrives Phnom Penh, now capital of Cambodia. Expedition is received by King Norodom in royal palace. Set off for the interior two weeks later. Cross Tonle Sap Lake. Continue explorations north of great lake.

An hour passed. Prescott rang room service for a pot of tea, then – remembering he had missed lunch – rang back to add a round of sandwiches to the order.

Fortified, he resumed his perusal of Delaporte's narrative. There were some strange parallels, he thought. Here were Delaporte and his men crossing lakes, fording rivers, trudging through the jungles to find ruined temples which no man (or certainly no westerner) had ever set eyes on before. And here he, Prescott Glover, was trying to hack his way through a thicket of ornate French prose, whose vocabulary and syntax strained his linguistic skills to the limit. A voyage within a voyage, he reflected.

Delaporte had provided no index to the book. There was no short-cut. He could, Prescott supposed, have broken the book's back, ripped out the pages and scanned them to a computer before using the search key to pick out any references to Ta Keo. But he doubted he would save time in the end and, as a course of action, it seemed too close to vandalism. Prescott laboured on. Another hour passed:

Delaporte's lieutenant, M. Faraut, he wrote, leaves main party and heads for Battambang. LD presses on. Party is five days march north (or north-east?) of Siem Reap. LD not good on directions or distances. Wildlife. Birds. Crocodiles. Natives with canoes (pirogues)...

He allowed his eye to run down the page. Suddenly, he recognised the passage where Delaporte described finding the head of Shiva. The words leapt out at him. Ta Keo!

'Christ, I've found it!' Prescott spoke out loud.

He didn't trust his notetaking skills any longer. Instead, he painstakingly transcribed the key passages from Louis Delaporte's book. By the time he had finished, Prescott knew that he had in a sense re-discovered what Louis Delaporte had discovered a century and a quarter earlier.

Delaporte, in looking for Ta Keo, had had only the faintest of references (an unconfirmed sighting of jungle-covered ruins by one of de Lagrée's men). He had ended up exploring and describing an archaeological site larger, more complex and certainly earlier than Angkor Wat itself. And was this city indeed (as Delaporte believed) Amarendrapura, Jayavarman II's capital, a place frequently referred to in Khmer inscriptions but whose location remained one of archaeology's most tantalising secrets?

Prescott got up from the desk and walked over to the window. After the afternoon lull, the traffic had begun to thicken in La Place de la Concorde. The outline of the great obelisk had begun to grow blurred against the darkening sky.

Fifty years earlier, thought Prescott, a young man named Hong, studying archaeology in Paris, had made the find of a lifetime. Whether by accident or design, he had come across the key passages in Delaporte's book which described the discovery of Ta Keo. When he returned to Cambodia, Hong Soeung had a secret life, as a key member of the Khmer Rouge. But he also had a public life which was not just a "cover," a convenient fiction.

Archaeology – by now Prescott, like Su, was totally convinced – was Hong Soeung's consuming passion. Given his job in the Cambodian Ministry of Culture, he was ideally placed to search for the ruins which Delaporte had described but which had effectively disappeared from view for more than a century. And for the last several decades, Prescott was convinced, Hong Soeung had been up in the jungle at Ta Keo waiting to announce the most extraordinary archaeological event of the new millennium.

Standing there, with a cup of cold tea in his hand and his notes strewn over the desk behind him, Prescott felt suddenly overwhelmed. What a mighty tree had sprung from an idly scattered seed! He had a firm sense, at that moment, that he was just a player in a much larger drama. He was beginning to see now, far more clearly than he had a few days ago, the full dimensions of the play. But still there were elements, major elements, that he did not understand.

Delaporte had discovered Ta Keo. Hong Soeung had re-discovered Ta Keo. But he was still no closer to knowing the place's location. Talking about, 'three day's march' and 'being greeted by natives in canoes' and 'vast ruins' didn't amount to a map reference or even a compass bearing.

Why the hell hadn't Delaporte drawn some maps, he wondered? There were maps in *Treasure Island*, for Christ's sake. X marks the spot!

He picked up the *Voyage au Cambodge* and threw himself into an armchair. He couldn't face the effort of more notetaking. Besides, he couldn't see where it would get him. Delaporte's description of the return journey to Siem Reap was no more informative, from the point of view of navigational information, than his description of the outward journey.

Damn it! Prescott was overcome by a sense of despondency. This was like looking for a needle in the proverbial haystack – not a Cleopatra's needle either!

He tossed the book onto the bed, where it landed awkwardly face down, with some of the pages visibly crumpled. Prescott was mortified. That was pretty childish, he thought.

Certainly, no way to treat a precious object.

The book had fallen open at page 381. Prescott glanced at it idly, smoothing the surface as he did so. Then he stopped and stared, his attention rivetted. He was looking at a map. A box in the bottom-right corner said: *Carte de I 'Indo-Chine Meridionale: Ancien Royaume du Cambodge ou Royaume Khmer.*

Beneath the legend was a red box and next to it the words: *La teinte rose indique l'emplacement des Ruines Khmers explorées jusqu'à ce jour.*

Wow! Prescott breathed deeply. This could be it! Still standing by the bed with the book in his hand, he studied the old map. He picked out the names he recognised. Battambang, Banone, Angkor... Grand Lac... that would be what the French explorers called the Tonle Sap Lake...

'Go north-east from Tonle Sap,' he told himself, 'five days march. What was the scale? How far was five days' march on the map? An inch? An inch-and-a-half?'

Then he saw it. Ka Keo next to a mountain range marked

Coulen (Kulen?). For a moment he was puzzled. Ka Keo? Why not Ta Keo? He scrabbled back through the pages of the book. There was a footnote somewhere he remembered reading.

He finally found it on page 95. Delaporte wrote, a propos the name he had used for his extraordinary discovery:

> C'est ainsi que nous appelons ce monument Ponteay Ka Keo (la Fortresse de l'Île Précieux Joyeux). De même le commandant de Lagrée avait appelé primitivement Ta-Keu, une célèbre pyramide Ka Keo, voisine d'Angkor, pour laquelle il adopta définitivement le nom de Ta Keo. Le mot Keo se reproduira plusieurs fois dans le cours de ce recit; il designe ordinairement des statues sacrées. On remarquera, d'ailleurs, que les noms des localités de l'Indo-Chine Meridionale varient avec les voyageurs qui les ont visitées, suivant la nationalité de ceux-ci ou celle de leurs guides.

Prescott heaved a sigh of relief. Ta Keo and Ka Keo were one and the same place. That much was clear. It was the earlier, not the later name which appeared to have stuck.

He turned back to page 381 and once again studied the map. Just how useful would it be as a guide, he wondered? Certainly, better than nothing. The needle was now considerably larger, and the haystack was considerably smaller but still it wasn't exactly a well signposted route map showing the way from A to B.

★★★

All Prescott's attempts to contact Su over the weekend ended in frustration. On the one occasion where he managed to get a line through to SAVE's Siem Reap clinic, there was no reply (he hadn't really expected one). He left another message on Su's mobile but, wherever she was, he doubted she was picking up her voicemail.

Sunday dawned wet and windy and after a rapid walk up the Champs-Elysées to the Arc de Triomphe and back, he spent much of the day in the hotel.

The excitement he had felt the previous day when he discovered the map in the Delaporte's book was now tempered with the realisation that, as a navigational tool, the chart left much to be desired. Even if it was accurate (which it might not be) the scale of the map did not permit precise identification of Ta Keo's location or of the route to be taken to find the place. Delaporte's description of the way he and his team hacked their way through the jungle, forded rivers and streams, dealt with the natives and Cambodia's assorted wildlife which included snakes, tigers and elephants, was colourful and at times even poetic but you couldn't go out there with the book in your hand and hope to retrace Delaporte's route. There wasn't a single grid reference in the whole text. They probably didn't have grid references in those days, Prescott thought. And GPS – the global positioning system – would have been the wildest science fiction.

By mid-afternoon, Prescott was feeling decidedly gloomy. He felt quite convinced by now that Su had headed off somewhere looking for her father. Somehow, she had discovered, or thought she had discovered, where Hong Soeung was. Maybe she had found out the location of the elusive Ta Keo and was trying to make her way there. Prescott shuddered at the thought. If Ta Keo was where it seemed to be from Delaporte's map, Su would be making her way through territory which could hardly be said to be controlled by the central government. The closer you got to the Kulen mountains, the stronger would be the influence of bandit elements, including the Khmer Rouge remnants. If you weren't blown to pieces by stepping on a mine, you ran the risk of being kidnapped and held hostage.

As the sky darkened outside, Prescott flipped on the television. CNN had live coverage of the President of the United States boarding Air Force One at Nice Airport after his weekend in the South of France. Among the dignitaries lined up on the tarmac Prescott recognised the smirking face of Jean-Claude Mercier. What a coup for Mercier, he thought, having the President of the United States and the First Family over for the weekend.

Half an hour later, he was still watching television when the telephone rang.

'Isn't it time we talked?' a voice said – in English.

'Who is this?' Prescott asked.

'Jean-Claude Mercier, of course. I think we are both looking for the same man, *n'est-ce-pas?* Isn't it time we joined forces?'

Prescott glanced at the television screen. Thirty minutes earlier, Mercier had been at Nice airport saying a fond farewell to President George W. Bush.

'Where are you?'

'Twenty-five thousand feet above Cahors, I would say,' Mercier replied. 'I'll be in Paris within the hour. Come to the office at nine this evening. They'll be expecting you. You know the address, don't you?'

'I'll be there,' Prescott said. He replaced the receiver. Suddenly his mood lightened. He wasn't sure what Mercier's interest in Hong Soeung was. There were lots of layers on this particular onion. That much was already clear. But Mercier had power, he had resources, he could make things happen. The key question was: how much time did they have? It might already be too late.

Not wishing to leave such a valuable object lying around in his hotel room, he picked up Delaporte's *Voyage au Cambodge* and put it in his briefcase to take with him.

CHAPTER 22

'I owe you an explanation,' Mercier began, pouring Prescott a stiff whiskey-and-soda. 'I realised some time ago that the Hong Soeung affair was the key – or the clue if you like – to the whole situation. I should have shared that knowledge with you much earlier.'

The two men were sitting in deep, white leather armchairs in Mercier's office on the top floor of the JCM headquarters building on Boulevard Haussmann. Almost directly in front of them, the Eiffel Tower soared spectacularly into the night sky. If he turned his head a few degrees to the right, Prescott could glimpse the top of the Arc de Triomphe. The view from the other side of the room was equally impressive. A mile or two away, he could see the soaring white dome of Montmartre's Église du Sacré-Coeur. Hanging on the wall in the space between the great plate glass windows Prescott counted two oil-paintings by Matisse and one by Picasso, as well as a Degas drawing.

Jean-Claude Mercier came straight to the point. 'You met Jules Barron in Cambodia, didn't you?'

'Of course. He worked for SAVE. He was one of Su's colleagues.'

Mercier nodded. 'I've known Barron for a long time. My father knew his father. It was Barron who first tipped me off that something major was in the wind. We were having dinner together in Phnom Penh at Le Royal. It was an emotional occasion. Jules feels these things very passionately. He is a grandson of the great French Marshal de Lattre de Tassigny who led France's Indo-Chinese campaign. His father died at Dien Bien Phu. Jules's point of view is quite simple. He believes it is high time for France to receive some kind of reward or recompense for the part she had played in safeguarding Cambodia's future. Which country toiled and suffered in Indochina for more than a century, creating – as Jules sees it – order out of chaos? The answer is: France. And which country strained every sinew to arrange the Paris Peace Conference of 1989? France, again, of course. Yet France has received almost no recognition for all that effort. France has become a distant memory in Cambodia. Even the French language has virtually disappeared as a means of day-to-day communication.'

Prescott listened, fascinated. He had met Jules Barron on several occasions during his time in Phnom Penh but he had never had a proper conversation with him, never found out what made him tick. Now it turned out that Barron had been heavily implicated in the unfolding of events. As the ancient tragedians put it, character was plot, he thought. Journalists would do well to remember that. You could spend too much time concentrating on the facts. You had to look at the people behind them.

'What precisely did Barron tell you?' Prescott asked.

While Prescott sat back in his chair sipping his drink, Mercier summarized the message Barron had passed on to him. 'As we agree,' he began, 'Barron works for SAVE. Because of this, he knows that Su Soeung is coming to Cambodia. He can't quite understand why she is coming. He knows she has been appointed Congressional Liaison Officer or whatever, but the circumstances of the appointment puzzle him. Why is the job given to Su without being advertised, at least internally? What exactly is she going to do while she is in the country? What exactly is she going to do when she goes back to Washington?'

Prescott nodded: 'I have to say, I wondered about that too.'

Mercier held up his hand. 'Let me continue. Barron's attitude turns from puzzlement to outright suspicion when Su arrives in Phnom Penh and seems to spend much of her time, not on her assigned tasks with SAVE, but on a very personal quest to track down her father. Even when he is not present himself, Barron gets a full account of developments from his girlfriend, Lina Chan, who works for DC-Cam. He believes right from the start that there is something fishy about the whole thing. Su has a photograph of her father with her and, hey presto! she finds a match in the DC-Cam archive. His suspicions mount when the Hong Soeung confessions are conveniently discovered in the Tuol Sleng archive. Long before those confessions are revealed to be fraudulent, Barron is convinced that there is a plot afoot. He forms the view that the Minister of the Interior, Khin Lay, is probably deeply implicated. Khin Lay has the authority; he has the means. Above all, he has the motive.'

'Barron, as I said, came to see me. Henri Le Blanc from Le Monde was with him that night. In the event it was clear that Barron's analysis was right. This was a "put-up job" if I may use that expression. The Hong Soeung affair led directly to the collapse of the case against the Khmer Rouge criminals – Duch and Ta Mok – and the withdrawal of the United Nations team. Khin Lay's position has been enhanced enormously compared with that of Hun Sen. Hun Sen was clearly identified with the tribunal – some kind of tribunal anyway, even if it wasn't a full-blown International Court of Criminal Justice.'

Prescott nodded thoughtfully. 'I had a feeling Le Blanc knew something I didn't know. I ran into him at the tribunal hearing, the morning it all went pear-shaped. He was confoundedly smug.'

'Don't torture yourself. It wasn't all down to Barron's superior powers of deduction. He has his own sources inside the Ministry of the Interior. He didn't tell me what those sources were, and I didn't ask. I saw him again just before I left Cambodia. He said that he believed, on the basis of what his sources had told him, that Hun Sen was soon to be expelled from office if he wasn't assassinated first. In his view Khin Lay would take over. He said there was an opportunity here for France to re-establish herself in the region, to strike a deal with the new regime. French-language schools could open up again all over the country. The tricolore would fly over public buildings in Phnom Penh on the Fourteenth of July as a mark of public respect...'

'And what did you say to him?'

'I told him I agreed with him. Simple as that,' Mercier nodded emphatically. 'Of course, I look at the situation more from a businessman's perspective. With the change of regime in Phnom Penh, there will be enormous opportunities for those who play their cards right. Why should all those opportunities go to the Americans?'

'You think Americans were also involved in the Hong Soeung affair, working with Khin Lay to ensure the right outcome?'

Once again Mercier nodded. 'I think some Americans were involved. Specifically, Andrew Mossman. Who wrote to your friend Su in the first place, offering her a job? It was Mossman, wasn't it? What about Mossman's collection of Cambodian antiquities? There's talk on the streets of some special arrangements which have been made between Khin Lay and Mossman, using SAVE as a cover. Don't you think Mossman will be anxious to strengthen those links by helping Khin Lay come to power in Cambodia?'

'I'm not so sure,' Prescott sounded dubious. 'The Mossmans are close to the Clintons. Hillary was severely humiliated by the Hong Soeung affair. It doesn't ring quite right to me.'

Mercier dismissed Prescott's objections out of hand. 'You're being too sentimental. As I see it, from the Mossmans' point of view, Hillary Clinton was expendable. They deliberately set her up for a fall. The dogs bark and the caravan moves on. You say the Mossmans are friends of the Clintons, supporters of the Democrats. Are you quite sure? Might they not be, after all, closet Republicans, admirers of the President? Might there not be a White House interest here too? There must be people around the President who find the thought of discrediting Hillary Clinton extremely attractive.'

As Mercier spoke, Prescott remembered Larry Steinbeck's cryptic comment in the bar of the Hotel Crillon a couple of evenings previously. *The President's very pleased with what you've been writing, Prescott.* Was this all a deep-laid plot to ensure that Senator Hillary Rodham Clinton ended up with egg on her face? He wasn't convinced. Not for the time being anyway.

'Let's forget about Senator Clinton for the moment,' Prescott said. 'Let's concentrate on Cambodia. Let's assume that you and Jules Barron are right and that Minister Khin Lay, possibly with the assistance of Andrew Mossman, was behind the Hong Soeung affair and that whole affair was designed to discredit the current regime in Cambodia? Where does that get us? How do Khin Lay and his friends come to power? There aren't going to be elections in Cambodia for another two years, so they must be planning on something else?'

Mercier stood up and walked over to the window, admiring the view. After a few seconds, he walked to the sideboard and poured himself another drink, then he came back to his chair. He leaned forward, confidentially.

'I had a telephone call on my mobile yesterday afternoon from Jules Barron,' he said. 'It was a sunny day down south. We were all of us playing boule on the terrace. The President was winning as I remember but the girls were also doing pretty well. I couldn't talk for long and Barron didn't want to. He uses a scrambler. We both do. But you can't be too careful.

'Barron told me that he has had absolute confirmation from his source that Khin Lay is going to mount a coup d'état within the next few days. He is going to oust Hun Sen and take over the reins of power.'

'How the hell is he going to do that? Hun Sen is not going to be a pushover. They don't call him the "strong man of Cambodia" for nothing.'

'Correct, again,' Mercier nodded. 'I called Barron from the plane, just after I called you. I put exactly the same question to him? How is the coup going to be engineered? Of course, I didn't ask that in so many words. I said something like: how is the package going to be delivered? but he got my meaning.'

'What did he say?' Prescott had no difficulty imagining the conversation between the two men. There was Mercier, on the one hand, flying above France in his private jet, high in every sense (after all, he had just been entertaining the President of the United States in his modest country chateau). And there, on the other, was that dark horse, Jules Barron, sitting on his veranda in Phnom Penh ten thousand miles away, huddling over his mobile.

'He didn't know,' JCM replied. 'He genuinely didn't know. Either his informant was keeping him in the dark about the finer points or else the source was himself ignorant of the mechanics of the operation. The only thing Barron could tell me was that Hong Soeung was definitely still alive and that somehow he would be a key player when Khin Lay took over in Cambodia.'

Mercier paused. 'If that's the case, I want to meet Hong Soeung now.'

'You want to be in on the ground floor with the new regime. Is that right?'

'Exactly so! You and I have precisely the same immediate objective, which is to find Hong Soeung, though our longer-term goals may differ.'

'Why do you need me?' Prescott asked. 'You said you wanted to join forces. Couldn't you find him on your own?'

Mercier laughed out loud. 'Don't underestimate yourself, Prescott. I know you know where Hong Soeung is! Share your knowledge. We will be much stronger if we work together.'

'How do you know I know where Hong Soeung is?' Prescott asked.

Mercier hesitated as though pondering how much to reveal. 'You really want to know?'

'I do really want to know. I think you owe me that.' Prescott was beginning to be irritated by Mercier's air of self-satisfaction.

'It was simple really,' Mercier explained. 'When I came back to Paris from Cambodia the other day, I was still engrossed in the Hong Soeung affair. I thought that if I could trace his history, I might get some clues as to his whereabouts.'

'You mean you thought he might still be alive even before you had a tip-off to that effect?'

'I did. I worked out – as you must have done – that if Hong Soeung had actually been in Tuol Sleng but had somehow escaped, it might be because of Khmer Rouge connections. One afternoon I went to the Bibliothèque Nationale and the rest as they say is history.'

'What do you mean?'

'When I heard you had been there too, I knew I was on the right track.'

'How did you know I had been there? Did you have me followed?'

'Remember the librarian? The young woman you spoke to. I met her too when I was at the library. She agreed to call me if anyone else came by looking for early accounts of the Cambodian Communist Party or whatever. I have to admit my people have been following you all weekend. As I say, we know you went to the Bibliothèque Nationale. We know you visited the Pol Pot house on Rue Letellier and talked to Madame Lefarge. I congratulate you on that. I sent a man there but he never talked to the woman. I don't actually think he got beyond the bar in the Café. We know you visited the Musée Guimet and the bookshop on the Quai Voltaire. And yes, we know you know the place where Hong Soeung is to be found.'

Prescott remembered the message he had left on Su's voicemail, telling her about the map in Delaporte's book and how he was convinced he now knew the location of Ta Keo. Could Mercier somehow have been picking up Su's messages on her cell phone? Surely not. Even if the cell phone wasn't working, she would still have it with her.

Then another idea occurred to him. JCM Enterprises owned the Hotel Crillon and bugging a hotel guest's telephone was the kind of thing that Mercier, a notoriously tough and un-scrupulous operator, would not flinch from if the need arose.

'Don't tell me!' he spluttered.

Mercier laughed. 'Don't be indignant! What do you expect? We are playing for high stakes. Very high stakes. So, will you help us? You want to find Hong Soeung. I want to find him. Let's find him together.'

Prescott swallowed his indignation. He saw the logic in what Mercier was suggesting. 'Why should I trust you?' he asked. 'By your own admission, you've been following me and bugging my telephone.'

'Mutual interest, surely?' Mercier replied. 'Isn't that the best basis for a trusting relationship?'

'In your world, perhaps,' Prescott muttered. He realised he had no choice. Su was out there in the jungle somewhere. Heaven alone knew what was happening to her. He had his briefcase with him and took out Delaporte's book. Opening it at page 381, he pointed to the red circle around Ta Keo.

'As you know if you listened in to the message I left on Su's cell phone, Hong Soeung is there up at Ta Keo. I'm sure of it. From Delaporte's description of the place this is the same Ta Keo that Soeung was writing home about. But still we have to find him. Even if this map is accurate, it only gives us the broad coordinates. We could spend a long time looking for Soeung if this is all we have to go on, and we might never be successful. From what I understand, you can be right on top of one of these temples in the jungle and still not realise they are there.'

Mercier took the book from Prescott and studied the map. 'You might not see much on the ground,' he agreed. 'But with the right kind of aerial photographs it can be a different matter.'

He went to his desk and tapped at the keyboard of a computer. 'JCM Enterprises has a major telecommunications division as you probably know. We have our own commercial satellite up in the sky there over Asia. People in this country and I suspect in many others, are fed up with running to NASA cap in hand every time they want a photo. We offer a cheaper, better service. Over the last six months we have accumulated satellite images of the whole of former Indochina. Colour as well as black and white. Infra-red too. The problem with all this stuff is knowing where to look and what to look for. If you don't know that, these images are not much help. There's just too much to analyse. But if you know what to look for, it's a different story. Thanks to you, we now do know where to look and we know what to look for. Look, this is Angkor Wat. See the lake, see the roads, see the temples.'

Prescott watched fascinated as Mercier brought up one image after another of the great Angkor Wat complex. He could now see the pattern of the temples in the jungle, the rectangular lakes, the water-filled moats, the encircling jungle.

'Now give us the co-ordinates for Ta Keo from Delaporte's map,' Mercier instructed. 'As near as you can. We'll try to pinpoint it this way.'

Prescott screwed up his eyes to read the small print at the margins of the page. 'North 15' 50. East 102' 60.'

'That's close enough,' Mercier said. He tapped at the keyboard again.

They looked at the photographs first. Full-colour photographs taken on a cloudless day. Mercier used the mouse to centre the image.

'Read off those co-ordinates again,' he instructed.

Both men gazed at the screen. 'Jungle. Nothing but bloody jungle,' Mercier commented.

'Take it closer,' Prescott thought he could discern beneath all the greenery a series of patterns in the forest, some oblong, some square. He jabbed with his finger at the screen. 'Look, here and here! There has to be something there under the trees!'

'Let's see what it's like in infrared,' Mercier said. 'The jungle will show up in red, but if there are buildings or temples or any other kind of stone construction there beneath the canopy, they'll show up in grey or black.'

As he spoke, he manipulated the keyboard. Suddenly, Mercier let out a gasp of astonishment. 'What on earth is that?' he exclaimed. An intricate pattern of images filled the screen. 'Christ! This is even bigger than the Angkor complex!'

'It's Ta Keo. That's what it is,' Prescott said quietly. 'And it's not just one temple. It's hundreds of temples. Delaporte believed that Ta Keo was the site of Amarendrapura, the lost city of Jayavarman II, the man who styled himself, "Emperor of the World." This could be the most important architectural discovery of the new millennium. If Hong Soeung has been working away all these years up there, if he's still there, he's going to become an international celebrity overnight when the news gets out – Albert Schweitzer, Dr Jonas Salk and Magic Johnson all rolled into one. I'd say Khin Lay knows this. He's going to use Hong Soeung to add legitimacy to the new regime. Hong Soeung is going to be an international super-star and he's going to be right there, sitting at Khin Lay's right hand.'

Mercier clicked away with the mouse, saving the images to disc.

'We can get the detailed locations from these,' he said. 'My people will work out the best route in. They're good at that kind of thing. They've got all the tools we need.'

For a moment, Mercier studied the screen. He fiddled with the mouse, zooming in on a corner of the screen then pulling down and enlarging the image. He pointed with his finger. 'I'm not an expert but I'd say there's a cleared area here which looks big enough. We're going to need that. '

'What for?' Prescott asked.

'To put the helicopters down, of course,' Mercier replied, surprised by Prescott's question. 'We can't just hover at tree-top height, can we?'

CHAPTER 23

Su learned that the man's name was Ung Pa. He was pleased as punch with his new leg and determined to get home as quickly as he could to show it off. But he either couldn't, or wouldn't, give a description of the route he planned to take.

'First the lake, then the river, then a small river, then we walk,' he told them.

As far as the logistics were concerned, Su left it to the experts. When, the previous evening, she had told her guide, Heng, that she planned to try to visit Ta Keo, he had insisted on coming with her.

'All my life I have heard rumours that such a place exists,' he said excitedly. 'I would like to come with you. It would be better for you to have an escort you know even if this man, Ung Pa, is reliable.'

Su had not needed much convincing.

As it turned out, Heng relished the responsibilities which Su had entrusted to him. 'We're going to need a boat,' he told her. 'My firm can organise that. We'll follow the north shore of the Tonle Sap lake, then go upriver. The tricky bit is going to be navigating the creeks and the waterways once we leave the main stream of the river. We're going to have to hope that Ung Pa is as good as his word and that he knows the way. There won't be any road signs.'

It took Heng two days to put everything in hand. Su became

increasingly impatient with the delay. She sensed the pressure building. Some of that pressure, she recognised, came from within. Though Ung Pa had been unwilling to talk in detail about life in Ta Keo, on two occasions at least, he had spoken about a "wise leader" who had lived in the area for many years and whom the locals regarded with a respect bordering on reverence. Su was totally convinced that this "wise leader" was none other than her father and the prospect of meeting him filled her with a strange combination of joy and dread. Joy, because she found the idea of seeing her progenitor again after so many years literally overwhelming. But dread too in terms of what she might still discover. So much was still unexplained about the past. Had Hong Soeung really been part of the Khmer Rouge movement? What role had he played? Had he known that Su and her mother had survived the Killing Fields? If so, why had he not tried to contact them?

These were all questions which she had rehearsed a hundred times, a thousand times, in her own mind. The answers still eluded her.

Su was sufficiently self-aware to recognise that her normal sense of equilibrium had been seriously jolted by recent events. But she also had the strong feeling that there were other external factors at play. She felt that they were in a race against time. The local Siem Reap newspapers which she had glanced at from time to time in the hotel lobby had been dropping hints about the 'rapidly evolving political situation' and had been running prominent photographs of Khin Lay as though determined to signal that, if push came to shove, the Minister of the Interior could rely on his local power base to stand up and be counted. You didn't stick your neck out, Su reflected, if you thought it was about to be cut off. Whatever might be the situation in Phnom Penh, up here in the boon-docks, a lot of people clearly believed that Khin Lay was about to take over the country and were making their dispositions accordingly.

Of course, coups could be bloodless. Power could move from one man to another or from one group to another with-out any accompanying violence. If a coup was in the offing, Su prayed that it would indeed be non-violent.

From a purely selfish point of view she feared that an out-break of political turmoil would scupper her plans to find Ta Keo and her father. If the expedition (as she thought of it) was still in Siem Reap when the balloon went up and Khin Lay made his move, it might never leave town. On the other hand, once they had crossed the Great Lake and were nosing their way upriver into the Kulen mountains, it might be a different story. The warring factions, if it came to that, might have oth-er things to think about.

Once or twice, she tried to get hold of Prescott. She wanted to tell him what she was doing and where – approximately – she was going. Admittedly she still had no idea of the precise location of Ta Keo, but at least she had established that Ta Keo existed. That was a piece of news which she longed to impart to Prescott. She wanted to bask in his admiration. How many hours had they spent – both of them – pouring over maps and then, a man hobbles into the clinic and lets the cat out of the bag!

Her cell phone resolutely refused either to receive or trans-mit. She simply wasn't getting a signal. Once the hotel oper-ator managed to get her an international line, but Prescott's own mobile seemed to be uncontactable. In the end she got through to *The New York Times* office in New York and left a message with the news desk.

'Please tell Prescott that I'm still in Cambodia,' Su told them. 'Tell him I'm going upriver to Ta Keo. He'll know what I mean.'

The man who took the message didn't give his name, but he had a great sense of humour. 'Sounds like *Apocalypse Now*. Remember that great scene when they find Mr Kurtz, played by Marlon Brando, amid the ruins. The horror, he whispered melodramatically, the horror...'

Su slammed the phone down in frustration. There seemed to be no way of getting a message through to Prescott in time.

Later, when she had calmed down, she realised it didn't really matter. If Prescott knew where she was going, he would try to stop her, to talk her out of it. Su's jaw was set. She was a big girl now. This was her show.

★★★

They finally left Siem Reap at dawn on the first Friday in December.

'We'll leave the jeep by the lake,' Heng told her. 'We often do that when we take tourists to see the floating villages. We have people there to guard the vehicles.'

'We could be away some time, couldn't we?' Su was worried. She was defraying the whole cost of the expedition on her Visa Gold guard (happily accepted as a means of payment by Heng's company) but she didn't want to cover the loss of a FWD Hyundai as well.

Heng reassured her. 'A week or ten days at the most if all goes well. Our boat has a motor. We won't have to paddle.'

'I don't think I'd mind a bit of exercise,' Su said. 'I rather like the idea of paddling.'

They drove out of town into the countryside. The road, as ever, was severely potholed but passable. Houses gave way to fields and, as the sun rose, the farmers were already making their way into the paddy fields.

They reached the Great Lake, where their boat was waiting for them, and by nine in the morning, they had transferred their supplies and were ready to leave.

Heng and Su together helped Ung Pa aboard.

'How's the leg holding up?' Su asked, looking at the shiny new prosthesis fitted to the man's left knee.

'Fine, really fine,' Ung Pa replied.

An extraordinary transformation seemed to have taken place in the man's demeanour. Whereas during his time in Siem Reap, Ung Pa had been reticent, even surly, now he was cheerful and almost talkative. The prospect of going home had obviously cheered him up enormously. He settled himself in the bow of the boat.

'Can you see all right?' Heng shouted, taking the tiller.

The man gave a thumbs-up sign.

'We'll be all right on the lake,' Heng explained. 'But when we go up-river, we can run into sandbanks or submerged trees. Ung Pa knows the way, but that doesn't mean you don't have to keep a lookout. We certainly don't want to run aground.'

'I imagine not,' Su said. She was grateful that Heng sounded so confident. He had probably been messing about in boats all his life, she thought. If you lived in Cambodia, boats were a necessity. Half the time the place seemed to be under water. No wonder the ancient kings had been able to build all those amazing temples. They just floated the stones downstream.

She noted that Heng had slung a rifle over his shoulder. She pointed to it. 'What's that for?'

'Tigers, snakes, bandits!' Heng smiled. 'Are you sure you want to do this?'

'Am I ever!' Su replied.

Heng pulled on the rope and the engine roared into life.

***

They spent the whole of the first day crossing the Great Lake. For Su, it was a magical experience. The sheer expanse of Tonle Sap amazed her.

'During the rainy season, the lake covers over ten thousand square kilometres,' Heng told her. 'Now the water is flowing out. By the time the dry season comes, the lake will be less than three thousand square kilometres.'

Su remembered the rowers in their huge pirogues thrashing up and down the river outside her hotel during the great Water Festival which celebrated the annual reversal in the direction of the flow of the Tonle Sap River. These rituals had a point, she thought. It made sense to celebrate, to offer up incense, to scatter flower petals on the water. There were good reasons for thanksgiving. As they puttered along the shoreline, she could see that the water which was now flooding out of the Great Lake was leaving behind a treasure-trove of biological riches. The fishermen were out in force, some using nets, some using fish traps suspended from trees. Along the shoreline, the floating villages rose and fell with the water level in the lake.

You could have fish for breakfast, lunch and dinner without getting out of bed, Su thought. Just lean out of your hammock and pull a net through the water.

When she suggested as much to Heng, he shook his head.

'It may look idyllic,' he said, 'but this is a hard life. Illegal fishing methods are damaging the spawning beds in the forest. That, and reduced water levels in the Mekong, have led to big reductions in the catch.'

They stopped for lunch at one of the floating villages, tying up on the outskirts and clambering up a wooden ladder into one of the houses.

'My aunt,' Heng explained, introducing Su to a toothless old lady who welcomed them with surprising enthusiasm. 'I often bring visitors to see her when I'm on the lake. She has a crocodile farm. She sells the young crocodiles and skins in Thailand.'

Su gave a start when she realised that the crocodiles were in mesh cages directly underneath the house. She peered down through a crack in the floorboards.

'Drop your lunch down there and you'll see an explosion!' Heng said.

He tossed a fish-head into the water and Su felt the boards beneath her shake as the crocodiles went for it.

'Don't do that again,' she instructed. 'That frightens me!'

Heng laughed. 'You'll get used to it.'

One of the things Su didn't get used to was the mosquitoes. That evening, before dusk, they tied up alongside another floating village. Though she had liberally doused herself with repellents, the moment the sun set, the mosquitoes arrived in voluminous, black clouds.

'Christ almighty,' Su exclaimed, as she lashed out wildly. 'Can't you spray these things with insecticide?'

Heng was less than sympathetic. 'If you spray the lake, you poison the fish. Besides, we need the mosquitoes. In their larval form, they consume organic matter. That prevents eutrophication.'

Su wrapped herself from head to toe in a sheet and retreated, muttering, to her hammock.

Around mid-morning on the second day, the colour of the water in the lake changed. Sandbanks had built up along the shore.

'This is where the Stoeng Chikreng river flows into the Tonle Sap Lake. Ung Pa told me that we would be following the river upstream from here.'

'How long for?' Su asked.

'He didn't say. I've been on the Stoeng Chikreng once before, but only a little way. This will be different.'

As he was speaking, Ung Pa signalled to him to turn the boat into the current and head upriver.

It was eery, Su thought, what a difference just a few minutes could make. One moment they were on the wide-open lake; the next the forest was hemming them in on either side. Except for brief glimpses, the sun was eclipsed by the canopy of trees. They could hear the squawk of parrots and the gibber of monkeys above the sound of the engine.

At the point it debouched into the Tonle Sap Lake, the Stoeng Chikreng river had been at least two hundred yards wide. By the time they had proceeded five miles upstream, the river was barely fifty yards wide. They steered a middle course trying to avoid shallow waters, sunken trees and other obstacles. Su had to admire the skill with which the two men navigated. Ung Pa, from his vantage-point in the front of the boat, used hand signals to guide Heng at the tiller. You had to watch like a hawk, Su realised, if you didn't want to end up stuck in the sand with nothing for it but to try to push the boat off the shoals with a load of crocodiles snapping at your legs.

Once, when Heng reacted too late to a hand signal, they did hit a sandbar. The boat juddered to a halt and Ung Pa, perched precariously in the prow, was almost pitched overboard.

The man shouted and swore and Heng apologised profusely.

From time to time, Su sensed that they were not alone. She had a strong feeling that their progress upstream was being observed. Her skin crawled.

'Do people live in the jungle?' she asked.

'They do, but you won't necessarily see them,' Heng said. 'We're in a boat with a motor. In their eyes, that means we probably represent the authorities. For tribals, that's usually trouble of one kind or another, so they'll keep out of the way.'

Su was only moderately reassured. 'What about the Khmer Rouge?'

'We'll just have to wait and see,' Heng said.

He sounded more confident than he felt. Back in Siem Reap, the idea of setting off into the jungle to discover the long-lost site of Ta Keo had seemed challenging enough. Now he wasn't so sure.

'How much further before we leave the river?' he called out to Ung Pa.

'Four hours, five hours,' the man replied.

An hour before dusk, they turned off the main stem of the now much shrunken Stoeng Chitreng onto a smaller watercourse which appeared to run into the river from a north-easterly direction.

Thirty minutes later, when the gloom of night had already reached the forest even though the sun had not yet set, they made camp for the night.

Heng got a fire going and Ung Pa, using a primitive bamboo pole and metal hook, landed some fish for their supper.

When the fish had been grilled, they sat around the fire. Su ate with one hand, using the other to swat away the mosquitoes and other insects.

Ung Pa's good humour had stayed with him. He was clearly delighted with his new leg and even more delighted to be on his way home.

'Do your people know you are coming?' Su asked him, as she used her chopsticks to scoop the last of the fish into her bowl.

Ung Pa nodded.

'How do they know?'

'They will smell the smoke from our fire.'

'How do they know we are friends, not enemies?'

'They will see me. That's how they will know,' Ung Pa said.

Soon after that, they turned in for the night. Su lay on her back in the hammock, staring into the darkness. Christ, how noisy the jungle was at night, she thought! The monkeys seemed to be having a party next door. The night-owls shrieked ominously every few minutes and once she fancied she heard the none-too-distant roar of a tiger. Cambodia still had up to a thousand tigers, she remembered reading some-where. As far as she was concerned, just one tiger prowling around the camp was too many.

Next morning, they set off again as soon as it was light enough to see what they were doing. The going was tricki-er now. There was no question of making a stately progress upstream by sticking to the middle of the river and watching the vegetation on either side pass by at a safe distance. The channel had grown so narrow that at times they had to use their long curving knives, like machetes, to clear the branches which impeded the passage of the boat. Anyone who wanted to hide behind a tree and fire a poison arrow at them at point-blank range would have a field day, Su thought.

Just how lucky they were to have Ung Pa as a guide, soon be-came apparent. On more than one occasion, they had a choice of routes. The stream they were following would branch into two and they would have to decide which watercourse to fol-low. Ung Pa hardly hesitated. He seemed to know the way in-stinctively, signalling vigorously when the need arose so that Heng could swing the tiller to right or left.

The ambush, when it happened, took even Ung Pa by surprise. Sometime around mid-afternoon, they rounded a bend and almost immediately found their way blocked by a tree. Whether the tree had fallen naturally in that position or whether it had been felled on purpose, they did not have time to establish.

Before they were able to react, certainly before Heng could lift the gun to his shoulder, half a dozen men with red ker-chiefs around their necks jumped onto the boat from the bank, almost causing it to capsize.

'What the hell is happening!' Su exclaimed. 'Who are these people?'

'They're the Khmer Rouge,' Heng replied, standing next to her. 'I'm not sure what happens next, but we're certainly not going to fight. I think Ung Pa is going to talk to them.'

Moments later, things looked much better. Ung Pa, it turned out, was well known to the Khmer Rouge. They had been expecting him for days and had realised only the day before that he was on his way back.

'You didn't have to give us a fright like that,' Ung Pa protested.

'Just practising,' a tall, young man who appeared to be the leader of the Khmer Rouge group replied. He laughed heartily, showing a flash of white teeth.

If that was what passed for a joke up here, Su thought, it was a pretty poor effort.

Happily, the young man seemed to have his team well under control. One or two of the band eyed her hopefully but Su felt confident that the Khmer Rouge's almost legendary sense of discipline would prevail. They might ask her some tricky questions about who she was and what she was doing but she didn't think she was going to be assaulted.

In the event, within less than ten minutes, it was smiles all round. Ung Pa proudly showed off his new limb, demonstrating his newly recovered agility by leaping from the boat to the bank and back again. The Khmer Rouge were both amazed and delighted. And when Ung Pa explained that Su's organisation and indeed Su herself had been responsible for this magical transformation, their admiration knew no bounds.

They set to and unloaded the boat, stacking the cargo on

the riverbank. The leader of the band solicitously helped Su to the shore. Once she was on terra firma, he decided to make a little speech.

'We are honoured by your presence among us,' he said. 'We respect the work which you and your organisation are doing in our country. Welcome to Ta Keo!'

Su didn't have to expend a great deal of mental energy in working out what to say in reply.

'I too – and my good friend Heng – are honoured to be here. We are pleased that we have been able to help Ung Pa return to his people.'

***

Su sounded more confident than she felt. Not so long ago, she recalled, a party of tourists visiting one of the temples in the jungle not far from Angkor had been taken hostage by the Khmer Rouge and at least two of them had been murdered in cold blood. Having Ung Pa with them was, she supposed, some kind of a guarantee. But things could still go wrong.

They walked for three hours through the jungle, then, with at least two hours of daylight left, they began to climb. The path twisted and turned and though Su tried to memorise the way, she soon gave up the attempt. That they were heading towards a Khmer Rouge stronghold in the Kulen mountains she had no doubt. But she was equally sure that, unaided, she would never find her way there again.

At one point, the KR leader, who was walking immediately in front of her, turned round and admonished her for being about to take a shortcut.

'Be careful!' he shouted. 'Follow in my steps. Don't deviate!'

Su quickly stepped back onto the path.

'What's the matter?' she asked.

By way of reply, the young man pointed to some almost invisible tripwires made of fine steel wire strung across the track she had been tempted to take.

'Mines' he explained. 'They'll blow you to pieces.'

Su shuddered. She didn't have to be told about the effects of landmines. Fragmentation mines, directional mines, bounding mines – in her short time in Cambodia she had become aware of the full horror of this particular weapon of war. The fact that the Khmer Rouge were still using these devices to protect their mountain stronghold was not surprising. She doubted whether any of them had even heard of Princess Diana and the Landmines Treaty. That was another world.

For the rest of the climb, she stuck scrupulously to the footprints of the man in front of her. She hadn't come all this way to be blown up at the last moment. They marched on for another four hours. Su imagined they would stop for the night, but they didn't. The moon rose early, a full moon, and with the thinning of the forest the track was easier to follow.

Around nine in the evening, they came to a mountain pass, a narrow saddle of land between two summits. While the rest of his band helped the now struggling Ung Pa to cover the last few hundred yards to the vantage point, the young KR leader stood beside Su and pointed to the vast saucer-shaped tree covered valley which lay beneath them.

'Down there is Ta Keo,' he told her. 'That's where we are going.'

Su stood in silence, gazing down into the valley. So, this was it, she thought. The elusive Ta Keo, the place which her father had stumbled on a quarter of a century earlier. Was he still there now?

'Why are we waiting?' Su asked. Ung Pa had joined them at last. He looked tired from his exertions, but he gave her a warm smile.

'Do you want to rest, or do you want to go on now?' the KR leader asked.

'Let's go on,' Ung Pa replied. 'I want to see my wife to-night. I want to show her my new leg.'

'Just the leg?' one of the soldiers joked.

The young KR leader ignored him. 'Let's go then,' he or-dered.

On the way down into the valley, Su could glimpse in the moonlight the outline of vast structures, huge crumbling monuments overgrown with vegetation.

Heng caught up with her. He was staggered by the size and number of the monuments. Even in the darkness he was able to grasp the sheer scale of the place. This was Angkor Wat and Angkor Thom, the Bayon and Ta Prohm all rolled into one.

'Good Lord!' he exclaimed, staggered that this extraordi-nary complex of ruins had lain undiscovered all these years. 'This is much more than Ta Keo, much more than just one jungle temple. This is a whole city.' He could hardly speak for excitement. 'This must indeed be Jayavarman II's long-lost capital – Amarendrapura!'

Su had other things on her mind at this moment. She turned to the Khmer Rouge leader. 'Can you take me to Hong Soeung?'

The young man smiled. 'He is waiting for you. He knows you are coming. He sent us to find you.'

For a moment, Su was at a loss for words. How on earth could Hong Soeung have known that she was coming? How could he have known she even existed?

Finally, she managed a staccato reply. 'Good. I'll follow you then,' she said.

The young man led her across a clearing in the forest towards a tribal long house set back among the trees.

CHAPTER 24

He was standing in the middle of the room, waiting for her. He held out his arms and hugged her to him. Tears streamed down his cheeks.

'I can hardly believe it,' he said. 'Until two months ago, I had no idea that you were alive and now you're here!'

She clung to him. The years fell away. She was still a child and he was still daddy. She couldn't speak. Didn't trust herself to speak. Just held on to him, sobbing.

After a while, he pushed her gently away, took out a handkerchief and gave it to her so that she could dry her eyes.

'You look wonderful,' he said. 'So beautiful, so young.'

'You're not looking bad yourself.' She smiled at him through watery eyes.

Of course, he had changed. His hair had gone grey, there were lines around his mouth. One of his teeth was missing. She didn't remember that. But he was still her father, still Hong Soeung. She didn't doubt that for one moment. She had recognised him the moment she saw him. This was a face she had loved, still loved. There was nothing to say. There was too much to say. She didn't know how to begin.

Hong Soeung helped her. 'Tell me about your mother,' he said. 'Is she well? I read the article in the paper. *The Washingtonian*? That was it, wasn't it? It was a good piece. Sita sounds happy in Seattle. And you are obviously a star. I am so proud to have a famous daughter.'

'You read the article?' Su at last found her tongue, incredulous. 'Why didn't you contact us if you knew we were still alive?'

'I did contact you,' Hong Soeung replied gently. 'That's why you are here. So that we can talk. So that you can understand.'

They went outside and sat on the veranda. Hong Soeung took out his pipe and lit it. The smell of the tobacco seemed so familiar to her that she could almost believe she was back in the house at 14, Street 310, getting ready for bed with her father deciding which goodnight poem to recite.

'Perhaps you had better begin at the beginning,' she said.

They talked for hours that night.

'You say, "begin at the beginning." But what is the beginning?' Hong Soeung asked. 'Is it our family life in Phnom Penh before the Khmer Rouge took over? That's your beginning, of course. You were born in 1970 at the time Lon Nol came to power. But your beginning is not my beginning. You have to understand that.'

'What is your beginning?' Su asked.

Hong Soeung puffed at his pipe. 'For present purposes, Paris, I suppose. Paris in the 1950s. I don't know if I can explain to you how exciting it was. We were all there. Saloth Sar, whom of course you know as Pol Pot. Ieng Sary. Thion Mumm. Khin Lay.'

'Khin Lay too?' Su asked.

'Oh yes. Khin Lay was my best friend. I shared digs with Pol Pot in the Rue Letellier, but I was never really close to him. He was too much of a cold fish. But Khin Lay was like a brother.'

'Why was Paris so exciting?'

'We believed we had a chance to change the world. It was as simple as that. We knew that sooner or later the French would have to pull out of Indochina. The rise of the nationalist movements there was irresistible. Ho Chi Minh had himself been to Paris and had returned to Vietnam to found the Vietnamese Communist Party. The Pathet Lao had begun to fight in Laos. That left Cambodia. Why should Cambodia be left behind? We were a small group of Cambodian students, meeting in the cafés and on the boulevards of Paris but we knew we could give Cambodia a future too, a future our country deserved.'

'A communist future?' Su interrupted.

'Yes, why not? Communism wasn't a dirty word then, not for us.' If Hong Soeung felt on the defensive, he did not show it. 'When we were in Paris, Pol Pot founded the Cambodian Communist Party. Secretly, of course. We didn't put up posters in the streets. Those of us who were in France at that time became the very first members of the party. Pol Pot was Brother Number One, Ieng Sary was brother Number Two, Khieu Samphan was Brother Number Three, Khin Lay was Brother Number Five.'

'And Brother Number Four? Who was Brother Number Four?'

'I was Brother Number Four.'

'Oh my God!' Su exclaimed.

'Don't be shocked,' Hong Soeung told her. 'It was only later things went wrong. At the start, as I said, we were full of idealism. When we emerged from the colonial era, we wanted to build a new country. We saw that they had tried it in France and that it had worked. *Liberté, fraternité, egalité*. That's what we believed in.'

'They didn't massacre two million people in France,' Su protested.

Hong Soeung sighed. 'I'm not trying to defend what happened, Su.'

It was the first time her father had called her by her name in more than a quarter of a century and she felt her heart turn over. But she wasn't ready to forgive. Not yet.

'You deserted us, didn't you?' she challenged.

Hong Soeung sighed again. 'How often have I wished it could have been otherwise! I can't forgive myself, but at least I can try to explain. When I came back from Paris, no-one except for the four I have mentioned – Pol Pot, Ieng Sary, Khieu Samphan and Khin Lay – knew I belonged to the Khmer Rouge and was a founding member of the Cambodian Communist Party. That was a strict secret. The idea was that I would be a "sleeper," rising to a senior position within government, to be deployed only when the moment was ripe.

'And that was precisely how it happened. In Paris, I had already made a name for myself as a student of archaeology. When I returned in 1952 to Phnom Penh, I was offered a job in the Ministry of Culture. And that was where I stayed. I quickly rose to the top in the Ministry and by the time Lon Nol came to power in 1970 I had become the senior civil servant there. This meant I knew all the secrets of the Lon Nol regime. The top civil servants from all the ministries met together every week. In reality, we ran the country. The Ministers, even the King, were mainly figure-heads.'

'And you betrayed them all?' Su hated having to hurt him when she already felt so close to him, but she knew she had no alternative. To understand all might be to forgive all – *tout comprendre, c'est tout pardonner* – but first she had to understand.

A wounded expression came over Hong Soeung's face. She had hurt him.

'Who did I betray?' he countered. 'Lon Nol and some other corrupt generals who were bent on bleeding the country dry? My friends, my classmates, were out there in the countryside, raising the standard of revolt. Risking their lives. They were not evil men. Not then, at least. Their methods may have been rough, but they were fighting to win, to change centuries of history overnight. If Mao Zedong could do it in China, we believed we could do it in Cambodia. If I had not helped the movement at that point, that would have been a betrayal, a much greater betrayal.'

Su listened to what Hong Soeung was saying. She tried to imagine what it must have been like to have been a young man in Cambodia thirty years earlier, fighting the system. If she had been there then, might she not have joined the Khmer Rouge too?

'If you were a party member, why did they arrest you then that day?' Su asked. 'Why did they cart you away when I was screaming for you to stay with us? If you had told them who you were, they would have let us all go.'

Hong Soeung shook his head. 'How I wish I could have done that, but it was impossible. As I said, for almost twenty years, I had been living under the deepest cover. Even your mother had absolutely no inkling that I was cadre. Of course, she knew I had been in Paris. She knew I had met other Cambodian students there, but I never talked about those days, never mentioned Pol Pot or Ieng Sary or the others.

'Don't think I don't remember that day in April 1975

when the men came to our house. I shall never forget it. It was the worst day of my life. I have often asked myself what else I could have done. If I had blurted out then and there that I was a Khmer Rouge operative, they wouldn't have believed me. Why should they have believed me? It was just what they would have expected a frightened man to say and they would have punished us for it. The likelihood is that we would all have been shot or beaten to death on the spot.'

'So they took you away and threw you into Tuol Sleng? That wasn't an invention?'

Hong Soeung nodded. 'No question about that. I have the scars to prove it.'

He pointed to his mouth. 'They beat me up, knocked my teeth out, tortured me for days. I was desperate to get out, desperate to find out what had happened to you and your mother. I was in there a week before they released me.' He shuddered. 'I never want to go through that again.'

'How did they realise their mistake?' Su asked.

'We all had to write confessions. That was part of the policy. They tortured you to extract a confession and then, when you finally had written what they wanted, they killed you. I wrote the truth. It was the only thing I could do. I wrote that I was a Khmer Rouge agent, not just a Lon Nol functionary. I hoped that someone from Santebal – that was the Khmer Rouge leadership – would see it. Someone who knew who I was and my place in the party.

'One day, Duch came into my cell, shouting and swearing and they let me go. They took me to Pol Pot. To his villa in the suburbs. He had taken over the US Ambassador's residence. He poured me wine, fine wine from the cellar and greeted me like an old friend. We were old friends. He wanted me to join the new government then and there in Phnom Penh but I refused. I said I had work to do up-country. I was shocked and horrified by what I had seen on the streets of Phnom Penh, by what I saw in Tuol Sleng. I heard of the carnage which was taking place in the countryside as they moved the people out of the city. I never dreamed it could be like that. Of course, I didn't tell him all that. I kept quiet. As far as I was concerned, Pol Pot was already a madman. A dangerous madman.'

Hong Soeung paused. 'There were times when I thought I myself would go mad, literally mad. When I left the city, I looked everywhere for you and your mother, but it was hopeless. There was no way of telling where you had gone. The whole country was in chaos. I realised as I pursued my enquiries that I risked being arrested again and this time there might be no one to get me out. In the end, after months of searching, I came to the conclusion that you had died in the horror of the Killing Fields. So many thousands of others had died. Hundreds of thousands. How could you have escaped?'

'And you came here to Ta Keo?'

'Yes, I came here to restore my sanity, to recover my self-respect if you like. This place is a total secret. I discovered it almost by accident in 1950 when I came back from Paris. I'll tell you the whole story later. All I need to say now is that I realised that there was a lifetime's work here at Ta Keo and I said to myself that this is what I would do – indeed – for the rest of my life. Bury myself in work. Ah, yes, and it has worked. Not just as therapy. We have achieved something here, Su. Tomorrow I will show you what we have achieved. We have discovered one of the wonders of the world and soon the world will know about it.'

As the hours passed, they continued to talk. There was so much else Su needed to ask, so much to understand.

'You said you learned we were still alive from the article in *The Washingtonian*. Who showed you the piece?'

'Khin Lay did. We have stayed in touch over all these years. He is a big man now, the leader of FUNCINPEC. You know that don't you?'

Su nodded. 'We met Khin Lay. An impressive man. The press – or parts of it – seem to think he's going to oust Hun Sen to become the next Prime Minister.'

'I know. We don't get the printed papers up here, but we can get onto the web. We have a satellite link-up. Ancient and modern rolled together.'

Hong Soeung laughed. His eyes were warm and smiling. This was a man still full of energy, of vitality.

'So Khin Lay emailed you the article, did he? Just that?'

Hong Soeung put his arm round his daughter. 'No, he came to see me. He had a plan. He wanted me to help.'

For the next few minutes, Hong Soeung gave Su the benefit of his own view of Cambodia's past, present and future. He spoke of the origins of the civil war, of the continued factionalism, of the danger of a renewed outbreak of internecine warfare.

'Khin Lay was convinced,' he said, 'that the efforts being made to bring the Khmer Rouge leaders – Duch and Ta Mok – before an international tribunal, or even a national tribunal, would end in disaster. Admittedly, the policy was being foisted on Hun Sen as a result of outside pressure, but still he was going along with it for his own purposes as a way of consolidating his power. Khin Lay reminded me that the United Nations had already appointed its overlord, an Australian, Geoff Jackson. Jackson was a good man, Khin Lay said. Too good. He was determined to see the tribunal open for business. The jury was about to be empanelled. As Khin Lay saw it, the day the tribunal declared Duch and Ta Mok guilty would be the day this country, once again, tore itself apart.'

He half-turned to face her. 'What you have to understand, Su, is that you can't just wipe the Khmer Rouge out. That means civil war. Even today, their supporters are everywhere. They may not wear red kerchiefs. They are not necessarily wedded to violence. But they believe passionately in a fairer society. Call it communism, if you like. Others call it common sense.

So, we have to work with, not against them,' he continued. 'That was and is Khin Lay's Point of view. Of course, he does not belong to the Cambodian Communist Party any longer – how could he? He's the leader of FUNCINPEC – but he knows where they are coming from, if you see what I mean. Having been a communist himself once, he understands the mindset. He knows that this country has to be governed not by one party, but by a coalition of all the talents.'

Su was fascinated by Hong Soeung's passionate exposition. It was so easy, she thought, to fly in with one's American set of values. Tribunals and human rights – good; Khmer Rouge and communists – bad. Things were not so simple. Do-gooders, especially do-gooders with ulterior motives, could often make things worse.

'How did Khin Lay think you could help him?' Su asked quietly.

'As I said, Khin Lay came here secretly to see me. About two months ago. He brought the article with him. Our embassy in Washington had circulated it. That's what they mostly do, Khin Lay said. Send back the press cuttings. But this was one press cutting which Khin Lay happened to read with attention. He realised at once who you were and of course he knew he had to tell me. In person. Even though I was and still am – his closest friend, we have not seen much of each other over the years. He has for the most part stayed in Phnom Penh, except when he comes to Siem Reap to make sure his own domestic power base is secure. As you know, I have been locked away in this hidden valley, this secret kingdom for decades, concentrating on my work. Khin Lay sees this as a good moment to renew our friendship. He comes up to Siem Reap and then, when his business there is done, comes to find me.'

Su found it difficult to imagine the Minister of the Interior spending days on the river, then hiking through the jungles and the mountains to reach Ta Keo.

'How did Khin Lay get here?' she asked. 'Your hideout seems pretty inaccessible.'

Hong Soeung gestured to the clearing in front of the long house. 'His helicopter landed right there.'

'So, he knew where you were?'

'Khin Lay has always known where I was. He covered for me when I left Phnom Penh in 1975. Made sure the Khmer Rouge stuck to their side of the bargain, which was to leave me alone to get on with my life and my work.'

For a moment Hong Soeung seemed lost in thought, as though contemplating the passage of years. 'Let me continue,' he said at last. 'Khin Lay comes here with the article from

The Washingtonian. He is witness to my joy, my ecstasy I should say, when I learn that both you and your mother are still alive. I want to get in touch with you both straightway. I want to fly to Seattle, to Washington to meet you again. You have no idea what the news means to me after all these years.

'But Khin Lay stops me. He appeals to me as a friend and as a patriot. He puts a proposal to me, a proposal which – if things work out – will ensure that you personally come to Cambodia, come here to this very valley, and at the same time achieve what Khin Lay sees as the overriding political objective: namely, the shelving of the plans for the tribunal and the humiliation of Hun Sen.

'Of course, I continue to protest. I have no idea how you're going to get here. I have no idea whether Sita – your mother – is even well enough to travel. I see Khin Lay's face harden. He reminds me that I am deeply in his debt, so deeply that it is impossible to argue further.'

'Why?' Su almost shouted. She found it hard to imagine the circumstances which had kept Hong Soeung from them, once he knew they were alive.

'Isn't it obvious?' Hong Soeung replied quietly. 'You seem to have understood so much. Haven't you understood this too?'

'Understood what?'

Hong Soeung spelled it out for her. 'Khin Lay, my brother-in-arms, was the man who ensured that I was freed from Tuol Sleng. He saw the confession I had written for Santebal. He went to Pol Pot and pleaded for my life. Pol Pot was furious. Threatened to have Khin Lay himself executed. Pol Pot said if I had been hob-nobbing with the likes of Tom Enders,

I deserved to die. Pol Pot hated Enders with a passion. Enders would personally call in the airstrikes on the Pol Pot positions. In the end, Pol Pot, shouting and swearing agrees to Khin Lay's request, but their relationship is never the same.

'Honouring Khin Lay's request was a way of repaying a debt of honour?'

He turned to her, pleading for her understanding. 'How could I say no? When he pleaded with Pol Pot, Khin Lay risked his life for me. Pol Pot would have people executed for much less. And how could I ignore the political circumstances? This country is on the verge of collapse. Khin Lay is probably the one man who can save us. And I would say that even if he wasn't my friend.'

Things were starting to become clearer to Su now. 'So together you cook up the Hong Soeung confessions, is that right?' she asked. 'Some new confessions. You have already written one set, but these are different. Khin Lay brings the pen and paper with him, but he takes care to ensure the ink is of the modern variety so that scientific examination will in due course show that these so-called confessions cannot possibly be genuine.'

Hong Soeung laughed. 'I must say that at first I was sceptical. The whole thing seemed too far-fetched. But Khin Lay was persistent. He built up a case. In the end, I could see how the scheme would work. Had to work. All the elements were there.'

'What do you mean?'

Hong Soeung's pipe had gone out. He stuffed some tobacco into the bowl and puffed away noisily until he was sure it was alight.

'You know Andrew Mossman?' he asked.

'Of course, I do. He runs SAVE. He gave me a job. That's why I'm in Cambodia now.'

'Exactly. Mossman and Khin Lay know each other, so Khin Lay told me. They do business together. For SAVE to operate effectively in this country, it needs the support of the Ministry of the Interior. Mossman and Khin Lay have developed a working relationship of some kind.'

As Hong Soeung spoke, Su remembered Prescott's account of the magnificent stone head he had seen in Andrew Mossman's study in Washington. Did the Mossman-Khin Lay relationship include the issuing of export permits for priceless Cambodian antiquities?

'Go on, please,' she urged, as Hong Soeung once again started fiddling with his pipe.

'He said Mossman agreed to offer you a job,' Hong Soeung continued. 'A job which would bring you to Cambodia.'

'Damn Mossman!' Su's pride was hurt. She had been naive enough to believe that she had earned her position on merit, not as a part of some political machination.

'Don't be upset,' Hong Soeung sensed her reaction. 'We needed to be sure that you would start looking for me, that you would visit DC-Cam and Tuol Sleng prison, that you would find the Hong Soeung confessions.'

Su blushed deeply beneath her tan. She felt humiliated, used. 'How could you be sure that I would find all the clues, follow the trail you so cleverly laid?'

'How could you miss the trail?' Hong Soeung replied, 'It was so obvious, you had to see it. And if you missed a marker or two, there were plenty of people to set you straight.'

'Professor Haq, Lina Chan, the guard at the prison, what was his name. Bun? Sarin Bun? Were they all in on this? Do they all work for Khin Lay in one way or another?' Su could feel her anger mounting.

'Su, listen to me,' Hong Soeung tried to calm her. 'This is how it had to be. You had to be convinced and then you would convince others.'

'Like Senator Clinton?'

'Exactly. If you think you have been humiliated, think about Senator Clinton. Think about that Press Conference. If Mrs Clinton had not made a worldwide issue out of the Hong Soeung confessions, the collapse of the tribunal would have been much less spectacular and the damage to Hun Sen might not have been fatal.'

'And the death-list? The list of potential victims which you were supposed to have passed over to the Americans, and which the Americans in turn are meant to have delivered to Pol Pot via their embassy in Beijing and the good offices of George Walker Bush, now President of the United States – was that all part of the same scam, the same charade?'

Hong Soeung didn't meet her eye, didn't answer her directly. 'Khin Lay told me what to write. We had to create a scandal, the biggest possible scandal. The death-list, the possible involvement of President George W. Bush – these were elements designed to ensure that the story had the maximum possible momentum. We needed to build it up, Khin Lay explained, so that the crash when it came would be all the more dramatic.'

'The higher they fly, the harder they fall?'

'You could say so.'

Hong Soeung obviously hoped that Su would let the matter drop, but she wasn't quite ready. For her, it was a matter of knowing what to believe and what not to believe about her father.

'So, there was no death-list at all or if there was a death-list, it didn't come from you? Is that right?'

At last, he looked her in the eye. 'I can give you an assurance about that. Yes, I dealt on a daily basis with the Americans. Yes, I knew Tom Enders and his successors. Yes, I used various methods to communicate with Pol Pot and the others in the field including on occasion passing messages via the American embassy which they would then transmit to their people in Beijing who would in turn be in touch with Sihanouk or Ieng Sary or whoever. Yes, George W. Bush might conceivably have been involved in this chain of communication although personally, I doubt it. But, no, I did not write any death-list at any time for Pol Pot and his men to use on the day they captured Phnom Penh.'

'But Pol Pot had a death-list that day, didn't he?' Su felt that she had to press him. She needed to know that her father was not a murderer, not complicit in murder.

'Please don't persist in this, Su,' he begged her. 'What good does it do? We have to bury the past if we are to live together. I wrote what Khin Lay told me to write that day. I told you. What Khin Lay knew, I cannot say. We were trying to create a document which would take the world by storm. I am not responsible for the detail.'

Hong Soeung was clearly agitated by the turn the conversation had taken. He strode up and down the veranda. 'Don't you see,' he almost shouted, 'we had to produce something that would create a stir. Evidence that the United States supported Pol Pot almost from the start was dramatic enough. Add in the death-list and we had a truly explosive cocktail.'

'And now that the so-called Hong Soeung confessions are discredited, are we to believe that all these elements including the possibility of US backing for Pol Pot and the Khmer Rouge are also to be discounted?'

Hong Soeung flung himself down in his chair once more. 'Why not?' he said. 'Our ultimate purpose was not to discredit the United States, but to remove Hun Sen.'

Su had to let it go. She felt calmer now. She was beginning to see that she had been just a cog in the wheel. But maybe she had been a useful, even essential, cog. 'I feel sorry for Senator Clinton,' she said. 'In order to get rid of Hun Sen, you exploited her ruthlessly, didn't you? That must have been a fairly humiliating experience for her.'

Hong Soeung did not seem to be too concerned about Senator Hillary Clinton's discomfiture.

'Senator Clinton will recover,' he said. 'You can be sure of that. Happily, Hun Sen will not recover. As far as he is concerned, the clock is already ticking.'

The sky was beginning to brighten over the trees. Dawn could not be far off. Somehow, they had managed to talk through the night.

'I'll fetch some tea,' Hong Soeung said.

When he returned, Su asked him a question which had been on the tip of her tongue for a long time.

'Did you know I would come here, to Ta Keo? Were you sure of that too?'

'No, I wasn't sure of that. But I knew you would be looking

for me. I knew you would work out that I might still be alive. After all, I had been in Tuol Sleng, but the confessions were false. Possibly I had not died there.'

'But why would I have come to Ta Keo?' Su persisted.

'I knew the name Ta Keo might mean something to you. I knew you might have read the letter I wrote to your mother about having a life's work in front of me here. When I heard you had come to Siem Reap, I sent a man to the clinic.'

'You mean Ung Pa, the man who brought us back here?'

'Why not?' Hong Soeung shrugged. 'It seemed as good a way as any. I couldn't send a helicopter for you. We may have email and radio and satellite telephones here, but we don't have a helicopter. Besides, when we met for the first time in a quarter of a century, I wanted you to see me as I am. I wanted you to see where I live, how I live. If we are to get to know each other again, you have to understand these things.

'But we have talked long enough. You must be tired. Would you like a rest?'

'Yes, please,' Su replied. She felt exhausted, drained. It was not just the physical effort involved in reaching Ta Keo – the river journey, the trek through the mountains, the descent into the great, secret valley. There was the emotional strain too. Though she had done her best to anticipate it, nothing had really prepared her.

'We must talk more later.' She paused. She wasn't sure what to call him.

He noticed the hesitation. 'I hope you will call me father,' he said. 'I *am* your father, after all.'

'Thank you, father,' she said.

He led her back inside and showed her the bedroom which

had been prepared for her. The sun had already risen, and light was streaming through the window. Hong Soeung closed the curtains.

'When you wake up, we will go up the temple-mountain. Then you will understand what I mean when I say we have discovered a whole new world.'

CHAPTER 25

It was mid-morning when Su awoke. When she had washed and dressed, she walked out onto the veranda to find her father sitting in a bamboo chair with a sheaf of papers in his hand.

She smiled at him. 'Good morning, father. What are you reading?'

'I printed out the last *New York Times* webpages. Thought you might like to look at them. Find out what your man has been up to.'

Of course, during their long and sometimes rambling conversation the previous night, she had told him about Prescott and his job on *The New York Times*, told him that they hoped soon to be married. 'When that happens,' she had added, 'you'll have to give me away. The father always gives away the bride.'

He had hugged her then. 'But I've only just got you back. It's much too soon to give you away.'

He poured her tea, and fussed over her, while she glanced at the print-out. As far as she could see, there was nothing from Prescott in the paper. The G8 summit was over. The captains and the kings had departed. If Prescott was still in Paris, he wasn't filing stories. Later, she thought, she would ask Hong Soeung if she could send an email. If he could access the internet, he would be on email too.

Looking around in daylight, Su could see that there were others, besides herself and Hong Soeung, in the long house. In one of the rooms at the back, she glimpsed a couple of women at work. At the top of the wooden steps which led down from the veranda to the forest floor, a slim, dark girl of about twelve years of age stood, gazing fixedly at her. Su smiled at her and the girl smiled back.

She had to ask him. She had meant to ask him the previous evening but had held back. Hong Soeung had been so keen to have news of her mother, so pleased to know that after all her trials and tribulations, Sita had achieved a life of peace and dignity in the United States, that it seemed a shame at that moment to appear to be too inquisitive. But she knew her mother would be bound to enquire. She would want to know every last detail. As a matter of fact, she realised, she herself needed to know too. It was a material consideration. She had won her father back. How much else had she gained besides?

'It has been twenty-five years, father,' she said. 'All that time you thought my mother was dead. You could have married again. Under the law, that would have been allowed.'

'No, Su, I never married again. I always held your mother in my mind. Though I was certain she was dead, marriage was not an option. But I have not been entirely alone, as you can see. Come, Keav, come and say "hello."'

The young girl stepped shyly onto the veranda, came up to Su and pressed the tips of her fingers together, bowing her head as she did so.

'This is your sister, Su,' Hong Soeung explained. 'She is called Keav. Her mother and I were never married but we lived together for ten years.'

'Where is her mother now?' Su asked, trying to keep the tremor out of her voice.

A look of immense sadness came over Hong Soeung's face. 'She died two years ago. She had gone alone into the forest to pick the wild fruits. Rith – that was her name – loved the forest. That's where her people came from. They were *Montagnards*. She grew up in the forest. After we met, she came and lived here with me and we were happy. But sometimes, when I was about my work, she would slip back into the jungle. She was following a trail through the trees one day when she stepped on a mine. She bled to death before she was found. I look after Keav now. We have a school – there are five or six families here. Of course, I try to teach her myself as much as I can.'

Su held out her arms to the girl and hugged her. She was filled with a sense of joy and wonder. She not only had a father; she had a sister too.

Hong Soeung was still speaking. He sounded anxious, almost pleading. 'Will Sita understand? I do hope your mother will understand.'

If there was one thing Su was completely sure of, it was that her mother would rejoice, as she had rejoiced, in the knowledge that Hong Soeung had had some loving companionship during those long, lonely years in the jungle. She would love Keav as she loved Su herself, as her own daughter.

'Mother will understand,' Su reassured him. 'She will understand perfectly.'

★★★

Later that day, when the sun had passed its zenith, the three of them walked up to the top of the temple-mountain.

Su had wondered where Heng was, but Hong Soeung had given her an evasive reply. 'He will stay here for a few more days,' was all he said. 'When it is all over, he will be able to return to Siem Reap. In the meantime, he will be well looked after.'

'When what is all over?' Su had asked.

'Wait and see,' Hong Soeung replied. 'You will know soon enough.'

As they climbed, Keav held Su's hand. Su wondered how old her mother had been when she died. She wished she could have met her.

'I always dreamed of finding this place,' Hong Soeung told her when they paused for breath. 'When I was an archaeology student in Paris in the early 1950s, I stumbled upon a book by the great French explorer, Louis Delaporte, in which he described how he had once visited Ta Keo. That was a long time ago. In 1873. Delaporte was actually following a clue left by an even earlier French explorer, Commandant de Doudart de Lagrée who explored the Mekong in 1866.

'Delaporte described this fabulous ruin and even shipped some of the statues back to Paris. They were exhibited in the museum there. One of them, in particular, attracted my interest. It was the most beautiful head of Shiva that you can ever imagine, and I knew at once from the style and carving that this was pre-Angkorean.'

He turned towards her to make sure he had her full attention. 'Can you imagine how exciting that was? I realised then that there was a chance that Delaporte had stumbled upon the long lost capital city of Jayavarman II. Scholars knew, of course, that Jayavarman II's capital had been somewhere in the Kulen mountains, but the site had never been located. The problem was Ta Keo itself had over the intervening century totally disappeared from view. Since Delaporte, no-one had been there. Though Delaporte had included a rough map with his description, it was hardly a reliable guide.'

'Go on,' Su urged him, totally immersed in Hong Soeung's story.

'Well, one thing was obvious to me,' Hong Soeung continued. 'When you are on the threshold of an archaeological discovery of this magnitude, you don't shout about it from the rooftops. Archaeologists are the supreme prima donnas. Why do you think we talk about Heinrich Schliemann's Troy, Arthur Evans' Knossos, Howard Carter 's Valley of the Kings? It's because these great men played their cards very close to their chest. They didn't trumpet their discoveries until they were ready to do so. Archaeologists are also quite ruthless. If they can piggyback on someone else's work and grab the credit for themselves, that's exactly what they will do!'

'So you kept your knowledge to yourself?'

'Exactly. In 1952 I came back from Paris to Cambodia to my job at the Ministry of Culture. Whenever I could arrange it, I organised my own expeditions and in 1953 I found the path through the mountains and came upon this hidden valley. I knew then that I had found Amarendrapura, the long-lost capital of Jayavarman II. I was quite convinced of it. But I also knew that it would take decades of work to establish this irrefutably. We would need to map the whole site, explore all the ruins, penetrate the jungle where we had to. As I said, this was a lifetime's work and I was ready for it. In my dreams, I was going to make an even bigger splash when the moment came than Schliemann, or Evans, or Carter ever did!'

By now they were halfway up the temple-mountain. The forest floor spread out beneath them. The vast array of structures which Su had sensed rather than seen the previous night stood revealed in all their magnificence. Monument after monument, temple after temple stretched out across the saucer-shaped valley filling the forest floor from the central point where they stood towards the encircling mountains. The site was awesome, breathtaking. If she looked at it a thousand times, Su thought, she would never cease to be overwhelmed.

'What convinced you that you were on the right track?' she asked him. 'Was it the fact that the ruins here matched Delaporte's description?'

'Exactly so. Even more important, I found the second of the three heads – the head of Brahma – which Delaporte had described.'

It was all coming together in Su's mind. 'That was the piece which you presented to King Sihanouk when he made his famous journey from China to Cambodia, the piece which Ting Wei-Ju now has.'

This was news which Hong Soeung, well-informed though he appeared to be on most matters, had not heard. They paused in mid-climb while Su filled him in with the details.

Hong Soeung was intrigued. 'I remember Ting Wei-Ju well. A remarkable young man. I thought then that he would go far and he obviously has. I'm not surprised Sihanouk passed the piece on to the Chinese. He could hardly have brought it back to Cambodia when he returned in 1975 to become, in effect, the prisoner of the Khmer Rouge.'

'Why did you present the piece to Sihanouk?' Su asked.

Hong Soeung looked at her sharply. 'I suppose it's hard for you to understand the reverence which Cambodians felt for the monarchy at that time. Sihanouk was our King; he was our Emperor. It seemed the right thing to do. I felt comfortable with it.'

Still, she pressed him. 'The head of Siva was in the museum in Paris. The Chinese had the head of Brahma. How did Andrew Mossman acquire the head of Vishnu?'

This time Hong Soeung seemed even more intrigued. 'This is marvellous news. Not that Andrew Mossman has it but that the piece has survived at all. It went missing years ago. It certainly wasn't here when I came back in 1975, after I escaped from Tuol Sleng. I thought then that it might have found its way onto the international art market and it obviously did. How marvellous it would be to bring it back here! How marvellous it would be to bring all three heads back to Ta Keo where they belong!'

Hong Soeung led them up the last three hundred feet to the summit. The precipitous flights of huge steps climbed a succession of levels, with each level having its own array of temples and sanctuaries.

Once again, they paused.

'A Khmer temple is an *imago mundi*.' Hong Soeung told them. 'It is an image of the world. In the Brahmanic concept of the world, there is a central continent, called Jambudvipa, at the heart of which rises the cosmic mountain, Meru, surrounded by the planets. Jambudvipa is encircled by six continents in the shape of concentric rings, the seventh of which is bounded on the outside by a large stone wall. On the sum-

mit of Meru is the city of Brahma, the world of the gods, surrounded by the eight guardians of the points of the compass.

So this is what Jayavarman II built here, the finest temple-mountain, the most splendid *imago mundi* in the whole
history of Khmer architecture. This is where, we now know
for sure, he founded the city of Amarendrapura. And it is here
in the Kulen mountains that he founded the empire of Angkor
and had himself consecrated "King of Kings," – *chakravartin*
in Sankrit.'

★★★

Hong Soeung strode ahead up the last flight of steps to the
third and final level of the temple-mountain. As they climbed,
Su was overcome by the breathtaking beauty of the bas-reliefs,
finely chiselled on the walls; she was staggered by the array of
piers and plinths, a thousand pediments displaying the glory
of the gods or recounting their exploits.

'Good heavens!' she exclaimed. 'This is superb. Even at
Angkor Wat I never saw anything like this.'

'Just wait,' Hong Soeung said.

Five minutes later, they stood in front of the central sanctuary, the mountain peak, the home of the gods. Su craned her
head back to look at the tower soaring high above, silhouetted
against the piercing blue of the sky. Two large birds – eagles,
Su supposed – circled lazily on the thermals.

'The central sanctuary is forty-eight metres high,' Hong
Soeung said. 'That means it is six metres higher than that of
Angkor Wat. And the inner chamber – the *cella* – is also bigger
than the inner chamber at Angkor Wat. The dimensions here

are at least seven metres square and twelve metres tall. Come.'

He led them inside.

'Oh my God!' she exclaimed. The *cella* was lit by shafts of light coming through narrow, slit windows. Looming above them was a gigantic gold statue. She held her breath. She had never seen anything so magnificent in her life.

'That, of course, is a statue of Buddha,' Hong Soeung said. 'Apart from the rock carved Buddhas in southern China, it is probably the largest statue of Buddha in the world. It is certainly the most important. Look at the moulding of the torso, look at the serenity of his expression, look at the way the hands are brought together. This is supreme artistry, is it not?

There is nothing like this at Angkor.'

They walked around the base of the statue, admiring it from all sides.

'What a lot of gold they must have used, daddy,' Keav said, 'to paint it like that. Lift me up so I can look closer.'

Hong Soeung picked the young girl up and put her on his shoulders.

'It's not gold paint,' he said.

'What is it then?' Keav asked.

'It's gold. Pure gold. Through and through.'

'Can I touch it?'

'Yes, you can touch it. We are the guards today!' Hong Soeung moved closer to the statue so that Keav could feel the texture of the metal.

'I've never touched a God before,' Keav said. 'Do you think he'll mind?'

'I don't think so,' Hong Soeung said, lifting her down gently.

They stayed on the last level but one for a good ten minutes, surveying the scene. In her imagination, Su could see not just one temple-mountain, but a whole city, a whole civilization.

'If you look carefully,' Hong Soeung said, 'you can see the outline of the great barays, the vast reservoirs which surrounded the city. During our research, we have traced the canals used to water the paddy fields and to fill the moats around the sanctuaries. Thousands of people lived in this valley. Probably tens of thousands. Of course, it is all jungle now.'

'You have worked with the tribal people all these years?'

'Of course. This is their inheritance too. When this place is open to the public, as soon it will be, they will be the guardians. And I will make sure they derive a benefit from it.'

Su looked at her father as he spoke. He seemed so sure of himself, so confident. There was an inner strength there which she admired and envied.

'How do you know what's going to happen?' she asked.

'It is all planned, Su. Now is the time. We are ready.'

'What do you mean?'

The Ta Keo temple-mountain followed the classic square-shaped alignment. Hong Soeung walked with her to the northern rim of the square, all the way to the parapet, and pulled out a pair of field glasses from his pocket.

'This parapet runs exactly east-west,' he said. 'Take the binoculars and look more or less north-east. You will see there is another pass through the mountains there. That pass leads into Laos. There is a road across the mountains. Try and pick it out. It's only a dirt road of course. More of a rough track, than a road. Have you got it?'

Su fiddled with the focus, trying to find the track Hong

Soeung was talking about. 'I'm not sure I see what you mean.'

Hong Soeung took the glasses from her and looked through them. 'They're there alright. Bang on the dot. Coming through in force.' There was a note of fierce satisfaction in his voice.

He handed the binoculars to Su again and this time she picked up the convoy, a long snaking train of vehicles coming over the mountain and down into the forest.

'Most of the time, you wouldn't see them,' Hong Soeung said. 'They'll have had tree cover all the way from southern China through Laos. It's when they have to cross the mountains in daylight, as they're doing now, that they risk detection.'

'Who are they?' Su asked, keeping the glasses to her eyes. There were no tanks as far as she could see, no half-tracks. From a distance they looked like armoured cars. She counted at least one hundred before she gave up.

'Who are they?' she asked again. 'Why do they all have Red Cross markings?'

'It's the Chinese Army, the People's Liberation Army, the PLA,' Hong Soeung replied. He looked at his watch. 'Their timing's perfect. Khin Lay has done a deal with China. He has agreed to let the Red Army enter Cambodia for a crash de-mining operation. The PLA are experts. They have the men. They have the equipment. Every Cambodian province which still has unexploded mines will be gone through with a fine-tooth comb. It would have taken decades to rid this country of mines. Now, thanks to the terms Khin Lay has agreed with the People's Republic, we shall be able to do it virtually overnight. The column of vehicles you see is just a start. They are heading for Siem Reap, Preah Vinear and Battambang provinces. But other columns even as I speak are heading south and east and west.'

Su wished, more than ever, that Prescott was with her. There were implications here she wasn't sure she understood. Prescott with his keen nose for the great geo-political themes would have known which questions to ask.

Still, she did her best. 'I know Khin Lay is Minister of the Interior and a power in the land. But does he have the authority to strike that kind of a deal with China? I recognise clearing the mines is an overriding priority. That's why organisations like SAVE exist. But inviting the Chinese Army in! Hundreds of vehicles, thousands of soldiers! How can he get away with it? Did Hun Sen agree?'

Again, Hong Soeung checked his watch. 'By now Hun Sen should be on a US destroyer somewhere in the Gulf of Siam. As I understand it, the US has offered him a safe haven in exchange for a promise to go quietly.'

'Why didn't he resist?' Su asked.

'Would you resist?' Hong Soeung replied, 'when the Chinese Army has just entered your country in force and when the majority of your own field commanders have made it clear that they are going to side with Khin Lay?'

'What about Vietnam?' Su asked. 'Aren't the Vietnamese ready to fight to keep their puppet in place?'

'The Vietnamese have told Hun Sen that he's on his own. Escape or die. That's the message. No, Su, it's a done deal.'

Hong Soeung broke off and swivelled on his heel. 'Look!' he instructed.

Coming in low and fast over the mountains from a south-westerly direction, they could see a helicopter.

Su wasn't an expert on helicopters, but she knew this wasn't a Huey gunship. It was a darting dragonfly, not a lumbering giant moth. As it banked steeply to circle the mountain temple where they were standing, she caught a glimpse of the markings – the distinctive logo and the letters JCM stencilled on the fuselage.

The machine hovered, twenty or thirty yards away. Su felt sure that she recognised Jean-Claude Mercier himself at the controls. There was another man in the seat next to the pilot, but she didn't get a good look because of the way the sun glinted on the side-window.

'Jesus Christ!' she exclaimed. She had imagined that the helicopter, if it alighted anywhere, would land on the cleared ground in front of the long house. But instead with a roar and a down-draft that would have ruffed the skirts of the apsaras if they had been wearing skirts, the helicopter came to rest twenty yards from where they were standing, right in front of the towering central sanctuary.

With the rotors still turning, the helicopter door opened.

Prescott Glover leaned out of the door, holding out his hand.

'Jump in, folks!' he shouted. 'You're needed in Phnom Penh. We've been sent to pick you up.'

Su looked at Hong Soeung. Keav looked at Hong Soeung. Soeung didn't hesitate.

'Keep your heads down,' he shouted, running to the machine and beckoning to them to follow him. 'It's going to save a lot of time if we do it this way.'

Keav hesitated. The noise of the helicopter's engine and the whirring of the rotors alarmed her. As Hong Soeung picked the young girl up, she threw her arms around his neck.

'Hold on tight, darling,' Hong Soeung shouted above the noise.

CHAPTER 26

As the helicopter lifted off, Su tried to make herself heard.

'Prescott, this is my father, Hong Soeung. This is my sister, Keav.'

Prescott helped Su and Keav into the rear of the machine and then joined them there himself.

Hong Soeung took the left-hand front seat which Prescott had vacated.

'Welcome aboard, sir,' he shouted. 'I'm so glad to meet you at last.'

Hong Soeung smiled. 'Me too.'

When they reached cruising altitude, the noise of the engine lessened.

'I tried to get in touch with you, Prescott.' Su still had to speak up but at least she didn't have to shout. 'Did you ever get the message I left with your office?'

'Yes, I got it. That's why we're here.'

Hong Soeung turned in his seat to talk to them. 'I wasn't expecting to be picked up till tomorrow. I thought the army would come for me.'

Prescott nodded towards the pilot. 'Mercier talked to Khin Lay earlier today, seeking permission to fly in. Khin Lay seized the opportunity. Told us to bring you along. Apparently, the schedule has been changed. Khin Lay is broadcasting to the nation tonight at six p.m. His first speech as the new Prime Minister. He wants you there beside him.'

Twenty minutes later, they were clear of the forest and crossing the southern part of the Tonle Sap Lake. Ten minutes after that Hong Soeung found himself gazing down at the rice-bowl of Kampong province. Mile after mile of green paddy fields stretched below. Even from five thousand feet, he could see the peasants digging the ditches and tending the watercourses, while the patient bullocks hauled their carts along the raised embankments. This is my country, he thought. These are my people. After so many years of exile in the forest and mountains, he was coming back.

They flew over Ponchentong airport after receiving clearance to land in the grounds of the Royal Palace.

Mercier removed his headphones for a moment to brief them on what was expected. 'They've just told me that there'll be a guard of honour when we touch down. Hong Soeung is going straight to the Prime Minister's office for the broadcast. The rest of us are being escorted to the Cambodiana Hotel, where rooms have been reserved. They'll be in touch with us later.'

Even if he hadn't been to Phnom Penh before, Mercier would have had no difficulty locating the Royal Palace. If you aimed for the junction of the Mekong and Tonle Sap rivers, you flew right over the shimmering roof of the Silver Pagoda and the Royal Palace was next door.

They landed at precisely five p.m. As they disembarked, a guard of honour saluted. Hong Soeung, returning to his hometown for the first time in almost thirty years, squared his shoulders and returned the compliment. He turned to give his companions of the hour a brief, grateful smile.

'Thanks for the ride,' he said. Then they ushered him to the waiting jeep.

'There's a man who has a rendezvous with destiny.' Prescott put one arm round Su and with the other held Keav's hand. 'Time to go.'

★★★

The four of them walked along Sisowath Quay towards the Foreign Correspondents Club of Cambodia with twenty minutes to go before the six p.m. deadline. Su remembered the first time she had visited the FCCC during the great Water Festival. What a long time ago that seemed! How much water had flowed down the Tonle Sap River and into the Mekong since then!

'The place is bound to be packed,' Prescott said.

It was. It was standing room only by the bar. The expatriate community was out in force. Prescott recognised many of the usual suspects. Henri Le Blanc from *Le Monde*, Mark Kelly from CNN's Bangkok office, for example.

'Back again then, Prescott?' Le Blanc said, with his habitual half-sneer. A look of surprise crossed his face when he realised that Jean-Paul Mercier had come in with Prescott and Su. Why was Mercier making common cause with Prescott Glover?

Fortunately, there was no time for his journalistic colleagues to probe the mystery of Prescott's reappearance. A series of gongs reverberated from the huge television screen which had been erected in the corner of the room and moments later, a Cambodian announcer solemnly intoned the words: 'His Excellency Khin Lay, Prime Minister, will now broadcast to the nation.'

Of course, Su Soeung and her half-sister Keav and the other Khmer speakers present could follow what Khin Lay had to say without the benefit of subtitles. For Prescott, Mercier and many, if not most, of the other foreigners present, the running subtitles which the Government of Cambodia's Information Office provided on that occasion proved invaluable.

'I speak to you in a solemn hour,' Khin Lay intoned in Churchillian fashion, sitting behind the Prime Minister's desk in the Prime Minister's office. 'Today His Majesty King Norodom Sihanouk has entrusted me with the responsibility of forming a new administration, an administration of all the talents and all the parties. I believe the time for factionalism is over. We must bury the past. We must move forward...'

Wow! Prescott thought, as he listened. Out of habit, he began to scribble in his notebook.

You didn't have to be a very close observer of Cambodian politics to understand the coded meanings. Khin Lay's announcement that he was forming an administration 'of all the parties' meant that he was letting the Khmer Rouge or at least their successors in title back into the government. That was news!

'Of course,' he heard Khin Lay say (via the subtitles), 'the tribunal has already been scrapped. Whatever the outcome might have been, the process of the trial itself would have been supremely divisive. Brother would have been set against brother. Husband against wife. This country might once again have faced civil war. On my orders, all charges against Duch and Ta Mok have been dropped. They will be joining other Khmer Rouge leaders, such as Ieng Sary and Khieu Samphan, in their current location...'

Wait for it, Prescott thought. Just releasing Duch and Ta Mok and sending them off to join the other Khmer Rouge leaders up at Anlong Veng or wherever was hardly the same as building a new coalition. There had to be more.

There was. Half-way through his remarks, Khin Lay paused dramatically. The camera panned across the room as Hong Soeung, kitted out in a sober suit, white shirt and pale blue tie, entered the Prime Minister's office to be embraced with fraternal warmth by Khin Lay. The two men kissed each other on both cheeks, visibly moved.

Resuming his seat at the Prime Ministerial desk, Khin Lay began by introducing – or reintroducing – Hong Soeung to the Cambodian nation.

'This is the man, the very man,' he said, 'about whom you have heard so much in recent days. This is the man whose devotion to his country has never been questioned, whose career has been untainted by any of the evils with which we have been, alas, all too familiar.'

Khin Lay went on to describe his own relationship over several decades with Hong Soeung. 'He is my brother, my spiritual brother,' he said. 'That fact that I have persuaded him today to leave his self-imposed exile to take up the post of Minister of the Interior which I myself have vacated on becoming Prime Minister is a source of the most profound personal satisfaction. Hong Soeung will become my right-hand man in our mission to rebuild Cambodia...'

Khin Lay continued in that vein for a few more minutes. Prescott, who had been briefed by Su about the full extent of Hong Soeung's extraordinary discoveries at Ta Keo, wondered if Khin would use this occasion to play his trump card or whether he would save it for later. Under his breath, he urged the new Prime Minister on. *Go for it now, you'll never have a better moment.*

'Today, I am pleased to announce what is probably the most significant discovery in a thousand years of Cambodian history. Under the leadership of Hong Soeung, the long-lost capital city of Jayavarman II has at last been located...'

In the crowded bar of the Foreign Correspondents Club of Cambodia, there was almost total silence. Those who had been clinking the ice in their drinks desisted. The low murmur of conversation which had accompanied Khin Lay's earlier exposition of the goals of his administration and his vision of the future of Cambodia subsided. You didn't have to be a Cambodian, thought Prescott, to realise what an astonishing impact Khin Lay's announcement must have. Even the casual observer could see that this was a land where the sense of the past was all-pervasive, where traditions – many of them based on historical or mythical events occurring centuries before – were at the heart of the nation's life. Most of these traditions had to do with the great empires and great king-emperors of Cambodian history. As the founder of the Angkorean empire, Jayavarman II – even Prescott by now recognised – was in a league of his own.

'I offer you all a new celebration of Cambodia's future,' they heard Khin Lay say by way of peroration, 'a future built on the greatness of its past.'

As the camera-shot of the Prime Minister faded, a fanfare of trumpets erupted from the television and a series of ever more fantastical images occupied the screen.

'What the hell's that?' Prescott asked Su. 'That's Ta Keo,

isn't it? That's where you were when we came to get you to-day?'

Su watched the stunning kaleidoscope unfold. 'Yes, that's Ta Keo. That's Amarendrapura, Jayavarman II's capital.'

'Jesus!' Prescott exclaimed. Whoever made that particular film, he thought, knew his or her trade. The camera soared over the towers and pinnacles of the temple-mountain, rushed along the bas-reliefs, and dwelt lovingly on the detail of the carvings, picking out the subtle features of the apsaras, the dancing girls, then suddenly zooming in on the serene visages of the Gods.

By way of a climax, the camera leapt up the great temple, the cosmic mountain, from level to level until it entered the inner chamber of the central sanctuary and came to rest on the mighty statue of Buddha.

By some trick of photography, while the great gold Buddha was still standing centre-screen shedding light on the world, Khin Lay was shown leaving the Prime Minister's Office arm-in arm with Hong Soeung. As the two men stood together on the steps outside, the crowd which had gathered there erupt-ed into applause. By now, night had fallen. The television showed great bursts of fireworks exploding in the night sky.

Some of the journalists present, professional cynics though most of them were, started to clap.

'That was my daddy, wasn't it?' Keav asked. For the last hour she had been gazing entranced at the television screen. It was probably the first television she had ever seen.

'Yes, that was your daddy,' Su replied. 'Mine too. Some daddy, don't you think?'

Jean-Claude Mercier had the last word. He took Keav's hand and solemnly shook it.

'Ton papa, chérie, c'est un vrai personnage.'

'Merci, monsieur,' Keav smiled shyly.

Mercier asked the young girl who had taught her French.

'Papa, naturellement.'

Jean-Claude nodded in satisfaction. So many things, he thought, were coming right.

★★★

There was a message waiting for them when they returned to the hotel. The Prime Minister had invited them to a private dinner at his residence. They would be picked up at eight o'clock.

The crowds were still celebrating in the streets as they drove out along Norodom Boulevard. Peering down the side street, Su caught a glimpse of her old house. Where would her father live now, she wondered? Did the Minister of the Interior have an official residence? Would Keav live with him? Who would look after her?

Khin Lay himself was waiting at the door for them as the car drew up. 'Welcome to my humble abode!'

Not so humble, Su thought, noting the graceful exterior of the building and the spacious lawns sweeping down to the river.

Khin Lay seemed to sense her comment. 'This is just going to be a family evening, nothing formal. Two old friends getting back together again after so many years.'

The Prime Minister was as good as his word. The mood was joyous, light-hearted. There would be long and arduous tasks for both men if they were to do all that they set out to do, but tonight was an occasion for celebration.

Of course, speeches were made, and toasts were drunk. More than once Khin Lay rose to his feet with his glass in hand and more than once Hong Soeung replied. Khin Lay thanked Hong Soeung for discovering Jayavarman II's vanished capital.

Hong Soeung thanked Khin Lay for all his help in the past.

'He means helping him out of Tuol Sleng, doesn't he?' Prescott, sitting next to Su, murmured.

'He does,' Su whispered in return. 'But he's not going to say so in so many words. Nobody links Khin Lay with the Khmer Rouge explicitly, whatever they may think or know privately.'

Prescott knocked back another glass of fiery rice wine. The clear liquid burned his throat. Cambodian politics was desperately complicated, he thought. He wondered if he would ever understand.

After the dinner, Khin Lay took Su aside for a moment. 'I hope you understand what an important role you have played by coming to Cambodia, Ms Soeung. I am sorry for the inconvenience.'

Su wanted to laugh. Inconvenience! That was hardly the word she would have used. Containing herself, she smiled politely. 'I have found my father at last, that is the important thing.'

'I'm so glad you understand, my dear,' Khin Lay said. 'It was the way things had to be.'

Su stood there for a moment as the Prime Minister moved on. Was it really the way things had to be, she wondered? Could there not been some other way of achieving their objective?

Hong Soeung came up to her at that point. 'This is the happiest evening of my life. I have you. I have Keav. And I have just spoken to your mother, Sita, on the telephone. She is flying here next week. She wants to come home. For good. The Cambodian consul in Seattle is going to escort her personally!'

Su's face lit up. 'That's wonderful news. Marvellous. I'm so pleased.' She tried to absorb the implications of what her father had just said. So her mother would be coming back to Cambodia, to pick up the threads of her old life and to start a new one. What courage that would take at her age!

Hong Soeung himself seemed to be choked with emotion. 'She told me she had never forgotten me. Never given up hope. God has brought us back together. She doesn't want to waste time now. And besides,' Hong Soeung added mischievously, 'she says she wants to be here for the wedding.'

'What wedding?'

'Yours and Prescott's, of course. I can't tell you how much I like him, Su. A fine man. I know you will be happy. As happy as your mother and I were.'

Su smiled. This was the fairy tale ending. 'This is Cambodia, not America. You have to give your formal permission first. Has Prescott asked you?'

'He just did. While you were talking to the Prime Minister.'

Hong Soeung picked up a glass of wine, tapped the rim and called for silence.

'There's one more piece of good news this evening. It is my pleasure to announce the betrothal of my daughter, Su, to Prescott Glover of *The New York Times*. What's more, I have just spoken to my wife, Sita, in Seattle and she will be coming over for the wedding. Indeed, she will be returning to Cambodia permanently.'

Hong Soeung could barely finish his sentence. 'Thank you, my friends. Thank you so much. Thank you so very, very much.'

★★★

Later that night Su and Prescott sat on the balcony outside their hotel room.

'It will have to be a proper Cambodian wedding,' Su said. 'You realise that don't you?'

Prescott smiled. 'Anything that makes you happy.'

Su hugged him. 'All's well that ends well?'

'Maybe,' Prescott sounded dubious.

'What's the matter?'

Prescott went inside and poured himself a nightcap. When he came back, he said: 'What I don't understand is how Khin Lay got there without a shot being fired. It seems to me that this takeover was set up for quite some time. The United States, for example, had to be involved at the highest level. You don't send warships to carry Prime Ministers off into exile without getting clearance. And don't tell me that we didn't know about the PLA moving down through Laos into Cambodia with hundreds of military vehicles and fanning out across the country. Those trucks may have Red Cross markings but everyone knows what they are. Don't tell me our satellites didn't pick it up? The trucks couldn't have been hidden by the trees all the way. Besides, the satellites have infra-red capability. They'd register the vehicle exhausts. And what about the

Vietnamese? Why did they let Hun Sen go just like that after supporting him all these years?'

Su was beginning to be cross with him. She was thinking about her wedding.

'For heaven's sake, Prescott, drop it. Whatever's done is done. We may never know the whole story.'

Prescott put his drink down, walked over to her and kissed her. 'You're right, Su. I could dig around for years and still not come up with the right answer.'

'That's better,' Su cuddled up to him. 'Now about the wedding. Traditionally, the festivities last a week. Nowadays, there's a shortened version of the ceremony couples can use.'

'How long does that take?'

'One and a half days. Minimum. The first day of the wedding encompasses a whole series of separate rituals. In the morning, gifts of betel, fruits and cakes are carried from the groom's shelter to the bride's home.'

'What does the groom get?'

'The girl's family presents certain traditional gifts, such as heavy silk sarongs and a scarf, to the groom.'

'Then what?'

'Guests have a simple mid-day meal. Then there's the hair-cutting ceremony. The "achaa" – that's the man who presides – ritually snips a lock of hair from the bride and the groom, then they have a general trimming. There's a splendid evening meal but the most important rite of the day is the *cong day* or tying of threads upon the couple's wrists for good fortune. First the bride in her home, then the groom in his shelter, lies semi-recumbent holding a betel nut crusher and betel leaves in cupped hands, while the achaa and various kinsmen and friends tie threads upon his or her wrists and offer best wishes. After that, there's merrymaking with music and dancing.'

'Good Lord!' Prescott exclaimed. 'How do you know all this?'

'Every Cambodian woman knows these things,' Su replied. 'That is the way we do things in our country.'

Prescott looked at her sharply. Was Su "going native" he wondered?

'What happens on the second day?' he asked gloomily.

If Su noticed Prescott's glowering expression, she didn't comment.

'We start extremely early,' she replied cheerfully. 'There's a pre-dawn ceremony when we bow to the rising sun and the achaa blesses us. More dancing while we hold betel nuts in our hands. Spectators throw coconut seeds. The music gets loud and louder. Right at the end, the bride rises and rushes to her chamber, followed quickly by the groom who must catch the end of her scarf as she goes.'

'And that's it at long last, is it?'

'More or less. The achaa gives us a brief lecture on marital and filial duties and a midmorning meal rounds the whole thing off.'

'You have been boning up on this, haven't you? You didn't learn all this at your mother's knee, did you?'

Su bridled at the accusation. 'So what if I've been refreshing my memory about how things are done. We have to get it right, don't we?'

Prescott groaned. 'Are you sure your father gave his permission?'

Su laughed. 'He did. Mother too. I've spoken to her.'

'You've got it all wrapped up, haven't you?'

'It was time, Prescott, wasn't it? We couldn't go on the way we were.'

'You're right, darling. Of course, you're right.' He was ready, in the end, to concede with good grace. If that was the way she wanted things to be, that was the way they would be.

'What do I wear?' he asked.

She was touched by his willingness to see things her way. 'You could begin in western dress, a suit for example. Then you could change to a casual sarong. You could wear a royal robe for the final ceremony.'

'And you?' Prescott smiled, playing along.

Su looked wistful. 'I might appear as a princess dressed in gold. With a tiara. Yes, I'd like a tiara.'

Prescott took out his notebook. *Get tiara,* he wrote.

Su had one last little bombshell in store for him.

'Do you realise,' she said, quite seriously, 'that a betrothed couple are not allowed to sleep together until the wedding is over?'

'Now that is really going too far!' Prescott spluttered.

★★★

Two days later, Sita Soeung arrived in Phnom Penh to a joyful reunion with her husband. Su thought her mother might crumble under the strain of the long journey from Seattle and the shock of being reunited with Hong Soeung. But the old lady proved remarkably resilient.

Hong Soeung came out to the airport to meet her. He had given instructions that only immediate family were to be present, so – besides Hong Soeung himself – the welcoming party consisted of Prescott, Su and Keav.

Before leaving for the airport, Hong Soeung had consulted Su about whether or not they should take Keav with them. Su had been emphatic.

'Mother knows everything,' she teased him (already they had achieved an easy familiarity). 'I have talked to her. I think she is as excited about the idea of meeting Keav and having another daughter to bring up, as she is about meeting you again!'

Hong Soeung had laughed. 'I am so happy,' he said.

And the man was happy. They could all see that. Joy shone from his face. Looking at her father, Su was sometimes re-minded of Nelson Mandela. Mandela had spent even longer than Hong Soeung locked away from the world, yet he had emerged with an inner strength that somehow radiated from him and energized all those whom he encountered. Hong Soeung was like that too, she thought. And like Mandela emerging from Robben Island, he seemed to know that his best years were still ahead of him.

Of course, when she saw her mother step down the ramp, and drop painfully to her knees to kiss her native soil before rising to throw herself in her husband's outstretched arms, Su lost control of herself entirely. She tried to choke back the tears, but she couldn't. This was her mother. This was her fa-ther. These were her parents, for Christ's sake!

'Hello, darling,' she heard her mother say to the man she hadn't seen for almost thirty years.

'Welcome home, darling,' Hong Soeung said. He bowed his head, stretched out his arms, and held her to him.

'For heaven's sake, help me!' Su clutched Prescott's arm and he steadied her as she was about to fall.

'Mother!' Su cried, hugging the old lady as Sita in turn hugged Hong Soeung. 'You've made it. I never imagined I would see this moment.'

'It's thanks to you, Su,' Sita said. 'You never gave up.'

'That's true,' Hong Soeung added, holding his wife with one arm and his daughter with the other. 'She never gave up. Su is tenacious. Even when she was a little girl, once she made up her mind to do something, she would do it.'

They were all crying now, great geysers of tears. Even Prescott felt overwhelmed. Thank God, he thought, the photographers had been kept away.

Through the mists of happiness, Sita Soeung caught sight of Keav, hiding shyly behind Prescott.

'You must be Keav. Hello, Keav. I'm so pleased to see you.' Sita bent forward and held out her arms. 'I'm your mother, your grandmother. I don't know what I am today, I'm so confused and happy, but I shall love you as I love my own daughter.'

There are moments, Prescott thought, pulling out a handkerchief and wiping his eyes, when a chap has to know when to make himself scarce. This was one of them. He gave Sita Soeung a quick but warm embrace. 'See you later,' he said. 'We've got so much to talk about.' Then he tiptoed away across the tarmac.

CHAPTER 27

While Su stayed on in Phnom Penh to be near her newfound family and to make preparations for the wedding, Prescott flew back to New York, spent a day at the office there, then caught the shuttle to Washington.

It was a brilliantly clear morning, the last Monday before Christmas. Though air traffic had been restricted for some months following the September 11 attacks, National Airport, also known as Ronald Reagan Airport, was fully operational once again. As they came in to land, Prescott could see that the commuter traffic on the roads and bridges was heavy. He caught a glimpse of the still gaping hole in the side of the Pentagon. It would be years before they made good the physical damage, he calculated. As for the psychological damage, that didn't even bear thinking about.

Minutes later, they were on the ground.

Looking back at that day, Prescott would readily admit that it was that reminder of the horrendous damage inflicted on the nation's capital by the September 11, 2001 attacks which allowed him finally to understand what had been going on over the last few weeks. It was a question, he supposed, of making the necessary connections. When you came to think about it, so many things could be traced back to that one day. Why should the Hong Soeung affair be any different?

He hailed a cab at the kerb and went back to his apartment.

Once they were married, he knew, Su and he would have to decide where they were going to live – was he going to go to her place, was she moving in with him, would they buy or rent a new apartment? – but there wasn't time for that now. He dumped his bag, quickly checked the mail – nothing urgent, and went out again. The cabdriver, as instructed, was still waiting for him.

'Massachusetts Avenue and 17th Street, please,' he said. 'That's the Johns Hopkins SAIS campus.'

Prescott didn't know whether Bob Jesson would be at his desk that morning. He could have called ahead but he didn't. He wanted to surprise the man.

★★★

Jesson looked up from his desk as Prescott walked in unannounced. 'Good Lord, I wasn't expecting to see you, Prescott. I thought you were still in Cambodia.'

'Are you sure, Bob?' Prescott said icily. 'I think you've known pretty much on a day-to-day basis where I was and what I was doing.'

Jesson laid down his pen. He was one of those old-fashioned academics who would sometimes still draft by hand. It was not difficult to sense Prescott's hostility. It positively radiated from him

'You're right. I was expecting you. Sooner or later, I knew you'd figure things out.'

'In my case, it was later than sooner,' Prescott said. 'I was making progress, but it wasn't until about an hour ago, when we were coming in to land at National and I saw the Pentagon, that I finally got there.'

'What on earth do you mean,' Jesson played for time.

'I mean what the Hong Soeung affair was really all about.'

Jesson sighed, looking for a way out but not finding one. He could see by the look in Prescott's eyes that he wasn't going to let this one go.

'This is going to be tricky, Prescott.' Jesson sounded gloomy. 'You're not cleared for this. I shouldn't be talking to you about this at all.'

Prescott bridled. He wasn't going to be mucked about. Not now. Not by Bob Jesson. 'If you don't talk, Bob, I'm going to write what I know. Maybe I'll speculate a bit. That could be worse. That could hurt you.'

Professor Robert Jesson thought for a moment. His hand reached out for the telephone as though he was about to call some higher powers to request authorisation, then he pulled back.

'What the hell,' he said. 'I'll take the responsibility. This has to be deep background though.'

'Unattributable?'

'Not just unattributable. Unpublishable in any form. We're talking national security here. Top-level stuff. Agreed?'

It went against all Prescott's journalistic instincts and training. The one thing he hated was doing an interview where it had already been established that none of the product could be used. But this was one time when he knew he would have to sign up to the terms Jesson was imposing. They had put Su through the wringer. His own professional reputation had for a time been in shreds. He needed to know the reason, Su needed to know. If they didn't know, there was a danger that the anger would go on burning, like a subterranean fire, deep in the soul.

Jesson moved out from behind the desk to sit down in an easy chair opposite Prescott. 'Maybe it would be easiest for me if you told me how much you know, how much you have already worked out.'

'The Deep Throat technique? You nod if I'm right, and shake your head if I'm wrong?'

Jesson gave a strained laugh. 'I don't think we need take it that far. I'll talk if I have to.'

'Okay,' Prescott agreed. He marshalled his thoughts.

'It's the motive which still puzzles me,' he began. 'Khin Lay wants to get rid of Hun Sen and seize power in Cambodia. He's not just a careerist. He is probably a good and capable man, in as much as you can say that about any politician.'

Jesson nodded. 'Agree with you there.'

'Khin Lay is the current leader of FUNCINPEC, but he profoundly believes Cambodia needs a government of national unity and he knows you can't achieve that in Cambodia without including the Khmer Rouge or their political legacy in any new deal. And that's not just because in the dim and distant past Khin Lay was a party member. It's an article of faith. The problem is: Hun Sen is moving in exactly the opposite direction. Pushed by both international and Vietnamese pressure – remember Vietnam and Cambodia are traditional enemies and many see Hun Sen as a Vietnamese puppet – Hun Sen is committed to holding an international tribunal and putting at least two former Khmer Rouge leaders, Duch and Ta Mok, on trial. Khin Lay knows – or at least he fears – that if Hun Sen follows that path, there's going to be another bloodbath in Cambodia.

'So he cooks up a scheme. His old pal, Hong Soeung – a

man he probably personally sprang from prison in 1975 – has a daughter, Su, and that daughter is alive and well and living in the United States. Khin Lay and his friend, Andrew Mossman, cook up the Hong Soeung confessions, I write my disgraceful pieces for *The New York Times*,' – here Prescott laughed ruefully – 'the whole thing explodes, and the net result is exactly what Khin Lay wants, namely the dismantling of the tribunal and, as a consequence, the discrediting of Hun Sen.'

Prescott paused. 'Here's the problem as I see it. Hun Sen is not known as the "Strong Man of Cambodia" for nothing. Why doesn't he fight back? Why is he such a pushover? Does Khin Lay have all the cards? And if so, why? Is the US backing him? Is Russia backing him? Is China backing him?

'For a time, I wondered whether this was all a complicated plot by President George W. Bush and his people to embarrass Senator Hillary Clinton and to make sure she doesn't get the foreign policy triumph she has been looking for. Bush is going for a new term and Hillary Clinton may well decide to run against him. But I wasn't really convinced by that theory. Humiliating Hillary in this way might have been a plausible objective in the days of cut-throat party politics but that's not where it's at today. After the events of September 11, everyone's trying hard to be bi-partisan. Ostensibly anyway. There's another angle to this, isn't there?'

'You tell me,' Jesson murmured, 'I'm all ears.'

'I should have guessed,' Prescott continued, 'that you personally were a key player when I bumped into you in Beijing. I should have asked myself what the hell were you doing there at precisely that moment. I should have worked it out at the time. You were there to make sure things didn't go wrong, weren't you?

'Looking back, I should probably have rumbled you when I made that slip-up about Ieng Sary. We were walking across Tienanmen square and I told you that I'd discovered Ieng Sary had been in Peking Union Medical College Hospital in July 1975, at the same time as George W. Bush. That didn't make sense, did it? Since we met in Beijing, I've been checking my facts. Should have done it earlier but better late than never. Ieng Sary had already left Beijing by July 1975. I agree he was there right up till April that year. But when Phnom Penh fell to the Khmer Rouge on April 17, 1975, Ieng Sary left China for Hanoi and had the pleasure of telling the North Vietnamese that Phnom Penh has fallen two weeks ahead of Saigon! On April 23 he arrived in Phnom Penh where Pol Pot was waiting for him and together they surveyed the scenes of devastation. So how could he have been having a secret meeting with Dubbya in Beijing three months later? There was no way you wouldn't have known about Ieng Sary's movements in 1975. This is your period, dammit. It's what they pay you for. Yet you kept quiet.

'And then there was Paris. You told me to go to the Bibliothèque Nationale to look for the early history of the Cambodian Communist Party. You knew what I was going to find there. You'd already read the book. You probably have a copy in your library here. You'd checked Hong Soeung out. You knew about his time in Paris. You probably knew where he's been since. If Hong Soeung was going to be part of the new all-inclusive settlement in Cambodia, you needed to be sure you were backing the right man.'

Jesson realised the game was up. If he wanted Prescott's cooperation in keeping the lid on the story, he would have to come through with the goods now.

He leaned forward in his chair. 'It wasn't just my idea,' he began. 'As you've probably already guessed, Andrew Mossman played a key part. I've known Andrew a long time. One day, when we were having lunch at the Club, he told me that Khin Lay wanted to kill two birds with one stone: eliminating the UN tribunal and weakening, if not destroying, Hun Sen in the process. He said Khin Lay had approached him for help. Khin Lay wanted to set up a "Hong Soeung affair" as we now know it and, for best results, he wanted to use Hong Soeung's own daughter, Su, whom he'd read about in the paper. That *Washingtonian* article. That meant that someone had to have a plausible reason for bringing Su to Cambodia and setting her down, like a game-dog, to follow the trail. Khin Lay thought that Mossman and SAVE would fit the bill nicely.'

'You helped draft the Hong Soeung confessions, didn't you?' Prescott Glover challenged him. 'All that detail about US foreign Policy in the late 60s and early 70s. That all sounded true, or at least plausible, because you – personally – worked on it. Am I right?'

Bob Jesson gave a modest shrug. 'Let's just say I acted as a technical adviser.'

'What was in it for Andrew Mossman?' Prescott asked after a pause, while he tried to absorb the meaning of what he had heard.

'Ah, that was intriguing. Mossman, as you may know, is a very smart operator. Have you seen Andrew and Caroline's place out in the country? That's some establishment. Mossman has made a lot of money over the years and I suspect that some of it has come from acquiring and selling antiquities originating in countries where SAVE operates.'

Prescott nodded. He remembered the evening he had visited the Mossman residence in Georgetown and seen the magnificent stone head in Mossman's den. He also remembered the story Su had told him a few days earlier about the SAVE storeroom in Siem Reap and the army trucks drawn up outside one Saturday morning.

'A lot of pieces have gone missing at Angkor over the years,' he said. 'The Depository may have been raided and a whole lot of sculptures and stonework shipped out, possibly under cover of SAVE consignments. Su suspected that Mossman might have done a deal with Khin Lay. SAVE and the Ministry of the Interior have an MOU. Mossman signed for SAVE; Khin Lay signed for the Ministry.'

'I know what you're talking about,' Jesson said. 'But it's not what you think. Mossman hasn't been lining his own pocket.'

'Where's the money been going then? If Mossman has been flogging off pieces from the Angkor storerooms, someone's been getting rich.'

'We've been monitoring this closely, I can assure you,' Jesson said. 'We wouldn't want to get into bed with Mossman if Mossman was corrupt. No way. But we're in the clear there. Mossman may have dabbled in the antiquities market trading pieces here and there but all the money Mossman has made on his side-deal with Khin Lay has, we believe, been ploughed back into SAVE. It has paid for the staff, paid for the prostheses – thousands of them. It probably paid for Su's trip to Cambodia. The way Mossman sees it – and he was quite open about this with me when we talked – Cambodia has antiquities coming out of its ears. There are thousands of sites which have never been discovered, let alone explored. If he can save Cambodian lives by selling Cambodian artwork, he believes that is what he should do. He said he saw it as a moral duty. SAVE raises money as a charity, but not nearly enough. He said he had to fill the gap somehow.'

Prescott was still not convinced. 'So that's why he cooperated with Khin Lay, to keep the sweetheart deal alive, not to fill his own pocket or Republican Party coffers? We had the Iran-Contra scandal. Why shouldn't we have a "stolen-artworks sold for party funds" scandal?'

'I admit there was more to it than just keeping the kettle on the boil. But it's not what you think.'

'What is it then? What's the bottom line?'

Jesson glowered at him. 'Deep background, remember? Unattributable. Unpublishable. Is that clear?'

'Of course, it's clear.'

'Okay, I'll give you the bottom line. The whole thing began almost as a joke. Mossman and I were talking over lunch some time back. He said agencies like SAVE could work in Cambodia for a hundred years and they would still barely have scratched the surface of the problem. SAVE could mend damaged limbs till kingdom come but what you really needed was the Chinese army to conduct a massive de-mining operation in every single Cambodian province where mines were still a problem. He had a map in his pocket and he pointed out all the places where the sappers were needed. The PLA had the equipment, they had the men. They were right next door. If Khin Lay ever came to power, Mossman suggested almost flippantly, all he had to do was send China an official invitation.

'I didn't take him seriously at first,' Jesson continued. 'But then I got to thinking. Maybe Mossman's idea was exactly what we needed. Not just in terms of the Cambodian people who would benefit by having the mines cleared, though of course that was important. Tremendously important. Princess Diana was right about that. No, I was thinking in terms of global realpolitik and the key objectives of US foreign policy.'

'Keep going.'

'Let me put it this way,' Jesson went on. 'For months we'd been sitting around thinking how we could pay back the Chinese for their help in the War Against Terror. As you know, having China in the anti-terror coalition was essential. As a matter of fact, it was vital. We needed their constructive acquiescence at least, if not their positive approval. Remember, we were invoking the self-defence provisions of the UN Charter to justify the war against Osama bin Laden and the Taliban. China is a permanent member of the UN Security Council. Having China on our side made all the difference. But it wasn't just a question of Chinese diplomatic support, though that was essential. That was just one of the reasons we needed them on board. There were some vital military considerations as well. People forget that China shares a sixty mile land border with Afghanistan.'

Prescott whistled, 'I thought we used Uzbekistan as a launch pad for the strikes against Osama bin Laden and the Taliban. Are you telling me we used China too? Did our ground forces cross over from Chinese Xinjiang into Afghanistan's Wakhan corridor and the High Pamir Mountains in case Osama bin Laden was holed up there?'

'I'm not getting into the details,' Jesson said firmly. 'I

can't. What I can say is that the Hong Soeung affair presented us with a golden opportunity to strike a deal with China. Why do you think that President Bush went to Shanghai in October 2001 for the APEC meeting? Christ, the President of the United States has never been to an APEC bull-session before and probably never will again. And he did that just a few weeks after the attack on the World Trade Centre and the Pentagon, when there were the strongest possible reasons for staying at home.'

'You tell me why.'

'Bush went to Shanghai for one reason and one reason only, to meet Chinese President Jiang Zemin. They met in public several times. And they also met in private. In those private meetings, Jiang made it absolutely clear that Chinese support in the fight against terrorism would depend crucially on what he termed, "progress in the US-Chinese relationship." Of course, he didn't say precisely what he meant. He left that to us to figure out.'

'Us?' Prescott asked.

'We were all involved. Dick Cheney chaired a top secret inter-agency task force. State, Defense, CIA, NSC, NSA, Homeland Security, other agencies I can't speak about because officially they don't even exist – they were all in on it. I was co-opted as an expert on the region, the outside adviser. We met twice a week, sometimes more. Our mandate was to find out what we could offer China. The President had made the promise in Shanghai. Now we had to deliver.

'It was tough, I can tell you. There were those who argued that the President shouldn't have made any deal with Jiang at all in Shanghai. They said it was a screwball idea. China had a moral duty to help us without thought of a quid pro quo. Well, that point of view had a hearing but it didn't prevail. The President hadn't been specific but he'd made a clear commitment that he'd come up with something. Jiang had eyeballed him. He'd eyeballed Jiang. They'd shaken hands. There was no getting out of it.

'So we agreed we had to come up with something. We fixed some ground rules. Number One, US fingerprints shouldn't be all over whatever we came up with. We'd done a lot of bombing recently in Afghanistan, as we sought out Osama bin Laden and tried to get rid of the Taliban. People are only too ready to accuse the United States of using bully-boy tactics even when they worked. This time we wanted to go for something more subtle.

'Number Two, clearly we weren't going to give China the earth. Of course, what we came up with had to be significant, but it certainly shouldn't affect the balance of power in China's favour. Ideally, we wanted to do something which was as much in our interest as China's.

'Within those parameters, the question was: what do we do? Some members of Cheney's group argued that what the Chinese really wanted was more concessions on Taiwan. Taiwan is the running sore in the US-China relationship. China is dedicated to the recovery of Taiwan and its reintegration with the mainland. But the US has sold Taiwan guns, we've sold them destroyers, we've sold them a missile defence system, and we've allowed the Taiwanese President to visit America as though he were the head of an independent state. The time has come, some members of the Committee argued, to look again at our pro-Taiwan policy. They suggested that could play very well with China.

'Well, we spent quite a bit of time on that one but in the end we concluded it was a nonstarter. If anything, the pressures were in the other direction, to beef up Taiwan's weaponry, sell them new submarines, new planes. Never underestimate the power of the pro-Taiwan lobby in this town, Prescott, even now.'

Prescott nodded. His mind went back to the afternoon he had spent in Hangzhou, in Ting Wei-Ju's lakeside villa and to the polished lecture the old man had given on that occasion about the niceties of the US-China relationship.

'I guess the President made it even more difficult when he said the US would do "whatever it takes" to defend Taiwan,' Prescott commented.

'Exactly. That statement was a hostage to fortune if ever there was one. With Taiwan off limits, what were we left with? Chinese accession to the WTO? That was in the bag before September 11. We couldn't, in all conscience, offer them that. That would be paying twice with the same coin.'

'What about the Uighurs?' Prescott suggested. 'You could have promised to turn a blind eye to Beijing's oppression of its Muslim minorities.'

Jesson nodded. 'We thought about that too. There were some people on the group who said we should forget about the Uighurs. Let them twist gently in the wind. But it's not as simple as that. Here are 8 million Muslims living in China who overwhelmingly practice a moderate form of Islam and are strikingly pro-Western. Even if they weren't, there was the human rights angle. We're meant to be against the persecution of racial minorities.'

'So finally, you came up with Cambodia?' Prescott said, quietly.

'Right. And I have to say it really was my idea, sparked off by that conversation with Mossman.'

Try as he might Bob Jesson couldn't keep the note of self-satisfaction out of his voice. 'The more I thought about it, the more I realised that Cambodia exactly fitted the bill. It wasn't a question of handing Cambodia over to the Chinese. Nothing like that. It was more a question of achieving a modest but important shift in the balance of national interests – a shift in China's favour. You have to see this in historical perspective. For more than a thousand years, China's main enemy in the region was Vietnam. The Vietnamese empire and the Chinese empire clashed repeatedly and, of course, the Indo-Chinese peninsula was the main area of conflict. Who supported the Vietnamese in the Vietnam war? It was the Soviet Union, not China. And when the North Vietnamese took over the whole country in 1975, Chinese anxieties reached fever pitch. Their worst fears seemed about to be realised. If the Vietnamese pushed on to Phnom Penh and then Bangkok, it would be game set and match to the ancient foe.

'Why do you think the People's Republic offered a safe haven to the Khmer Rouge during the Lon Nol years? Why did they wine and dine Sihanouk and give him one of their finest houses during his years of exile? Why did they back Pol Pot and the Khmer Rouge so persistently? Because they care passionately about Cambodia. At the very least, they have always seen a non-Vietnamese Cambodia as a vital element in China's national security. And, of course, the Chinese have very long memories. For centuries, Cambodia was known as Funan and was part of China. They don't forget these things. With the Chinese, it's visceral.'

'How did you sell the idea to the Chinese?' Prescott asked.

'It didn't take much selling. When I put the idea to Dick Cheney and the Committee, they jumped on it. I was authorised to talk to Ting Wei-Ju, the Chinese Ambassador here. You know Ting, don't you? One of the cleverest diplomats I've ever met. When that US spy-plane was forced to land in Hainan, he sorted things out brilliantly.

'Ting Wei-Ju got the point immediately. What's more, he saw that US interests and Chinese interests exactly coincided. The United States, like China, has never been happy with the Hun Sen regime. The Vietnamese brought Hun Sen to power in 1979 and basically have sustained him in power ever since. So for the US it has been, in a sense, a double humiliation. We lost Vietnam and de facto we lost Cambodia too. Of course, once information about the Killing Fields and the horror of the Pol Pot years was in the public domain, the US situation was very difficult. For years, we backed the Khmer Rouge claims to Cambodia's UN seat, but we were on a hiding to nothing. The human rights lobby could always cry foul.'

'So Khin Lay's new regime offers the ideal solution, for the United States as well as China?'

'It does indeed. China gets what it wants. A friendly non-Vietnamese-led government in Cambodia with a guarantee that if things go wrong, some of those mine-clearing vehicles with Red Cross markings may suddenly sprout guns. The United States is happy because China is happy and a big debt has been settled. And our national interest is certainly not threatened by the change in the balance of power in Cambodia. Quite the reverse. France is happy too, by the way. Almost fifty years after Dien Bien Phu, France has regained a foothold in Indo-China. Jean-Claude Mercier is opening supermarkets and department stores all over the place. Air Cambodia has been renamed Air Cambodge. It's now part of the JCM empire and, unlike most airlines nowadays, looks set to turn in a tidy profit, not least because of the vast expansion in international tourism that is bound to occur now that Amendarapura has been rediscovered by our good friend, Hong Soeung.'

'Are the Russians happy?'

'Yeah, they're happy as well,' Jesson said, 'though, being Russian, they don't like to show it. There was a time when they cared about losing influence in Vietnam and therefore, by proxy, cared if Vietnam lost a trick or two. But the world has changed. Gorbachev pulled the Soviet Union out of Hanoi years ago and they're not going back. To make assurance doubly sure, Putin made it absolutely clear to the Vietnamese that a little geo-political engineering was about to take place and the time had come to let Hun Sen go. The Russians are getting their own pay-off for co-operating in the War Against Terror.'

'Such as?' Prescott was curious.

'That's another story,' Jesson replied cryptically. 'I'm not going to get into that now. Just throw in all the elements you can. Imagine NATO, pipelines, economic aid, technology transfer – then double the number you first thought of.'

Prescott let it go. Russia was indeed another story. It would keep. 'The Vietnamese certainly are not happy at the way things have turned out,' Prescott commented.

'I'm not sure a lot of people around here are bothered about that,' Jesson replied drily. 'We lost fifty thousand service men and women in Vietnam.'

'What about the international human rights lobby?' Prescott asked finally. 'The reality is the Khmer Rouge have been let off the hook in Cambodia. In one way or another, they're part of Khin Lay's new government. Are you sure bodies like Amnesty International won't make trouble in the future, press for a restoration of the tribunal, that kind of thing?'

Jesson shook his head. 'No, they've shot their bolt. They wouldn't get the votes in the UN to set up a new tribunal, not with all the great powers opposed, including China. Besides, Khin Lay has his alibi, his lightning conductor.'

'Hong Soeung?'

'Yes, Hong Soeung. Can you imagine what a star that man has turned out to be? He has been on the front cover of Time and *Newsweek*. The man who discovered the lost city of the great Emperor, Jayavarman II. The former Khmer Rouge leader – Brother Number Four, indeed – whose hands are squeaky clean! Cambodia's new figurehead! I wouldn't be surprised if Khin Lay doesn't find a way of making Hong Soeung the titular Head of State.'

'He'd have to get rid of King Sihanouk first,' commented Prescott.

'True,' Jesson agreed. 'But Sihanouk's not going to live forever. He's over eighty as it is.'

'He probably chews a lot of betel. That will keep him going!'

After a while, the two men went out to lunch. It was that time of day. 'Zbig's going to be at the Club today,' Jesson said. 'I'm sure he'd like to have a word. He told me he read your stuff with interest.'

'Delighted,' Prescott muttered. If the great Zbigniew Brzezinski – President Jimmy Carter's one-time national security adviser – wanted to talk to him, who was he to say no? Maybe Henry would be there too. Prescott's pulse quickened in anticipation.

They had paused to wait for the WALK sign at the junction of 18th and Massachusetts Avenue, when Prescott said by way of wrapping things up: 'So the only real loser was Hillary Clinton then? She ended up with egg all over her face, didn't she? Her friends, the Mossmans, really let her down, didn't they? I can't imagine she talks to them anymore.'

'Oh, is that what you think?' Jesson sounded complacent, as though he had yet another surprise in store for Prescott and couldn't wait to produce it.

★★★

Prescott saw them almost as soon as he entered the Cosmos Club dining room. Hillary Clinton, Senator for New York was sitting at a table with Andrew and Caroline Mossman.

'Prescott! Bob! Come over here and say hello! Great to see you.' Three voices with one message rang out simultaneously.

A waiter brought over two extra chairs. Bob Jesson and Prescott Glover joined the Senator's small party, conscious of the covert but interested stares of the other diners in the room. It wasn't just Prescott who had been speculating about Hillary Clinton's relationship with the Mossmans and how it might survive the Phnom Penh debacle. Washington is still a small town and the rumour mill needed a new supply of grain each day.

'What a coincidence, Senator!' Jesson exclaimed as they shared a round of drinks. 'Prescott was just asking me about you as we walked in, wondering how you and Andrew could still be on speaking terms after he landed you in the deep doo-dah out there in Cambodia.'

Prescott kicked Jesson under the table. Shut the fuck up, he mouthed.

'Oh, come off it, Prescott,' Hillary Clinton said. 'You don't really believe I didn't know what I was doing? That Andrew didn't tell me? If you believe that, you'll believe anything. I certainly did know. Did Bob tell you about Dick Cheney's Committee. He shouldn't have, but I bet he did. Well, I was on that Committee. Right from the outset. Bob has probably been telling you that the whole thing was his idea. Well, don't believe everything Bob says. The rest of us had quite a hand in it.'

Prescott felt his ears burning. He sensed yet another humiliation approaching at express-train speed.

He knew he was missing the point but he couldn't help asking the – to him – obvious question: 'Senator, if you knew the Hong Soeung confessions were a fake all along, why did you publicise them like that at the Press Conference in Phnom Penh that day? We all wrote that you were looking for your first foreign policy triumph. And then you ended up with a spectacular public relations disaster.'

Senator Hillary Rodham Clinton gave him a withering look. 'What you see is not always what you get. I agree my staff got all excited. Jessie Low and Jack Rosen were wetting their pants at the thought of scoring one over the Republicans, implicating previous Republican administrations, Henry Kissinger, George Bush Senior, even the current President himself, as supporters of the detested Pol Pot and Khmer Rouge. But don't you see, Prescott' – and here she leaned across the table confidentially and put her hand on his arm – 'that was the way it had to be. My staff weren't in the loop. We couldn't risk that. Capitol Hill leaks like a sieve.'

Prescott tried to take in what the Senator was saying. 'What you're saying, Senator, is that you were ready to be publicly humiliated at a later stage as long as you could play the role you were asked to play by Dick Cheney's Committee in launching the worldwide coverage of the Hong Soeung confessions by means of that press conference in Phnom Penh?'

Hillary Clinton nodded, still smiling. 'Don't you guys call it "giving a story legs?" That's what I did. I gave it legs. And then it ran around the world.'

'You paid a price in political terms. A heavy price,' Prescott persisted. 'It could have damaged your own political prospects.'

The Senator looked at him sadly. 'You journalists sometimes make a terrible mistake. You judge politicians by your own standards. What we're talking about here is *patriotism*. I was asked to put my country before my own personal and political interests and that's precisely what I did. Of course, I knew I would look a fool to some people, but not to the people who count. Remember, Prescott,' the Senator stared at him with a fixed, intense expression which reminded him of former British Prime Minister Margaret Thatcher, 'we are all patriots first and foremost. That was always true. It is even more true now, when Osama bin Laden is still at large and the War against Terror has still to be won. Politics, personal ambitions – these have to be a secondary consideration.'

Perhaps realising that she was laying it on a little heavily, the Senator made a conscious effort to lighten up. 'Besides, as we all know, in this town the truth has a habit of seeping out.'

While the Senator was speaking, Andrew and Caroline Mossman stared at the linen tablecloth. Their expressions were so firmly fixed that Prescott wondered for a moment whether they were trying to stop laughing. He didn't doubt that the Mossmans would find a way of helping with the seeping-out process in due course.

Good grief, he thought. How many other little dénouements would there be before the Hong Soeung Affair had finally run its course?

'Of course, Senator,' he sounded like a naughty pupil apologising to teacher. 'You're quite right. Patriotism must always come before politics. Especially now.'

Bob Jesson heaved a sigh of relief. Prescott had had to face some incoming, but he wasn't going to make trouble. Not now, anyway. 'Attaboy!' he muttered.

Prescott Glover and Bob Jesson lingered a few more minutes at the Senator's table. Inevitably, the conversation turned to Christmas.

'What are your plans, Prescott?' Mrs Clinton asked. Now that the stern lecture had been delivered, she was full of charm and gaiety.

'Back to Cambodia,' Prescott said. 'Su and I are getting married.'

'Oh,' Mrs Clinton pricked up her ears. 'I love weddings. What day are you talking about? I could try to be there. I got an invitation this morning from the new Prime Minister to visit Phnom Penh again. I have a feeling Mr Khin Lay wants to make amends.'

Prescott gulped. What the hell, he thought! If the Senator wanted to come to the wedding, why shouldn't she? It seemed as though half Cambodia would be there.

'Actually, it takes rather more than a day to get married in Cambodia. The full wedding ceremony takes about a week, Su told me, but there's a shortened version too. Lasts a day and a half.'

'Go the whole hog, Prescott,' the Senator laughed. 'It's a once in a lifetime event. I should know! You'll never regret it.'

Prescott was suddenly struck by the force of the Senator's remarks. Why go for some ersatz variety when you can have the real thing?

'You know, Senator,' he could see the funny side of it now, 'you could just be right!'

An hour later, as Bob Jesson and Prescott Glover left the Cosmos Club, Jesson said: 'Sorry Zbig wasn't there.'

CHAPTER 28

When Prescott had informed Senator Hillary Clinton that he saw her point about "going the whole hog" he meant what he said. A few days later, having tidied up his affairs in Washington, he returned to Cambodia and told Su that, if he could chew betel nuts for two days, he could chew them for seven.

'Let's do it the proper, traditional Cambodian way,' he said, 'trimmings and all.'

Su had been thrilled. 'You have no idea what this will mean to my mother.'

As it turned out, it wasn't just Su's mother who had been delighted by Prescott's gracious capitulation. Deprived of festivals, and festivities, for so many years under the dark days of Pol Pot, the people of Phnom Penh – indeed the Cambodian populace at large – welcomed the prospect of an additional cause for national celebration. The Hong Soeung story had received top billing not just in the international press but back home in Cambodia too. The newspapers, TV and radio were full of Soeungs of one kind or another. If Hong Soeung himself was the chief celebrity, mother and daughters – both Su and Keav – were not far behind. There were even some Soeung websites wholly devoted to chronicling the progress of the 'Soeung family'. The forthcoming wedding became the focus of intense public interest.

'Looks like it is going to be the biggest thing to happen

here since Madonna visited Angkor Wat,' Prescott commented, scanning the morning press soon after his return. 'The guest list is going to have to be as long as your arm.'

In the circumstances, the choice of venue was highly problematical. Several family conclaves on the subject were held. Various options were canvassed, but no firm decision was taken. Three weeks before the wedding, the matter was conveniently solved for them. Perhaps sensing the surge of popular enthusiasm for the forthcoming event, His Majesty Preah Bat Samdech Preah Norodom Sihanouk, King of Cambodia, and Her Majesty Preah Reach Akka Mohesey Norodom Monineath Sihanouk graciously consented to allow the Silver Pagoda to be used for the ceremony and the grounds of the neighbouring Royal Palace for the public reception afterwards. Their Majesties had also lifted the ban on photography.

A week before the official start of the celebrations (the kick-off date itself had been chosen in consultation with the Royal Astrologer), Prescott returned to Phnom Penh for a round of visits with tailors, hairdressers and Buddhist priests. Happily, he was also able to spend time with Su even though, as Su had predicted would be the case, they were kept apart at night. While he himself continued to live at the Cambodiana Hotel, Su moved in with her parents and half-sister, Keav. Hong Soeung, appointed Interior Minister in Prime Minister Khin Lay's new administration, was offered an official residence, but he refused. Having reached an amicable settlement with the current occupants, the Soeung family returned to the ancestral home at 14, Street 310, off Norodom Boulevard. Though there was inevitably a police presence at both ends of the street, the Soeungs tried to live as normal a life as possible. Most evenings, the Minister could be observed smoking a quiet pipe on the veranda.

Hong Soeung was sitting there one day when the Royal Cambodian Post Office arrived with a Special Delivery letter. It was postmarked Tucson, Arizona. Hong Soeung opened it and read the letter.

Dear Hong, he read, I cannot tell you with what joy I have learned that you and your lovely family are still alive and well and that you have all been able to return to your house in Phnom Penh. I remember you all so well. If Tom were still alive, I know he would join me in wishing you every happiness for the future. Please give my very best to Sita and, though she will not remember me, to your daughter, Su. I understand she is going to marry a New York Times journalist. I hope they will be very happy.

I enclose a copy of a photograph which I took of the Soeung family before Tom and I left Phnom Penh. I sent one to Sita at the time, but I doubt whether she still has it given everything that has happened!

I am living in Arizona now. Hot and dry. About as different from Cambodia as you could imagine. But good for my old bones!

Very best wishes to you all. Tanti auguri!
Gaetana Enders

Hong Soeung fished in the envelope and found the photograph. He held it up to the light and studied the picture carefully. How much had hinged on that one photograph, he thought. If *The Washingtonian* hadn't used the image Gaetana Enders took so many years ago, would he now be sitting where he was?

He took the pipe out of his mouth. 'Sita, Su,' he called.

'What is it, Hong? I'm cooking dinner.' Sita Soeung came out onto the veranda with Su not far behind.

'Gaetana Enders has written us a letter and sent us a photo,' Hong Soeung said.

The day after he received the letter from Gaetana Enders, Hong Soeung invited his prospective son-in-law to have a quiet lunch with him in a small French restaurant on Sisowath Quay. In the course of the meal, Hong Soeung opened up. 'Of course, you know I was a member of the Party. You know about my life in Paris. You went there. You visited my old digs in Rue Letellier, didn't you?'

'Yes, I did. Madame Lefarge said to say hello and that you still owe her 200 francs.'

Hong Soeung laughed. 'I'd like to go back to Paris myself one day. I'll settle that debt. Better late than never! We weren't monsters, you know. Even Pol Pot wasn't a monster, not then. We were zealots, yes. We were enthusiasts. We were freedom fighters. We thought the time for independence had come and if the route to independence lay through the Communist Party, so be it. We could see that Mao Zedong had liberated China from centuries of oppression. We thought it was our turn. Of course, later, it was another story. One must never condone the Pol Pot atrocities. And believe me, I won't. But we have to move on.'

The two men sat at the table a long time that day. Hong Soeung had been fascinated by Prescott's sleuthing activities.

'You found Louis Delaporte's great work: *Voyage au Cambodge*. That's exactly what set me looking for Ta Keo. His description of finding the head of Shiva rivetted me. Mind you, we've done better than Delaporte.'

'What do you mean?'

'Delaporte found the heads of the three statues: Shiva, Vishnu and Brahma. We've found the bodies too. We've pieced them together and reassembled them, put them back in the sanctuaries. One day we may be able to reunite the heads with the bodies. That is my dream.'

'That could be a long wait.' Prescott didn't want to deflate Hong Soeung's sense of optimism, but he didn't realistically see how Soeung's dream could come true, at least in the foreseeable future.

✶✶✶

After that lunch, Prescott decided the more he saw of Hong Soeung, the more he came to like and admire the man. He welcomed Hong Soeung's honesty, the way he had come to terms with the past without denying it; he appreciated the sheer joy and wholeheartedness with which Soeung had re-established a loving and trusting relationship with Sita and Su; he was captivated by the bond that clearly existed between Hong Soeung and young Keav.

'My, what a stunner that young girl is!' he commented to Su one day as they enjoyed a rare, quiet moment together after a family reunion. 'Can we have her as a bridesmaid?'

'Now don't go falling for Keav!' Su had joked with a faint undertone of menace.

As far as Prescott was concerned, one of the high points of the week was the private audience he and Su had with the King. They met in the Khemarin Palace, within the Royal Residence Compound. After offering their heartiest thanks for His Majesty's generosity in making available the Silver Pagoda and the grounds of the Royal Palace for their wedding, they listened to a half-hour discourse from the monarch which Prescott decided was one of the most extraordinary speeches he had ever heard.

The old King was over eighty, his health was not good, but he spoke with the energy and vitality of a much younger man.

'You have no idea how much it means to me to have your father back,' he said to Su. 'Did you know I met him in the Kulen mountains in 1973? He presented me with a most magnificent stone head – a head of Brahma, as I recall. He had found it at a place called Ta Keo he said. Of course, your father probably didn't realise then just what it was he had discovered. The whole amazing archaeological complex. None of us did. I gave the head to the Chinese as a token of my appreciation of their hospitality to me. Do you know that after I was deposed by Lon Nol in 1970, Chinese Premier Zhou Enlai came out in person to Beijing airport to greet me?'

The King paused, and then added: 'I wonder whatever happened to that marvellous head of Brahma. You know in the Hindu Trinity, Vishnu is the Protector, Shiva is the Destroyer, but Brahma is the Creator. A statue of Brahma will have four heads, each one facing a cardinal direction. It would be so good to see that piece again after all these years. I rather wish

I had not presented it to my Chinese hosts!'

King Sihanouk chuckled as though he had said something rather naughty. The old man's mind was as sharp as a razorblade, Prescott thought, as he listened. He might sound as though he was rambling, but he wasn't. He didn't waste words. What's more, there was usually a subtext. You just had to know how to read it.

What an extraordinary person the old man was, Prescott thought. All the complexities of Cambodian politics seemed to be embodied in his life story. He had ascended the throne in 1941 at the age of eighteen. He had been Prince, then King, then President, then Prince and King again. He had spent years in Beijing; indeed he still had a house there. One way or another, he had supported – or at least acquiesced – in the rise of the Khmer Rouge. And yet, when he came back to Phnom Penh in late 1975, his children had been killed by the Khmer Rouge and he himself had been virtually imprisoned in the Royal Palace.

'The roof had leaks everywhere,' Sihanouk was describing those dismal days. 'Each time it rained we couldn't sleep. But they gave us two koupreys. Do you know what koupreys are? They are rare grey oxen, almost extinct in Cambodia. Thanks to these animals, there was no need to cut the grass!'

Recognising a royal joke when they heard one, Prescott and Su laughed politely.

'We also had a mango tree,' Sihanouk continued. 'It grew behind the palace. We all took great care of it. We wanted to enjoy the fruit. But when the mangoes were ripe, the Khmer Rouge appreciated their taste. They came and took them all, leaving us only with bananas.'

***

Later that day, as they enjoyed a drink together by the pool of the Cambodiana ('what time's your curfew, Su?') Prescott tried to replay in his mind the conversation they had had with the King.

'I can't quite work out why he wanted to see us,' Prescott said. 'Do you think it was just politeness, a kind of tribute to your father? A way of showing that he approves of Khin Lay's choice?'

'I think there's more to it than that,' Su said slowly. 'There was a message there somewhere. I'm not sure we got it.'

An hour later, after Su had left, Prescott was reading his email in his hotel room. He gave a whoop of delight when he got a memo from Harry Schumberg at *The New York Times* telling him that, if that was what he wanted, he could be reassigned from Washington to Phnom Penh to serve as a roving Asia correspondent.

Prescott punched a fist in the air. Good for you, Harry! he exclaimed. Su had already decided that she wanted to stay with SAVE in Cambodia and Andrew Mossman had agreed. He had even offered her a rise in salary, so now there would be work for both of them out here. They could sell or rent out their apartments in Washington and get a place in Phnom Penh. Already Prescott had dreams of green, manicured lawns stretching down to the river, with a pool and tennis court thrown in, if possible... nothing too ostentatious, of course. Journalists had to watch it, nowadays; charity-workers even more so.

He was about to send off an ecstatic reply when he paused.

The thought of Andrew Mossman put him in mind of something. What the hell was it? Yes, he had it now. The statue in Mossman's den. Sihanouk had been talking about a statue that afternoon. Maybe that's what the message, the sub-text was...

Prescott looked at his watch. What time was it in the US? Mid-morning or thereabouts. Bob Jesson should be at his desk. This would take a bit of doing, he thought, but basically it was do-able. There wasn't a lot of time, though. In fact, they were damn nearly out of time. Still, it was definitely worth having a go. Jesson would have to talk to Cheney, of course, and it might even have to go higher than that.

Prescott picked up the telephone and dialled Bob Jesson's number in Washington, DC.

CHAPTER 29

The Silver Pagoda, so named because the floor is covered with over five thousand silver tiles weighing one kilogram each, is one of the loveliest structures in all Cambodia. As the wedding procession approached the great, Italian, marble staircase and made its way inside, Prescott marvelled at the strange chain of events that had dictated that his first visit to this architectural gem should be as the bridegroom in Cambodia's Wedding of the Year. Cheers rang out from the crowds which lined Samdech Sothearos Boulevard. As Su sat on the velvet cushion in the palanquin next to him, Prescott squeezed her hand and smiled encouragingly.

'I think we're going to make it,' he said.

It was the last, the positively final, day of the wedding. As far as Prescott was concerned, it seemed that they had explored and exhausted every conceivable, Cambodian nuptial tradition. They had feasted and danced, had threads tied to their hands, then untied; they had distributed betel leaves and – yes – chewed betel nuts. Prescott had had his hair trimmed yet again and monks had sprinkled holy water on the happy couple. They had performed the ceremony of 'drinking coconut juice' – *puk tu dong* – in which the achaa feeds three spoonfuls of coconut juice to both bride and groom; they had also undertaken the ritual of 'doing the teeth'. As far as the latter event was concerned, Prescott had dug his feet in when informed he would have to lacquer his teeth black.

'I don't mind brushing my teeth,' he said firmly. 'I do that morning and evening. But I'm not going to paint them black.'

Su had smiled back at him. In her glittering bridal costume she looked positively radiant. Whatever Prescott's hesitations, Su had found herself entering wholeheartedly into the spirit of the occasion. She felt more Cambodian than ever, more at one with this suffering, yet indomitable Khmer race, than she could ever have imagined might be the case. Somehow, all those years in America seemed very far away.

'Thank you so much, darling,' she whispered. 'You didn't have to go through all this, but you did.'

Su and Prescott dismounted from the palanquin in front of the Emerald Buddha, made of Baccarat crystal, which sat on a gilt pedestal mounted on the dais. In front of the dais stood another Buddha, this one life-size, covered with diamonds from head to toe.

'Please stand here,' the achaa instructed the bridal couple, motioning to them to take their places side by side next to the gold Buddha.

Su and Prescott held hands. Hong Soeung stood next to Prescott and Sita Soeung, whitehaired but erect, stood next to Su. Little Keav, enchantingly dressed as a young apsara complete with robes and crown, managed to slip in between her father and new brother-in-law, clutching their hands as the achaa, in a small ad hoc addition to the traditional ceremony which Prescott had insisted upon, pronounced Su and Prescott man and wife.

'Where's the scarf?' Prescott whispered. 'You've forgotten the scarf.'

★★★

An hour later, it was all over. The guns sounded from the Royal Palace. Ships on the Mekong and Tonle Sap Rivers sounded their hooters. Balloons rose into the air and fireworks exploded on all sides.

Prescott had been waiting for someone to say, 'You may kiss the bride,' but that didn't seem to be part of the ritual. But he did it, anyway, hugging Su to him as they stood there in front of the Emerald Buddha. Then he kissed Sita and Keav.

Hong Soeung was still standing there. From the expression on his face, his thoughts could have been a million miles away. Perhaps he was thinking of those dark days in Tuol Sleng prison or the long years at Ta Keo when he didn't know whether his wife and daughter were still alive, and when his true solace had been work, work and nothing but work. Or perhaps Hong Soeung was thinking of the young men and women he had known, full of ideals, who had somehow seen those ideals corrupted and their lives destroyed.

Prescott didn't know whether to kiss the man or to shake his hand. In the end, he did both.

'I want to thank you for allowing me to marry your daughter,' he said.

★★★

The reception was held in the grounds of the Royal Palace, immediately adjacent to the Silver Pagoda. It seemed to Prescott that the whole cast of characters had assembled. One after another, they came up to congratulate him and Su and, of course, Hong and Sita Soeung. He recognised Professor

Haq and Lina Chan from DC-Cam, Jules Barron and Dr Borei Pen from SAVE, Mark Kelly, Graham Bender and Henri Le Blanc from the Press corps, Narong Sum, the painter... they all seemed to be there. It was like the last act of an opera, he thought, with the whole cast assembling before the final curtain. Only Geoff Jackson was missing, but that was hardly surprising given that the UN had been virtually run out of town. Still, Jackson had taken the trouble to send them a telegram of congratulations from some sheep station in the Outback. The man was a class act, Prescott reflected. Sooner or later, he would re-emerge on the international stage. Maybe one day they'd organise an international tribunal for the Taliban with Jackson presiding...

Suddenly he saw Senator Hillary Clinton. 'Welcome, Senator!' He saluted her. What a woman! She probably would run for President one day, he thought. She certainly had what it takes.

'Congratulations, Prescott,' she kissed him on both cheeks. 'I told you I'd try to get here. Just don't write any stories about me this time!'

Prescott laughed. 'I've got the week off.'

At that moment, Prime Minister Khin Lay came up, congratulated the bride and groom and swept the Senator away.

After a while, as the tempo of the celebrations increased and as the crowd grew in size, Prescott grew vaguely worried. This could get out of hand, he thought. You needed something to break it up, change the rhythm. He hoped they weren't going to ask him to make a speech. He was damned if he was going to do that.

Oh God, he thought, as the Great Gong sounded from the Throne Room, that's just what they're going to do. They're going to ask me to make a bloody speech.

But it wasn't that. It wasn't that at all. Through the haze of alcohol and sheer emotion, he remembered what was about to happen. Christ, he'd set it all up, hadn't he?

Over the loud speaker, a voice announced in English and in Khmer: 'Your Royal Highness, Ladies and Gentlemen, the Ambassadors of the United States, France and the People's Republic of China will now make their presentations in honour of this occasion. Please make your way to the Throne Room.'

'Here we go,' thought Prescott.

The other guests stood aside as the wedding party, led by the bridal couple, followed the three Ambassadors up the steps of the Throne Room.

Prescott had time to glance at the splendid murals, showing scenes from the *Reamker*, the Khmer version of the Ramayana, which lined the walls on every side. He had time to admire the tall ceiling and superb array of pillars.

Then the Master of Ceremonies, a splendidly bedecked courtier, was speaking again. He had turned to face the Royal couple, sitting side by side on their bejewelled sandalwood thrones.

'Your Majesty Preah Bat Samdech Preah Norodom Sihanouk,' he began, bowing to the King, 'Your Majesty Preah Reach Akka Mohesey Norodom Monineath Sihanouk,' he continued, bowing to the Queen, 'with your permission, the three Ambassadors will now unveil their gifts to you and to the Cambodian people.'

The MC stepped aside.

Willard Price, the American Ambassador, came forward to the microphone. Total silence had fallen on the great hall. Between the three ambassadors and the royal couple stood three plinths. There was an object mounted on each plinth, hidden under a velvet drape.

'Your Majesties,' Willard Price began, reading from his notes, 'by mutual agreement I am making an introductory statement on behalf of myself and my colleagues from France and China. We would like to take this occasion to stress the undying friendship our countries hold for your great country, as well as our many shared interests.'

Prescott felt his attention wandering. It had been a long day. It had been a long week. Get on with it, he urged.

About ten minutes later, the Ambassador finally came to the point. 'So, I conclude by saying that the time has come to repair the ravages of the past. We cannot always heal the damages to men's minds, but where we can make amends, we should do so. I can announce today that in a spirit of reconciliation and in recognition of the great future that lies ahead of a new, unified Cambodia, the three governments represented here today by the three of us are returning to the Cambodian nation and people three key treasures from Cambodia's heritage.

'As far as the United States is concerned, I can tell you the United States government has been able to acquire from a private collection one of the most remarkable pieces of Cambodian sculpture. We have flown this piece out to Phnom Penh in the last few days and I am proud to be able to present it to the Cambodian nation today.'

Ambassador Price stepped forward to pull the string attached to the right-hand plinth. Seconds later, the head of Vishnu stood revealed in all its glory.

The room burst into applause.

How much did Andrew Mossman sting the government for that, Prescott thought? Apparently, he had tried to drive a hard bargain. Jesson had called him a day or two ago to say that Dick Cheney had had to do some serious arm-twisting. The Vice-President had threatened Mossman with charges of illegally importing antiquities under the SAVE umbrella unless he was 'flexible' in terms of compensation demanded. But Jesson hadn't said how flexible Mossman had proved to be. At least, thought Prescott, Mossman wouldn't be raiding the larder anymore. With the Chinese de-mining teams hard at work all over the country, he shouldn't have to.

It was the Frenchman's turn next.

Serge de la Boulaye, France's Ambassador, a tall, silver-haired gentleman, wearing as decoration only the small bouton in his lapel which indicated that he belonged to the highest rank of the Legion d'Honneur, stepped up to the microphone. He spoke in his own language, *bien entendu.*

'I am pleased and proud,' de la Boulaye said, 'to be able to announce that the French government is handing back to Cambodia today, the famous head of Shiva which was first removed from this country by a French citizen in 1873 and which is now in the Musée Nationale des Arts Asiatiques in Paris. I will not repeat here all that Ambassador Price has said. Let me just add that my country believes, Your Majesty, that her destiny and the destiny of your great country, are inextricably intertwined. *Vive la France! Vive le Cambodge!'*

With a flourish and a bow, the French ambassador stepped forward to the middle plinth and jerked the string to reveal the marvellous sculpture, the superb head of Shiva, which had so beguiled Louis Delaporte when he first set eyes on it and which over the decades since then had delighted countless visitors to the Musée Guimet.

Once again, the applause which followed de la Boulaye's presentation was thunderous.

As he stood there, clapping vigorously, Prescott marvelled at the beauty of the piece and at the similarities between this head of Shiva and the head of Brahma which the United States Ambassador had just unveiled. He remembered Delaporte's description of the extraordinary moment when he had discovered the head of Shiva in the ruins of Ta Keo. He could recite the text almost word for word even now:

> *a priceless discovery awaited us among the ruins. We noticed the remains of candles, cleared the ground and soon unearthed a limestone cylinder with a very smooth grain, then a skull cap decorated with braid, then a face and finally the remains of a head. There could be no mistake: these were the heads of the major Brahminic divinities and each one of them must have occupied one of the three sanctuaries...*

Finally, it was China's turn. The last time he had seen Ting Wei-Ju, Prescott thought, had been at Ting's luxurious villa by the lake in Hangzhou. The time before that had been in Washington, at the Smithsonian reception. Now here he was in Phnom Penh, China's newly appointed Ambassador to Cambodia. Some people might have seen this as a demotion, but Prescott knew that Ting, who had his own power base in China, would not have accepted the post on those terms. It must have been made clear to him that China had a very major stake in the new Cambodia and that he, Ting, was the man to ensure that China's position was not jeopardized. Who would really be running the country, Prescott wondered? Khin Lay or Ting Wei-Ju? He wouldn't like to take a bet on it. Not at the moment. They were both pretty canny customers. And of course, there would be other watchful eyes in the background. The US would give China a good deal of leeway in Cambodia – that was obviously part of the deal, as Bob Jesson had explained. But that didn't mean China would have a totally free hand. And France also had to be taken into consideration. There was a new wind blowing.

Ting Wei-Ju stepped up to the microphone. He looked as suave and as spruce as ever, Prescott thought. You'd never believe the man was well over seventy.

Ting began his remarks by addressing himself directly to King Sihanouk.

'You may remember, Your Majesty,' he said, 'that almost thirty years ago a young Chinese diplomat accompanied you and your party on a visit from Beijing to Cambodia. I was that man.'

He paused. The King didn't speak. Instead, he bowed his head very deliberately and clasped his hands together to indicate that he remembered, remembered very well.

'Your Majesty may recall that we camped in the Kulen mountains,' Ting Wei-Ju continued, 'some thirty miles northeast of Angkor Wat. One evening, a young Cambodian scholar and archaeologist arrived at the camp to pay his respects to Your Majesty. That young man was Hong Soeung whose daughter's wedding we have celebrated today. Hong Soeung brought with him a stone head of Brahma which he had recently located somewhere nearby. He presented that head to Your Majesty as a token of esteem.'

Again, Ting Wei-Ju paused, waiting for Sihanouk's slow nod of acknowledgement. This time, there was a round of applause.

When silence had once more descended, Ting continued. 'Your Majesty, I know, will remember that piece. I myself remember it very well. We carried it back with us together to China so many years ago. Though Hong Soeung had presented the head of Brahma to Your Majesty, you very generously handed it over into my safe keeping. So it gives me great honour, on behalf of my country, to be able to return to the people of Cambodia the third and final member of the Trimurti, represented by this superlative head of the great god Brahma!'

This time, as Ting Wei-Ju jerked the cord to reveal the magnificent, four-faced head of Brahma, the applause grew to an all-time record. The King heaved himself from his throne, tears streaming down his face. He beckoned to Hong Soeung to come forward, then he put one arm round him and the other round Ting Wei-Ju.

A flunkey held the microphone for him. 'Thank you, everyone,' King Sihanouk said in his perfect French. 'Thank you so much. This means more to me than I can say. I am hereby instructing our new Minister of the Interior, our beloved Hong Soeung, who is responsible for these matters, to ensure that these three statues are returned at the earliest possible date to their rightful home, my great ancestor Jayavarman

II's holy city of Amendarapura. They must occupy there the sanctuaries which were prepared for them so long ago. Thus may Cambodia's great future be united with her glorious past. Minister Hong Soeung, you can do that, can't you?'

'Upon my life, sire,' Hong Soeung replied, bowing his grizzled head, 'there is nothing I would rather do.'

Hong Soeung shook hands with Ting Wei-Ju. 'Thank you so much. Thank you so very much.'

Three out of three! Prescott thought. The jackpot! Jesson must have worked his butt off. Did they have to lean on Ting too, he wondered? It must have hurt a lot for the old man to give up the piece. It had looked pretty nice there in his study in Hangzhou. Did Cheney call him while he was still in Washington? Did it go still higher? Did Bush call Jiang Zemin? Maybe he'd never know.

With the presentations over, the party resumed. Prescott and Su continued to receive the congratulations of all and sundry.

Jules Barron, his voice choking with emotion, came over, shook Prescott warmly by the hand and kissed Su on both cheeks. 'This is a proud day for France. Thank you so much. We are at the top table again, here in Indochina.'

'*Vive la France!*' Prescott said, straight-faced. 'His father died at Dien Bien Phu,' Prescott murmured to Su, as Jules withdrew. 'Today, it is clear that France is back as a player, at least in Cambodia. That must mean a lot to him.'

At one stage, the British Ambassador came up to offer his respects and congratulations. He fished a paper from his pocket. 'I've just had a message from London. You may like to know that in the light of events here tonight, Greece has just renewed its request for Britain to hand back the Elgin Marbles.'

By then, Prescott was on a high. 'Does it really matter, Ambassador, if you lose your marbles?'

Jean-Claude Mercier, who had enjoyed the day's events as much as he had enjoyed anything in recent months (he had struck several business deals during the reception and laid the groundwork for several more), had once again received permission for his helicopter to land in the grounds of the Royal Palace.

Around midnight, as the crowds were beginning to thin out, the darting JCM dragonfly hovered over the Silver Pagoda, before alighting on the debris-strewn grass in front of the Chan Chaya Pavilion.

'It's all yours,' Mercier said, helping them on board. 'The pilot has instructions – and clearance – to take you wherever you want to go. Sihanoukville? Bali? Timbuktu? You decide.'

As they lifted off, Prescott and Su could see the strangely foreshortened figures of Hong Soeung and Sita and little Keav waving up at them.

'You're sure you have the merchandise?' Hong Soeung shouted.

Prescott turned round to check the storage area behind the passenger seat. He gave the thumbs-up sign. 'All aboard,' he called.

'I love you all. We'll be back soon,' Su shouted, looking down.

The helicopter hovered over the Royal Palace grounds for a moment or two to the continued cheers of the crowd, then turned north to follow the Tonle Sap upstream

Su held Prescott's arm tightly as they encountered some momentary turbulence, then as they continued north, she asked: 'Where are we going by the way?'

'Give you one guess.'

Su pondered for a moment, then glanced behind 'We've got the statues on board, haven't we? That's why father asked you if you had the "merchandise," isn't it?'

Prescott smiled. 'It was the least we could do. Your father knew perfectly well that if he left them behind in the Royal Palace, the people of Cambodia might never see them again. Sihanouk might just hang on to them. Or else they'd be nicked overnight. So, we're taking them back to Ta Keo, back to where they belong. Did you know that Hong has found the bodies which go with the statues, all three bodies? He's put them back in the sanctuaries waiting for the heads to arrive. That's one of the reasons I so much wanted to help him. You see the disembodied heads of all these statues in museums or in private collections because people found it easier to saw off the heads and carry them away, leaving the trunks and torsos behind. But it's not the same thing, is it, as having the head and the body together? If you were Brahma or Shiva or Vishnu you wouldn't just want to be a head. You'd want to wave your arms and legs around as well. We talked about it at lunch one day and then later we met King Sihanouk and he said how glad he was to have the head of Brahma back and to see the return of the other pieces and how he hoped that heads and bodies might be reunited. So, I thought, well, let's give it a go. I think the statues will be safe up at Ta Keo or at least as safe as they'll be anywhere. Your father's people up at Ta Keo are, by all accounts, ferociously loyal to him. They'll guard the place with their lives.'

'Anyway,' he added. 'I think Ta Keo is a great place to begin our honeymoon. I want to see that great gold Buddha you told me about, with the dawn light streaming in through the windows...'

Su was so moved by what he had done for her father, for all of them, that for a while she couldn't speak. Then, as the first, moon-lit shimmer of the Great Lake, the Tonle Sap Lake, could be seen below them, she asked: 'But how did you do it, Prescott? It was marvellous. Completely marvellous. If you could have seen my father's face when the three Ambassadors handed back the statues. As a matter of fact, I think that meant as much to him as the wedding itself.'

'I read the Cambodian wedding handbook,' Prescott joked. 'Page 43. *Traditionally, groom gives huge present to bride's father!* Actually, I just made a phone call or two. Bob Jesson did the donkey work. I guess he called Dick Cheney. And I can tell you, when the Vice-President decides something needs to be done, it gets done!'

'I still don't understand,' Su persisted. 'This must have involved some top-level diplomacy. France, China, the US government itself – they all had to be brought on board pretty quickly for those pieces to get back here in time. Why did Cheney come through? What kind of pull do you have with him?'

'You're forgetting something, Su.'

'What am I forgetting?'

'You're forgetting they owed us one. A big one. You and I may have been suckers, but we were necessary suckers. If we hadn't done what we did, wittingly or otherwise, their whole scheme would have gone up the spout. There wouldn't have been a Hong Soeung affair. They might have had to pay off the Chinese in a different coin altogether. Or not pay them back at all, which might have been worse given that those guys have very long memories indeed.'

'So as far as you and I were concerned, it was payback time?'

'Well, that's how I put it to Bob Jesson,' Prescott said. 'I'm pretty sure he agreed.'

They were over the mountains now. Prescott started fumbling in the back.

'What are you looking for?'

'I just wanted to be sure we hadn't forgotten the hammock when we were getting the other stuff on board.'

'Just one hammock? What about me? What about us? Curfew's over now, isn't it?'

She hadn't kissed him since that moment, earlier in the day when they were leaving the Silver Pagoda, so she did so now.

When she at last released him, Prescott answered her question.

'It's a double-hammock, actually,' he said.